KERRELYN SPARKS

SECRET
LIFE
OF A
Vampire

An Imprint of HarperCollins*Publishers*

AVON BOOKS
An Imprint of HarperCollins*Publishers*
10 East 53rd Street
New York, New York 10022-5299

Copyright © 2009 by Kerrelyn Sparks
Excerpt from *Forbidden Nights With a Vampire* copyright © 2009 by Kerrelyn Sparks
ISBN 978-0-06-166785-5
www.avonromance.com

First Avon Books paperback printing: April 2009

Printed in the U.S.A.

10 9 8 7 6 5 4 3 2 1

*His gaze flitted down,
then back to her face.*

"I am very tempted to give you a try."

Her pulse speeded up. "Must you do that? Twist everything I say into some sort of sexual challenge?"

"Yes, I must." His eyes gleamed as he leaned forward. "It is only foreplay when you feel it."

This man was outrageous. "I don't feel anything."

"I think you do. Your heart is racing."

How did he know that? "Give me the clip for my gun."

"So you can shoot me?" He touched her hair and rubbed a strand between his thumb and forefinger. "Your hair is like a fiery nimbus. What is your name, *bellissima?*"

She moved out of his reach. "I'm Officer Boucher to you. And I want my clip back."

He stepped toward her. "I bet you have a lovely lyrical name to match the beauty of your face. A rich, melodious name that rolls off the tongue and reminds me of the luscious curves of your delectable body."

She stepped back and bumped against the wall.

He planted his hands on the wall, hemming her in . . .

By Kerrelyn Sparks

SECRET LIFE OF A VAMPIRE
ALL I WANT FOR CHRISTMAS IS A VAMPIRE
THE UNDEAD NEXT DOOR
BE STILL MY VAMPIRE HEART
VAMPS AND THE CITY
HOW TO MARRY A MILLIONAIRE VAMPIRE

Coming May 2009
FORBIDDEN NIGHTS WITH A VAMPIRE

To my agent,
Michelle Grajkowski of 3 Seas Literary Agency,
with my thanks for your
unfailing support and friendship.

Acknowledgments

*M*y world of vampires would still be a secret if not for the fabulous experts at HarperCollins. My thanks to executive editor Erika Tsang and the entire editorial staff; publisher Liate Stehlik; the art department for the best covers an author could ever wish for; publicist Pamela Spengler-Jaffee and the publicity department; and the staff of the marketing and sales departments, who work tirelessly behind the scenes to make each book in the Love at Stake series a success.

Closer to home, I have a personal support team that is always there for me. My love and gratitude to my husband, Don, and children, Jonathan and Emily; critique partners MJ, Vicky D, Vicky Y, and Sandy; travel buddy Linda Curtis; and the ever-supportive members of the West Houston and Northwest Houston chapters of Romance Writers of America.

And finally, my gratitude to all those incredibly smart people who read the Love at Stake books. My vamps continue to thrive thanks to you!

Chapter One

I don't want to die . . . again," Laszlo groaned.

Jack knelt beside Laszlo's sprawled body. "Can I fetch you anything? A warm cup of Type O?"

Laszlo covered his mouth. "Don't talk about food."

"Mi dispiace." Jack patted the Vamp on the shoulder, the only spot on the guy's shirt that wasn't soaked with spewed Blissky. Poor Laszlo. He'd only drunk one glass of the whiskey-flavored synthetic blood when everyone had toasted the groom, but obviously the little chemist was better at making Vampire Fusion Cuisine than ingesting it. He'd promptly thrown up all over himself.

There wasn't much anyone could do for the poor guy, so the bachelor party had raged on in full force while Laszlo rolled on the floor, his face clammy and pale.

"Shall I help you move to the couch?" Jack asked.

"I might get blood on it," Laszlo mumbled.

Jack frowned at the rich upholstery on the Louis XV-style furniture. "It's already stained." What a mess. How would he ever clean this up?

He rose to his feet with a growing sense of doom. It had seemed like a great idea when he'd reserved an Edwardian suite at the Plaza on Fifth Avenue to celebrate Ian MacPhie's last night as a bachelor. But now he realized the hotel's housekeeping service would wonder how an innocent party could produce so many bloodstains.

Things had gotten out of hand after Dougal arrived with his bagpipes. Ian had insisted on teaching everyone a Scottish jig. A dozen tipsy Vamps hopping around with glasses full of Blissky had resulted in a few collisions and even more stains on the carpet and furniture.

And then the phone call had come. The ladies were at Romatech Industries having a bridal shower, though Jack had heard that Vanda was bringing a male stripper from her Vamp nightclub. The ladies' party had come to an abrupt halt when Shanna Draganesti had suddenly gone into labor.

Before teleporting to Romatech, Roman Draganesti had lamented that he was too inebriated to help his wife in her time of need. This had caused the other guys to rally around, declaring their undying support with a rowdy fight song. Then a dozen drunken male Vamps had teleported to Shanna's side to cheer her on to victory.

Jack grinned as he imagined Shanna's reaction, but the moment quickly faded. He had two hours before the sun rose to get this hotel suite back to normal.

A noise from the adjoining bedroom drew his attention. Had one of the guys stayed behind? Good, he could use the help. He strode into the luxurious bedroom and frowned at the naked VANNA lying on the bed, dripping Bleer on the satin comforter.

That had been Gregori's bright idea. He'd arrived at the party toting two Vampire Artificial Nutritional Needs Appliances, otherwise known as VANNAs. The lifelike rubber females were sex toys in the mortal world, but for Vamps, they'd been modified with a battery-operated circulatory system. Gregori had filled the two sexy dolls with beer-flavored synthetic blood, and then he'd invited the guys to have a bite. From the looks of the lacy clothes strewn about, the guys had had more fun undressing VANNA than nibbling on her.

A man's voice drifted from the bathroom. "Oh, yeah, baby. Take it off!"

Jack knocked on the bathroom door. "The party's over."

"The party's never over for Dr. Phang." The door opened, revealing Phineas McKinney. "What's up, bro?"

The young black Vamp looked debonair in his maroon velvet smoking jacket and white silk cravat, although the cavalier effect was marred somewhat by his SpongeBob boxer shorts. Like any vampire, Phineas didn't reflect in the bathroom's gold-framed mirror, but the second VANNA did. The dark-tinted doll was sitting on the white marble vanity, wearing nothing but red silk panties and a silly grin on her face.

Jack was distracted for a moment when he noticed the words on Phineas's shorts. *Ladies dig the Sponge.* "Ah, sorry to interrupt."

Phineas's face turned a bit red. "I was just practicing, you know. When you're the Love Doctor, you gotta keep your mojo in top condition."

"I understand."

"I bet you do." Phineas grabbed the black VANNA off the vanity. Her legs jutted stiffly forward like a Barbie doll, and he pushed them down. "I heard you're a real Casanova."

"So they say," Jack muttered. He could never escape his famous father's reputation. "I suppose you were too busy to hear, but Shanna went into labor. All the guys left with Roman. Except Laszlo. He's still sick."

"No shit?" Phineas strode into the bedroom with the black VANNA clasped under his arm.

"The sun will rise soon, so we need to clean up."

Phineas glanced at the white VANNA on the bed in a pool of Bleer. "Damn, bro. We need professionals for this. How about Vampy Maids? They clean Roman's townhouse."

"That would be great. Can you ring them?"

"Don't remember their number, but they're in the *Black Pages*."

They would never find the vampire version of a telephone book in the Plaza hotel. "Do you—" Jack was interrupted by a loud knock on the door.

"Expecting someone?" Phineas's eyes lit up. "Maybe some *real* women?"

"NYPD," a male voice shouted. "Open the door, please."

Jack sucked in a deep breath. *Merda.*

"Hot damn," Phineas whispered. "It's the po-po." He looked around frantically. "We're in deep shit."

"Relax," Jack whispered back. "I'll use mind control to get rid of them."

"I don't do well with the police." Phineas backed away. "I'm outta here, man."

"You're leaving?" Jack winced as the pounding on the door grew louder.

"Open the door now!" the police officer yelled.

"I'll be right there," Jack shouted.

"Look, man." Phineas tossed the black VANNA into the bathroom and shut the door. "I'll go to the townhouse and call the Vampy Maids. I'll come back later to help you, okay?" His body faded away as he teleported.

"*Grazie mille*," Jack muttered. He strode into the living room, considering his options. He could grab Laszlo and teleport away, but the police would still come in and see the bloody mess. The suite was reserved under his name, so they might want him for questioning. No, it was better to take care of this now and use vampire mind control to erase the police officers' memory.

Laszlo struggled to sit up. "This is terrible." Sweat beaded his brow. "I think I'm going to puke again."

"Hang in there," Jack whispered. "I'll get rid of the cops."

"I'll call the manager up here to open the door," the police officer yelled.

"I'm coming!" Jack cracked the door two inches and quickly assessed the uniformed patrolman. Young, nervous, easily handled with vampire mind control. His gaze swept to the second officer.

Santo cielo. He forgot to breathe for a moment. Not that lack of oxygen could actually hurt him. His first impression: she was stunning. His second impression: she was trying very hard to minimize her looks. Golden red hair pulled back severely in a tight French braid. Fresh, creamy skin, a few adorable freckles, and big blue eyes. She wore very little makeup. And she was still stunning.

Her eyes widened as she met his gaze. Her mouth opened slightly, drawing his attention to her pink, sweetly shaped lips.

"*Bellissima*," he whispered.

She came to her senses with a heart-pounding jolt that Jack could actually hear. Her mouth closed with a frown. Her chin tilted up. Her hands gripped her belt. No doubt, she meant to intimidate him with her hands so close to her sidearm and baton, but he was more impressed by the way her belt accentuated her lovely hourglass figure.

She should be draped in the finest silks. She should be displaying her curves like a goddess. The fact that she was doing the opposite, covering herself from chin to toe in a mannish blue uniform, was intriguing.

The world had changed in two hundred years. If this lovely police officer had lived centuries ago in Italy, she would have been sought after by every artist who wished to immortalize feminine beauty on canvas. But here she was, trying to look tough and powerful. Didn't she realize she was already powerful? A woman like her could bring a man to his knees and make him grateful for being there.

The male officer cleared his throat. "Sir, we received a call from hotel security. You and your friends have been way too loud and rowdy."

"We were having a party," Jack explained. "A bachelor party."

"Hotel guests from three floors were calling to complain," the male officer continued.

"It was a very good party." Jack smiled at the female officer. "I'm sorry you missed it. Perhaps next time?"

She wrinkled her nose. "I can smell the whiskey from here."

"Your neighbors complained about a bagpipe," the male officer said. "And some loud clashing noises. Someone thought you might be having a sword fight."

"There's nothing to be concerned about, officer. Everyone has left." Jack raised his voice when Laszlo let out a low moan. "It's very quiet now."

"I think I heard someone," the female officer whispered to her partner. "He sounds injured."

"Thank you for stopping by." Jack started to shut the door, but the male officer wedged a booted foot in the way.

He pressed a hand against the door. "We'd like to take a look inside, if you don't mind."

"I do mind." Jack unfurled a wave of psychic energy. *Both of you are under my control.*

The male officer's arms dropped down by his sides, and a blank look stole over his face. The lovely woman stumbled backward. She grimaced and pressed a hand against her brow.

I am sorry to cause you pain, he said mentally. *What is your name, bellissima?*

"Harvey Crenshaw."

"Not you," he told the male officer.

Laszlo moaned again.

The female officer lowered her hand. "I knew it! There's someone in there. Step aside, sir."

Jack's mouth fell open. What the hell? She was supposed to be under his control. *You will not enter.*

"We will not enter," Harvey repeated.

"Of course we will." The woman shoved at the door.

Jack was so shocked, he stepped back as the woman barged in. *Nine circles of hell!* "Wait. You can't come in here."

She spotted Laszlo on the floor and immediately clicked the transmitter on her shoulder. "We have a stabbing victim. I need an ambulance—"

"No! No ambulance," Jack protested, but she was already giving the suite number to the operator. *Merda.*

Now he'd have to erase more memories. And why the hell wasn't she obeying him?

He hurled a wave of psychic power at her. *You are under my control.*

She shivered as she knelt beside Laszlo. "Hang in there, sir. Medics are on their way."

"Oh God, no." Laszlo gave Jack a beseeching look. *I can't go to a hospital! Make her go away!*

I'm trying. Jack concentrated hard. *You will leave this instant.*

"I will leave this instant." Harvey stepped back into the hallway.

"Harvey!" The female officer jumped to her feet and jabbed a finger at Jack. "You stay put." She dashed into the hall and grabbed her partner's arm. "Harvey? What's wrong with you?"

He just stood there, his face blank.

She shook him. "Harvey! Snap out of it!"

With a sigh, Jack reeled back his power. Keeping Harvey under his control would only make the female officer more suspicious.

Harvey blinked. "What? What happened?"

The female officer pointed at Jack. "Cuff him."

"*What?*" Now Jack wished he hadn't let Harvey go. "I didn't do anything."

The woman glared at him as she marched back into the hotel room. "We have a stabbing victim, and you're the most likely suspect."

"I didn't stab him." Jack aimed psychic energy once again at male officer. *You will not cuff me.*

Harvey halted next to him, the blank look once more on his face. Jack clasped his hands behind his back so the female officer would think he was handcuffed. She hadn't noticed, for she was kneeling beside Laszlo, ripping his shirt open. "Where were you stabbed, sir?"

"He wasn't stabbed," Jack insisted. "He just threw up."

"A pint of blood? Do I look stupid to you?" She glowered at Jack. "Where did you stab him? In the back?"

"I didn't stab him!"

I've tried controlling her, but it doesn't work, Laszlo told him mentally.

I know, Jack answered. She was every Vamp's worst nightmare. A beautiful woman who could not be controlled.

Perhaps she has psychic power, Laszlo continued. *Or she could suffer from some sort of mental defect that's blocking our power.*

"Did your mother drop you on your head when you were a baby?" Jack asked.

Harvey sniffed. "Yes, she did."

"Not you," Jack muttered.

The woman studied him suspiciously as she rose to her feet. "Harvey, watch that guy. Harvey?"

The male officer flinched. "What?"

"Watch him." She pointed at Jack. "Don't let him move. I'm going to check the rest of this place."

Harvey nodded. "Up against the wall."

Jack backed up so the woman couldn't see that he wasn't cuffed.

She scanned the area next to the wall-mounted flat-screen TV. "Someone was stabbed here. This is blood splatter."

"It's not mine."

She narrowed her lovely eyes. "Whose blood is it?"

"A friend's. He . . . cut himself accidentally." After guzzling down an entire bottle of Blissky, Angus

MacKay had decided to become a blood brother with every guy in the room. He'd taken his Highland dagger to nick his wrist, but accidentally punctured an artery and spurted blood in a wide arc across the wall. He'd promptly wrapped a towel around his wrist and replaced his lost dinner with another bottle of Blissky.

"Right. An accident." The female officer stopped beside the crossed swords on the carpet. "And these are your weapons."

"They're not mine," Jack protested.

"Right."

"They're Scottish claymores," he told her. "They belong to the groom. And there's no blood on them. The guys were using them to do a Highland sword dance."

She studied the swords, frowning. "You could have cleaned them."

"I didn't stab anyone." At least not tonight.

She surveyed the room, and her gaze lifted. "What's this?"

Jack winced at the sight of VANNA White's red silk bra dangling from the chandelier.

The female officer climbed onto the coffee table and used her expandable baton to dislodge the bra. "There were women at this party?"

"I wouldn't call them *real* women."

"Female impersonators?" She gave him a wry look as she waved the bra in the air.

He scowled at her. "It's not mine."

She tossed the bra on the couch and stepped down to the floor. "What's in the bedroom?"

Jack squeezed his eyes shut as he bombarded her with all the psychic power he could muster. *Do not go in there.*

"Do not go in there," Harvey repeated.

She shivered. "It's damned cold in here." She slipped into the bedroom. "Oh my God!"

Jack groaned.

She stuck her head out the door. "Harvey. Harvey! Call for backup!" She went back inside.

Harvey shook his head. "Huh?" He gave Jack a questioning look. "Who are you? Where am I?"

"There's a body on the bed," the woman called from the bedroom. "Female."

"It's VANNA White," Jack explained.

"Oh my gosh, she . . . she's not alive," the female officer continued.

Harvey blinked. "You killed Vanna White? You bastard." He reached for his transmitter.

You will not call for backup, Jack told him.

Harvey lowered his hand and resumed his deadpan face.

"She was never alive." The female officer appeared in the doorway, holding the doll. "It's a sex toy." She tossed it on the floor and gave Jack a look of utter disgust. "You sick pervert."

"It's not *mine*," he growled.

With a huff, she headed back into the bedroom.

This had gone far enough. Jack focused on Harvey. *You will leave this place and go back to your car. You will forget you were ever here. You will forget me and everything you have seen here.*

Harvey nodded, then slowly wandered down the hall.

Now to take care of the beautiful but strangely resistant female. Jack followed her into the bedroom. "Miss—"

She whirled around, and her eyes widened at the sight of his free hands. She immediately reached for her gun. "I thought you were cuffed."

Jack stepped toward her. "There's no need to——"

She drew her weapon. "Stay back. *Harvey!* Where are you?"

Jack could hear her heart racing. "Relax. I only want to talk. And there's no need to yell for Harvey. He left."

Her pulse jumped. "My partner wouldn't leave me alone. What did you do to him?"

"Nothing. He simply left."

"I don't believe you." She lifted her gun an inch, aiming at his head. "More police are on their way."

"No, they're not. I didn't let Harvey call for backup."

She gulped audibly. "You didn't *let* . . . Who are you?"

He opened his palms. "I will not harm you."

"What did you do to Harvey?" she shouted.

"Nothing. He's on his way to the car. He knows I'm harmless." Jack lifted his hands and moved closer. "Think about it, Miss . . . ?"

She stepped back. "Officer Boucher."

She pronounced it the French way, like *bouchey*. It sounded pretty, coming from her, even though he knew it meant "butcher." "There was no crime committed here. And while it is true that my friends were too loud and messy, I'll clean everything up and pay for any damages. You have my word on that."

She kept her gun pointed at him. "There's blood everywhere. A sure sign of violent crime. Just because I haven't found the body doesn't mean it didn't happen."

"There is no body."

She edged toward the bathroom. "I haven't finished checking everywhere yet."

He sighed. "Don't go in there."

She lifted her eyebrows. "Sounds like an invitation to me." She reached behind her to ease open the door.

She glanced back and gasped at the sight of VANNA Black sprawled on the tile floor.

With vampire speed, Jack lunged forward and snatched the gun from her hand.

She gasped again. Her eyes grew wide. He could hear her heart racing dangerously fast.

Merda. Did she really think he would kill her? "*Bellissima*, you wound me." He ejected the clip and handed it to her. "I would never hurt you."

She stared at him, then at the bullets in her hand. Her heart still pounded, but he could hear it slowing down.

She glanced at VANNA Black. "Another sex toy? How many do you need?"

He gave her a wry look. "It's not mine."

"Right."

He concentrated all his efforts on one last attempt to take over her mind. She stumbled back, knocked off balance by the strength of his psychic power.

You will leave immediately and forget you were here. You will forget you ever met me. The reality of that last command pricked him with a twinge of regret. He almost wished his mind control would fail.

With a grimace, she pinched the bridge of her nose. "Ouch."

He should be careful what he wished for.

She lowered her hand and gave him a confused look. "There's something really strange going on here."

"Tell me about it." In two hundred years, he'd never encountered this problem before.

"I thought I heard your voice—never mind." She stepped back, eyeing him warily. "Who are you?"

"I am Giacomo. My English-speaking friends have called me Jack for so many years, that I think of myself that way when I'm speaking English. You may call me Jack."

"I'm not your friend." She shivered from the cold psychic waves surrounding her.

He stepped toward her. "What is your full name?"

She stared at him, her eyes wide, as if she were completely entranced, but he knew she wasn't. He couldn't breach her mind. He had no idea what she was thinking.

A noise in the hallway drew his attention. He peered into the living room just as two paramedics rolled a gurney inside.

He shot a wave of psychic power at them. *You will leave the hotel, go back to your ambulance, and have no memory of ever being here. Go now.*

The two men turned and rolled the gurney down the hall.

"How did you do that?" Officer Boucher whispered.

He turned toward her. "I know none of this makes sense to you, but you must believe me. No one was harmed tonight. Nothing bad happened here."

She frowned. "What about the guy on the floor?"

"He's sick. I'll take care of him. You didn't find any wounds on him, did you?"

"No. But there's so much blood."

"I'll make sure it's all cleaned up." He offered her the empty gun. "Please go, Officer Boucher."

She accepted the weapon. "I—I don't feel right about this. I can't just act like nothing happened."

"There's nothing you can do but go. I'm sorry."

She stood there, chewing her lip and frowning. "This isn't right."

"Your partner is outside waiting for you. Good-bye, Miss Boucher."

She wandered toward the door and glanced at Laszlo. "You'll be okay?"

He waved good-bye. "I'll be all right. Thank you."

She paused at the door to give Jack a pointed look. "This isn't over. We have unfinished business, Jack." She strode down the hall.

A part of him, a very old and lonely part of him, hoped she was right.

Chapter Two

*W*ait!" Lara Boucher ran after the paramedics as they rolled their gurney into an elevator. She caught up with them just as the doors slid shut. She could have stopped the elevator doors, but she froze when she saw their faces. They had the same zombielike expressions that she'd seen on Harvey.

A shudder shot down her spine. It must be a residual effect from the icy cold hotel room she'd just left.

Who was she kidding? She was totally freaked out.

She punched the down button for another elevator and jammed the clip back into her automatic pistol. *Coward.* If she had any guts at all, she'd march back to that room and take the mysterious Jack in for questioning.

Another shudder racked her body as she recalled the moment he'd taken her weapon. It had been scary enough when he'd ambled calmly into the bedroom with no cuffs on to announce that Harvey had abandoned her and no backup was on the way. But when he'd grabbed her weapon, she'd thought for a second that her life was over. And if that wasn't terrifying enough, she'd thought she'd heard his voice in her head, although she couldn't make out the words.

She glanced down the hall. Should she go back for him? The man was dangerous. Strangely compelling, but at the same time frightening. Confusing, unworldly. And incredibly handsome.

She jumped when a dinging noise announced the next elevator. She hurried inside and pushed the lobby button. *Coward. You're running away.*

What else could she do? Harvey had left her. And Jack had disarmed her so easily. He would simply do it again.

She snapped her sidearm back into the holster. She had a strange feeling Jack had been in control of the situation all along. He could have killed her, but instead, he'd seemed insulted that she'd thought him capable of it.

After the elevator doors opened, she dashed into the lobby and spotted the paramedics leaving the hotel. She rushed through the revolving door and met them as they were loading the gurney into the back of the ambulance.

"Hey, guys. What's going on?"

One of the paramedics gave her a blank look. "Hello, Officer. We're on call tonight."

"You were called here, to the Plaza hotel."

The paramedic shut the back doors on the ambulance. "We've never been to the Plaza."

Lara's mouth fell open. Didn't they know where they were?

The paramedic climbed into the driver's seat. "Good night, Officer."

She inhaled sharply as the ambulance drove away.

What had Jack done to them? Did he have some sort of strange power over people's minds? Her skin prickled as if a thousand eyes were focused on her in the dark. *Keep it together. You're not losing it.* Unfortunately, she knew too well how fragile a person's brain could be.

She spotted the patrol car parked by the curb and jogged over to it.

Harvey frowned at her as she climbed into the front passenger seat. "Where have you been? I've been waiting forever."

"I was in the hotel." She buckled her seat belt. "With you."

He snorted. "I've never been in a hotel with you. I'm a married man."

"I didn't mean—"

"If that's some kind of joke, it's not funny." He turned on the ignition and pulled out onto Fifth Avenue.

"Harvey, I have the utmost respect for you and your marriage." *And absolutely no attraction to you.* "You don't remember the Plaza asking us to check on some guests who were too rowdy?"

"Hotel security would take care of that."

"Normally, yes. But when someone reported an alleged sword fight going on, they called us."

He laughed. "A sword fight in a hotel room? You need to cut back on the caffeine."

"You don't remember the guy with the sex toys?"

Harvey gave her a dubious look. "You're crazy. Our last call was a drunken brawl in Times Square."

Her skin chilled. "I'm not crazy." *It did happen.* Just because Harvey and the paramedics couldn't remember it, that didn't mean it hadn't happened. Somehow Jack had erased their memories. What manner of man could do that?

At least he hadn't screwed with her head like he had

the others. Or had he? Was she remembering something that hadn't even happened?

Oh God, not again. She'd already spent six months of her life in utter confusion, unable to tell reality from dreams. After the car accident, reality had seemed fuzzy, and her dreams had seemed real.

She had to know. She had to go back and face Jack.

Two blocks ahead of them, a car swerved onto Fifth Avenue. It skidded across two lanes, sliding dangerously close to a yellow cab before speeding away.

Harvey eased on the accelerator. "What do you think? Drunk driver?"

"Or stolen vehicle." Lara grabbed the radio mike to call the dispatcher. "I need a ten-fourteen." She read the license plate number as they continued to follow.

The radio crackled. "That's a ten-seventeen." The dispatcher reported the vehicle was not stolen.

"Roger," she answered. "Looks like a DWI."

"Let's get him." Harvey hit the lights and siren.

Lara's nerves tensed. You never knew how people would react. Luckily, the driver cooperated, and twenty minutes later, they were hauling his drunken ass into headquarters.

As the sun rose, Lara finished her paperwork for the night. She double-checked the log Harvey had kept. No reference of them ever going to the Plaza. She drummed her pen on the desk, debating what to do. If she included the Plaza incident in her report, then her supervisor, Captain O'Brian, would question why it didn't appear in the log or in Harvey's report. She'd never get promoted to detective if they started doubting her grip on reality.

She strode to the water cooler and took a long drink. Maybe she should visit a neurologist and see if it was possible to have a relapse.

Dammit, no! She crushed the paper cup in her hand and tossed it in the trash. She'd fought too hard to overcome her head injury. That was six years ago, and she was over it. She hadn't dreamed this up. For one thing, she could remember everything about Jack. All sorts of details.

Thick, black hair brushed back from his wide brow. The ends curled slightly where they touched his shirt collar. And that black silk shirt—it had clung to him, clearly outlining his broad shoulders and rock-hard abs. He was as gorgeous as any model she'd ever seen in a magazine.

And his voice had intrigued her. Soft and melodious, with an Italian accent, but also crisp and polite, as if he'd learned English from the British. The dual accents hinted at a man who would be complex. Fascinating, even. He was both Jack and Giacomo. *Bellissima*, he had called her.

She closed her eyes and mentally roamed up his body from his expensive Italian leather shoes. Long legs. Narrow hips. Trim waist. Broad shoulders with a lovely curve to his neck that made her want to nestle her face into the crook. Strong jaw with a shade of dark whiskers, just enough to make her want to touch. Expressive mouth. She'd found herself using his mouth to gauge his reactions. One corner of his mouth would curl up when he was amused. His lips would part when he was surprised, then press together when he was annoyed.

And his eyes—they were a warm, golden brown that radiated both intelligence and courage. He'd watched her every move with an intensity that bordered on . . . hunger.

"Hey, don't fall asleep standing up."

She jerked her eyes open to find Captain O'Brian regarding her curiously. "Sorry. It was a long night."

"It takes a while to adjust to the graveyard shift, but you're doing fine. Finish up and go home, Boucher."

"Yes, Captain." She hurried back to her desk to finish her report without the incident at the Plaza. But it had happened. Jack might look like a dream, but he was real.

She usually changed into civilian clothes before taking the train back to her apartment in Brooklyn. After a long night of dealing with drunk and disorderly people, she just wanted to fade into the crowd unnoticed. But this morning, she kept her uniform on and took the subway back to the Plaza hotel.

"I need information on Room 1412," she told the registration clerk.

"Just a moment." The young man typed on his keyboard. "That's one of our Edwardian suites. Would you like to reserve it?"

"It's already occupied. I want to check on it."

He frowned at his computer screen. "That suite is vacant at the moment."

"Well, maybe they checked out, but they were there last night. They had a wild party. Hotel security called the police."

He gave her a confused look. "I don't know what to tell you, Officer. According to our records, that room was vacant last night."

Lara swallowed hard. How far had Jack gone to erase his steps? "Is the night manager here? I'd like to speak to him. And hotel security, too."

The story remained the same. The night manager had no record of Suite 1412 being occupied. Lara asked him to check on any room reserved by a man named Giacomo, but no such name emerged in their files.

Hotel security was even worse. They got all huffy when she claimed they had called the police. They could handle matters on their own, thank you very much. And there hadn't been any wild parties the night before.

She insisted on seeing the room for herself, so they reluctantly gave her a key. On the fourteenth floor, she opened the door slowly and let it swing open. She inhaled, expecting to encounter the odor of whiskey.

It was gone. But the strong smell of disinfectant and cleansers filled the room. She walked in and looked to the left where the man had lain on the carpet, covered in blood. He was gone. The carpet was clean.

She wandered through the room, eyeing the upholstery and carpet. No stains. Her gaze shifted to the wall. No blood splatter. She moved closer. Either she was off her rocker, or someone had done a phenomenal cleaning job.

He had said he would clean it up.

She touched the wall. It looked so fresh. Had they repainted it? Too bad she couldn't get a CSI team in here. There was no way Captain O'Brian would okay that, not when hotel management insisted the room had been empty.

She strode into the bedroom. The satin comforter was spotless. How had Jack managed that? She peered into the bathroom. No sex doll. She scanned the mosaic floor and white marble vanity for any sign of blood. The twenty-four-carat-gold faucets gleamed. The towels were neatly folded. No one would ever believe this room had been occupied.

She strode toward the door to let herself out. Somehow, Jack had tampered with the memories of all the hotel staff. Had he bothered with the guests?

She knocked on the next door down the hall. A droopy-eyed, yawning couple told her that everything had been quiet the night before, then slammed the door in her face. If it had been quiet, why were they so sleepy?

Well, that was easy. They could have been up all night making love. Lara sighed. Just because she was going without didn't mean other people were.

Close to the elevator, a man in a business suit emerged from his room, carrying a briefcase.

"Sir." She jogged to catch up with him.

"Yes?" He gave her that wary look so many people give the cops, like they know they've done something wrong and they're hoping she doesn't know.

She gave him a friendly smile to put him at ease. "I wanted to ask you about last night. Did you hear anything out of the ordinary?"

"You mean the damned bagpipes? Some idiot was playing them at three in the morning."

Lara's heart lurched up her throat. She wasn't crazy! And Jack had missed someone. "Yes, exactly. Do you remember anything else?"

"Just that I couldn't sleep. I finally went out to a bar to get a drink."

And that was how Jack had missed him. "Thank you."

"Well, I just hope my presentation today doesn't suck," he grumbled as he lumbered toward the elevator.

Jack was real. But how could she find him? She glanced at the local newspaper in front of the door. "Sir?" she called after the businessman. "Do you mind if I take this paper?"

"Be my guest." He stepped into an elevator.

Lara picked up the paper and turned to the section on wedding announcements. It had been a bachelor party with bagpipes and claymores. Chances were good that the groom was Scottish.

Today was Saturday, so there were plenty of weddings listed. MacPherson, Ferguson, and MacPhie. Three weddings with Scottish-sounding grooms.

Lara took a deep breath. She was about to become a wedding crasher.

Lara rushed up the stone steps as fast as her high-heeled red sandals would allow. After three months on the beat, she wasn't used to dressing up. She stopped before the carved wooden doors and mentally braced herself.

She could do this. She'd crashed the MacPherson wedding with no one realizing it. Of course, that had been a huge affair. The Ferguson wedding had been scarier. With only fifty people in attendance, she'd been painfully aware of the curious looks cast her way. She'd slipped away as soon as possible, leaving behind one of the three wedding presents she'd purchased that afternoon.

She adjusted the bodice on her red cocktail dress. Maybe she shouldn't have worn red. Or this low neckline. It was bound to draw attention. But this was a late wedding, starting at nine P.M., so she assumed it would be more formal than the afternoon weddings she'd attended. The red dress was the fanciest one she owned. The only fancy dress she owned. After leaving home, she'd sworn never ever to wear a full-length formal gown again.

Too bad she had to lug this canvas tote bag with her. Her uniform and weapon were inside, since she'd have to leave soon for work. Her shift started at ten, but she'd make it on time. It would only take a few minutes to see if Jack was here. She believed he was real, but she'd feel a lot better if she could verify that in person. And she wanted to know how he had managed to erase his tracks at the hotel. He was an intriguing mystery, with his ability to control minds. So naturally, as a wannabe detective, she just had to investigate him. The fact that he was also gorgeous and incredibly sexy didn't factor into it.

Yeah, right. She shouldn't lie to herself in church.

She pulled open the heavy wooden door and slipped inside the vestibule. Rows of red glass votives flickered, casting a warm glow against the stone walls. Her stiletto heels wobbled on the uneven pavement as she moved quietly toward the nave. Two saintly statues flanked the entrance, frowning at her for sneaking in uninvited.

Those who were invited seemed like a happy bunch. She remained half hidden behind the door, watching them as they laughed and talked. The ends of the pews were decorated with white ribbons and lilies. Another floral arrangement rested on the altar. She scanned the small crowd, looking for Jack. She didn't see him, but she did spot the guy who'd been sprawled on the floor covered with blood just the night before. How strange. He was perfectly fine now.

"May I help you?"

She jumped and turned toward the man who'd spoken behind her. A big redheaded Scotsman. "Hi there."

" 'Twill begin soon. May I escort you to yer seat?"

"Sure." She figured he must be one of the ushers. This was definitely a Scottish wedding. The guy was wearing a black-and-white-plaid kilt, white lacy shirt, and black jacket. A single red rosebud was pinned to his lapel, and his long hair was pulled back with a thin black ribbon.

He regarded her curiously with his light green eyes. "Ye're a friend of the bride?"

Lara's mind went blank as she desperately tried to

remember the name of the bride. Cheryl? No, that had been the MacPherson wedding. Dammit. She'd paid more attention to the names of the grooms. And this groom had seemed familiar somehow. "I'm a friend of Ian MacPhie."

The Scotsman's eyebrows lifted. "Ye know Ian?"

"Sure. We go way back. I . . . used to date his cousin."

"I see."

Shoot, this wasn't working. She'd have to distract this guy. She brushed her long hair behind her shoulder to show off some cleavage and gave him the dazzling smile her mom had spent a small fortune on. "I don't believe we've met. I'm . . . Susie."

"Delighted to make yer acquaintance. I'm Robby MacKay." He took her hand. "Since ye're a friend of Ian's, he'll want to see you right away."

"Oh, that's not necessary." She tried to remove her hand, but Robby's grip tightened. "Surely it can wait till after the ceremony."

"Come with me." He pulled her across the vestibule.

Oh, shit. "Isn't the wedding about to start? We need to take our seats."

He opened a door and gently pushed her inside a dark room. "Wait here." He flipped on a light and as she quickly looked about, he grabbed her canvas tote bag.

"No!" Dammit, her weapon was in there. "I need that."

"Ye'll get it back." He started to shut the door.

"Wait! Is Jack here?"

Robby paused. "Jack?"

"Yes. Giacomo. His English-speaking friends call him Jack. I need to talk to him."

Without bothering to answer, Robby shut the door in

her face. An ominous click sounded like a key turning a lock.

Dammit! Lara looked about the dimly lit room. A storeroom, she guessed. A row of high-backed, carved wooden chairs rested against the wall to her left. A bookcase filled with dusty old hymnals lined the wall to the right. The wall across from her was bare. No other door. Just as well. She couldn't leave without her uniform and weapon.

Damn, damn, damn! She paced across the small room. How could she have been so stupid? That Scotsman had moved incredibly fast. He'd wrenched the bag away before she'd known what was happening. But she had suspected he was onto her. She should have done something. But what? Drawn her weapon in a church at a wedding she was crashing?

She tried the door and sure enough, it was locked. How long would they keep her in here? What if she was late to work? What if she couldn't get her uniform and sidearm back? What a lousy cop she was turning out to be.

On the other hand, if Jack was here, then she was a damned good cop for managing to find him.

Male voices murmured on the other side of the door. She took a few steps back and drew in a deep, steadying breath.

Click. The door swung open to reveal Robby and . . . Jack.

Her breath caught. Good God, he was even more handsome than she'd remembered. His elegant gray suit looked tailor-made. His golden brown eyes widened as he looked her over.

"Ye know this woman?" Robby asked.

"*Si.*" Jack never took his eyes off her.

"Lucky bastard." Robby shoved her tote bag into Jack's arms and strode away.

Jack continued to give her that look, the one she could only describe as hungry. A chill crept up her bare arms. Oh yeah. It was more than intellectual curiosity that had driven her to hunt him down.

"*Bellissima.*" Jack shook his head. "*Mi dispiace.* I—I forgot all my English for a moment. You look so . . . *bella.* You would make the Mona Lisa cry with envy."

Her heart stuttered in her chest. *Get a grip. You're here to question this guy.* "Hello, Jack."

"I thought I would never see you again."

She lifted her chin. "I told you it wasn't over."

He walked into the room and shut the door. "Then you wish to start something with me?"

Chapter Three

*L*ara ignored the flutters in her stomach and the tingling sensation on her skin. She was not about to let this man know how flustered she was. "I'm here on business, Jack. This is an investigation."

He smiled slowly. "I'm flattered. I didn't realize I warranted so much personal attention."

The cad was trying to flirt with her, but she would remain professional. "You can answer my questions here or down at the precinct."

"I don't want to miss my friend's wedding."

"Then talk to me now. I want to know how you did it."

"Did what?" He ambled over to one of the high-backed chairs and set her tote bag on the red-cushioned seat.

"You know what. I went back to the Plaza this morning, and the room was spotless."

"I told you I would clean it." He peeked in her bag, then glanced at her. "I'm a man of my word."

"If you're honest, then you'll tell me how you did it."

"I cannot take full credit. I was helped by some very

efficient maids." He removed a gift-wrapped box from the tote bag. "You brought a wedding present. How thoughtful of you. Especially when you don't know the bride or groom."

Her face grew warm. "It was the least I could do. Now back to the matter at hand. When I questioned the hotel staff this morning, none of them could remember you."

He shrugged. "I suppose I am a forgettable sort of guy."

"On what planet?" she muttered, then blushed when he gave her a sexy grin.

He shook the wedding present. "What's inside, Officer? Some handcuffs?"

"Very funny." And the rascal kept changing the subject. "I'll answer your question, but then you have to answer mine. I gave them some silver-plated salad tongs."

"Silver?" He chuckled. "Ian will love that."

"I couldn't afford anything fancier. I had to buy three presents today."

"You went to *three* weddings?" His eyes twinkled with humor. "Were you invited to any of them?"

She crossed her arms, glaring at him. "I went to every wedding I found listed in the paper that had a Scottish groom. Ian MacPhie's name seemed familiar somehow."

Jack set the wedding gift down on another chair. "Ian became a bit of a celebrity about six months ago when he was declared the most eligible bachelor in the city on an online dating service."

"Oh, that's right. Now I remember." Lara's roommate had shown her that site at a cyber café. All the girls in the coffee house had drooled over Ian.

Jack glanced at her with a wary look. "Were you one of Ian's admirers?"

Was he worried about competition? Lara affected a dreamy look. "You have to admit Ian is incredibly hot."

Jack frowned at her. "He's taken. That's why his bride insisted on putting the announcement in the paper. She wants everyone to know he's no longer available."

Lara's curiosity got the better of her. "What about you? Are you taken?"

"I am single, but I wouldn't call myself available."

An odd answer. She wanted to know more, but she needed to stay professional. "Back to my original question. How did you erase all those peoples' memory?"

Jack rummaged around inside her tote bag. "So you crashed weddings with Scottish grooms until you found me? That's a fine piece of detective work. I'm impressed."

Lara's heart swelled at the compliment, then realized he'd done it again. "You didn't answer my question."

He pulled out her police hat. "Charming."

"Leave that alone. And answer my question, please."

He removed her folded blue shirt and pants. "You are going to work soon?"

"My shift starts at ten. Jack, how come no one remembers you?"

"I didn't want them to. Ah, your gun." He retrieved her belt, holster, and automatic pistol from the tote bag. He flipped open the holster to remove her gun.

She reached for it. "Give that to me."

He ejected the clip and handed her the empty gun.

She lifted her brows. "Do you think I would shoot you? You wound me," she repeated his words from the night before.

His mouth curled up. "*Brava, bellissima.*" He unbuttoned his suit jacket and slipped the clip into his trouser pocket. "You're very clever and talented."

"I plan to be a detective someday."

His smile grew. "Then we will be in the same business. I'm an investigator, too. For a private company."

"What company?"

"MacKay Security and Investigation." He peeked inside the tote bag. "There's something else in here. How interesting." He pulled out a lacy white bra.

"Put that back." Lara transferred the empty gun to her left hand, then made a grab for her bra with her right.

He moved quickly, whisking it out of her reach.

"*Bellisssima*, why would you pack a bra in your bag?"

"So I can wear it, you creep. Now hand it over."

His gaze dropped to her low neckline. "Does this mean you are currently . . . without?"

"It's none of your business." She extended her hand, palm up. "Give it to me."

He continued to study her breasts. "I believe you are wearing a corset of some kind."

"I am not going to discuss my underwear with you."

His eyes lit up. "Then I'm afraid I will have to search you."

"*What?* Don't you dare."

He gave her an innocent look. "What choice do I have? You crashed my friend's wedding and brought a weapon with you. How do I know you don't have a knife strapped to your thigh?"

She gritted her teeth. "Because if I did, it would already be sticking in your chest."

His mouth twitched. "And then there is the questionable area surrounding your breasts. You must be wearing some sort of contraption, though I cannot detect any sign of one." He stepped toward her. "I will be forced to investigate further—"

"It's a Nu-Bra," she blurted out, then winced. How had this conversation veered so far off course? She ought to clonk him on the head with her empty gun.

"A new bra?"

"Nu-bra. Polyurethane cups that stick to your breasts. Now back to my original question——"

"They *stick* to your breasts?" He looked appalled, then focused once more on her chest. "Surely you did not glue them to yourself?"

"Of course not. There's an adhesive backing."

He grimaced. "Like duct tape?"

"Would you please stop ogling me?"

He lifted his gaze. "But when you rip them off, does it not hurt?"

"This is entirely inappropriate."

"*Scusi, signorina*, but it is entirely inappropriate for you to harm your breasts. They are very sensitive, no?"

She glared at him. "They're tougher than they look."

His gaze dropped once more to her chest. "Then you would not object to rough handling?"

The nerve of this guy! "I'm not discussing that with you."

"A little nibbling, perhaps?"

She snatched her bra from his hand and turned her back to him as she dropped it into the tote bag. "I shouldn't have come. You're impossible to talk to. I swear, you have a one-track mind."

"Perhaps." He sighed. "People have always said I cannot escape my heritage. My father seduced hundreds of women in his lifetime. My mother was his last conquest."

"Sounds like a real Casanova." Lara set her empty gun down, then stuffed her uniform back into the bag.

"Exactly," he said wryly.

She dropped her hat back into the bag. "Since you refuse to answer my questions, I'm leaving." She picked up the empty automatic.

"I wish I could answer you."

She turned to face him. "Then do."

"I . . . cannot."

"Try me."

His gaze flitted down and then back to her face. "I am very tempted to give you a try."

Her pulse speeded up. "Must you do that? Twist everything I say into some sort of sexual challenge?"

"Yes, I must." His eyes gleamed as he leaned forward. "It is only foreplay when you feel it."

She stiffened. This man was outrageous. "I don't feel anything."

"I think you do. Your heart is racing."

How did he know that? "Give me the clip for my gun."

"So you can shoot me?" He touched her hair and rubbed a strand between his thumb and forefinger. "Your hair is like a fiery nimbus surrounding an angel of vengeance. What is your name, *bellissima*? Robby said it was Susie, but he thought you were lying."

She moved out of his reach. "I'm Officer Boucher to you. And I want my clip back, so I can leave."

He stepped toward her. "I bet you have a lovely, lyrical name to match the beauty of your face. A rich, melodious name that rolls off the tongue and reminds me of the luscious curves of your delectable body."

She stepped back and bumped against the wall. *Damn.*

He planted his hands on the wall, hemming her in. "Your beautiful name, *bellissima*. What is it?"

She narrowed her eyes. "Butch."

He blinked. "Butch?"

"The guys at the precinct call me that. It's short for Boucher." She shoved at his shoulders, but it didn't move him an inch. His body was like a boulder of granite. His head, too, no doubt.

"Butch," he murmured. "You're full of surprises. I like that."

Since he couldn't be budged with brute force, she'd have to try another tactic. "Tell me, Jack." She wrapped her right arm around his waist so that the gun rested against his back. "What else do you like about me?"

The gold flecks in his eyes gleamed. "I like your persistence. And your cleverness."

He hadn't mentioned her looks. She liked that. She gazed at his mouth and licked her lips. "Tell me more, Jack."

He lowered his head till his mouth was a mere inch from hers. She could feel his breath upon her cheek. She leaned into him and eased her left hand into his trouser pocket where he'd stashed the clip.

"*Bellissima.*" He rubbed the tip of his nose against hers. "You're driving me crazy."

Was she really? Good. She liked that. She also liked the feel of the clip safely gripped in her hand. She eased her hand from his pocket and brushed her cheek against his whiskered jaw. "Kiss me, Jack."

"Before or after you shoot me?" His hand latched around her wrist. He lifted her arm so he could see the clip in her hand. "Shame on you, Butch."

"Shame on *you*. Refusing to answer my questions. Embarrassing me about my bra. I ought to drag you to the precinct and stick you in holding for a few days—"

He grabbed both her wrists and pinned her against the wall. "You refused to answer my question, too. What is your name?"

"How did you erase their memories?"

"Drop it," he growled. "You don't want the answer."

"I'm a good detective. I'll figure it out."

He gave her a beseeching look. "Just leave it be, Boucher. Go away from here and forget you ever met me."

She searched his face. "How can I forget you? Who are you? What are you up to?"

"I do not harm anyone. Can you leave me be?"

Could she? Could she walk out of here and never think of him again? No, she couldn't. She would wonder about him for months. Years. "What about *you*, Jack? Do you want to forget me? Do you never want to see me again?"

His eyes darkened. He stroked the inside of her wrist with his thumb, and it sent a delicious shiver down her spine. "If you knew what you're doing to me, you would run. You would run like the hounds of hell were after you."

Run? She couldn't manage to move an inch. "Aren't you being a little overly dramatic, Jack?"

"Am I?" He leaned close, and his chin grazed the edge of her brow.

The scrape of his whiskers sent a shiver down her arms, prickling her skin with gooseflesh.

"I believe you asked for a kiss, Butch," he whispered in her ear, then drew back to look at her mouth.

Her breath caught when she noticed the reddish glint in his eyes. That couldn't be normal.

A knock sounded on the door. "The ceremony is starting," Robby's voice called out.

Jack released her and stepped back. "I have to go." He walked over to pick up her tote bag. When he turned to face her, his eyes had resumed their usual golden brown color. "You should go, too." He handed her the tote bag.

She quickly loaded her gun, then checked the safety before snapping it back into the holster. As she carefully placed it in her tote bag, a defeated feeling dragged her down. She was a lousy interrogator. She'd found Jack, but she still knew next to nothing about him. He dressed well. He was gorgeous. He apparently had issues with his parents, but then, who didn't? And he could make people forget. "Why didn't you do it to me? Why did you make everyone forget but me?"

He gave her a sad look. "I tried, *bellissima.* You are immune to me."

She hugged the tote bag against her chest. "Not entirely." He'd just admitted to causing mass amnesia. She shivered. Was he some kind of psychic? Or worse? And how could she feel attracted to him?

"Would you accept this?" He drew a business card from the inside pocket of his suit jacket. "My cellphone number is on there."

He wanted to see her again? Her heart expanded in her chest. She took the card and examined it. *Giacomo di Venezia.* Was his last name Venice, or was that his hometown? Beneath his name, it read *MacKay Security and Investigation.*

"I want you to call me if you're ever in trouble."

She glanced up at him. "*Only* if I'm in trouble?"

He frowned at her. "Especially if you're in trouble. I am worried about your safety."

She flicked the card into her tote bag. "Now you sound like my father." She strode toward the door.

He opened it for her. "I am serious, Boucher. It is a dangerous world out there. More dangerous than you know."

She glowered at him. "I'm not incompetent, Jack. Just because you managed to disarm me, it doesn't mean anyone else can."

"*Signorina*, you have disarmed me."

She swallowed hard. Did she actually have an effect on him? Or did he just say these things to keep her constantly off balance?

She walked into the vestibule and halted at the sight of the bride. She was a lovely young woman with long blonde hair partially hidden beneath a gossamer white veil. She clutched a huge bouquet of white lilies and roses. Her eyes glittered with excitement, and she glanced their way with a brilliant smile.

The "Wedding March" began, and she started down the aisle. The train of her elegant white gown skimmed the floor behind her.

"Wow," Lara whispered. "What a beautiful bride. She was absolutely beaming with joy."

Jack rested a hand against his chest and smiled. "*Amore*. It makes people glow from the inside."

"You believe in true love? And happily ever after?"

His smile faded. "Ever after is a very long time. It hasn't been that happy for me." He led her to a side door.

What had happened to Jack? Damn, but she wanted to know more. She wanted to know everything about him.

She glanced back. "I left the gift in the storeroom. Will you give it to the bride?"

"Yes." He held the side door open. "Will you call me if you're in trouble?"

"Maybe." She glanced at him, and their eyes met. Her heart stilled as if time had stopped. And in that timeless moment of a few seconds, she knew she would call him. She would not be able to resist him. There was something about him that awakened her senses and made her ache with want.

But how could she trust a man who could manipulate peoples' minds? And what if he was manipulating her? Was her attraction to him real, or was he tricking her?

He touched her hair. "Be careful out there, Butch."

Her heart squeezed in her chest. "My name is Lara." She hurried down the steps, but heard his whisper float toward her on a night breeze.

"Lara Boucher. I knew it would sound beautiful."

Chapter Four

*J*ack winced at the blood-curdling shriek. How could such a tiny bundle of humanity be so loud? And so terrifying? "I don't think she likes me." He quickly handed the newborn back to her father.

Roman Draganesti chuckled. "You were holding her like a sword being used to knight someone." He cradled his tiny daughter close to his chest and jiggled her up and down.

Jack stepped back, afraid that more than noise would emerge from the babe's mouth. "That jostling doesn't make her ill?".

"It soothes her." Shanna Draganesti gave them a weary smile from her hospital bed at Romatech Industries. "It reminds her of being inside of me."

"She's a bonny lass." Angus MacKay gave the newborn an appraising look. "She'll be needing a godfather, no doubt?"

Angus's wife, Emma, laughed. "Now that was subtle."

She perched on the hospital bed next to Shanna. "How are you, dear?"

"I'm fine," Shanna said. "But I hated missing the wedding."

"I was there!" Her two-year-old son, Constantine, sat at the foot of the bed. "I was the ring bearer."

"And you did a great job," Jack said, then turned to Roman. "What have you named your daughter?"

"Sofia." Roman swayed slightly as the baby fell asleep in his arms. "After my mother."

"A lovely name for a lovely little girl," Emma said.

Jack kept a tactful silence. The babe looked too fragile and frightening to him. But then, he hadn't had any experience with infants before this.

After the wedding ceremony, there'd been a short reception at the church to keep up appearances for the bride's mortal friends and family. Then the party had moved to the banquet hall at Romatech Industries where the Vamps could be themselves and toast the newlyweds with Bubbly Blood, a mixture of synthetic blood and champagne.

Jack had congratulated Ian and his bride, then wandered down the hall to the Romatech clinic where Shanna Draganesti had given birth to her second child.

He still marveled over the recent changes in the Vamp world. All his bachelor friends were suddenly succumbing to the lure of *amore*. Roman and Shanna seemed quite content. His boss, Angus MacKay, was deliriously happy with his wife, Emma. Jean-Luc had found Heather, and now Ian had married Toni.

You would think there was something in the water, but none of the Vamps drank water. They all survived off synthetic blood, first invented by Roman in 1987.

Only their enemy, the Malcontents, continued to feed off mortals, often killing them in the process.

Roman lowered his sleeping daughter into the bassinette next to the hospital bed.

"Isn't she beautiful?" Shanna whispered. "She has her daddy's dark hair."

Roman tucked a pink blanket around the baby. "I'm sorry I missed her arrival. I wanted to take the Stay-Awake drug."

"And I said no." Shanna smiled at her husband. "All you missed was me groaning and cursing men to hell for half the day. And when I was done screaming, Sofia took over."

"Look what I can do." Constantine tugged on Jack's suit jacket.

Jack glanced down just in time to see Roman's son vanish.

"Ta-da!" Tino reappeared across the room.

"*Santo cielo*, that's amazing!" Jack had already heard about Constantine's ability to teleport, but he figured the little boy was in need of some attention after the birth of his sister. And it truly was amazing. As far as Jack knew, Tino was the only mortal on earth who could teleport.

"Just remember not to do that tomorrow when your grandpa and grandma come to visit," Roman warned his son.

"I know." Tino hung his head. "Grandpa won't like me if he knows I'm different."

"He loves you," Shanna insisted. "We all love you. Grandpa just has trouble . . . understanding."

That was an understatement. Jack considered Shanna's father a loose cannon. As the head of the CIA Stake-Out team, Sean Whelan had started off wanting to kill all the Undead. Now that his daughter was married and having children with a powerful Vamp, Sean had reluctantly backed off the Vamps and was concentrating on the Malcontents.

Jack patted the little boy on the shoulder. "I think your grandpa would be jealous. You can do so many amazing things that he could never do."

Tino's blue eyes lit up. "Really?" He turned to his godfather. "Uncle Angus, when can I have a sword? You said you would give me one."

"Oh great," Shanna muttered and fell back against her pillows.

Emma chuckled. "We won't let him get hurt."

Angus swung the boy up into his arms. "Ye have to be able to lift a sword before ye can wield it."

Constantine wrapped his hands around Angus's neck. "I'm hungry."

"There's some food at the reception. Would ye like to go with me?" Angus asked.

"Oh yes!" Constantine squirmed in his godfather's arms. "I want to see Toni!"

"Verra well." Angus headed toward the door. "I'll bring him back in a little while."

"Thanks," Shanna said. "And please ask Ian and Toni to stop by before they leave. I was so sorry to miss the wedding."

"I'll tell you all about it," Emma said.

"*Scusi.*" Jack bowed to the ladies and nodded at Roman, then followed Angus out the door.

"I've reconsidered your offer," he told his boss as they walked down the hall. "I'll be happy to fill in for Ian." Since Ian was leaving for a three-month-long honeymoon with Toni, the position of head of security at Romatech Industries was temporarily vacant.

"Excellent." Angus set a squirming Tino down and let the boy run ahead of them. "But I'm wondering why ye changed yer mind. Last night at the party, ye told me ye were eager to return to Europe to search for Casimir."

Jack shrugged. "Our leads are dead. Literally." All of the recent sightings of Casimir had been in Eastern Europe, although the Vamps had never been able to pinpoint his exact location. Whenever one of Casimir's men turned informant, they never survived more than a few nights. "We're no closer to finding Casimir now than we were two years ago."

"Aye, 'tis verra frustrating."

Damned frustrating. Jack had serious doubts they could ever capture the leader of the Malcontents, not when he could simply teleport away if they got anywhere in his vicinity. "I thought about what you said, and you're right. The Russian-American coven will seek revenge."

Jack had helped Ian and Toni defeat the local Russian Malcontents when they'd taken over the Digital Vampire Network. That had been five months ago, just before Christmas. "Since I was involved in the incident at DVN, I should be here for the repercussions."

Angus nodded. "Did ye know they're calling the battle at DVN a massacre?"

"I'm not surprised." Jack could hear music as they approached the banquet hall. The band was playing a waltz. What a shame he couldn't invite Lara Boucher here. How glorious it would feel to hold her in his arms and swirl around the floor till they were both breathless and dizzy. He'd tighten his embrace until her soft breasts—

"Zoltan told me ye killed six Malcontents that night," Angus continued.

Jack frowned as the lovely mental image of Lara wavered and disappeared. "Zoltan talks too much.

I stopped counting the dead years ago. What's the point?"

Angus snorted. "The point is for every Malcontent ye kill, ye are saving countless mortals who would have been his victims."

"Oh right." Jack smiled wryly. "I'm one of the good guys." He doubted Lara Boucher would believe that. There had been two mortal women in his past, and they hadn't believed it.

Angus slapped him on the back. "Ye're a good lad, all right. I'm glad ye decided to stay in New York, but I'm wondering if yer decision has something to do with the pretty mortal who crashed Ian's wedding. I believe Robby said her name was Susie?"

"Robby talks too much."

"Robby was right to report a potential threat. She came to the wedding looking for you and carrying a weapon. Did she mean to do ye harm?"

Jack groaned inwardly. He should have known Robby would check that bag before handing it over. "Don't worry about it. I can handle her."

"How do ye know her?"

"She's a police officer."

"The devil take it," Angus muttered. "How much does she know?"

"Nothing. She and her partner were called to the hotel when our party got a little too rowdy." Jack gave his boss a wry look. "You all left me with a mess to clean up. Thank God Phineas came back with the Vampy Maids."

"Ye got the room back to normal?" When Jack nodded, Angus continued. "And ye followed standard protocol?"

"Yes. I erased all signs and memories that we were ever there. The hotel has no record of us. The paramedics who came for Laszlo have no memory of it. Even the dispatcher who called the police to the scene cannot remember it."

Angus paused outside the open doors to the banquet hall. "Why did paramedics come for Laszlo?"

Jack winced. Now he had talked too much. "She called them."

"Susie?"

"Her name is Lara." Jack didn't give out her last name. Somehow he felt possessive of that knowledge. He wanted to be the only one who would investigate her.

"Look!" Constantine pointed across the banquet hall. "There's Bethany and her mom. Can I go see them?"

Angus glanced at Jean-Luc's mortal wife and step-daughter. "Sure, lad." As the boy scampered off, Angus turned to Jack. "Laszlo told me she couldna be controlled with our psychic power."

"Laszlo talks too much."

Angus narrowed his green eyes. "Then it is true? Ye couldna erase her memories?"

Jack shifted his weight. "No. She's immune some-how."

"She's a threat——"

"No. I can handle her. The situation is under control."

Angus stared at the waltzing couples as they twirled about the dance floor. "How was she able to track you?"

"She knew from the claymores Ian left in the hotel room that the groom was Scottish," Jack began.

"So she crashed weddings with a Scottish groom till she found you?" Angus turned his attention back to Jack.

"Yes." Jack kept his face blank, aware that his boss was studying him carefully.

"She sounds clever. Robby said she was passing fair."

Jack snorted, then resumed his bland expression.

Angus arched a brow. "No comment?"

Jack gave him an annoyed look. "I've known you almost two hundred years, Angus. You're fishing."

Angus's mouth twitched. "Verra well. Robby actually said she was verra lovely."

Jack felt a strange sense of pride on Lara's behalf. "That would be correct."

Angus leaned back against the door frame and folded his arms. "Does she realize all signs of the party were erased?"

"Yes."

"And being a clever lass, she has questions, no doubt." Angus frowned. "I would order you never to see her again, but I'm afraid ye would disobey. I doona want to fire you. Ye're too valuable to the company."

Jack remained silent.

"So I'll suggest ye doona see her again," Angus continued. "Whatever ye do, doona tell her about us. That is an order."

Jack nodded. "I understand." There was no way he could tell Lara about vampires. He'd made the mistake twice in the past, telling his mistress in 1855 and another one in 1932. They'd both reacted so badly that he'd been forced to erase their memories. They'd gone on with their lives, blithely unaware of him and the heartache he'd endured for losing them.

It would be even worse with Lara. He couldn't erase her memory. A confession to her would be a giant leap forward that could never be taken back. Not only would he lose her, but she would remain a threat.

Angus rested a hand on his shoulder. "Be careful, lad. Be verra careful." He sauntered into the banquet hall.

Jack sighed. Telling Lara the truth would put his life and the lives of all his Vamp friends in jeopardy.

The full extent of his dilemma became painfully clear. He couldn't trust Lara enough to tell her the truth. And she would never trust him as long as he refused to tell her the truth. A no-win situation. He should follow Angus's advice and never see her again.

A small voice deep inside him whispered *no*. It repeated the word a bit louder and louder till it was shouting in his head. *Merda.* If she called him, if she needed him, he would rush to her side in a second.

Over the next week, Jack adjusted to his new job as head of security at Romatech Industries. It wasn't difficult. In fact, it felt like a vacation after two years of hunting for Casimir in Eastern Europe.

He'd arrived in New York City at the beginning of May in order to attend the annual spring conference and Gala Ball. Then, with Ian's wedding only a week away, it had made sense to stay in New York. Now that he was filling in for Ian, he'd remain here another three months.

Romatech was a bustling place during the day, with two hundred mortal employees making synthetic blood that was shipped to hospitals and blood banks. At night, about fifty Vamp employees arrived. A few, like Laszlo, were brilliant scientists who assisted Roman. The others, not so brilliant, packaged and shipped synthetic blood and Vampire Fusion Cuisine to Vamps around the world. It was Jack's job to keep them safe from the Malcontents, who considered Romatech a prime terrorist target.

Phineas McKinney was there to help him. Dougal Kincaid, who had been stationed at Romatech for five years, was reassigned to Eastern Europe to help Angus search for Casimir. Connor Buchanan was on hand to advise Jack. As personal bodyguard to Roman and the Draganesti family, Connor was often at Romatech.

Whenever Phineas made the rounds, Jack found himself alone in the security office, and his thoughts always wandered back to Lara Boucher. She hadn't called, so hopefully, that meant she was safe. He was tempted to call her, but always managed to resist. Instead, he appeased his curiosity by researching her on the computer.

He knew where she lived. He knew she worked from the Midtown North Precinct. But the more he found out about her past, the more confused he became. She didn't make sense.

She was from a town in northern Louisiana, where her father had served as mayor and her mother resided on the board at the local country club. Lara could be living a charmed life there, so why did she move to New York City? At the age of seventeen, she'd won the title of Miss Teen Louisiana. Why would she give up a pampered life to become a police officer?

On the third night of his investigation, he located a newspaper article that was six years old. FORMER MISS TEEN LOUISIANA NEARLY DIES IN CAR ACCIDENT. His heart tightened in his chest. *Santo cielo*. The photo showed a crumpled car turned upside down. Lara had been inside that? He scanned the article. *Intensive care. Not expected to live.*

Merda. What pain and horror had this poor girl endured? He reached for the phone to call her.

No. He'd begged her to leave him alone, and she had. He closed the browser window and paced across the office. He should avoid her like Angus said. No good could come from contacting her. Instead, he should be grateful that she'd recovered from the accident. She was alive and well.

And risking her life every night on the street. He pulled his cell phone from his pocket. She could have called during the day while he was in his death-sleep. No messages. He entered her home and work numbers into his phone's directory. Just in case.

Nine circles of hell. What a fool he was. Seven nights had passed, and he still wanted to see her. He almost wished she would get into trouble.

It was just after eleven Sunday night when Lara and her partner arrived at a fifth-floor condo overlooking Hudson River Park. Mrs. Kelsey Trent had called 911, asking for help before abruptly hanging up. Lara could hear the screaming voices from the hallway. A man and a woman.

Harvey knocked on the green-painted door. "NYPD!"

Lara waited about four feet away from Harvey, her weapon drawn and ready if her partner was attacked.

The door swung open. "What the hell do you want?" A middle-aged man stood there in plaid pajama bottoms and a navy T-shirt. His eyes narrowed at the sight of their uniforms. "You must be at the wrong place. There's nothing going on here."

"Are you Mr. Trent?" Harvey asked.

"Maybe. What do you want?"

The man reeked of alcohol, and Lara noted the bloody knuckles on his right hand.

"We received a call," Harvey said. "May we come in?"

"A call?" Mr. Trent gave them a confused look, then his expression cleared. He looked over his shoulder. "You stupid bitch, did you call the police?"

Lara heard a feminine groan from inside the condo.

She raised her voice. "Mrs. Trent, do you need medical attention?"

"There's nothing wrong with her," Mr. Trent insisted.

Lara lifted her chin. "We're not leaving, Mr. Trent, until we have properly assessed your wife's physical condition."

"Well, aren't you the feisty one," Mr. Trent sneered at her. "Then come in, sweetcakes, and properly assess. Assess your little ass off."

Harvey stepped into the foyer and neatly maneuvered the drunken man to the side so Lara could enter. "Can you tell me what happened, sir?"

Mr. Trent ran a hand through his thinning hair. "Kelsey slipped in the shower. That's all."

Lara quickly surveyed the foyer. An oriental rug ran the length of the polished wooden floor. Against one wall rested a wooden console table, topped with a brass lamp that illuminated the narrow hall. Arched openings led into a living room on one side and a dining room on the other. There were closed doors at the back of the foyer and a cushioned bench.

A woman sat there. Kelsey Trent, Lara assumed. Her peach-colored silk bathrobe matched her slippers. She'd folded her arms on her knees and was leaning over to rest her forehead on her arms.

"We heard your voice raised in anger," Harvey told the drunken husband.

"I was yelling at Kelsey for being so clumsy," Mr. Trent grumbled. "Because I care so much, you know."

Lara holstered her sidearm and sat on the bench next to the wife. "Mrs. Trent, are you all right?"

She lifted her head. Her left eye was puffy and bruised, and her lip was cut. She cast a wary glance at her husband. "I . . . fell in the shower."

"See?" Mr. Trent said. "That's what I told you."

"Let's go to the kitchen and fix you an ice pack." Lara helped the woman stand and gave Harvey a pointed look.

Harvey would understand. He would commiserate with the husband, trying to lure him into a confession of assault and battery. They could go ahead and arrest Mr. Trent on suspicion, but a confession would make it easier to convict him in court.

"Kitchen's in here." Kelsey Trent opened a door and led Lara into a brightly lit room.

Lara grabbed a dish towel off the gray granite countertop and opened the freezer door. "Do you have any other injuries?"

"No, I'm fine." Kelsey sat at the kitchen table. "I just slipped and fell."

Lara deposited a handful of ice cubes in the center of the towel. "Let's be honest about this, okay? If you had fallen in the shower, it wouldn't be just your face that was hurt."

Kelsey's shoulders drooped.

Lara folded the towel, encasing the ice inside. On the way to the table, she noticed the empty vodka bottle in the sink. "You called us for help, Kelsey. We can't help you if you won't tell us the truth."

"I—I shouldn't have fussed at him for drinking so much."

Lara handed her the ice pack. "This is not your fault. How many times has he hit you?"

Kelsey dabbed the ice pack against her lip. "This is only the second—no, third time."

"One time is too many." Lara sat beside her. "You need to put a stop to it. Press charges."

"No! That would make Charlie so mad. It would get even worse then."

"No, it would be better. He'd be in jail."

Kelsey's bruised face contorted with horror. "But what would I do without him?"

I don't know, live? Lara tamped down on her growing frustration. "Listen, he's going to keep using you as a punching bag. In fact, you can count on him getting more and more violent."

Kelsey glanced at the open door. "What's that officer doing to him? He won't arrest Charlie, will he?"

"They're just talking for now—"

"He'd better not make Charlie mad," Kelsey continued, growing more agitated. "Charlie has a gun in the living—"

"*What?*" Lara rose to her feet. "Stay here."

She unsnapped her holster as she peered into the foyer. No sign of Harvey or Charlie Trent. They must have moved into the living room. She raised her voice. "Harvey? Can I speak to you for a minute?"

"What are you doing?" Kelsey shouted. "Don't shoot my Charlie!"

"Quiet," Lara hissed. She heard male voices shouting. "Harvey!"

BAM! A gun fired.

Kelsey screamed.

Lara's heart lurched in her chest, and she drew her weapon. "Harvey, answer me!"

"Goddammit!" Charlie roared from the living room. "You stupid bitch! This wouldn't have happened if you hadn't called the police!"

Lara could hardly think with Charlie bellowing and Kelsey shrieking. Panic seized her as she mentally pictured Harvey dying on the living-room floor. *Get a grip.* Harvey needed her to stay calm. She'd gone through a jillion simulations like this at the academy, but still, she wasn't prepared for the sheer terror of real people dying.

She punched the transmitter on her shoulder. "Shots fired. Officer down. Requesting an ambulance and immediate backup."

"Ten-four. They're on their way," the dispatcher said.

Even so, it could take five minutes or more for the cavalry to arrive. Lara's heart thundered in her ears as she positioned herself next to the door frame and readied her pistol. "Charlie Trent! Put down your gun and step into the foyer with your hands up!"

"I'm not going to jail for this!" Charlie shouted. "Goddammit! This is Kelsey's fault. I'll make her pay."

A chill crept down Lara's back. Charlie was planning to take everyone down with him. She shut the kitchen door. It would take Charlie a few seconds to open it, and in those few seconds, she would have to shoot. She glanced around and spotted two more doors. One looked like it led into the dining room. What if Charlie attacked from that direction? And then, there was a third door. She rushed over to Kelsey. "Where does that door lead?"

"It's a back entrance."

"Then I want you to leave. Now."

Kelsey shook her head, whimpering.

"I'll kill you, you stupid bitch," Charlie yelled. "And the children, too."

Children? Lara's heart plummeted. "You have children?"

Kelsey burst into tears. "My babies."

This was a nightmare. Lara fought to remain calm. Was Harvey dead? Would Charlie attack his wife first or the children? Oh God, she couldn't think. She needed to act now. She had to stop Charlie before he killed anyone. Dammit! If only there was another option . . .

If you're ever in trouble . . .

He couldn't come here immediately. Or could he? Jack was so . . . different.

"I'm coming for you, Kelsey!" Charlie yelled.

Lara heaved at the thick kitchen table and it fell onto its side with a loud crash. She squatted behind it with Kelsey. With shaking fingers, she retrieved her cell phone from her shirt pocket. Three days ago, she'd told her roommate about Jack. LaToya had urged her to call him, but Lara had refused. Then LaToya had swiped Lara's phone and entered Jack's number on speed dial at number one.

What did she have to lose? Lara pressed *1*, then set the phone down and readied her weapon.

Charlie's heavy footsteps pounded across the foyer.

"*Pronto?*" Jack's voice emanated from the phone.

"Jack—"

The kitchen door burst open and shots exploded across the room.

Chapter Five

*L*ara's heart slammed in her chest as she crouched behind the thick table with Kelsey Trent. Charlie had taken a few wild shots as he'd entered the kitchen, probably to keep her from shooting him. A bullet whizzed over her head and thudded into the wall behind her. Kelsey screamed.

Lara's chest constricted, making it hard to breathe. The thought of sticking her head out was terrifying. But she had to see to take aim. She struggled to remember all the instructions that had been drummed into her head at the academy. Dammit. She'd thought the simulations were scary, but they were child's play compared to the real thing.

The shots stopped.

Now or never. Lara leaned to the side of the table and aimed her pistol. Time suddenly slowed to a crawl. A cold sweat chilled her skin while her ears filled with a buzzing noise. All she could feel was her right index finger crooked against the trigger, ready to kill.

God, no. Forced to kill someone. She'd known in

theory that this could happen, but she'd foolishly believed that somehow, if she was careful enough, it never would.

Charlie spotted her and aimed his gun.

This was it.

The air wavered in front of Lara.

"What the hell?" Charlie stumbled backward.

He saw it, too? Lara's knees shook in her semi-crouched position. The multicolored pocket of air took shape. Human shape. *Jack.* She gasped.

"Oh my God!" Charlie pointed his gun.

With a blur of super speed, Jack knocked the gun from Charlie's hand and slammed him down onto the tile floor.

Lara blinked, stunned by Jack's speed. In the milli-second it took to reopen her eyes, Jack had Charlie pinned down and his hands pulled behind his back. *Jack be nimble, Jack be quick.*

"Get off me!" Charlie squirmed, but couldn't budge his captor.

A wave of cold air swirled around the room.

Jack's eyes narrowed, gleaming with a golden inten-sity. "Be still. Be quiet."

Charlie went limp. Kelsey slumped against the table with a blank expression. Lara shivered. *Jack.* He was doing his mind tricks again.

"Lara, pass me your handcuffs," Jack demanded.

Icy cold vapor crept along her skin. Oh God, it had been cold in the hotel room, too. Was Jack doing that? And how had he magically appeared out of thin air?

He glanced at her. "Are you all right?"

"I—" She stumbled, and her pistol knocked against a table leg. She glanced at it, confused and disoriented by a reality that had suddenly zoomed forward at warp speed.

"Put the gun away, Lara," Jack spoke softly. "And give me your handcuffs."

She holstered her sidearm, then walked stiffly over to Jack and handed him the cuffs. "Thank God you came." She hadn't had to shoot. Jack had saved her from killing. Jack may have saved her life. And the lives of everyone else in the house. Including her partner . . .

"Harvey!" She ran from the kitchen and located him on the floor in the living room. He was barely conscious, his hand pressed against his blood-soaked shirt.

She spotted a laundry basket full of folded clothes on the coffee table and grabbed whatever was on top. A bath towel, good. She knelt beside her partner and pressed the towel against the bullet wound in his side.

"Butch," Harvey gasped. "Thank God. I heard gunshots. I was afraid you were—"

"I'm fine. Everything's under control. You just hang in there, okay? The bus is on its way."

Harvey grimaced. "I was stupid. I saw his gun, but I hesitated. I—I've never had to shoot anyone before."

"I know." Lara's vision blurred with tears. "I didn't want to shoot, either." What a relief Jack had arrived when he did. But now that she was away from him, she could feel the cold fog clearing from her mind. She realized Kelsey and her crazy husband were staying perfectly still and quiet because Jack had ordered them to be that way. He'd taken complete control of the situation without even wrinkling his expensive suit.

She shuddered. What sort of man could magically appear? Or move as fast as lightning? Or control people's minds? At least he was on her side. Otherwise, he could be a really dangerous man.

Lara's attention snapped back to Harvey when his eyes flickered shut. "Harvey? Harvey, hang in there."

"He's unconscious." Jack strode into the room. "He'll

need a transfusion right away." He closed his eyes briefly and drew in a deep breath. "He's Type O positive."

"How can you tell?" Lara kept the towel pressed against Harvey's wound as she looked Jack over. He looked so normal, if you could count extreme good looks as normal.

He knelt beside her. "I assume you called for backup and an ambulance?" When she nodded, he continued, "The man and woman won't remember me. I've altered their memories—"

"How? How do you do it?"

"It's hard to explain." He raised a hand when she started to object. "Not now, Lara. We're short on time, and we need to make sure your story matches up."

"You expect me to lie?"

"This is the truth for the couple in the kitchen. After the man shot your partner, he came after you. You hid his wife behind the table while you waited just inside the door. He barged inside, shooting wildly, and you knocked him on the back of the head with your baton."

"That's the way they remember it?"

"Yes. The guy fell unconscious on the floor. You cuffed him, then ran in here to help your partner."

"I don't think the guy was ever unconscious."

"He will be soon." Jack removed a white handkerchief from an inner coat pocket. "Give me your baton."

"He's already restrained. You're going to hit him?"

"Lara, the story has to make sense. It'll be more believable that you subdued an armed man who's bigger than you if you first rendered him unconscious."

He was right, though Lara didn't like to admit it. Sirens wailed outside. Backup was arriving, and hopefully, an ambulance for Harvey. "Here." She handed Jack the baton. "But don't hit him too hard."

Jack's mouth curled up. "You're too sweet for this line of work, *bellissima*." His smile faded. "That man tried to kill you. He deserves more than a knot on his head."

Jack left the room, holding the baton with the handkerchief. Lara wondered if he was right, and she cared too much. But if she didn't care, how could she be a good cop? She tensed, waiting for a sound.

Clonk. She winced. Harvey hadn't yelped or even moaned. He had obeyed Jack's order to remain quiet. In a few seconds, Jack was back and handing her the baton.

She wedged it under her belt. "How do you move so fast?"

He dragged a hand through his thick black hair. "There's no time to explain now."

But she wanted answers *now*, dammit. She knew the rest of tonight would be taken up with paperwork and hospital visits to check on Harvey. "Okay. Tomorrow."

She turned her head as footsteps pounded down the hallway outside. It sounded like a herd of elephants charging to the rescue. She could almost picture Tarzan riding on one of their backs. No, wait. The wildly handsome hero was already in the room.

"You'd better tell me everything tomorrow." She turned back to Jack.

He was gone.

"Oh, that smells good!" LaToya Lafayette dropped her handbag and keys on the console by the door. "What's cooking, girl?"

"Blackened redfish." Lara carefully turned the fish filets in the skillet.

"Great!" LaToya removed her purple LSU Tiger hoodie and fluffed up her glossy black corkscrew curls.

"It's been raining all damned day." She draped the damp sweatshirt over the back of a chair in their tiny living room. "So how come you're cooking? Not that I'm complaining. I love your cooking. But I was planning to take you out to celebrate."

"I don't want to make a big deal out of it."

"But it *is* a big deal." LaToya strode into the kitchen. "You saved that woman's life. Her children, too. And Harvey."

"I didn't save Harvey. The doctors did that."

"You're too modest, girl." LaToya washed her hands in the kitchen sink. "Everyone was talking about you at my precinct. I heard they're going to do a press conference with the chief of police giving you a commendation."

"Oh God, I hope not." Lara added chopped parsley and chives to the bowl of mashed potatoes.

"You know they'll milk this for all it's worth. Three months out of the academy and you're saving the day. You're like the poster child for how successful their training program is."

"But I didn't do anything!" Lara smashed a clove of garlic with the flat edge of a knife. "Jack did it."

"You know that. I know that. But nobody else does." LaToya leaned a hip against the counter. "Now don't look at me that way, holding a knife, girl."

Lara snorted as she scraped the smashed garlic into the potatoes. After a few hours of filling out forms and being interviewed by the detectives that had taken over the case, then another two hours spent at the hospital to check on Harvey, Lara had finally dragged home to her Brooklyn apartment about eight-thirty in the morning.

She'd recounted the story to LaToya before her friend had left for her job in the twenty-sixth precinct. Then

Lara had showered and climbed into bed. But even in her state of exhaustion, she'd had trouble sleeping. Gunshots and screams bounced around in her head along with visions of Harvey, bleeding on the floor.

And she'd kept wondering about Jack. She'd decided the best way to thank him for charging to the rescue was a home-cooked meal, Louisiana style. She'd called his number, but he hadn't answered the phone. She left a message inviting him to dinner, then headed to the grocery store. She tried calling again about five P.M.

He never called back.

"What's in this salad?" LaToya studied the wooden bowl as she carried it to the table.

"Spinach, fire-roasted tomatoes, and pine nuts."

"Ooh, fancy." LaToya's gaze wandered over their best china, cloth napkins, and candlesticks. "You went to a lot of trouble here."

"I was bored." Lara loaded up two plates with fish and potatoes. "The captain ordered me to take some time off."

"With pay? You lucky dog." LaToya struck a match and lit the candles. "Even so, this seems awfully . . . romantic."

"Let's eat." Lara set the plates on the table.

LaToya's brown eyes narrowed as she blew out the match. "You did this for Jack, didn't you?"

Lara heaved a sigh as she sat at the table. There was no point in denying it. "All right. I invited him to dinner, but he never returned my call. That doesn't mean I wasn't planning to eat with you."

Latoya sat across from her. "Girl, I know when three's a crowd. I would have left you alone with the mystery man. But you say he never called back?"

"Nope." Lara heaped some salad into their salad bowls. "And I left *two* messages on his voice mail."

"Maybe he didn't get them."

"I'm not calling him again. That would sound desperate. And I'm not desperate. At all." *Liar.* She had really wanted to see him again.

LaToya drizzled balsamic vinaigrette over her salad. "That jerk. I'm tempted to call him myself and give him a piece of my mind."

"*No!*"

LaToya smirked, then strode toward the refrigerator. "I have the perfect solution for this. Wine. It's multipurpose. We can toast your heroic feats and drown our sorrows over disappointing men all at the same time."

"I'll drink to that." Lara stabbed at her salad. The food looked and smelled great, but her appetite was lacking. Damn that Jack. He didn't make any sense. He'd risked his life to help her, and now, he couldn't even return her call?

LaToya brought two glasses filled with white wine to the table. She sat and raised her glass. "A toast. To my best friend, a real hero."

"I'm not a hero. It's bad enough to hear it at work, but I don't want to hear from you, when you know the truth."

LaToya scowled at her. "Yeah, girl, I know the truth. If it wasn't for you, I'd still be a clerk in a convenience store in some town no one's ever heard of. You kept me going when I didn't think I could. You *are* my hero."

Lara's eyes misted with tears. She'd first met LaToya when they'd shared a hospital room together after her car accident. LaToya had been shot during a robbery at the convenience store where she worked. Whereas Lara had lived a pampered life before the accident, LaToya had struggled to survive years of abuse. "You hated me at first."

LaToya smiled. "I thought you were a spoiled little white girl. Miss Teen Louisiana."

Lara winced. "And I'm sure it didn't help matters when my mom came to visit wearing a tiara and sash."

LaToya laughed. "Your mom is wack, girl."

"That's for sure." Lara's mom was still entering beauty pageants at the age of fifty-two. "You helped me, too, you know. It would have been so much harder to rebel against my family and follow my dreams if I'd been all alone. I don't know what I would have done without you."

"To us." LaToya tapped Lara's glass with her own. "The two most bad-ass rookie cops in the big city."

"To us. Live long and prosper." Lara recited their favorite toast, borrowed from the Vulcans on *Star Trek*.

They ate in silence for a while, and Lara's thoughts drifted back to Jack. The rascal had altered Mr. and Mrs. Trent's memories so that their statements made her sound like a hero. And she had to make sure her story matched theirs. "I have to go see the department shrink."

"That's probably routine procedure." LaToya scooped some potatoes into her mouth.

"I suppose." Lara pushed her fish around the plate. "I'm kinda worried about it. I mean, what if I tell the doctor my story, and he realizes I'm lying?"

"He won't question it. Not when it confirms everything the Trents said."

Lara sighed. "I'm not at all comfortable with everyone thinking I'm a hero."

"Get over it already. That's why we wanted to be cops, remember? We wanted to catch the bad guys and make a difference. Besides, no one's going to believe that some strange guy magically appeared to save the day."

Lara set down her fork. "You believe me, don't you?"

LaToya's brown eyes softened, and she reached forward to touch Lara's hand. "I do. I watched you in the hospital when you struggled to learn how to read and write again. I was with you when we both struggled through classes at LSU. And I survived the academy with you. I know you're not going to lie to me, no matter how strange it sounds."

"Thank you." Lara squeezed her friend's hand, then picked up her fork. "I have to be very careful talking to the shrink. I don't want him thinking that I'm still suffering from my brain injury."

"You're not. That was six years ago. You're over it."

"How can you be so sure? No one remembers seeing Jack but me. What if he's a figment of my imagination?"

"Then who knocked down Mr. Trent? And what about that business card he gave you? His phone number worked."

"That's true." She hadn't imagined the business card.

"You saw him at Ian MacPhie's wedding," LaToya continued. "And I know Ian MacPhie is real. I called him when he was on that dating website."

"You didn't."

"I sure did." LaToya took her plate into the kitchen. "Some lady took my message, then Ian called back really late, about midnight. I was kinda pissed, especially when he said he was already taken, but his accent was really cute."

Lara shook her head. "I can't believe you called him."

"*I* can't believe you didn't take me to his wedding." LaToya planted her fists on her hips. "I would have loved to see him. Is he as good-looking as his photo?"

"I didn't actually see him."

"Are you crazy? The guy is hot!"

"And taken, remember?"

LaToya sighed. "Yeah, I know. So how does this Jack look? Is he anywhere as cute as Ian?"

Lara couldn't quite recall how Ian had looked. It didn't matter. There was no way he could look better than Jack. She brought her dishes into the kitchen. "Jack is the most gorgeous man I have ever set eyes on."

"Really?"

"Which probably means that I *am* imagining him." Lara wrenched open the refrigerator door. "How about dessert? I made a Mississippi mud pie."

"Damn, girl, you went all out."

Lara set the pie on the counter. "I wanted him to answer my questions."

"Fine food, candlelight—sounds to me like you wanted to do more than just talk."

Lara shot her friend an annoyed look, then sliced two pieces of pie. "I was merely trying to set the mood so he'd be comfortable enough to spill all his secrets."

"Right." LaToya grabbed a fork and a saucer of pie, then headed back to the table. "Where I come from, Mississippi mud pie means let's get down and dirty, honey."

With a snort, Lara set her plate of pie on the table. She went back to the kitchen for a glass of water. "I'm afraid he's avoiding me 'cause he doesn't want to divulge his secrets."

"Hmmm." LaToya considered with a mouth full of pie. "We want to be detectives, right? We'll just figure out his deep dark secrets on our own."

"I've been trying to do that for a week." Lara sipped water on her way back to the table. "All I can figure out for certain is that he's psychic."

" 'Cause he messes with people's minds?"

"Yep." Lara sat. "But he's got other powers, too, that I can't explain. Like super speed."

"Then he's a superhero. You know, faster than a speeding bullet." LaToya shoved some pie in her mouth.

"This is the real world, not a comic book. How could a normal guy suddenly become a superhero?"

LaToya's eyes twinkled with humor. "Maybe he got zapped by lightning or fell into a vat of acid."

Lara laughed. "He might look delicious, but he doesn't look deep-fat fried."

"Then he's got to be an alien. That's how Superman got his powers."

Lara ate some pie while she mentally pictured Jack in a latex costume with a cape fluttering in the wind. Damn, he looked good. "I wouldn't be entirely opposed to a superhero if he looks like Jack. But it doesn't explain how he can appear and disappear at will."

"That's a tough one." LaToya stuffed more pie in her mouth, then her eyes lit up. "I got it! Astral projection."

"What?"

"It means he stayed in one spot while his spirit—"

"I know what it means, but Jack wasn't a spirit. He slammed Charlie Trent onto the floor and cuffed him."

"Okay." LaToya frowned. "Then he can't be a ghost."

"No." Lara recalled the way she'd rubbed against him in the church closet. "He is totally solid."

"You've touched him?"

Lara shrugged. "In the process of interrogating him."

LaToya snorted. "I bet. So the only explanation for the disappearing act is the guy knows how to teleport. Like on *Star Trek*."

"It would appear so, but teleportation hasn't been invented yet."

LaToya pointed her fork at Lara and gave her a knowing look. "That's what they want us to believe."

Lara grinned. "You think NASA or some secret branch of the government has discovered how to teleport?"

"Yeah. And this Jack is one of their secret agents."

"Hard to believe," Lara mumbled with her mouth full.

"I've got it!" LaToya's face beamed with excitement. "He's a secret agent from the *future*."

"Right. Teleportation and time travel together. That makes it much more believable."

LaToya glared at her. "Hey, it makes sense. People don't know how to teleport now, but they will in the future. *Ipso facto*, he's from the future."

"And he traveled back in time to throw a bachelor party at the Plaza hotel."

"All right, mock me all you like." LaToya took her empty plate to the kitchen. "But you won't like the alternative. Since humans don't know how to teleport, then your Jack has to be an alien."

"You can't be serious."

LaToya pointed a finger at Lara. "This is the second train of thought that's ended up with him being an alien. A coincidence?" She wagged her finger and her head. "I don't think so. Does he spell his name with an apostrophe? Like J'Ack instead of . . . Jack?"

"Why would he do that? It sounds exactly the same."

"All the aliens do it. It's part of their code."

Lara snorted. "He seemed awfully human to me."

"He wants you to think he's human, but it's all a façade. He's playing with your mind, making you see him as a human, when he's really a slimy creature with tentacles. And then, he'll impregnate you with his alien baby, and it'll rip right through your stomach—"

"Enough!" Lara took the rest of her pie to the kitchen and dumped it in the trash. "I just lost my appetite."

"Has he made a move on you? Has he tried to kiss you?"

"Not really. Well, sorta. But I asked him to." Lara chafed under the look of horror LaToya was giving her. "I didn't mean it. It was an interrogation technique."

LaToya scoffed. "I must have missed that lesson at the academy. But now that I think about it, you do need to make a move on him. Get him to take his clothes off."

"Why would I do that?" Although the prospect did sound rather appealing. "I have no interest in him that way."

LaToya gave her a skeptical look. "Are you going to tell me you never thought about jumping his bones?"

Lara's face grew hot. "Fine. But if he's really an alien, then we're probably not biologically compatible."

"Oh good Lord, you're right. He might not even be a mammal. He could be a reptile and have two . . . hearts."

Lara grimaced. "You've been watching too much science fiction. Just because Jack can teleport, that doesn't make him some kind of lizard."

The phone rang.

Lara jumped. Was Jack finally returning her call?

"It's the lizard," LaToya whispered.

"Don't be silly. He's as human as you and me." Lara hurried to the phone, then hesitated. "No, you answer it."

LaToya lifted both hands in the air. "I ain't talking to no alien."

"He's not an alien." The phone rang again. "I need someone else to hear him, so I'll know I'm not crazy."

LaToya heaved a sigh. "Okay. I'll do it for you." The phone rang again, and she grabbed the receiver. "Hello? You have reached the Boucher and Lafayette terrestrial home."

Lara groaned.

"You want to talk to Lara?" LaToya spoke with a high-pitched sweet voice. "May I ask who's calling? Why yes, Jack, I'll fetch her right away. Just a moment, please." She covered the receiver with her hand. "It's the talking lizard. And honey, he ain't selling insurance."

Chapter Six

Sometimes Jack wished he didn't have superior hearing.

"He's not a lizard," Lara whispered.

"Then he's another kind of alien," the other woman muttered. "And this Jack is jacking with your mind to make you see him as human."

He shook his head as the two women continued to discuss him in urgent whispers. Obviously, Lara had told her roommate about him. Now there were two mortals who knew too much. He could erase the roommate's memory, but Lara would probably resent his *jacking* with her friend's mind. And she'd simply tell her friend everything again.

He retrieved a bottle of synthetic blood from the mini-fridge and popped it into the microwave. Whenever he was in New York, he resided at Roman's townhouse on the Upper East Side. The Russian-American Malcontents were headquartered in Brooklyn, not far away, but luckily, they were laying low at this time. And the security system at Roman's townhouse had been improved to make it safe.

Jack usually stayed in a guest room on the fourth floor so he could use Roman's office and mini-fridge on the fifth. The microwave dinged, announcing his breakfast was ready. He poured the blood into a wineglass, then sauntered to the desk with his cell phone by his ear.

"Hello, Jack?" Lara finally answered. "Sorry you had to wait. I was . . . in the shower."

She was a lousy liar, but he considered that a virtue. "I hope you put something on, *bellissima*. Otherwise, my imagination will run wild." As if it wasn't already.

"I—I'm dressed. I'm glad you called. I left some messages on your phone this afternoon."

"I just heard them a minute ago." He sat behind the desk and booted up the computer. "I work at night, so I'm . . . asleep during the day."

"Me, too, but I had trouble sleeping today. So I decided to cook you dinner, but when you didn't call back, we . . . uh, we ate it. Sorry."

"That's all right." Jack sipped from his wineglass. He figured the dinner invitation was part of a plan to confront him with all her questions. Unfortunately, he couldn't give her any answers. "I'm sorry I missed it."

"That's okay. Maybe you could drop by for dessert?"

Merda. He wasn't sure how to handle this. Maybe he could put her off for a few months. Then Ian would be back from his honeymoon, and Jack could return to Europe. Lara would never be able to track him down.

He grimaced. Avoiding her till he could run away seemed cowardly. And the thought of never seeing her again was downright depressing. "I—I have to go to work soon."

"But I really wanted to see you *tonight*." Lara's voice sounded strained. "I can meet you somewhere when you go on break."

She wasn't going to give up. Normally Jack admired a person who stuck to a project till it was done, but when the project was *him*, he was beginning to feel as desperate as Lara sounded.

He didn't want to tell her where he was staying or where he was currently working. "I'll drop by your place for a few minutes." He typed in her address on MapQuest.

"Thank you! Do you need directions? Or does 'dropping by' mean you're going to magically appear in front of me?"

Jack winced. How could he deny his ability to teleport when she'd seen it? He studied the map to her apartment. "I'll drive. I should be there in thirty to forty minutes."

"You know where I live?"

"Yes." He would ask Phineas and Connor to cover for him at Romatech for an hour or so. He heard Lara whispering again to her roommate.

"I doubt he's driving a space shuttle," Lara muttered.

Nine circles of hell. Lara was going to be really angry when she realized he couldn't tell her anything.

"So, uh, I guess you have an Italian car?" Lara asked.

"Not here in America. I'll borrow a car from a friend." Roman always kept one at the townhouse.

"What kind of car?"

"Why do you ask?"

"Oh, no reason. But if it's really big, you might have trouble parking."

He couldn't resist. "*Bellissima*, it *is* big, but I've never had trouble parking it." He smiled as a period of silence stretched between them.

"O-kay," she finally said. "I'll see you soon." She rang off.

Jack finished his breakfast while he pondered her request for a description of his car. She was up to something. If she were a Malcontent, he'd suspect her of wanting to set a car bomb, but he didn't think Lara wanted to kill him.

Of course that could change if she learned the truth about him. He knew from experience that women didn't react well to the truth. He'd have to be a fool to repeat the same mistake and expect a different outcome.

"Hey, someone's parking down the street," LaToya reported on her cell phone. "Oh, I forgot. This is a stakeout." She switched to a low, urgent voice. "Possible sighting of male subject, driving a red Toyota."

"A Toyota? That doesn't sound very Jack-ish," Lara said. Thirty minutes had passed, and she was waiting anxiously in the apartment on the third floor, while LaToya was stationed on the street below. Their plan was for LaToya to spot Jack arriving so she could write down his license plate number. Then, while Lara interrogated Jack in the apartment, LaToya could run his plates.

Lara watched from the living-room window as LaToya wandered slowly down the street, pretending to window-shop. It was dark outside, but the streetlamps cast yellow pools of light that reflected eerily off the wet cement.

"Subject has exited his car," LaToya whispered into her phone. "Dark hair. Average height. Average looks."

"Jack has black hair," Lara said. "But I'd say he's taller than average. And way better-looking than the—"

"Average alien?" LaToya muttered. "Subject has entered the deli. Don't think he's our man. And it's starting to drizzle again, dammit."

"You want to come in?"

"Negative. I'm on a mission. Possible alien incursion." LaToya pulled the hood of her LSU sweatshirt over her head. "Hey, I wonder what aliens eat. I hope your Jack isn't here to harvest us for food."

"Jack is *not* an alien." But Lara wasn't sure what he was. She glanced around the apartment to make sure it was presentable. The dishes had been rinsed and stashed in the dishwasher. The kitchen opened onto the living room, which was so small, it was easy to keep clean. Her bedroom was a little messy, but she didn't intend to invite Jack there, even though LaToya insisted she should strip him to check for multiple belly buttons or hidden scales and gills.

Lara's heart speeded up at the mere thought of seeing him again. How would he explain things to her? And how would she react? What if he actually confessed to being an alien? She snorted. LaToya's silliness was getting to her. There had to be a reasonable explanation for Jack's bizarre abilities. *Please let it be reasonable.*

She wanted him to be human. And available. And interested in her. Oh what the hell, she wanted him to worship the ground she walked on.

"Dammit, would you look at that?" LaToya growled.

"What?" Lara strained to see out the window. "Have you spotted him?"

"No. I'm looking in the window at Mrs. Yee's bakery. She swears everything is fresh every day, but this cream puff with the chocolate icing has the same little black spot on it that the one yesterday had. I'm telling you it's the same one."

"LaToya, you've been lusting after those cream puffs

for a week. Just buy one and eat the damned thing."

"Are you kidding? You know how many calories that is?"

Lights flashed across the dark, wet pavement as a new car turned onto the street.

From Lara's vantage point, she couldn't spot the car yet. "Can you see it?"

"Affirmative. Black four-door sedan. Windshield wipers on. Driving slow, like he's looking for a place to park."

Lara tensed as it drove by. "I think it's a Lexus. Could be Jack."

"Windows were tinted," LaToya continued. "I couldn't see the driver. Wait. He's parking at the corner by the magazine stand. I'll head that way."

Lara watched as LaToya strolled past the shops.

"Oh my God," LaToya whispered.

"What? Are you all right?" Lara asked. Her friend had stopped in her tracks.

"Oh my God." LaToya turned to look into a shop window that was, unfortunately, empty. "He's across the street at the end of the block. And he is so *hot!*"

"It must be Jack." Lara's heart pounded faster. Good God, this was ridiculous. She was acting like a teenager with a crush on the best-looking boy in school. She needed to get a grip. There'd been plenty of good-looking boys who had wanted to date her after she'd won Miss Teen Louisiana. It hadn't taken her long to realize that they'd merely wanted to boost their own ego and reputation. Any beauty queen sufficed. She'd been an object, not a person, and after the car accident, they'd all quickly disappeared.

"Status report: totally hot subject is halfway to our apartment," LaToya whispered. "Too hot to be a cold-blooded lizard. I repeat, subject is *not* a lizard."

Lara pressed against the window, trying to catch a glimpse of him.

"Oh no!" LaToya hissed. "He just looked at me."

Lara gasped when a tall, dark-haired man jogged across the street, headed straight for LaToya. *Jack.*

"I told you, Bob," LaToya yelled into the phone. "It's over between us. Pack up your crap and move out!"

Lara held her breath to see if her friend's playacting would fool Jack.

"Miss." His voice could be heard over LaToya's phone. "You are Lara Boucher's roommate, no?"

"I—who?" LaToya huffed. "I don't know who you're talking about."

"I recognize your voice," Jack said.

He'd managed to hear LaToya's hushed voice from across the street? Lara wondered if super hearing was another one of Jack's unearthly abilities.

"I'm sure I haven't met you before," LaToya insisted. "And I'm busy talking to my ex, if you don't mind."

"Tell Lara I'll be there soon."

"Humph." LaToya strode away. "No, Bob, you're not taking the Courvoisier. It's mine!"

Lara spotted Jack crossing the street again, then disappearing into her building.

"Did you hear that?" LaToya whispered. "He knows who I am!"

"I don't know how he heard you whispering," Lara said. "He must have excellent hearing."

"Supersonic hearing. I bet you he's a Bionic man. You should get his clothes off so you can see which parts are real. He might be a man of steel." LaToya snickered.

"Very funny." Though a Bionic man would definitely have good stamina. A knock sounded on the door, and Lara jumped. "He's here! How did he get up three flights of stairs so fast?"

"He's freaking Superman, that's what. You be careful, girl, or he'll pull some super mojo on you. Okay, I'm next to his car now, so I'll get his plates. Call me if you need me." LaToya hung up.

Lara snapped her phone shut and set it on the coffee table on the way to the door. Super mojo? She had to admit, there was something very sexy about Jack. Maybe it was his incredible powers. Or incredible good looks. Or the mystery surrounding him. Or the whole package.

She opened the door, and her heart lurched in her chest. Oh yeah, the whole package was good. She'd always loved to unwrap pretty packages.

"*Buonasera*, Butch." His smile revealed white teeth and friendly laugh lines. He brushed a tendril of damp hair off his smooth brow.

She liked the way his smile reached his twinkling golden brown eyes. And the way the light rain had glued his black T-shirt to his broad chest and firm stomach. He was dressed more casually than usual, with worn faded jeans that hugged his hips and legs. His black boots looked worn but comfortable. He was a man who appeared comfortable with himself. Genuine and sincere. Gorgeous without pretense or vanity. She only hoped he could be honest with her.

His smile widened. "May I come in?"

"Oh. Yes. Of course." Lara stepped back. How long had she stood there gawking at him? She motioned to the living room. "Please have a seat. Can I get you something to drink? I made a Mississippi mud pie for dessert. Would you like a piece?"

He turned to her with a confused look. "You eat . . . mud?"

"It's chocolate. Nice and gooey." Lara grinned. "You've never had any before? You're in for a real treat."

"I—no, thank you."

Her smile faded. So she couldn't impress him with her cooking. "Something to drink then? We have a nice Chardonnay." If she couldn't sweeten him up for the interrogation, maybe some wine would loosen his lips.

"No, thank you." He touched his stomach, frowning. "I've been a little under the weather."

"Oh, sorry. You should drink lots of fluids."

His mouth twisted with a wry look. "I do. But please, go ahead and drink if you like."

"Okay." Another glass of wine might bolster her courage. She headed into the kitchen. "I wanted to thank you for helping me last night."

"You're welcome." Jack pivoted in the middle of her living room as he looked around. "How is your partner?"

"Harvey's going to be all right, but he'll be out of commission for a few months." Lara set her wineglass on the coffee table, then settled on the love seat. Her heart did a little flip when Jack sat beside her.

His gaze wandered over her, lingering here and there with apparent appreciation. "And how are you, Lara?"

"I—I'm fine." It was hard to talk with him so close. Hard to think when he spoke her name like it was an endearment. "The captain gave me some time off. And I guess I'm going to get some sort of commendation. It's really embarrassing that everyone thinks I'm a hero."

Jack extended an arm across the back of the loveseat. "*Cara mia*, you *are* heroic."

Cara mia? Lara had grown up hearing *ma cher* in Louisiana, but the Italian version sounded new and exotic. Even so, she shouldn't let it go to her head. Jack could use those words all the time without meaning them. "I'm not a hero. You're the one who saved the day. Then you programmed the Trents to make me sound like RoboCop."

"It was the best way to explain what happened. The important thing is that you're safe and unharmed."

"Yes, I am. Thank you. I don't mean to sound ungrateful. I—I'm just uncomfortable with taking credit for something you did." She was also uncomfortably aware of his hand resting just inches from the back of her neck. She felt a very slight tug. Was he touching her hair?

He smiled. "You're an honest person. I like that."

"What about you? Can you be honest with me?"

His smile faded. "I would like to be, but I-I'm in a bit of a bind, actually."

Her heart sank. "I don't get it. Why can't you just tell me the truth?"

"I'm truly sorry. I'm under orders from my boss not to talk about certain sensitive matters."

"Your boss? He would be with MacKay Security and Investigation?"

"Yes."

"I looked that up on the Internet. It didn't say much, just that the company was started in 1927 and was based in London and Edinburgh."

Jack nodded. "That is true."

Since he was responding, her questions were apparently dodging the *certain sensitive matters*. She decided to keep digging. "What does this MacKay company do?"

"We provide security services for clients around the world, and we specialize in investigation."

"That's what you do? Investigation?"

"Usually, yes."

"Are you investigating something here in New York?"

"No."

"Providing security?"

"Yes."

Lara sipped some wine. This was like pulling teeth. If only she could get him to loosen up a bit. "Are you sure you wouldn't like some wine? Or something stronger?"

His mouth curled up on one side, and his eyes gleamed with amusement.

Damn. He knew what she was up to. She needed a different strategy, but she couldn't bring herself to blurt out a question about him being an alien or a Bionic man. It just seemed too ridiculous.

But she could always try LaToya's suggestion of examining his body. "You poor thing. Your shirt's all wet. Why don't you take it off, and I'll toss it in the dryer."

He glanced down at his damp T-shirt. "It's not that bad."

"It's sopping wet. You'll catch your death of cold."

His mouth twitched. "I doubt that."

"I insist." Lara leaned forward to grasp his T-shirt and yank the hem free from his jeans. What was she expecting to find? Gills across his rib cage?

"Are you trying to ravish me, *bellissima*?"

Her cheeks flamed with heat. "Of course not. I just don't want you to get sick from wearing a wet shirt."

"How thoughtful of you." His eyes glimmered. "I believe my jeans are a bit damp, too?"

Her face burned hotter. "They seem all right to me."

"Let me know if you change your mind." He stood and finished tugging the black T-shirt free from the jeans slung deliciously low on his narrow hips. A trail of dark hair emerged from his jeans, striking for its deep contrast to his pale skin.

Lara dragged in a deep breath, forcibly avoiding any

mental pictures about where that trail of hair led to. Man of steel? No, she wasn't going to think about it. But the paleness of his skin did surprise her. How long had he been working the night shift?

He rolled the T-shirt up further, revealing a swirl of dark hair around his belly button. *One* belly button. Very touchable-looking skin. Nothing at all alien.

Her mouth went dry as the T-shirt rose higher. Surely an alien couldn't fake those stomach muscles, chest hair, and strong pecs. What scientist would stick chest hair on a Bionic man? She could always touch it to see if it was real. Give a few of those dark curls a tug to see if they were glued on. Just for the sake of her investigation, of course. Her hands curled into fists, resisting the temptation.

He was moving so slowly. Damn him. Was he purposely trying to emphasize how sexy he was? He lifted his arms, and muscles rippled and bulged across his chest and shoulders as he yanked the T-shirt over his head. Lara bit her lip to keep from moaning. Or drooling.

He dropped the shirt on the coffee table. "Your turn."

"Hmm?" She dragged her gaze up to his face. The gold flecks in his eyes were gleaming. "I-I didn't get wet."

His nostrils flared and his chest expanded as he took a deep breath. His voice was soft and deep. "Are you sure, *cara mia*?"

Lara pressed her thighs together. Oh God, what if he also possessed a super sense of smell?

He sat beside her on the love seat. "I should warn you, love. Even if you take me to your bed, I will not be able to tell you what you want to hear."

She gazed dumbly into his warm brown eyes for a

moment before his words clicked, then she gasped. "I wasn't intending to bed you for information. How dare you!" She snatched his damp T-shirt from the coffee table and marched into the kitchen.

He stood and slid his hands into his jean pockets. "I misinterpreted the situation." He ducked his head and studied his black leather boots. "I have insulted your honor. I apologize."

He actually looked embarrassed. A small fissure zigzagged across Lara's defenses and tugged at her heart. In spite of Jack's suave and sexy demeanor, she suspected there was a sweet and vulnerable man underneath.

She tossed his shirt into the small dryer unit that was stacked on top of the washing machine. "I only wanted to talk to you. I want to know how you can move so quickly. And how you can appear and disappear. And how you can control people's minds."

He followed her into the kitchen. "I am truly sorry, but I cannot explain."

So she was at a dead end. She punched the button on the dryer control panel, and a whirring sound filled the strained silence. How on earth could she let this go? "My roommate thinks you're an alien."

He gave her a wry look. "Do I look like an alien?"

"You could be hiding a different body underneath. Or given your ability to mess with people's minds, you could be manipulating everyone into seeing you as human."

He leaned back against the kitchen counter and folded his arms across his broad chest. "You see me as I am. I'm not able to influence your thoughts."

"I only have your word for that."

His brow furrowed. "I'm not lying about it. Believe

me, if I could erase your memory, I would have already done so. And we wouldn't be having this awkward conversation."

Awkward was right. "Can—can I touch you? I mean, just to see if you feel normal."

He uncrossed his arms and held them straight at his sides. "Be my guest."

She took a deep breath, then approached him and placed a hand over his chest where his heart should be. His chest hair was like a soft, silky cushion. Individual strands curled around her fingers as if welcoming her touch. "I can feel your heart. It's beating a little fast."

"You're touching me."

She had an effect on him? She liked that. She gave him a playful smile. "So you're not . . . hiding a second heart somewhere?"

The corner of his mouth quirked. "Hide and seek? Where would I hide it?"

Her throat constricted. Was he implying he *was* an alien? "I don't know. Where?" She slid her hand down his rib cage and pressed against his firm stomach. "I don't feel anything beating."

"A little lower."

"Here?" She reached the waistband of his jeans.

"A little lower."

She noticed the bulge beneath his zipper and snatched her hand away. "You Neanderthal."

He laughed. "You can't blame me for trying."

"Well, if that's your idea of a *heart*, I'll just have to be a heartbreaker." She lifted her hands and mimicked the act of snapping a twig in two.

He grimaced, although there was still laughter in his eyes. "Please. My heart is very sensitive."

She lifted her brows with an innocent look. "You're softhearted? How sweet."

"I haven't been soft since I met you," he growled.

She ignored the heat in her face. "Stick out your tongue."

"My tongue?"

"Yes. To make sure it's not forked like a snake."

He gave her a challenging look. "I'll show you mine, if you show me yours."

"*My* humanity isn't under question. How do you control people's minds? Are you psychic?"

"I suppose you could call me that."

She was finally getting somewhere. "How do you move super fast?"

"It's a gift." He arched a brow. "I can also move super slow. Shall I show you?"

She bit her lip to keep from saying yes. Good God, the man was far too tempting. Or was he doing something to her? "Are you sure you've never influenced my thoughts?"

"I haven't. I tried, but I can't control you at all."

"Ain't life a bitch?"

He grinned. "I'm starting to like it. I never know what you'll do or say. It's exciting. And I like knowing that your reaction to me is honest." He tilted his head, studying her. "I think you're truly attracted to me."

She snorted. "What an ego." She let her gaze drift south. "You must be thinking with your *heart*."

"Oh yeah, I've been thinking real *hard*." He chuckled when she rolled her eyes. "Even though I can't answer all your questions, I am truly honored by your interest in me."

"*Professional* interest."

"Of course. For my part, I find you equally intriguing."

She blinked. No, he couldn't mean that. "There's nothing unusual about me."

"I disagree. You could be living a pampered life in

Louisiana. You're certainly beautiful enough to win more pageants."

She winced. "You investigated me?"

"That's what I do." His eyes gleamed. "I'm amazed by your bravery and determination. You've given up an easy life to become a police officer."

"I wanted my life to mean something."

"*Cara mia*, you will always mean something."

The crack in her defenses widened. She glanced at his face. He was watching her intently, as if his gaze alone could touch her. She looked away, overwhelmed suddenly by a strange yearning. How could she want him to touch her when she knew so little about him?

"How do you do it?" he whispered.

"Do what?" Get totally flustered?

"Over the years, I have known women who were innocent and women who were not, but I have never met one who was both. Until you." He stepped toward her. "So pure and provocative at the same time."

She opened her mouth to disagree, but looked at his eyes and forgot to speak. There was so much desire in his gaze, so much hunger, it made her knees weak.

He took another step closer. "I wonder which side will win? The innocent or the seductress?"

"I—" Lara pressed against the dryer, and it vibrated against her back, making her skin tingle and beg to be touched.

He grazed his fingers along her cheek, and she shivered. His eyes were hooded as he focused on her mouth.

He's going to kiss me. Should she let him? Oh God, he was right. There were two voices at war inside her mind. The prim and proper one warned her not to get involved with such a mysterious man, but an inner primeval woman urged her to dive into the unknown and surround herself with his mysterious allure, his charm, his manliness. *Go for it.*

His forefinger skimmed over her bottom lip, and a deep longing flooded her senses. It consumed her body, making her greedy for his touch, his kiss. *Go for it.* She sucked his finger into her mouth.

He groaned. "Lara." He removed his finger and cradled her face in his hands. "*Cara mia.*"

"Yes." God help her, she wanted to be dear to him.

He leaned forward and brushed his mouth against hers.

Chapter Seven

*B*efore the invention of synthetic blood, Jack had preyed on women in order to survive. It was not something he was particularly proud of, but he had always made sure it was pleasurable for the woman. He would invade her thoughts and read exactly what she wanted. If she craved sex, he made sure she was fully satisfied. If she needed comfort and understanding, he gave her that. Then he would quietly take a pint of blood and erase her memory.

Lara was different. He couldn't tell what she wanted, and if he made a mistake, he couldn't erase it and start over.

It was terrifying. It was exciting. It was like being mortal again. All his senses were centered on *now*. He had to do it right, right *now*. That made him feel more alive than he had in many years. And more vulnerable.

His old insecurities crept back. Could he please her if he didn't know what she wanted? He was over two hundred years old, so he certainly had his technique down. But Lara was different. She deserved more than a practiced routine. This was a memory he couldn't erase, so it needed to be special.

He sucked her bottom lip into his mouth and caressed it with his tongue. That elicited a moan deep in her throat, and his heart swelled with joy. He *was* pleasing her. He swept his tongue across the seam of her lips.

They opened.

He was undone. How could he not fall for Lara? She was opening up to him without the use of vampire tricks. He molded his mouth against hers, and she kissed him back. She wrapped her arms around his neck and pulled him close. *Santo cielo.* She wanted Jack, the man. Not Giacomo, the Casanova. Nor Jack, the vampire. She wanted *him*.

With a growl, he enveloped her in his arms. Her answering whimper sounded sweet. Like a surrender. And that ignited a passion in him, a need long dormant, the need to possess a woman and lay claim to her. He swirled his tongue inside her mouth, and she stroked it with her own. She tasted of wine and chocolate, both tart and sweet. She was both vixen and angel, and he wanted to pounce on her and worship her at the same time.

He moved his hands down her back, his fingers splayed and pressing her against him. She melted in his arms and clutched his shoulders. So giving, yet so demanding. To hell with years of finesse and well-mannered seduction. He wanted it raw and honest. He wanted to make her scream.

He grabbed her buttocks and pulled her tight against his erection. She gasped, breaking their kiss. He trailed kisses to her neck. He could smell her Type A blood, pulsing wildly in the carotid artery. Her rapid heart-beat echoed in his ears. Her fingers dug into his skin.

"Lara," he whispered in her ear. "I want you."

She trembled in his arms.

He nuzzled his nose against her neck. God, he wanted to lick her. He wanted to set her over the edge. Normally, he could use mind control, coupled with vampire saliva, to bring a woman to climax just by laving her neck. It was an old trick to make the penetration of fangs feel orgasmic instead of painful. But he didn't need to feed, and he had no mental connection to Lara. He wasn't sure she would feel anything at all.

He pressed his lips against the pulsing artery. His gums tingled, aching to release his fangs. Even with a full stomach, she was a huge temptation. He dragged his tongue up her neck, and she shuddered.

"Jack." She raked her hands into his hair.

She *did* feel it. The old-fashioned way. Her reactions were honest, just like her. His erection strained against his pants. *Merda*. He was about to burst. He rested his brow against her temple and took deep breaths. Her breasts pushed against him as she also struggled to breathe.

"Wow," she whispered.

"*Santo cielo*," he breathed.

"What is that? 'Holy . . . sky'?"

"Heaven."

"Oh yeah. Definitely." Her hands smoothed down his back. "Good news. I have determined that your tongue isn't forked."

"That's a relief." He moved back a tiny bit to stop torturing his groin.

She gasped and pulled her hands away from him.

Merda. Too late he realized his vision was still tinted

rosy pink. He'd managed to hide it before the kiss, but now. . .

"Your eyes are red!" She scooted away from him.

"*Bellissima*, don't be concerned. It is nothing."

"Bull hockey! Red glowing eyes are definitely something. I don't know what, but you'd better tell me."

How could he explain this? "It is simply an indication that I'm . . . turned on."

She stiffened. "Turned on? Like an android? You're like Data?"

Jack hesitated. He wasn't sure what she meant. Unfortunately, Lara took his pause as an assent.

"I can't believe it, although it does explain a lot." She gave him a curious look. "I didn't think androids could kiss like that. You'll put real men out of business."

"Lara—"

"Do you have an on-and-off switch?" She reached behind him and raked her fingers through the hair at the base of his neck. "I think Data's switch was around here."

"Lara, I'm not an android. I have a heart, remember?"

"It could be an artificial heart. Or you could be like the Bionic Man, with just a few mechanical parts. It would explain your super speed and hearing." She dragged her hand over his shoulder and down his chest. "Where's the switch?"

She wasn't listening. Poor girl, she was too desperate to make sense of the situation.

She slid her hand down to his navel. "Is this it?"

He couldn't resist. "A little lower."

She glanced lower, and the bulge in his pants was larger than before. "Oh come on." She swatted him on the arm. "That's not a switch. Though it might be a little *off* button."

"It's more like a lever. And if you grabbed it, I would definitely get *off*."

She snorted. "You've got to be a normal guy. You've been trying to get a hand job all night."

He grinned. "*Bellissima*, when it comes to receiving pleasure, I always say ladies first."

Her cheeks flushed. "I should have known you couldn't be an android. No one would ever program a machine to be as outrageous as you."

"You wouldn't want me to be a machine, would you?"

"No, but I still don't know what or who you are." She turned and opened the dryer door. "You might as well get dressed. It's obvious you're not going to tell me."

"Lara." He touched her shoulder. "I am sorry."

With a sigh, she removed his black T-shirt. "I don't understand why you can't tell me."

He took the warm T-shirt. "It's a matter of security. There are . . . others who would be in danger if I said too much."

"Others like you?"

He pulled the T-shirt over his head. "I really shouldn't say."

"There's got to be a way around this." She shut the dryer door. "What if I did the talking, and if I'm wrong you can say so, but if I'm right, you say nothing."

That might be safe for a few questions. He seriously doubted she would ever guess he was a vampire.

"Are you an alien?"

"No." He tucked his T-shirt into his jeans.

"Do you have any metal parts, like the Bionic Man?"

"No."

She placed a hand on his chest. "You're a live, human male?"

"At the moment." His heart was beating now, but it would stop at sunrise.

Her mouth quirked. "You're only male at the moment?"

"If you doubt my masculinity, love, just slide your hand a little lower."

She laughed. "You never give up."

He touched her cheek. "I'm afraid I have to, for the night. I need to go to work."

"Where do you work?"

"Wherever I'm assigned."

She grabbed his shirt and squeezed the cotton in her fists. "You're driving me crazy!"

"*Cara mia.*" He slid his hand around the nape of her neck. "The feeling is mutual."

"Why can't you trust me?" she whispered. "You came to my rescue. You probably saved my life. We shared a really nice kiss—"

"*Nice?*"

"*Really* nice." She gave him an annoyed look. "Okay, it was super-duper *über*-hot. The point is, I would never do anything to hurt you. You can trust me."

His heart ached. He knew she meant the words now, but if she knew the truth, she'd consider him a monster. "Lara." He rested his forehead against hers. "I wish I could be the man you want me to be. The kind of man you deserve."

She touched his face. "What's stopping you?"

He closed his eyes. "Life . . . and death." She was one, and he was the other.

"I don't understand."

"I know." He pressed a kiss against her brow. It was best for him never to see her again. But the thought of never holding her in his arms again, never hearing the sound of her laughter, never gazing into the blue heaven of her eyes—it was wrenching his heart in two.

But what choice did he have? Either she could remain

ignorant and remember him fondly, or she could learn too much and recall him with disgust. The former option was the best for both of them. "Good night, Lara."

Good-bye, cara mia. He strode from her apartment, wishing he were dead. Unfortunately, that wish came true with every sunrise.

Five days passed with no word from Jack. Lara tried not to think about him, but how could she forget the most intriguing man she'd ever met? Or forget the hottest kiss she'd ever received?

Five long days. He had to be avoiding her. Obviously, he didn't want to tell her about himself, but couldn't they still be friends? Deep inside she felt he could be trusted. He'd come to her rescue. He'd protected her from harm. He'd been very apologetic about his inability to explain. He had to be a good man. And he was one hell of a good kisser.

LaToya kept bugging her to call him, but Lara resisted. LaToya had run his plates, so she knew his address, but Lara refused to go see him. She was hurt and disappointed that he hadn't confided in her, so she was avoiding him, too.

She wasn't supposed to return to work yet, so she spent the days cooking, cleaning, and watching DVDs, mostly romantic comedies. None of the heroes were as sexy as Jack. She avoided watching her stash of sci-fi reruns. It would be too annoying to watch the characters teleporting.

When the phone rang Sunday afternoon, her heart lurched. Was Jack finally calling? She lunged for the receiver, then mentally slapped herself. *Don't act desperate.*

She lifted the receiver to her ear in slow motion and assumed a bored voice. "Hello?"

"Hey, girl."

Her shoulders slumped at the sound of LaToya's voice.

"Hey."

"I'm getting off work soon," LaToya said. "Meet me at Morningside Park in thirty minutes."

"Why?"

"Can't explain now. See ya soon." LaToya lowered her voice. "Don't forget your badge."

"What?" Lara asked, but her roommate had already hung up. What was LaToya up to? She usually came straight home when her shift ended.

Thirty minutes later, Lara waited by the park's main entrance and spotted LaToya headed her way, still in her patrol officer's uniform.

"What's up?" Lara swung her handbag over her shoulder.

"I want to show you something." LaToya led her toward the entrance to Columbia University. "I didn't want to talk about it while I was still at work. The case has been turned over to some detectives there, so I'm not supposed to be involved with it anymore."

"What case?"

"A missing college student. Vanessa Carlton. My partner and I answered the nine-one-one call, then later, we turned it over to the detectives."

"So why are we here?" Lara asked.

LaToya adjusted her sunglasses against the late afternoon glare. "I was there when the detectives questioned the girls in the dorm, and it was really weird. I kept remembering the way you described Harvey and the paramedics when they were under Jack's mind control."

Lara flinched. "You think Jack is involved with this girl's disappearance?"

"I don't know what to think. And I couldn't tell the detectives about what happened to Harvey when he doesn't remember it. We would both look crazy."

"That's true."

"So I thought you'd better see these girls," LaToya continued. "You've seen mind control before, so maybe you can tell if that's what happened to them."

Lara's heart sank. "Okay." She'd always known Jack was different. Unusual. But she'd never thought he was a criminal. He couldn't be involved with this. *Please.*

She followed LaToya into the dormitory. A bulletin board covered the wall close to the entrance. Brightly colored paper announced seminars and parties.

Girls stood in small clusters in the hallway, whispering to each other. When they noticed LaToya in her uniform, they hushed, and a silent aura of fear hovered over them.

"Officer?" one of the girls asked. "Any news about Vanessa?"

"Not yet, sorry," LaToya said.

The girls nodded and filed into their rooms.

"This is Vanessa's room." LaToya knocked on Room 116, then raised her voice. "NYPD."

The door cracked, and a young woman peered out. Young, about eighteen, Lara figured. Round, chubby face and innocent eyes.

"Did you find her?" Her eyes were wide with hope.

"We're still working on it," LaToya said. "Megan, I brought another . . . detective here to ask you a few questions." LaToya motioned toward Lara. "Can we come in?"

"Sure." Megan opened the door. "But I already told the other detectives everything I know." She sat cross-legged on a twin-sized bed and set a bowl of M&M'S in her lap. "Want some?"

"No thank you." Lara sat at the desk chair that was situated between the two twin beds.

LaToya perched on the other bed and removed a pad of paper and a pen from her shirt pocket.

Lara began with questions about Vanessa's schedule, her girlfriends, boyfriends, enemies, her favorite pastimes or places to hang out. LaToya busily took notes while Megan answered between mouthfuls of candy.

"Do you have a recent photo of Vanessa?" Lara asked.

"Well, the other detectives took the best one." Megan grabbed a photo album off the desk and thumbed through it. "This one's pretty good." She handed it over.

Lara studied the photo. "Auburn hair, blue eyes, slim build."

"Yeah. Vanessa's really pretty." Megan gave her bowl of M&M'S a guilty look. "She's not overweight like me."

"Any trouble with guys?" Lara asked.

Megan shook her head, and her brown curls bounced about her face. "People are always assuming that Vanessa dates a lot, but it's not true. She . . . she's sorta picky. She wants to save herself for the right guy."

"I see." The missing girl didn't sound like the type to run off to have an affair. Lara turned to LaToya. "Has her family been contacted?"

"Yeah," LaToya said. "They have no idea where she is. They say she's never run off like this before."

"And the ex-boyfriend checked out?" Lara asked.

"Yeah. He has an alibi. And he's happily engaged to another girl. It's a dead end."

Lara focused back on Megan. "You have no idea where she could be?"

"Nope." Megan shoved more candy into her mouth. She filled her hand with more M&M'S.

"Did you go anywhere with Vanessa last night?" Lara asked.

Megan's hand went slack, and the M&M'S fell with a pattering sound back into the bowl. Her face went blank. "We were in our room, studying."

A chill crept up Lara's arms. Megan's face was expressionless, just the way Harvey's had been. The paramedics and the Trents had looked the same way. *God, no. Don't let Jack be involved with this.*

"I told you it was weird," LaToya whispered.

Lara cleared her throat. "Megan, it was Saturday night. Surely you went somewhere? Maybe to get something to eat?"

"We were in our room, studying," Megan repeated.

"And Vanessa never went out at all?"

"We were in our room, studying," Megan whispered.

"I understand." Lara stood and slipped Vanessa's photo into her jeans pocket. "Thank you for your time."

Megan blinked and looked surprised. "You're going?"

"Yes. I'll keep in touch." Lara headed for the door.

"Okay." Megan's eyes were once again eager. "I hope Vanessa will be okay. She . . . she's really nice to me, you know. She showed me the proper way to put on makeup."

LaToya led Lara down the dormitory hall. "You see what I mean by weird? Megan was acting normal, then she turned into a zombie."

"I know," Lara grumbled. "It looked like she'd been programmed."

"And we know only one person who's capable of doing that."

Lara winced. *Not Jack, please.* "There could be others

with that ability." Hadn't he said something about protecting others? Others who could be like him? But if his friends were capable of kidnapping, what did that say about Jack?

LaToya knocked on door 124. "Vanessa's friends live here. Carmen and Ramya."

Lara talked to the two girls. They were both pretty brunettes. Carmen looked Hispanic and Ramya came from India. They were clearly worried about Vanessa and eager to help in any way they could. Until Lara asked if they'd gone out the night before.

Their faces went blank and their eyes shuttered. "We were in our room, studying," they answered in unison.

Gooseflesh slithered down Lara's arms. "Thank you." When the door shut, she turned to LaToya. "Don't say it. It can't be Jack."

LaToya grimaced, then headed toward the stairs. "There's someone else I want you to meet."

Lara followed her up to the second floor. "All three girls were programmed to say the same thing. They must have all gone out together. But why was Vanessa abducted, and the other girls sent back?"

"Maybe the perp can handle only one vic at a time." LaToya turned right, down the hall.

"I don't think so. With mind control, he could handle a room full of women. He wouldn't even need restraints. They would just obey him like sheep."

"Well, that's a good point." LaToya knocked on a door. "This is Roxanne's room."

A girl with dyed black hair, heavy black eyeliner, and a lip ring answered the door. "Yeah, what?"

"I'll tell you what," LaToya said. "Megan, Carmen, and Ramya all claim they were in their rooms last night, studying."

"Well, I can't swear under oath about Carmen and

Ramya. I didn't go to their room. But I know Vanessa went out, so the other girls had to be with her. They follow her everywhere like puppy dogs. It's freaking pathetic."

"How do you know Vanessa went out?" Lara asked.

Roxanne rolled her eyes. "Look, I was really suffering from menstrual cramps, and Vanessa—she's like a freaking pharmacy down there. So I went to her room to score some Midol, and no one answered the door. It was locked, but I was really desperate, you know. So I jimmied the lock and went inside."

"What did you see?" Lara asked.

"A box of Midol in the top drawer of her dresser, so I took two pills. Left her fifty cents. I'm not a thief, you know." She slanted a worried look at LaToya. "You guys aren't going to arrest me, are you?"

"You're fine," Lara assured her. "But are you saying the room was empty? Vanessa wasn't there?"

"Duh. Vanessa and her chubby sidekick were gone."

"Any idea where they went?" Lara asked.

Roxanne snorted. "I don't know. Maybe she went shopping or to get her nails done. She really freaks out if her nails aren't perfect. Or her hair. She's got about fifty different tote bags for her books, so she can coordinate them with whatever she's wearing each day."

LaToya narrowed her eyes. "You don't like her much, do you?"

"Oh, brilliant detective work, Nancy Drew. But if you think I'd do anything to hurt Vanessa, you're crazy. She paid me three hundred bucks to type her papers this semester. I need her." Roxanne grimaced. "And the whole thing kinda freaks me out. The same thing happened last year to Brittney Beckford. She disappeared, and the cops never found her."

Lara exchanged a worried look with LaToya. Brittney had gone missing before they'd arrived in New York. How long had Jack been in New York? "Can you describe Brittney?"

"Typical spoiled rich preppie," Roxanne grumbled.

"In English, please?" LaToya pulled out her notebook and pen.

Roxanne sighed. "Long hair, bleached strawberry blonde. Fake tan. Blue eyes due to her contacts. Collagen lips. Fake friends who have forgotten her. The only thing real about Brittney was her low IQ."

"Thanks. You've been very helpful." LaToya stuffed her notebook back into her pocket and headed back to the stairs.

"Fascists," Roxanne muttered as she shut the door.

Lara and LaToya descended the stairs in silence, then strode down the hallway to the dormitory entrance.

"Vanessa seems to worry a lot about her appearance," Lara said.

"She and a million other girls," LaToya muttered.

"Yeah, it sounds like she and Brittney have a lot in common." Two missing girls with red or reddish blonde hair and blue eyes. Lara paused to look at the bulletin board. A pink paper drew her attention. "Look at this." She ripped it free.

LaToya read it out loud. "Do you want to stay young and beautiful forever? Free seminar. Room 4, Student Services Building. Saturday, nine P.M."

"That would be the kind of seminar Vanessa would go to." Lara studied the paper. "Let's check it out."

They located the room where the meeting had taken place, but it was empty except for a few plastic chairs and a dry-erase board. They talked to the building manager, and he checked the schedule.

"Room 4?" His face went blank. "There was no one in that room Saturday night."

Lara gulped. Whoever had run the seminar had erased his tracks. Much like Jack had erased all evidence of him and his friends at the Plaza hotel. *Damn!* She'd wanted so much to believe in Jack. She'd wanted to trust him.

Her gut churned as they walked across the campus. She couldn't believe he was involved. There had to be someone else with his abilities. "I need to talk to Jack."

"You're in luck." LaToya pulled out her notebook and flipped through the pages. "I have his address right here. That Lexus he was driving was registered to a Roman Draganesti. Upper East Side."

"Then let's go." Lara's heart squeezed in her chest. She'd wanted so badly to see Jack again. But now, she'd have to question him as a suspect.

"What did you learn about Jack in our apartment?" LaToya asked. "You didn't say much about it."

She hadn't wanted to talk about his kiss. It had been too glorious to cheapen with gossip. A vision flitted through her mind—Jack in his jeans and no shirt. His broad chest and strong shoulders. His warm brown eyes that glimmered with gold. Or glowed red when he was turned on.

She swallowed hard. "I'm not sure what he is."

LaToya shook her head. "It's looking bad for him."

"I know." Lara's gut clenched. *Please, God. Don't let Jack be a kidnapper. Or a murderer.*

Chapter Eight

*I*t was almost six o'clock when Lara and LaToya ascended the steps to Roman Draganesti's townhouse on the Upper East Side.

"Fancy place." LaToya scanned the neighborhood from the front porch. "Nice and quiet."

"Did you notice how heavily shuttered all the windows are?" Lara had hoped for a peek inside one of the windows, but the place was closed up tight.

She pressed the doorbell. The chimes echoed inside as if they were reverberating around an empty cavern. There was something not quite right here, but she couldn't put her finger on it. Maybe it was just an overactive imagination coupled with her current sense of gloom.

The subway ride and short walk hadn't done much to calm her nerves. A niggling fear had settled in her gut and a sick heaviness in her heart. She recognized the symptoms, having endured this pain once before. Disillusionment. Betrayal.

She had fought so hard after the car accident to rebuild her life and put the pageant days behind her. She'd met Ronny at LSU. She'd thought he understood her need for a new and meaningful life, had trusted him and believed him to truly love her. Until he had bragged to his friends and anyone else who would listen that he'd popped the cherry of a beauty queen. She'd been nothing more than a fancy title so he could mark a notch on his trophy case.

Dammit. She had thought Jack could be trusted. She'd thought he was different, that he admired her for her intelligence and strength of character. She'd thought he might be the one.

"We're being watched," LaToya whispered.

Lara looked up at the surveillance camera. The green light had come on. "Jack works for a company that specializes in security."

"I wonder what they're keeping secure," LaToya muttered.

A crackling sound emanated from an intercom next to the door. "May I help you?" a male voice asked.

Lara pushed the call button. "NYPD. We have a few questions."

"Yeah, open up!" LaToya shouted.

There was a pause. Lara's stomach knotted. *Please let Jack have an alibi for Saturday night.*

The door opened slowly, revealing a tall young man. The words *MacKay S & I* were embroidered on the left side of his navy Polo shirt. His khaki pants were belted low on his lean hips. His dark hair was pulled back into a short ponytail. A gold stud gleamed in his ear. He was almost as gorgeous as Jack.

"I am Carlos," he said with a slight accent. "How may I help you?"

"Can we come in?" LaToya asked.

His mouth quirked. "Do you have a warrant?"

"We have a few questions, if you don't mind." Lara gave him a friendly smile. "Is Jack here? Giacomo di Venezia, otherwise known as Jack."

Carlos tilted his head, studying her. "Are you the cop who crashed Ian's wedding? I heard about you."

Lara felt heat creeping up her neck to her cheeks. "I'm Officer Boucher, and I'm here on a professional matter. Jack is a . . . person of interest."

Carlos's eyes gleamed. "I bet he is."

"This is my associate, Officer Lafayette." Lara motioned to LaToya. "Is Jack here? We need to talk to him."

"He's not available at this time." Carlos's amused gaze swept down to her feet and back up. "Robby said you were pretty, but that's a huge understatement. He must be angry that Jack caught you first."

Lara stiffened. "I haven't been *caught* by anyone."

Carlos smiled. "I believe the net has been cast."

"Will you cut the bullshit and get Jack?" LaToya demanded.

"Miss Lafayette." Carlos's eyes glimmered as he considered LaToya. "Aren't you a little wildcat?"

Her brown eyes narrowed. "Sucker, I've got claws you don't want to see."

Carlos chuckled. "I'll tell Jack you stopped by. He has your number?"

"We need to see him *now*," Lara insisted. "I realize he sleeps during the day, but would you please wake him?"

"Easier said than done," Carlos muttered. "I'm afraid he's not really here. Not in the metaphysical sense."

LaToya jutted out a hip and planted a hand on it. "Where is he then? In the freaking metaphysical sense?"

"I've often wondered that myself." Carlos frowned. "Where exactly do they go when they're . . . *not here*?"

Lara exchanged a look with her roommate. Carlos sounded like he was one taco short of a combination plate. "Are you saying you don't know where Jack is?"

"Not exactly. But if you'll return about eight-thirty, he could see you then."

"We'll do that," LaToya said.

"Excellent." Carlos smiled. "It's been a pleasure to meet you, ladies. *Ciao.*" The door closed.

Lara heard the sound of deadbolts being shot into place. "That was interesting."

"I'll say." LaToya descended the steps to the sidewalk. "Between Ian, Jack, and Carlos, I can't decide which one is the hunkiest."

Jack, definitely. Lara checked her watch. "Let's grab some supper."

They walked toward Central Park, then turned south. As they passed by the Plaza, Lara remembered that the hotel had a business center inside. She and LaToya shared a pizza at a deli on Sixth Avenue, then returned to the Plaza, where the staff was happy to cooperate with New York's finest. They sat side by side in front of computers in the business center.

"I'll check out the Draganesti dude." LaToya typed on her keyboard.

Lara Googled Giacomo di Venezia, but all the links referred to Giacomo Casanova, the famous womanizer. That wasn't any help, although it did elicit a memory. When Lara had questioned Jack at the church, he'd mentioned his father had seduced hundreds of women, and that his mother had been the last conquest. What a strange coincidence.

Was Jack like his father? Did he make a sport of seducing women? Somehow, Lara had felt that his attraction to her was genuine. But wasn't that how these cads operated? They made all the women they seduced think they were special. And Lara had been fooled before.

It would really hurt to find out he was a womanizing pig. Unfortunately, it could be even worse. He might be a criminal.

No! She refused to believe Jack had anything to do with the missing girl. Lara didn't know him that well, but she couldn't believe he would ever abuse a woman. He'd saved her life. He was a protector of women, not an abuser.

"Well, Roman Draganesti sounds like a genius," LaToya said. "He figured out how to clone blood. According to this article, his synthetic blood is responsible for saving thousands of lives every year."

"Synthetic blood?" Lara thought back. "I was given some of that when I was in the hospital."

"Then this Roman dude saved you, too," LaToya continued. "He manufactures the stuff at Romatech Industries. He's got several factories around the country, but the biggest one is in White Plains, New York."

"That's close to us." Lara did a search on Romatech and located a news article that described a bombing at the facility last December. A car had exploded in the parking lot, but no one had been seriously injured. This was just the last of several attempts to bomb the place. "It looks like Romatech has some serious enemies."

"Maybe they're doing some kind of funky research that's upsetting people," LaToya suggested. "You know, stem-cell research or genetic engineering."

"They obviously need good security." Lara wondered if this was the security work Jack was doing. "I might check this place out." Thank God she was off work for a few more days.

"I'm supposed to work tomorrow, but I could call in sick and go with you," LaToya offered.

"I'll be fine. Don't worry." Lara checked her watch. "It's a little after eight. Let's go talk to Jack."

"Is something wrong?" Jack had just teleported into the kitchen at the townhouse. He'd been in the fifth-floor office, drinking his breakfast and catching up on e-mail when Carlos called on the intercom to request his presence downstairs.

"You bet something's wrong." Phineas sat at the kitchen table, wearing the official khaki pants and navy Polo shirt of MacKay Security and Investigation. "Carlos has gone crazy. I think he's been sniffing some catnip."

Carlos shook his head as he opened the refrigerator. He retrieved a bottle of water and twisted off the top. "Some cops came by while you two were . . . napping."

"And Carlos invited them back!" Phineas thumped a fist on the kitchen table, shaking his half-empty glass of blood. "They'll be here in fifteen minutes."

Jack frowned. "What do the police want?"

"Me, probably." Phineas gulped down the last of his breakfast, then slammed the glass on the table. "I—I have an outstanding warrant."

"Sheesh, Phineas." Carlos grimaced. "You should have warned me. How can I protect you if I don't know?"

As their daytime guard, it was Carlos Panterra's job to keep them safe during their death-sleep. Jack had been impressed so far by the Brazilian's vigilance. Like many of the mortal day guards who worked for MacKay Security and Investigation, Carlos had special skills. And a special secret. He kept quiet about the

Vamps, and they kept quiet about his shape-shifting ability.

Phineas's shoulders slumped. "I didn't want Angus to know. He believed in me enough to give me a job. I really like being one of the good guys."

"Don't worry. Angus is very happy with you," Jack assured him, then turned to Carlos. "Were the police looking for Phineas?"

"No, they didn't even mention him. He should be safe." Carlos sipped some water.

Phineas exhaled in relief. "Then I'm outta here."

"That's a shame." Carlos sat beside him at the table. "They were very pretty ladies."

Jack's heart speeded up. "The police were women?" Was Lara looking for him?

"Pretty ladies?" Phineas smoothed back his short hair. "This sounds like a job for the Love Doctor."

"Was Lara here?" Jack strode toward the table. "I mean Officer Boucher?"

"Yes. She was looking for you. And Officer Lafayette was with her." Carlos smiled at Phineas. "She's a lovely black woman."

"Hot damn!" Phineas's face lit up, then crumbled. "Why would a pretty young thing join the po-po?"

"They're clever, too," Carlos continued. "Somehow they figured out where Jack's living."

"That's the po-po for you, man. They'll track your ass down!" Phineas took his empty glass and blood bottle to the sink and rinsed them out.

Jack sat at the table as he thought back. He'd been careful not to tell Lara where he lived or worked. The car! That's why Lara's roommate had been waiting on the street. "They must have run the plates on Roman's car."

Carlos nodded. "They're smart."

"Relentless." Phineas jammed his empty glass and bottle in the dishwasher. "You'd better not talk to them, man. They'll drag you down to the precinct, where they have those interrogation rooms with one-way glass, and when you don't show up in the mirror, your ass will be cooked."

"I'll be careful." Jack glanced at the clock above the sink. They would be here in eight minutes. "Phineas, go on to work without me. Tell Connor I'll be there shortly."

"Okay, but I can tell you he's not going to like this." Phineas frowned as his body wavered and disappeared.

Jack sighed. Connor had strongly suggested he avoid seeing Lara again. Jack had tried to forget her, but it was impossible. Someone at Romatech would walk by wearing a blue shirt that reminded him of the color of her eyes. Or he would hear someone laugh and find himself longing to hear the sound of Lara's laughter. Whenever he showered, he recalled the feel of her hands on his skin.

And when he lay down to fall into his death-sleep, he imagined the sun rising, a fiery ball of gold and red. He could never see it again, but he could see Lara's hair, the way it gleamed red and gold, the way soft strands curled close to her brow. It felt like silken fire in his hands.

He wanted to see her again. *Santo cielo*, he wanted her.

"I hope you don't mind that I invited them back," Carlos said. "I thought it would be best to appease their curiosity. We don't want them coming here with a search warrant during the day."

Jack winced. "That would be a disaster." They would find dead bodies.

"You're awake now, so everything should appear normal."

"Are there any coffins in the basement?" Jack asked.

"No. Dougal took his with him when he was reassigned. Ian gave his coffin away to charity. He'd outgrown it."

Jack smiled. "And I doubt his new wife wanted to share one with him."

Carlos laughed. "No, Toni wouldn't go for that."

Jack glanced at the clock. Five minutes to go. "I'd better get ready." He teleported to his bedroom on the fourth floor. With vampire speed, he showered, brushed his teeth, and pulled on a clean pair of jeans and a maroon T-shirt. He was dragging a comb through his damp hair when he heard the doorbell chime below. *Lara.*

He glanced at the blank wall above the bathroom vanity. Even if a mirror were there, he wouldn't reflect in it. He rubbed the stubble on his jaw. He hadn't had time to shave. Hopefully, he would look all right to Lara.

He was gorgeous. A blur of motion had caught Lara's attention, and then Jack was suddenly there on the second floor landing of the grand staircase. She blinked. Had he been moving at super speed? He was standing still now and looking at her.

He smiled, and her heart squeezed in her chest. No way could this man be a kidnapper. All he'd have to do is crook his finger, and a woman would come running.

"Officer Boucher?"

A tap on her shoulder made Lara jump. "Yes?"

Carlos grinned. "I asked if you and your partner would like a tour of the premises."

"Oh." Lara winced inwardly. She hadn't heard Carlos the first time. She'd been too busy ogling Jack. When she and LaToya had arrived a minute ago, Carlos had ushered them into the spacious foyer. She'd noted the gleaming marble floor and grand curved staircase, and then Jack had appeared. Now he was slowly descending the stairs, his gaze still focused on her.

"I'll take the tour," LaToya announced. "Lara can talk to Jack."

Lara sidled close to her roommate. "Are you sure you want to . . . separate?"

"Don't worry, Officer Boucher," Carlos said. "Your friend will be safe with me."

LaToya snorted and crossed her arms. "You should be worried if you're safe with me."

Carlos's eyes gleamed. "So how do you want to do this? Shall we start at the top and work our way down?"

LaToya arched a brow. "Sounds good to me."

"Officer Lafayette." Jack bowed slightly as he reached the bottom of the stairs. "A pleasure to see you again. I hope your *ex* is no longer causing you trouble. I believe his name was Bob?"

"He's fine," LaToya grumbled. "But your ass could be in trouble." She stomped up the stairs with Carlos.

Jack turned to Lara, his eyebrows raised. "I'm in trouble?"

No, *she* was in trouble. Her skin was tingling, and he hadn't even touched her. "Is there someplace we can talk?"

"This way." He motioned to a room on the left.

She strolled into a living room. Three maroon couches

surrounded three sides of a large square coffee table. The fourth side faced a widescreen television.

"Would you like something to drink?" Jack asked.

"Some water would be nice." The pizza she'd eaten earlier was making her very thirsty. She sat at one end of the middle couch. She placed her handbag beside her so there would be something between her and Jack.

She noted a desk against the far wall, topped with a computer. To her left, maroon curtains flanked a large bay window that overlooked the street. Metal shutters were closed tight, as if they were worried someone might get a peek inside. But as Lara scanned the room, she couldn't see anything out of the ordinary. Maybe someone was extremely opposed to sunlight.

"Here you go."

Jack's voice caught her off guard. That was fast.

He handed her a glass of ice water, then placed a wooden coaster on the coffee table in front of her. "Shanna will have my head if we leave water marks on the table."

"Shanna? Who's she?"

"Roman's wife. They own this townhouse." Jack settled on the couch beside her.

"Roman Draganesti?" Lara sipped some water.

"Yes." Jack shifted sideways to face her and propped an elbow on the back of the couch. "You did your homework. I'm guessing you ran the plates on Roman's car."

"Yes." Lara drank some more water. "LaToya doesn't actually have an ex-boyfriend named Bob."

The corner of Jack's mouth lifted. "What a surprise."

Damn, he was cute. Lara set her glass on the coaster. "You're not thirsty?"

"No, I'm fine, thank you."

It seemed odd that he never joined her for a drink.

She glanced at the window. "I've never seen such heavy-duty shutters in a residence before. They look industrial strength."

"They cut out the noise from the city."

"That's for sure. It's as quiet as a tomb in here."

He rubbed his whiskered jaw. "You could say that." His gaze shifted to Lara with an intense look. "I missed you."

Her throat tightened. "You could have called."

"I've been trying to resist you."

"*Trying?* I would say you were entirely successful." Lara slapped herself mentally. She was sounding too needy. She waved a hand in a dismissive gesture. "Not that it matters. I was avoiding you, too."

He regarded her sadly. "That was wise of you."

"Why? Are you involved with someone else?"

"No." He touched her hair. "After meeting you, how could I want anyone else?"

She gulped. Did he really mean that, or was he just a smooth talker? She shoved her hair behind her shoulders and out of his reach. "This is a professional call."

"I see. How can I help you?"

"Where were you last night?"

His eyebrows rose. "Are you working a case?"

"Yes." She lowered her gaze to her clenched hands in her lap. Now she felt like a heel. "A college girl disappeared last night. She may have been kidnapped. And it looks like someone altered her friends' memories."

"And you suspect me?" he asked quietly.

"I don't—" She swallowed hard at the lump constricting her throat. "I don't want to, but you're the only one I know who can manipulate minds like that." She cast a nervous glance his way. "Are there others who can do it?"

"*Merda,*" he muttered, his brow creasing with a scowl.

"Tell me there are others. Tell me you have an alibi."

"Do you really believe I would kidnap a young woman?" He tossed her purse on the coffee table, then scooted closer to her.

She stiffened. "What are you doing?"

"If you think I'm a criminal, you obviously don't know me well enough." He scooped her onto his lap.

"Stop it." She tried to wiggle off his lap, but he held her tight. "You could get in big trouble for hindering an investigation—"

"Lara," he interrupted her, gazing fiercely into her eyes. "I was at work last night."

"At Romatech Industries?"

"Yes. We celebrate Mass there on Saturday night. There was a reception afterward." He gritted his teeth. "About thirty people were there, if you wish to question them."

"I-I'll do that." She couldn't find a place to set her hands other than his chest or shoulders. "You had a church service at work?"

"Yes. Father Andrew comes every Saturday night. Our . . . enemies know about it. They've attacked before, so I had to be there to provide security."

Enemies? That sounded over the top. But on the other hand, if Jack was at church, he couldn't be involved with Vanessa's disappearance. It looked like her prayers had been answered. "What about the mind manipulation?"

His frown deepened. "There are others with the ability."

"Friends?"

"Yes." His eyes hardened, the gold glinting with anger. "And enemies."

Gooseflesh skittered down Lara's arms. Friends and enemies with mind-control power? She shivered, suddenly feeling like she was teetering on a precipice, about to fall.

He touched her cheek. "This is shocking to me."

"Tell me about it." What on earth was she getting into? She tried to make sense of everything, but it was hard to think with him touching her and looking at her so fiercely.

He skimmed his fingers along her jaw. "I'm . . . stunned by how much it hurts for you to think ill of me."

She swallowed hard. "I didn't want to. It was making me sick. I-I didn't want to believe it."

"Then don't." He raked his hands into her hair.

"I want to trust you, Jack." But it was damned hard when his eyes were taking on a reddish glow.

"You can." He pulled her into his arms and kissed her.

Chapter Nine

*H*e must have turned masochistic in his old age. How else could he rage with desire for a woman who suspected him of being a criminal? Jack molded his mouth against Lara's, easing her lips apart so he could invade her with his tongue.

He rubbed his hands down her back. *Mine. Santo cielo*, he was becoming possessive. Possessive to the point that common sense no longer made sense. So what if they were wrong for each other? So what if every affair he'd had in the past had come to a terrible end? He no longer cared. She was Lara, and he had to have her.

He stroked her tongue with his own, and a surge of joy shot through him as she grabbed his shoulders and kissed him back. Yes! She wanted him, too.

"Lara." He dusted her face with kisses. Her cheeks, her brow, the little freckles on her nose. *"Cara mia."*

"Jack." She delved her hands into his hair. "I-I shouldn't let you."

"Don't be afraid," he whispered against her temple.

"But . . . you have strange powers."

"The better to love you with." He drew her earlobe into his mouth and suckled.

He knew from experience that a Vamp's saliva tended to make a woman more sensitive and titillated, but it usually required some mind control to work, and Lara was immune to that. He tickled her neck with his tongue.

She moaned.

He grew hard. She was so glorious, so responsive. Even without a mental connection, her body reacted to him as if. . .as if they belonged together.

He ran his hand down her hip to her thigh and squeezed.

"Mmm." She wiggled closer to him.

He winced as her hip rubbed against his erection. He'd reached the limit of how much torture he could bear.

"Time out." He shifted her lovely rump onto the couch beside him, so she was lounging sideways with her head resting against the side cushion and her legs draped across his thighs. Her pink tint warned him that his eyes were still red. He turned his face away from her and circled a hand around her ankle.

"I saw your eyes, Jack," she whispered. "They're glowing and red."

"I know." He massaged her delicate ankle bone. "It's a sign of how much I want you."

She took a deep breath and let it out slowly. "I want to know your secret. Who are you?"

He closed his eyes briefly. "Nine circles of hell. I'd tell you if I could."

She groaned. "This is so frustrating. At least tell me what's the deal with the nine circles of hell?"

"It's an old habit." He took her hand and stroked her fingers with his own. "When I was a young lad in Venice, my tutor was an old priest. He taught me to read with Dante's *Divine Comedy*. It starts with *Inferno* and the nine circles of hell."

She grimaced. "What a strange choice of reading material for a child."

He laced his fingers with hers. "Father Giovannni was trying to scare me into being good. He didn't want me to follow in my father's footsteps."

She gave him a wry smile. "Did it work?"

He smiled back. "Unfortunately, I found the descriptions of *Inferno* more interesting than *Paradiso*."

"Well, most kids would. It's the literary equivalent of a horror movie. So *nine* circles, huh? That's a lot of hell."

"According to Father Giovanni, there are a lot of sinners."

She snorted. "What a fun teacher. So which of the nine circles is waiting for your untimely demise?"

The question caught him by surprise. After living two hundred years, Jack no longer gave much thought to death. And that was a mistake. He could always die in battle with the Malcontents. And then, what would happen to his immortal soul?

Would he prove Father Giovanni right and end up in *Inferno*? He'd killed before, but only in self-defense. He'd fed off women, but he'd always tried to repay the favor. When it came to sin, only one loomed before him that he couldn't possibly deny.

"Jack." She squeezed his hand. "You look so serious. I was only joking."

He met her gaze. His vision was no longer tinted red. Nothing like thoughts of eternal damnation to kill the mood. "I would go to the second circle, and there,

I would spend eternity, being tossed to and fro by a violent storm."

She made a face. "That's awful. What sin have you committed to deserve that?"

He lifted her hand to his mouth and pressed a kiss into the palm. "Lust."

Her eyes widened. "That hardly seems fair. I mean, lust doesn't seem all that evil. At least *your* lust doesn't. Not when it's directed at me. It is me, right?"

"Oh yes." He rubbed his thumb over the spot he'd kissed, wishing he could permanently imprint his claim on her skin. "Definitely you. Only you."

Her eyes sparkled. "I like that." Her gaze swept over him with a seductive look. "Maybe we could find a way to appease your lust."

"Cure a sin by giving in to it?" He smiled as he wrapped a hand around her calf. "That's a novel approach."

"Hey, what good is a sin if you can't enjoy it?"

He chuckled. "What a naughty angel you are. But as tempted as I am, I don't believe your solution can work."

"Why not?"

"You're assuming my lust can be appeased." He gazed at her body with a wistful look. "There is no cure for this. The more I get, the more I want. Even so, I am touched that you would so nobly sacrifice yourself to save me."

Her face turned a deeper pink. "It wouldn't be entirely unselfish on my part. I'm afraid I'm suffering from the same sin."

He leaned toward her to touch her face. "Don't worry, *cara mia*. There is an easy way out. Easy, but also very rare. If lust grows into true love, then we would find ourselves in *Paradiso*."

"Jack, you're so sweet." She curved a hand around his neck. "There's something very old-fashioned and romantic about you."

He was definitely older than she thought. "You bring out the romantic in me."

She watched him with worried eyes. "There's so much about you that I don't know. I wish you would tell me more, 'cause I . . . I just don't know what to think."

"I understand." How could she trust him when he wouldn't confide in her? Maybe he could prove himself by earning her trust. He kissed her lightly on the lips, then straightened. "Tell me about this case you're working."

She groaned. "Okay." She told him about the college student who had disappeared Saturday night, and how the friends all appeared programmed to tell the same lie.

"Here, I have some stuff to show you." Lara slipped a hand into her jeans pocket, lifting her hips slightly in the air.

Jack groaned. "Have mercy, *bellissima.*"

She grinned. "You have a one-track mind." She handed him the photo, then unfolded a pink sheet of paper. "LaToya and I found this on a bulletin board. We checked it out, and the building manager did the same zombie act that the girlfriends did."

Jack studied the photo and then the flyer. *"Do you want to stay young and beautiful forever? Free seminar."*

"Yeah, I think that's how the perp attracts the girls. Then he picks one out like Vanessa and makes sure no one else can remember him. Roxanne said there was another girl last year who went missing."

Jack glanced at the photo. "Was the other girl a redhead like this one?"

"Close. Strawberry blonde."

A twinge of unease pricked at Jack's gut. Lara was exactly the kind of girl this kidnapper was looking for. And given the kidnapper's ability to manipulate minds, chances were good that he was a vampire. A Malcontent who preyed on pretty young women for food and sex. And like most Malcontents, he probably considered mortals a disposable food source. When he tired of one, he would drain her dry and toss her out like an empty milk jug.

If Lara came across him in the course of her investigation, he would want her. He would grab her and teleport away, and there would be no way to track him down.

Jack swallowed hard. He couldn't let Lara pursue this vampire. "This . . . criminal is dangerous. I think you should leave his capture to someone else." *Like me.*

"No way." She scowled at him as she swung her legs off his lap and sat up. "I want to be promoted to detective. If I can help with this case, it'll prove that I'm ready."

"Prove yourself on someone less dangerous."

She scoffed. "They're all dangerous, Jack. That's why they're called criminals."

He folded the flyer and handed it back to her. "Have you been officially assigned to the case?"

"No." She stuffed the flyer in her pocket. "Some detectives in LaToya's precinct are handling it. Normally, it would be a really big no-no for us to do our own investigating, but we feel compelled to do something because we know about the mind-control aspect. I don't think the detectives will ever figure that out, and I really don't know how to explain it to them without them wanting to lock us up in a psych ward."

Jack also doubted the detectives would figure out

that a vampire was involved. But if they did, it would be disastrous for all the good Vamps, who needed secrecy in order to survive.

He would explain the situation to Connor and Angus. They would agree that the matter needed to be resolved by Vamps, quickly and quietly with as little mortal interference as possible. "Since you are determined to work on this case, I would like to . . . assist you."

"Really?" Lara's eyes widened.

Actually, he was going to take charge, but he'd keep that to himself for now. "I have some experience in investigative work. And I could be considered an expert in mind control."

"Yeah, I noticed."

"I'd like to meet Vanessa's friends," Jack continued. "I might be able to retrieve their real memories."

"Oh my gosh!" Lara jumped to her feet. "That would be great. We could get a real description of the kidnapper."

"Then you agree. We will work together." And he could protect her from harm. He stood and motioned toward the foyer. "The car's out front. I'll drive."

"Great!" Lara dashed into the foyer. "LaToya!"

"What?" LaToya yelled. Footsteps pounded on the stairs. "I'm coming! Are you all right?"

"I'm fine," Lara shouted. "I'm going out with Jack. He wants to help us with the case."

"*What?*" LaToya halted on the second-floor landing and gasped for breath. Carlos stopped right behind her. She gave Jack a wary look. "He can't help us. He's a suspect."

"He's fine." Lara smiled at him. "He's a good guy."

Jack's heart expanded in his chest. "*Grazie, bellissima.*" He took her hand and kissed her fingers.

"Wait a minute." LaToya marched down the last flight of stairs, glaring at Lara. "You're going somewhere alone with this guy?" She glanced at Jack. "No offense, but you're not exactly normal."

Jack bowed his head. "I understand. And I applaud your desire to protect Lara. I feel the same way."

"Ain't that just dandy?" LaToya grabbed Lara's arm and pulled her away from Jack. "Girl, we need to talk."

"He has an alibi for last night," Lara explained as she was dragged into the living room. "He was at church."

LaToya snorted. "Right. He's a regular choir boy."

"What's going on?" Carlos whispered as he reached the bottom of the stairs.

Jack held a finger to his lips. He wanted to listen in on the conversation next door. Carlos nodded.

"Have you lost your mind, girl?" LaToya whispered. "One minute you think he's a suspect, and the next, you're ready to believe anything he says?"

"He has an alibi," Lara repeated. "A lot of people saw him last night."

"You only have his word for that. And what if he programmed those people to say they saw him?" LaToya asked. "What if he's messing with your mind, too?"

"I'm immune to him."

LaToya snorted. "Girl, if that man had the flu, you'd already be running a fever."

"He's an honorable man," Lara insisted. "I—I sorta offered myself to him, and—"

"*What?*"

"Shhh," Lara hushed her. She lowered her voice so that Jack had to strain to hear. "I offered myself to see how he would react, and he turned me down, even though it was obvious that he wanted me. It was so sweet."

"How special," Carlos whispered with a wry smile. "I feel strangely nauseated."

Jack shot a look at Carlos that said, *Butt out*. Still, he was surprised that the shape shifter's hearing was as good as his. "How did the tour go?"

"Fine," Carlos kept his voice low. "I made sure she didn't see any bathrooms with missing mirrors."

"Good." Jack focused once more on the conversation in the living room.

"He's going to help us find the kidnapper," Lara whispered.

"What if he's steering the investigation away from himself?" LaToya asked.

"He's not," Lara hissed. "Did you come across any imprisoned women upstairs?"

"No, but I haven't seen the basement yet. You know there's something weird about him."

Lara sighed. "Yes, I know."

"What *do* you know?" LaToya asked sharply.

"I know that I don't know."

"Well, I know that."

Lara moaned. "This is getting us nowhere. I'll be fine. Why don't you go home, and I'll be along later."

"All right," LaToya grumbled. "But before I leave, I'm going to finish checking this place out. If you need me for anything, call me."

Jack strode to the console and collected the car keys. "Are you ready, Lara?" he called.

"Coming." She rushed into the foyer, swinging her handbag onto her shoulder.

LaToya followed her and glared at Jack. "She'd better come back safe."

He nodded. "I would never do anything to hurt Lara."

"I'm holding you to that. I've got a cousin in New Orleans who's into voodoo. Don't make me start playing with dolls."

Jack looked at Lara and smiled. "I'll try to behave myself."

She leaned close and whispered, "Don't try too hard."

He squeezed her hand. "Whatever you say, *bellissima*. I always aim to please."

"Oh God." LaToya grimaced. "Y'all are so sweet, I'm going into hyperglycemic shock. Just kill me now."

Carlos laughed. "How about a beer?"

"Sounds good." LaToya crossed her arms, still watching Jack with a suspicious eye, while Carlos disappeared into the kitchen. "So, choir boy, what's in the basement?"

"A dead body or two, usually." Jack smiled. "But they're gone now."

Lara gave him an annoyed look. "That's not helping."

"Sorry," Jack said. "There's a washer and dryer downstairs."

"Of course." LaToya narrowed her eyes. "And plenty of bleach for getting out bloodstains."

"Exactly." Jack nodded. "I hate bloodstains."

Lara elbowed him in the ribs. "Would you stop kidding? She's going to believe you."

Unfortunately, he wasn't kidding.

"Here's the beer," Carlos announced as he returned from the kitchen. He handed an opened bottle to LaToya.

"Thanks." She took a swig. "So what is in the basement, Carlos?"

"A pool table. Would you like to play?"

"Sure." She followed him to the basement stairs and gave Jack an irritated look as she passed by. "Dead bodies, my ass. You've probably got a spaceship down there."

Jack strode to the front door and punched some buttons on the keypad to deactivate the alarm. "Shall we go?"

"Sure." Lara followed him out the front door. "Please don't mind LaToya. She's just very protective of me."

"I understand." He closed the front door and turned the alarm back on. "I feel the same way." There was a bloodthirsty vampire out there collecting redheads. He would do whatever it took to protect Lara.

Chapter Ten

*M*egan, this is Jack . . . Venezia." Lara realized she wasn't sure what Jack's last name was, which was a bit disturbing since she kept ending up in his arms, kissing him. "He's going to help us locate Vanessa."

"Okay." Megan's eyes widened at the sight of Jack standing at her door.

"How do you do?" He nodded politely. "May we come in?"

Megan stumbled back a few steps, still gawking at Jack. Lara knew how she felt. Jack had a way of taking over one's senses.

He closed the door. "Have a seat, please. This will just take a moment."

Megan retreated until she collided with her bed and fell onto her rear. Lara sat across from her on the other twin bed. She retrieved pen and paper from her handbag while she wondered what exactly Jack would do to this girl.

He leaned casually against the door. "So, Megan, you and Vanessa are good friends?"

"Oh yes. Vanessa's like the coolest friend I've ever had. I—I hope she's okay." Megan's bottom lip trembled and tears filled her eyes. "I'm so afraid for her."

"I'm sure you are," Jack spoke softly. "And where did you and Vanessa go last night?"

The change that swept over Megan's face was alarming. Lara's skin prickled with gooseflesh as she watched the young woman go from near tears to a totally blank expression in a matter of seconds.

"We were in our room, studying," Megan said with a dull, robotic voice.

An icy blast of air swirled around the room. With a shiver, Lara turned her attention to Jack. What kind of human brain could change the temperature? He was frowning, completely focused on Megan. The gold flecks in his eyes gleamed.

Lara swallowed hard. What did she really know about him?

He stepped toward Megan. "Where were you last night?"

"We were . . . in our room . . ." Megan swayed, her eyes closing.

A strange crackling static echoed in Lara's ears. Beneath the buzz, she thought she detected a low and masculine voice. It sounded like Jack, but she couldn't make out the words. Since his mouth wasn't moving, he must have been communicating telepathically.

"Yes," Megan whispered.

Yes, what? Yes, she would answer his questions truthfully, or yes, she would say whatever he mentally ordered her to say? Unease tickled the back of Lara's neck. Could LaToya be right? Was Jack programming Megan to lie for him?

He placed a hand on top of the girl's head and closed his eyes. "You will remember. Where did you go Saturday night?"

"We were in—" Megan grimaced. "We went to the Student Services building for a seminar. Vanessa wanted to go."

"Who was presenting the seminar?" Jack asked.

"He—" Megan slumped back.

Jack grasped her head, covering her temples. "Who was he?"

"Apollo," she whispered.

Lara wrote the name down on her pad of paper.

"Describe him," Jack ordered.

"Tall, blond, really good-looking." Megan wrinkled her nose. "Really pale."

Lara paused in the middle of taking notes. She'd always thought Jack was a little pale, too.

"What did Apollo tell you?" Jack asked.

"He showed us a PowerPoint presentation with pictures of a fancy resort and spa. We filled out a survey about our favorite spa treatments, and one lucky person was chosen to receive a deluxe spa package. One week, all expenses paid. Vanessa was the lucky one."

Lara shook her head. That kind of luck could get you killed.

"Did he say where the spa is located?" Jack asked.

"I don't know." Megan frowned. "It looked pretty. Classical Greek architecture. White marble buildings. It was in the country somewhere."

"Thank you, Megan. You will go to sleep now, and when you wake in the morning, you will have no memory of us being here. You will not remember answering my questions." Jack released her.

She fell sideways on the bed, and Jack pulled her up

to where her head rested on the pillow. The cold air in the room dissipated.

Lara rushed across the room to remove Megan's flip-flops. "Why did you erase her memory of us?"

Jack covered her with a blanket. "As long as she sticks to the story that Apollo programmed her with, she'll be safe. If he ever suspects she's been talking about him, her life could be in danger."

Lara nodded. "I understand." She headed for the door. "I doubt Apollo is his real name."

"I agree." Jack turned off the lights as he exited the room. "He probably thinks it goes well with the Greek architecture of this supposed resort."

"A free spa package would be hard for any woman to resist." Lara motioned down the hall. "Do you want to see the other friends?"

She led him to Carmen and Ramya's room. Ramya was at the library studying, so Jack did his spooky mind tap on Carmen. Like Megan, Carmen reported that Apollo was tall, blond, and handsome, and that he'd chosen Vanessa to win the free spa package. They left Carmen asleep and walked across campus to the Student Services building. There was no record of Apollo filling out any forms to rent a room, and the manager had no memory of him.

As they neared the exit, Lara spotted a vending machine. "I need a drink. Would you like something?" She fumbled in her handbag for her billfold.

"No thanks." Jack whipped out his wallet and inserted a dollar into the machine before she could unsnap her billfold.

He sure was fast. "Thanks." She punched the button for a Diet Coke. Once again, he was refraining from drinking with her.

"Shall I drive you home now?"

"Yes, thank you." She unscrewed the top from the cola bottle and took a sip while he opened the door.

She strolled across campus with him, mentally reviewing what they'd learned so far. Kidnapping college-aged girls was uncommon enough, but using mind manipulation to pull it off was definitely different. Apollo covered his tracks just as well as Jack had at the Plaza hotel. How many people possessed these powers? How many crimes were being committed on a daily basis that were so well covered up, no one knew they had even happened? It was the perfect crime, if the victim didn't realize he'd been victimized.

Lara suppressed a shudder. This whole train of thought was very disturbing. There could be a crime syndicate of secret mind manipulators who were abusing, raping, and killing the innocent. And if no one knew about it, how would they ever be stopped?

She gulped down some cola. "Jack, we have to find this guy. He could be a serial killer."

"I agree."

As they approached the parking lot, she realized Jack had also been quiet. He was frowning, apparently deep in thought. How much did he know that he wasn't telling?

"So what do you want to do next?" she asked.

"I'll find out more information." He glanced at her with a lopsided smile. "I'm an investigator, remember?"

"A secretive one," she muttered.

"That's the best kind." He punched his keypad to unlock the Lexus.

"If we're going to work together, you should tell me everything you know."

A pained look crossed his face as he opened the passenger door for her. "I'll do what I can."

Which translated as "not much," Lara figured as she slid into the passenger seat. He closed the door behind her and circled the car. Once again, she was struck by how old-fashioned he was. She buckled up and inserted her Coke bottle into a cup holder.

He climbed in and started the car. "I want to thank you, Lara, for telling me about this case."

"You're welcome." She fiddled with her handbag, gathering up her courage as he pulled out of the parking lot. "You know, when I introduced you to Megan and Carmen, I realized I wasn't sure about your last name. Is it really Venezia?"

"Venice is my home." He glanced at her with a smile. "Would you like to see it?"

She blinked. "Well, sure. Of course." She'd always thought it would be wonderfully romantic to float along in a gondola with a handsome Italian man. Who wouldn't? And the rascal was changing the subject on her. He was good at manipulation without using any psychic power. "About your last name—"

"I shall take you."

"Excuse me?"

He turned south onto Henry Hudson Parkway. "I'll take you to Venezia."

She gave him a dubious look. "If you insist, but you might want to top off your tank first. And I seem to recall an ocean somewhere along the way that could be a problem."

He chuckled. "I'm not prepared to go tonight."

"Duh. I don't have a plane ticket. And I can't really afford one, so even though I appreciate the offer, I'll have to pass."

"You won't need any money, *bellissima*. You can stay at my *palazzo*."

"Is that like a palace?"

"We'll ride in a gondola under the moonlight," he continued. "And I'll show you my favorite places."

"How can a guy who works as an investigator afford a *palazzo*?"

He shrugged. "It's not a very big *palazzo*. It's been in my family for years. And I work because I want to do more than merely exist. I want to do something meaningful, like rid the world of bad guys. We have that in common, yes?"

"Yes, but I don't have superpowers like you."

"You have power, *bellissima*. You can bring a man to his knees."

She snorted.

A corner of his mouth lifted in a half smile. "You might be surprised at what I can do on my knees."

Her cheeks grew warm. "So this *palazzo* of yours—do you have family living there?" she asked casually, hoping to get more personal information from him.

"No. I'm not there very often. I'm usually on assignment."

"Do you have any family at all?"

"I have a . . . distant cousin who runs the family business. I'm a major investor."

"And what is the family business?"

"Shipping." He slanted an amused look at her. "I am somewhat aware of the oceans out there."

"Good. I feel so much safer now."

He snorted softly. "*Cara mia*, you are never entirely safe with me."

Her skin tingled. "Are you threatening me?"

He gave her a wry smile. "Nothing painful. If I pounced on you, it would only be to give you pleasure."

"Oh." Her face burned as she turned to look out the window.

As the minutes ticked by, the tension in the car grew. Lights flashed and horns blared, but it all seemed distant, as if they were alone in the world, as if nothing could touch them in their private cocoon. It was only him and her and this strange magnetic energy that was pulling them together.

An odd sense of destiny overwhelmed her thoughts, making her feel as if her whole life had zoomed by for the express purpose of reaching this moment in time. This moment with Jack.

She thought remaining silent would help, but it didn't. Heavy desire surrounded her, swathing her in heat. It felt so dense, she would have sworn there was a physical connection between her and Jack. If he hadn't been driving, she'd be climbing all over him by now.

He turned onto Canal Street, going east.

She cleared her throat. "Jack?"

"Yes?" His voice sounded strained. Was he feeling it, too?

"If we ever . . . I mean, if I go to bed with you, I want it to be entirely my own decision." She turned to him. "Promise me you won't use any of your manipulative powers to sway me one way or the other."

"I promise." He gave her a sad look. "I would not have it any other way."

"Thank you." She took a deep breath. "What is your last name, Jack?"

"Good question. I go by the name Giacomo di Venezia, since my last name has always been debatable." His eyes twinkled with humor. "I'm a bastard, but I'm sure you've already noticed that."

She smiled. "Yes, it was painfully clear from the start."

He chuckled. "According to my birth certificate, I'm Henrik Giacomo Sokolov."

"You're kidding. You're . . . German?"

"Half Bohemian, from my mother. Her husband's name was Sokolov. I've never used the name since I'm not related to that cuckold, who refused to allow me in his house."

"Your mother's husband rejected you as a baby?"

Jack shrugged. "Why not? I was evidence of his wife's infidelity. He sent her back to her family in disgrace, and she died a few years later. I never really knew her."

"That's terrible!" Lara leaned toward him. Poor Jack. "What happened to you?"

"I was sent to the . . . place where my father was working. An old nurse raised me." Jack headed across the Manhattan Bridge. "It wasn't that bad, really. Nana Helga was a kind woman, and I saw my father whenever I could. He taught me Italian. I spoke Czech with everyone else."

"So your father's Italian?"

"He was. He died when I was seven."

"Oh my gosh, Jack." Lara touched his arm. "I'm so sorry."

"It's all right. My father was seventy-three when he died. He had a full life. A very full life."

"What happened to you then?"

"I was sent to Venice to live with an uncle and some cousins." He squeezed her hand. "I fell in love with Venice. I'd love to show it to you."

"Well, maybe. That would be nice." Lara realized he still hadn't claimed a last name. And something about his story seemed oddly familiar. "Your father was Italian, but he was working in Bohemia, where he met your mother?"

"He lived in many places, but he had a way of burning his bridges behind him." Jack approached her street in Brooklyn. "Can I see you tomorrow night? We can work some more on this case."

"You mean the kidnapping?" She'd become so intrigued with Jack's story that she'd almost forgotten about Apollo.

"How about eight-forty-five?" He turned onto her street. "Your place?"

"Okay." She gathered up her belongings. "Thank you for helping me."

"Lara." He stopped the car in front of her apartment building. "I want Apollo stopped. I pray the girls are still alive. But most of all, I am determined to keep you safe."

"I'll be fine." She unbuckled her seat belt.

He touched her cheek. Her heart stuttered in her chest.

"I want to kiss you," he said softly. "Is that all right?"

"Yes." Oh God, yes. She skimmed her fingers along his high cheekbone, then across the hollow of his cheek and the dark whiskers on his jaw.

He leaned forward and pressed his lips against hers. His mouth moved slowly, sweetly, molding her till she ached to open up to him. She slipped her hand around the back of his neck and ran her fingers into his soft dark hair. He was so delicious, so tempting.

He broke the kiss and settled back in his seat. "Good night, Lara."

The rascal. He had to know he was leaving her hot and bothered. The red tinge in his eyes let her know he was as turned on as she was. "Good night, Jack."

She climbed out of the car and hurried up the three flights of stairs to her apartment.

"So how did it go?" LaToya lounged against her bedroom doorway, wearing her pajamas.

Lara booted up the computer at her desk. "It was great. We now have a description of the perp. Tall, blond, and goes by the name Apollo."

"Cool." LaToya yawned. "And Jack behaved himself?"

"Yes." Lara connected to the Internet and Googled Giacomo Casanova. "You look tired. Go on to bed. I'll fill you in on the details tomorrow."

"Okay. Good night." LaToya closed her bedroom door.

When Jack had told her about his childhood, certain things had bothered Lara, and it had taken her a while to figure out why. Jack's father had lived such a naughty life that the old priest who tutored Jack had worried that he would follow in his father's footsteps. The man had been a womanizer who lived in many places. His last job had been in Bohemia, where he'd seduced Jack's mother. He'd died there at the age of seventy-three.

As Lara scanned Casanova's biography, her chest tightened. Her heart raced. Giacomo Casanova. Famous womanizer. He'd lived in many places until some sort of scandal forced him to move on. His last job was librarian at Castle Dux in Bohemia, where he died at the age of seventy-three. In 1798.

Lara's stomach roiled, and she pressed a hand to her mouth as bile rose in her throat.

No, it was some kind of strange coincidence. People didn't live to be more than two hundred years old. She was imagining things. But had she imagined Jack's super speed and hearing? His ability to teleport or control minds?

She jumped to her feet and paced across the living room. Who was he? *What* was he?

He had to be human. He had a beating heart. She'd felt it before. She'd felt his breath against her face when he kissed her. And she'd felt his erection under the zipper of his jeans.

She paced back and forth, but nothing was making sense. She collapsed on the couch and grabbed a legal pad off the coffee table. She could figure this out, dammit. If she was going to be a detective, she had to be smart enough to solve things.

She scrawled a title at the top of the page. *You Don't Know Jack.* Then she began a list of his characteristics. *Intelligent. Strong. Handsome. Witty. Sexy. Sweet. Gorgeous. Protective. Supportive. Generous. Naughty. Great kisser.* She frowned at the list, then marked a big X through it. It looked like a wish list for the perfect boyfriend, not clues to reveal his true identity.

Her gaze drifted over the list once more. Damn, he would be the perfect boyfriend if there wasn't something weird about him. What she needed was a list of his stranger characteristics. She began writing. *Teleportation; mind reading and manipulation; super speed, strength, and hearing.* These were the obvious ones. She needed to dig deeper. The truth could be hiding in the obscure.

Secretive. He definitely had something to be secretive about.

Hardworking. Motivated. She'd gotten the impression he didn't need to earn a living. He was fighting what he called the bad guys.

Has enemies. He'd mentioned enemies several times. And his friends and enemies all had the same ability to control minds.

What else? *Old-fashioned.* That made her cringe. He'd said he was seven years old when his father died. What if his father died in 1798?

Never drinks with me. Come to think of it, she'd never seen him eat, either.

Pale. Megan had said that Apollo was pale, too.

Eyes that can glow red.

Lara stared at the list. Her mind ticked off the possibilities LaToya had mentioned that night over dinner. Her ideas had seemed silly then, but not anymore. Superhero. Mutant. Alien. Bionic man.

Could Jack's secret have something to do with Romatech Industries? If Roman Draganesti had managed to clone blood, what other strange things had he accomplished?

Lara tossed the list on the coffee table and lounged back against the sofa. She rubbed her temples. Whatever Jack was, he was giving her one doozy of a headache. If she had any sense, she'd avoid him. But she knew she wouldn't. When it came to Jack, she was hopelessly intrigued. And falling fast.

Chapter Eleven

*W*ith the amount of mind manipulation involved, I believe we can assume Apollo is a vampire." Jack finished explaining the case of the missing college student.

"I agree." Connor tapped his fingers on the desk in the security office at Romatech Industries. "He could be a Malcontent. Instead of hunting for a victim every night, he lures them to his place and keeps them on hand."

"Yeah," Phineas said. "The dude's stocking his pantry."

Jack suspected Apollo was using the women for more than food. He paced across the office. After dropping Lara off at her apartment, he'd driven back to the townhouse. Then he'd teleported to Romatech and called this meeting.

Phineas lounged back in his chair. "Limp dick."

Connor arched a brow. "Excuse me?"

"I wasn't referring to you," Phineas muttered.

Connor continued to stare at him.

"The Apollo dude's a limp dick," Phineas explained. "He has to use mind control to catch a woman. If he was the Love Doctor like me, the ladies would naturally succumb to his sophisticated charm and manly physique."

Jack chuckled. He'd been in New York for almost four weeks, and in that time, he hadn't noticed any women succumbing to Dr. Phang.

Connor cleared his throat. "I believe it is time for you to make another round."

Phineas frowned. "I did one ten minutes ago."

"And a good job ye did, too," Connor said. "Off ye go, lad."

Phineas trudged toward the door. "I'm more than just a babe magnet, you know. I can tell you want to talk to Jack in private."

Connor's eyes twinkled. "Och, ye're verra astute."

"Yeah, you bet your plaid-covered ass I am." Phineas flipped up the collar of his Polo shirt. "Dr. Phang is one astute son of a bitch." He closed the door behind him.

Jack sat in the chair Phineas had vacated. "I hope you've trained Dr. Phang well. I would hate to lose him in battle."

"He's become a verra good swordsman. Ian and Dougal taught him." Connor narrowed his eyes. "He would benefit from some lessons from you. I would say ye're actually the best swordsman in Europe, but if Jean-Luc heard that, he would skewer me."

Jack smiled. Jean-Luc had been claiming himself the European champ for centuries. "I'll be sure to tell him. He's too vain, as it is."

Connor snorted, and turned his attention to the surveillance monitors.

Jack glanced at them and spotted Phineas leaving

through a side entrance. The Vamp's body blurred as he raced into the wooded grounds that surrounded Romatech. "I'll fit in a practice session with him before dawn."

"Good." Connor drummed his fingers on the desk, then stopped abruptly. "How much does the girl know?"

Jack wiped his face blank. "Nothing."

Connor studied him carefully. "Is she . . . intellectually challenged?"

His mouth ticked. "No."

"The more time she spends with you, the more suspicious she'll become. And the more ye'll be tempted to tell her too much."

"She knows nothing," Jack said. "It's the other police officers we need to be concerned about. So far, they don't know anything about Apollo. We need to keep it that way. We can't afford to let them actually solve this case."

"I agree. Nothing is more important than keeping our existence a secret." Connor gave him a pointed look.

Jack glared back. "She knows *nothing*."

Connor looked away, frowning. "I'll tell Angus about this Apollo problem. And I'll have Roman send out a memo to all the minor coven masters in America. Perhaps one of them will know of a resort with classical Greek-style architecture in their district."

Jack nodded. "Excellent idea."

"Hopefully, we can locate Apollo's resort in a few nights," Connor continued. "I assume the place will be fenced off and have a few daytime guards. Apollo's control over the ladies' minds may be weaker during the day, while he's in his death-sleep."

"True. And he can't afford to let any of the women escape." Jack frowned as he wondered how many women Apollo might have killed. "I'll compile a list of missing college students." Especially pretty redheaded females.

"Good." Connor glanced at the surveillance monitors. "Do ye know which police officers are working the case?"

"I could find out. They'll be working out of the precinct where Columbia University is located."

"That would be Morningside Heights. We should erase their memories." Connor looked at Jack. "We should erase the memories of *every* mortal who knows about this case."

Jack gripped the arms of his chair. "Lara is immune. Her memory cannot be erased."

"By you," Connor finished softly.

Jack gritted his teeth. "My psychic powers are as strong as any Vamp's."

"I doona mean to insult you, but I have to question if ye really tried. Deep inside, ye may no' have wanted her to forget you."

"I tried," Jack growled. "Laszlo tried, too. We couldn't get through to her."

"Then ye willna mind if I give it a try."

Jack shot to his feet. "*No.*"

Connor's eyebrows rose. "An interesting reaction."

"Don't play these games with me, Connor. You will leave Lara alone."

The Scotsman heaved a sigh and leaned back in his chair. "What the hell is wrong with you all? Roman, Angus, Jean-Luc, Ian—'tis spreading like a bloody plague. I've been wondering if a Vamp loses his mind once he reaches the ripe old age of five hundred, but I remain unaffected, thank God, and you—ye're just a youngster."

"Two hundred and sixteen years old," Jack said wryly. "Barely out of training pants."

Connor gave him an annoyed look. "There are at least five thousand law-abiding Vamps that we know of, and almost half of them are verra bonny and clever women. Why can ye no' dally with one of them?"

Jack shrugged. "I never intended this to happen."

"Do ye no' realize that ye risk the lives of every Vamp around the world when ye tell a mortal our secret? Ye doona have the right to endanger us all."

"I haven't told her anything."

"*Yet.*" Connor rubbed his brow. "I've seen this happen too many times now. Ye're acting just as sick as the others did."

"Love isn't sick. *Amore* is the most powerful and positive force in the universe."

"Ye've known her—what—two weeks? Ye canna call it love. 'Tis a bad case of lust, nothing more."

Jack paced across the room. No, he'd lusted before. He'd loved before. He knew the difference. "This is more than lust."

"It is folly," Connor grumbled.

Maybe so, but was it love? Jack halted and stared into space. How deeply was he falling for Lara?

"Can ye stop seeing her?" Connor asked softly.

Could he? There were only a few things he had to do to survive. Hide from the sun. Drink blood. When looked at that way, the life of a Vamp seemed endlessly monotonous.

Every day at sunset, his heart leaped to life in his chest, but for so long he'd felt dead inside. He'd given himself entirely to the cause of fighting the Malcontents, for it gave him a reason to climb out of bed every night. It was a dark life of constant conflict and bloodshed. It had lasted two centuries, and it could go on forever. *Merda*, he was living in a circle of hell.

Lara felt like an angel who had come to his rescue. All beauty and light. He was no longer living for death, but for *amore*. He was falling in love.

Love. He'd always believed in true love, but he'd always been unlucky in it. His first love, Beatrice, had died before he could marry her. Her loss had hit him with such devastation that many years passed before love found him again, in 1855. With high hopes he'd told his mistress his secret, only to have her reject him. He'd been forced to erase her memory, but his memory had remained intact, and the pain of losing her had taken years to get over.

In 1932, the same scenario repeated itself. The same pain of losing a woman he loved. He had no doubt that telling Lara the truth would mean losing her. He swallowed hard. He couldn't risk it. He couldn't bear the thought of never seeing her again. Just considering the possibility of losing her was causing his chest to clench painfully.

There was something so special about her. And he wanted to share something special with her, something that he loved. The idea of Venezia came back. "I have to be with her."

"I was afraid of that." Connor strode toward the door. "I'll tell Roman about the situation and start the hunt for Apollo's resort."

"All right." Jack circled the desk to sit in front of the computer. He would spend the next several hours compiling information on missing female college students. He glanced at the Scottish Vamp, who was halfway out the door. "Thank you, Connor, for understanding."

Connor snorted. "What I understand is ye're falling into madness. May God save yer soul."

"*Amore* can fill your heart with joy and peace," Jack said. "It can make you feel whole."

A pained look crossed Connor's blue eyes. "Or it can rip yer heart in two." He closed the door.

Jack sighed. He'd been there before, left behind with a heart ripped in two. He could only hope it wouldn't happen with Lara.

By late Monday afternoon, Lara was becoming increasingly bored. LaToya was at work, so she was all alone. She'd gone to the department shrink for a one-o'clock appointment, and he had declared her fit for duty, starting on Wednesday night. She considered going to work early so she could access the records on missing persons. But how could she explain that she was working a case she hadn't been assigned to?

She wondered how Jack was doing with the investigation. Actually, she wondered about Jack quite a bit. By four o'clock, she was lounging on the sofa and once again studying the *You Don't Know Jack* list she'd written the night before.

The first list gave all the reasons she was attracted to Jack. *Intelligent. Strong. Handsome. Witty. Sexy. Sweet. Gorgeous. Protective. Supportive. Generous. Naughty. Great kisser*. And he was so much more. He seemed attuned to her thoughts and feelings, much more than any other man she'd ever met. And he truly cared for her. She could see it in his eyes. When they weren't glowing red.

With a sigh, she read the second list. Psychic powers. Super powers. Old-fashioned. That made her wince. If his father died in 1798, that would make Jack born in 1791.

This was definitely freaky enough that she ought to be scared off. Even Jack had told her she should run like the hounds of hell were after her. But if he were truly a bad man, would he warn her? Maybe he was afraid that he'd accidentally hurt her with his super strength.

She tossed the list on the coffee table. Enough with this useless speculation. She needed hard facts. If she were a detective, how would she investigate him? First stop would be his workplace. She'd check out Romatech Industries and confirm his alibi for Saturday night. The trip would probably take a few hours, so she needed to let LaToya know she wouldn't be home for supper tonight.

She turned on her cell phone and noticed a missed call in her voice mail. Probably her mother again, begging her to give up this police nonsense and come back home to do something sensible with her life, like compete for the Miss Louisiana title.

When Lara had first moved to New York, her mother had called every day to nag her, so she'd resorted to turning the phone off when she wasn't at work. And now that she worked the night shift, she continued to keep it turned off so she could sleep during the day.

With a resigned sigh, she steeled herself for more nagging and activated her voice mail. Her heart leaped at the sound of Jack's voice.

"Lara, I've been gathering information on the case. I'd like to show it to you Monday night. I've also planned a . . . date for us. It would only take a few hours of our time, then we could come back and work some more. I'll call you Monday about eight-thirty to see if you're agreeable to going out with me. Sleep well, *bellissima*." He hung up.

A date? She listened to his message one more time. Yes, Jack was planning a date! She collapsed back on the couch and closed her eyes, enjoying the deep, sexy sound of his voice. Jack wanted to date her, and he wondered if she would agree? She snorted. That was like asking her if she was agreeable with world peace. Or a cure for cancer.

She glanced at the list on the coffee table, and the title mocked her. *You Don't Know Jack.* Should she be this eager to date a mystery man with strange powers? But wouldn't dating him give her the best opportunity to get better acquainted with him?

She checked the time of his call. He'd made it at five-thirty that morning. She glanced at the time now. Four-thirty P.M. She had four hours before he would call. It wouldn't take her four hours to get ready.

And what about her plan to go to Romatech? How could she fit that in? She had time to travel to White Plains, but it would be tight getting back in time. An idea struck her, and she called Jack. He didn't answer, so she left a message.

"Hi, Jack. I'll be happy to go on a date with you. And thanks for working on the case. I'm guessing you did all the work at Romatech, so I'll just meet you there at eight-thirty, okay? Bye."

She showered and after thirty minutes of deliberation, finally chose a blue sundress with a white straw belt. She topped it with a white crocheted shrug sweater in case the evening turned cool. She switched to a white handbag to match her white sandals.

She checked her makeup for the tenth time, and her conscience pricked her. There were kidnapped girls out there who needed her help, and all she could think about was this date. She was letting her attraction to Jack get out of hand.

But there will always be bad guys, she argued with herself. *How often does love come along?* She stared at herself in the mirror. Was it love? Could she really be falling in love?

Her chest tightened with a mixture of anticipation and uncertainty as she gathered her things and left the apartment. She took the subway to Grand Central Station, then boarded an express train to White Plains. It was almost seven when her taxi arrived at Romatech. The facility was bigger than she'd imagined, and completely walled off. The front gate was closed, with a guard station nearby.

When the guard approached the taxi, she rolled down the window and flashed her NYPD badge at him. "Hi, I'd like to talk to your head of security. And I have an appointment with Jack . . . Venezia, whenever he arrives."

The guard gave her a doubtful look. "I've never known the police to arrive in a taxi. And no offense, but you look more like a fashion model than a police officer."

Her face grew warm. She handed him her badge. "Check it out, if you must, then let me speak to your supervisor."

He studied her badge. "Lara Boucher? I've heard about you."

Heard what? Her face grew warmer.

With a smirk, the guard returned her badge. "Just a minute." He went to the guard station and spoke on a phone.

Lara groaned inwardly. She hadn't realized this place would be so hard to get into. And she should have realized that no one would believe she was pursuing a case when she was dressed like this. It was all too obvious that she was pursuing Jack.

The guard returned to the taxi. "Miss Boucher, Howard

Barr will meet you at the front door." He pushed a button on his remote control, and the iron gate swung open.

The taxi proceeded down a two-lane road that cut through a wooded area. Then, around a bend, the facility came into view. A small parking lot was in front and a larger one to the left by a side entrance. The building sprawled from the main entrance with several wings jutting out into the beautifully landscaped grounds.

A large man in khaki pants and navy Polo shirt emerged from the front door just as the taxi pulled to a stop.

Lara paid the cabbie and climbed out of the car. "Hello. I'm Lara Boucher." She extended a hand.

"Howard Barr." Smiling, he shook her hand. "I've heard about you."

"Um . . . thanks." She watched as he slid his ID card through a slot, then pressed his hand to a sensor pad. "You certainly have tight security here."

"Yep." A green light blinked on a keypad, and he opened the door. "Come on in."

She stepped into a wide foyer and noted a few potted plants resting on the marble floor and beautifully framed artwork decorating the walls. The scent of antiseptic cleanser lingered in the air, reminding her of a hospital. Not surprising, though, since they would need a sterile environment for the manufacture of synthetic blood.

Howard led her to a small table on the right. "I'm sorry, but I'll have to check your bag."

"I understand." She set her white straw handbag on the table. Thankfully, she'd left her handgun at home. "Jack mentioned that you have some enemies."

"Yep." Howard fumbled around her handbag with his huge hands, then refastened the clasp. "We've been bombed a few times, so it pays to be extra careful."

"Why would someone bomb this place?" Lara swung her bag onto her shoulder. "The synthetic blood you're making here is saving thousands of lives."

"Yes, but there are some . . . weirdos out there who object to it not being real blood. So, Miss Boucher, how can I help you? Jack won't be available for another hour or so."

"I'm investigating a college student who disappeared Saturday night."

Howard nodded. "Jack was working on that last night. He left the information on a laptop. Did you want to see it?"

"Yes, please."

"This way." Howard led her down a hall to the left. "I'll let you use a conference room. Jack mentioned that he was working with you, so it should be all right for you to look at the information he found."

Lara felt a twinge of annoyance. Of course it was all right. The missing girl was a police matter. "I suppose Jack was here Saturday night, working security?"

"Yes." Howard frowned. "Why do you ask?"

"Standard procedure," she murmured. She noted the labeled doors that they passed. *Restroom*, *Storeroom*, *Conference Room*. *Nursery?* She thought she heard a child's laughter behind that door. *Dental Office*. "You have a dentist here?"

"Yep. Shanna Draganesti." Howard motioned to the office. "She provides dental care for all the employees here for a fraction of the normal cost."

"That's nice. So what time was Jack here Saturday night?"

"All night long." Howard stopped. "You don't seriously consider him a suspect, do you? Jack's a great guy. And if he were guilty, why would he help you work on the case?"

Lara shifted her weight. "I don't mean to sound ungrateful, but it would clarify matters if you could provide actual proof that he was here that night."

Howard scowled at her. "Fine. I'll show you the security tapes from Saturday night." He led her to a door labeled *MacKay Security*. Once again, he swiped his ID card and pressed his hand against a sensor pad. "We've got a few weapons inside, so we have to keep it locked up tight."

"I understand." Lara followed him inside.

At first, it looked like a normal security office: desk, computer, file cabinets, a wall covered with monitors linked to surveillance cameras. But then she spotted the caged-off area in the back. Her mouth fell open.

A *few* weapons? She walked toward the padlocked cage, counting the assault rifles lined up on a rack. Twelve. Numerous handguns on a shelf. Bins filled with ammo on another shelf. But what really caught her eye were the swords. Gleaming broadswords and foils filled the wall on the left. On the right wall, lethal-looking daggers and knives were on display.

She curled her fingers around a chain link of the cage and studied the swords. Some of them looked really old. And what an old-fashioned way to protect a building.

Old-fashioned. Those words were starting to haunt her. "What's with all the swords? Are you expecting a horde of Vikings to attack?"

Howard snorted as he sat behind his desk. "The guys like to collect them." He typed on his keyboard. "Okay, I've got surveillance video coming up from Saturday night."

Lara turned to look at the monitors. They went fuzzy for a second, then cleared up. The numerical date for last Saturday was printed in the bottom right corner along with the time. Twenty-one hundred hours. Nine P.M.

Howard joined her by the monitors, holding a remote control. "As you can see, the building's fairly empty on Saturday night. Just security, and people going to Mass."

"I see." Lara had noticed that most of the monitors showed empty hallways. She recognized the main foyer. A few people were congregated there.

A blur of movement on a different monitor caught her attention. It looked like someone racing at warp speed through the wooded grounds. "How fast is that guy going?"

"Oh, it's just on fast forward," Howard muttered.

She wondered if one screen could be on fast-forward while the others weren't.

Howard pointed at a screen. "There's Jack, leaving this office."

She watched his graceful, long-legged stride. "How long have you known him?"

"Since I started working for MacKay S & I," Howard said. "About ten years, I guess."

Lara saw a little boy run into the hall. Jack swung him up into his arms. "Who's that?"

"Constantine Draganesti. Roman and Shanna's son," Howard explained. "That's Shanna coming out of the nursery with the new baby."

Lara smiled when she saw Jack step back. He'd looked perfectly comfortable around the toddler, but the baby seemed to terrify him. Shanna handed the baby to an older woman who had also exited the nursery. While the older woman returned the children to the nursery, Shanna strolled down the hallway with Jack.

"They're headed to the chapel for Mass," Howard explained. "I'll fast-forward."

Lara noticed Howard was wearing the same sort

of clothes that Carlos had been wearing at the town-house. "Are you wearing a uniform?"

"Yes. For MacKay guards."

"I've never seen Jack wear the uniform."

"Jack's one of our top investigators, and he works under cover a lot. He can do pretty much whatever he wants." Howard punched a button on the remote control. "You'll see them coming out of the chapel soon."

"It strikes me as a bit odd to have a church service here."

Howard shrugged. "Roman likes to do it. Okay, here they come." Howard motioned to the monitor as everyone exited the chapel. Most of them went into a room on the right. "That's the fellowship hall where we go for refreshments. There's no camera in there."

Lara spotted Jack in front of the chapel, talking to the kilted Scotsman she'd met at the wedding. Robby. The two of them strolled into the fellowship hall. The time in the corner of the screen said twenty-two hours. It looked like Jack did indeed have an alibi.

The older woman showed up on the monitor displaying the hall outside the nursery. She was walking with the baby in her arms, and the little boy was skipping by her side. They soon appeared in the monitor outside the chapel. The little boy jumped into his daddy's arms. Roman Draganesti hugged the boy, and Shanna took the baby. They were a lovely family and looked so normal.

All the people seemed normal and nice. Lara wondered if she was being too suspicious where Jack was concerned. Maybe she should just relax and enjoy being attracted to him.

She blinked when Jack suddenly walked into the hall. He had a glass in his hand, and he sipped from it. At last! Proof that Jack actually drank.

She pressed closer to the screen. "What is he drinking? Wine?"

The screen went blank.

"What—?" She glanced back at Howard and saw him set the remote control down on his desk.

"I assume that was enough to prove his alibi." He typed on his keyboard, and the monitors went back to real time. "Now would you like to see the information Jack compiled last night?"

"Yes, I would. Thank you."

"It's all in here." Howard picked up a laptop and strode toward the door. "You can use the conference room across the hall."

Lara grabbed her handbag to follow Howard and glanced back at the monitors. Was she just being paranoid, or had he tried to keep her from seeing something?

Chapter Twelve

Lara sat at the end of the long conference table and waited for the computer to boot up.

Howard hovered at the door. "Do you need anything to write on? Maybe something to drink?"

"I'll be fine, thank you." She did a double take at the computer screen. The desktop was surprisingly bare. There was only one non-system file, and it was labeled *Apollo*.

"I need to make a round," Howard said. "I'll check on you in fifteen minutes." He strode away, leaving the door wide open.

Security was certainly a priority around here. Lara turned her attention back to the computer. Jack had made sure there was nothing on this laptop pertaining to Romatech Industries or MacKay Security and Investigation. He obviously didn't want her trying to snoop around their business. What could they be hiding?

She'd gotten the feeling that Howard hadn't really liked her being in the security office or looking at the surveillance tapes. And what was the deal with all those weapons, especially the swords? She sighed. More questions to ask Jack.

At least he wasn't trying to hide anything from her regarding the Apollo case. Lara clicked on *Apollo* and two folders came up titled *Negative* and *Positive*. She opened the *Negative* file and found a brief description of five local women who had been kidnapped. She scanned down the page and realized they were all the wrong age or wrong hair color for Apollo.

She opened the *Positive* folder and gaped at the screen. There were twenty more folders. Jack had uncovered all this information in one night?

She opened the first folder and found a photo and brief report. A female student with dark auburn hair had disappeared from NYU last month. April.

Lara opened the second folder. A strawberry blonde had vanished from NYU the year before in June. The third folder showed Brittney Beckford from Columbia University, who had disappeared last July. The fourth and fifth folders showed two redheaded students who'd gone missing from Syracuse University.

Was Apollo kidnapping a new girl every month? Lara double-checked the dates. Each girl had disappeared on the fourth Saturday of each month.

How could something so blatant and horrible slip by the authorities? Apollo must be using mind control to cover his tracks so well that no one realized what was happening. In fact, most of these girls were merely listed as runaways. Thank God this criminal was finally coming to the attention of the police.

Lara frowned. Jack had worked awfully hard on this, but it wasn't his case to solve. It was a police matter.

She winced as she scanned the report in the sixth folder. The girl had been a student at the University of Pennsylvania in Philadelphia. The seventh girl was missing from Princeton, New Jersey. If Apollo was kidnapping girls across state lines, then the case belonged to the FBI.

Even so, she had to hand it to Jack. He was one hell of an investigator. She wasn't even halfway through all the folders, and she was skimming through them fast. She needed hard copies of all these reports so she could compare them to one another. And she needed hours to study the material.

What she needed was a copy of all this. She started to e-mail herself the entire *Apollo* folder, then hesitated. Would Jack mind? Surely not. He'd said in his phone message that he meant to show her all this information. They were working the case together. She clicked on *Send*.

"Hello."

She jumped in her chair and spotted a little blond-haired boy at the door. He looked like the boy from the surveillance video. "Hello."

He tugged at his blue-and-green-striped T-shirt. "My name is Tino."

Of course. Constantine Draganesti. "How do you do? I'm Lara Boucher."

He gave her an angelic smile. "I heard about you."

"Great." She turned off the laptop and rose to her feet.

"Tino!" a woman's voice called. "Oh, there you are." An older woman appeared in the doorway and noticed Lara. "I'm sorry. I hope Tino wasn't disturbing you."

"No, not at all." Lara approached them. "I'm Lara Boucher."

"Oh, I've heard about you."

Not again. Lara extended a hand. "How do you do?"

"Very well. My name is Radinka." She shook hands

and didn't let go. She peered closely at Lara, then smiled. "Yes. You and Jack will be very happy."

"Excuse me?"

Radinka released her hand, then yelled over her shoulder. "Shanna, you'll never guess who's here."

"Coming." A woman emerged from the nursery, pushing a baby stroller. She was blonde and a little plump from having recently given birth. The babe was a tiny newborn with pink, delicate skin and a fuzzy cap of black hair.

Lara leaned over the stroller for a closer look. "What a beautiful baby." A girl, she figured, from the baby's delicate features. The pink blanket was another clue. She raised her gaze to the baby's mother. "Hi. I'm Lara Boucher."

"Oh. I've heard about you."

"That's what they all say," Lara muttered.

Shanna laughed. "Don't worry. It was all good. By the way, I'm Shanna. My daughter's Sofia. And you met my son, Constantine?"

"Yes." Lara smiled at the little rosy-cheeked boy.

"She's the one for Jack," Radinka announced.

Lara gulped. "I-I wouldn't say that. I hardly know him."

"Well, we'll just have to gossip about him then, won't we?" Shanna's eyes sparkled with humor. "Robby said you were very pretty. He was definitely right."

"Connor said you were trouble," Constantine added.

"Tino." Shanna frowned at her son, then turned to Lara. "Connor's just worried about Jack getting hurt. We're all sorta like family around here. Would you like to have supper with us? We were just headed for the cafeteria."

"I'm gonna have macaroni and cheese!" Tino pranced around the hall.

"I'd love to come, but Howard might expect me to stay put." Lara motioned toward the conference room.

"Oh, don't worry about that." Shanna waved a dismissive hand. "He'll see you on the monitor and know you're with us. Come on."

Lara grabbed her handbag, shut the conference-room door, and accompanied them down the hall toward the foyer. She hadn't eaten yet, so she was hungry, and she was eager to hear some of the gossip Shanna had referred to. At the same time, she figured she'd better eat light. Jack had a date planned for later that night, and it might involve dinner. And other things . . .

They went down the length of the foyer, then turned right, then left, then another left. The halls were lined with windows on one side, and Lara realized they were circling around a courtyard and landscaped area. The setting sun cast a glare off the windows and lit up the bright red and pink geraniums that bloomed in pots around the courtyard.

In the nearly empty cafeteria, they settled at a table with the baby stroller parked at one end next to Shanna. Lara sat across from her and ate a small salad while she admired the two-week-old baby.

"You want to see what I can do?" Tino asked.

"Of course." Lara figured the little boy wanted some attention, too.

"Tino." Shanna shook her head, frowning.

"Oh. Okay." His shoulders slumped, and he pushed his macaroni around his plate.

Shanna watched him, still frowning, then her face brightened. "I know. You wiggled your ears the other day. You can show Lara that."

Tino sat up, grinning. "Yeah." He turned to Lara. "You want to see?"

"I'd love to." Lara laughed when the little boy's ears moved slightly. "That's amazing. I was never able to do that."

"I can read, too," Tino boasted.

"That's wonderful." Lara pushed back her empty salad bowl. "How old are you?"

"I was two in March." Constantine gulped down some milk.

Two? Lara would have guessed he was more like four, but then she didn't know very much about children.

Sofia suddenly let out a wail, and Shanna lifted her from the stroller. "There, there." She paced around the table, cuddling the baby. "You just had your dinner. Can't you let your mama have hers?"

Lara realized Shanna was only halfway through her meal. Radinka wasn't finished either. She pushed back her chair and stood. "I'll hold the baby."

"Oh, thank you." Shanna transferred the baby to Lara's arms. "She likes to be carried around. I guess it reminds her of being inside of me."

"I don't remember being inside you, Mama," Tino said.

Shanna chuckled as she sat down to finish her supper. "You used to roll around, doing somersaults."

"Cool." Tino attacked a bowl of red Jell-O cubes.

Lara strolled slowly around the table, enjoying the incredible softness of the baby against her chest. Sofia gazed up at her with clear blue eyes. Lara smoothed a hand over the baby's head and felt the downy black hair. Jack's children would have hair like this.

She sighed. What on earth was she doing, imagining Jack's future children? As crazy as it was, she couldn't seem to get too upset. There was something about holding this baby that made her feel very calm inside.

"You're good with children." Shanna scooped some mashed potatoes into her mouth. "Jack is, too."

"He would make an excellent father." Radinka pointed her fork at Lara to add emphasis.

Lara snorted, but she couldn't help but smile. "You two are a couple of matchmakers. But as good-looking as Jack is, I doubt he needs any help in the romance department." She hoped they would come back with something like *Jack hasn't been seeing anyone for years. Jack's been as chaste as a ninety-year-old monk.*

Shanna reached for her glass of iced tea. "I have to admit, Jack is a very good-looking man."

"Youth," Radinka muttered and shook her head as she cut up the last of her steak. "What's really important is character. Jack is a good man. He's kind, loyal, and dependable."

That sounded all fine and dandy, but Lara still wondered how many busloads of women had chased after Jack. She continued to walk around the table. "I suppose a guy with both good looks and good character would have a lot of women pursuing him."

"I suppose he would." Shanna's eyes twinkled.

Lara blushed. She was so obviously fishing.

Shanna chuckled. "Don't worry. I've never known Jack to have a girlfriend. He always comes to parties alone."

Lara's lungs expanded with a breath of joy.

"But of course, once he arrives, he flirts something terrible with all the women," Shanna added wryly.

Lara coughed when her throat suddenly constricted.

"He's just being kind," Radinka insisted. "He flirted with me at the spring Gala Ball and even asked me to waltz with him. I knew he was just being polite, but still, it made me feel wonderful. Like I was forty years younger."

"How long have you known him?" Lara asked.

"Since I started working here," Radinka said. "About eighteen years now. I used to be Roman's assistant."

"But then I stole her." Shanna looked fondly at Radinka, then turned to Lara. "I met Jack three years ago at my wedding. He goes to all the weddings and parties."

"He's an excellent dancer," Radinka added.

Shanna nodded. "And a good friend. When Angus and Emma were in trouble, he came to help. He helped Ian and Toni, too."

Lara knew who Ian was, but she wondered about the other people. Still, she didn't want to veer off the topic of Jack. "I know he's a sweet guy, but there are some . . . odd things about him. Exceptional things."

"Like exceptional good looks?" Shanna asked with a sly grin.

"And exceptional loyalty," Radinka said.

"And exceptional availability," Shanna added.

Lara stopped pacing and faced them. "I realize you may not know this, but . . . Jack has some strange powers. He can actually teleport and move super fast."

Radinka patted her mouth with her napkin, then carefully folded it. "We know about that, dear." She gave Lara a pointed look. "We also know you have nothing to fear from him."

"That's true," Shanna said quietly. "I'm sure Jack's abilities must seem awfully strange to you, but please don't let it scare you away. What really matters is how he uses his powers, and he always uses them for good. You can trust him, Lara."

Was it that simple? Could she just accept him the way he was and trust him? Apparently, Shanna and Radinka did. Lara was tempted to, but at the same time, she wanted answers. And she wanted Jack to trust her enough to give her those answers.

"Well, speak of the devil . . ." Shanna nodded her head toward the cafeteria entrance.

Lara whirled around and saw Jack standing at the open door. Her heart lurched in her chest. He was definitely exceptional. He was everything she'd ever wanted in a man. *You can trust him, Lara.*

He walked toward her slowly. He was dressed in faded jeans, a black T-shirt, and black leather jacket. His hair was still damp and combed back from his face. Dark whiskers shaded his jaw. He looked as if he'd hurried here as quickly as possible. His gaze drifted to the babe in her arms, then returned to her face with a heated, golden gleam. She stepped toward him as if drawn by a magnet.

"Oh yes," Radinka announced behind her. "Those two will be very happy."

Lara halted as heat invaded her face. She knew the amused smirk on Jack's face meant he had overheard Radinka's remark.

"Here, I'll take Sofia." Shanna rushed over to relieve her of the baby.

"Hi, Jack!" Constantine ran up to him, and Jack swung him into his arms.

"Hey, buddy. How's it going?" He tousled the little boy's blond curls.

Tino leaned close and whispered loudly, "Radinka says Lara is the one for you."

Lara bit her lip as she grew increasingly annoyed. These people acted like she would automatically fling herself into Jack's arms. It wasn't like the man was irresistible. She could resist him.

On what planet? An inner voice chided her.

Radinka shook her head as she stacked their empty dishes onto a food tray. "If only I could find the one for my son."

"I don't think Gregori's ready to settle down," Shanna whispered.

"Well, he'd better hurry it up," Radinka grumbled. "I won't live forever, and I want to see some grandchildren."

"How are you, ladies?" Jack set Tino down, then gave Shanna and Radinka each a peck on the cheek. "How is Sofia?"

"She's fine." Shanna smiled. "We dragged Lara to supper with us so we could gossip shamelessly about you."

"I see." He turned to Lara, and the corners of his mouth curled up. "*Bellissima*, you never cease to surprise me. I didn't expect you to come to Romatech."

She shrugged. "I wanted to get some work done on the case."

"And you checked my alibi for Saturday night."

She lifted her chin. "Yes, I did. It's standard procedure."

His eyes twinkled with humor. "Did I pass?"

"I believe so."

"That's good. I wouldn't want you going on a date with a criminal." He drew closer to her as his gaze wandered over her blue sundress, bare legs, and white sandals. "You look very beautiful tonight."

"Thank you." She forgot to stay annoyed. It was hard enough not to automatically fling herself into his arms.

He touched her arm where it was covered with the white crocheted shrug. "This is pretty, but it may not be warm enough for where we're going."

"Where *are* we going?"

He smiled. "Not to worry, love. I'm sure we can find something warmer for you." He turned to the others and inclined his head. "*Ciao*, ladies, Tino. I must steal Lara away from you now."

There was an old-fashioned courtesy about the way he bowed. Lara groaned inwardly. Those words *old-fashioned* kept popping up. She grabbed her white handbag and looked at Shanna and Radinka. "It was nice to meet you."

Shanna patted her on the shoulder. "I have a feeling we'll be seeing you again."

"Definitely." Radinka nodded. "Enjoy your date."

"Oh, we have business to take care of, too," Lara said. "Police business."

Radinka snorted and muttered, "You mean monkey business."

"Can I have a cookie?" Constantine hopped around the table, obviously not in need of any sugar.

"*Scusi, signorini.*" Jack bowed again, then with a light touch on Lara's back, he ushered her from the cafeteria. "I was halfway through my breakfast when Carlos told me that Howard had called and you were here, waiting for me. I came as quickly as I could."

"Thank you. I left a message on your cell phone, too."

"I heard it." He smiled at her as they started down the hallway. "I'm delighted you want to go on a date."

She shrugged. "It's just for a few hours, right? Then we'll get back to work."

"As you wish. Howard said he showed you the laptop."

"Yes. I was amazed by how much information you discovered. It's very impressive."

"*Grazie.*" He turned right and led her into another

hallway. "I am determined to find Apollo as soon as possible. I believe he kidnaps a new girl on the fourth weekend of each month."

"I noticed that, too. In a few weeks, he'll strike again."

Jack nodded. "We'll catch him before that."

We? Lara bit her lip. She hated to tell Jack that this was strictly a matter for the police and FBI, especially after all the hard work he'd done. "You know, I go back to patrolling the streets on Wednesday."

Jack halted. "You'll work at night?"

"Yep. Looks like we'll both be working the grave-yard shift."

He frowned. "I won't be able to see you very much."

He would miss her? Lara liked the thought of that. "Don't worry. I get a night or two off each week. I might even agree to go out with you again, although that'll depend on whether tonight's date is any good." She gave him a teasing smile.

His frown deepened. "I hope it'll be good. I wanted to share something special with you. A place that I care deeply about."

"Oh." Her smile faded. "Okay."

"But we'll be limited in how long we can stay there." He glanced around the hall. "If it's all right with you, I think we should leave right away."

"Really?" She watched as he opened a door and peeked inside.

"Oh, sorry." He'd interrupted someone at work. He strode down the hall to the next door. "We can always work on the Apollo case later. I've already made a lot of progress, don't you think?"

"Yes, you have." She frowned as he opened the door to a storeroom and peered inside. "Did you lose something?"

"I just don't want us to be seen. Come. This will do."

He caught her arm and dragged her into the store-room.

Was this his idea of a date? Making out in a closet? She had a brief glimpse of shelves filled with office supplies before Jack shut the door and enclosed them in darkness. "Whoa. I thought we were going someplace special."

"We are, *bellissima*. I have it all planned out." He wrapped his arms around her. "Gianetta and Mario are very eager to meet you."

"Who are they?"

"They take care of the *palazzo* for me."

She swallowed hard. "But that's in Venice."

"Yes." He brushed her cheek with his knuckles. "That's where we're going."

Her mouth fell open, then snapped shut as she shook her head in disbelief. "We can't go to Venice. It's about a ten-hour flight, isn't it?"

"We'll need to hurry. We have about three hours at the most."

"Before the plane leaves?" The reality of the situation finally caught up with her. "Then what are we doing here?" Her heart started to race. This was so sudden. And so exciting. "I need to go home and pack. I need my passport." She pushed away from him to get to the door.

He pulled her back so suddenly, her handbag tumbled to the floor. "*Bellissima*, we're leaving now."

A sudden suspicion snaked through her, and the tiny hairs on the back of her neck rose. "What—what do you mean?"

"I need you to trust me." He wrapped his arms around her tight.

Her skin chilled in spite of the warmth of his body. "Why are we in this closet?"

"So no one will see us teleport."

Lara gasped. *"No."*

"Yes. You saw me do it before. It's perfectly safe."

"It's perfectly crazy!" She pushed against his chest.

"Lara." He held her by the shoulders. "I would never do this if it could hurt you. I care for you too much to let anything harm you."

He cared? Her heart melted. Unfortunately, the rest of her was still freaked out. "I don't know how to teleport. It scares me. What if I get put back together all wrong?"

"You'll be fine. As long as you're in my arms, you'll be safe."

She swallowed hard. "Wouldn't a plane be safer?"

"Cara mia, we could be in Venice in two seconds."

"That seems hard to believe. And for someone who's been pretending to be normal for the last two weeks, you're suddenly okay with showing me your true self?"

"Yes." He eased his arms around her. "It's a step forward, don't you think?"

He was finally ready to be honest with her? How could she refuse that? "I—I want to move forward."

"Then come with me." He embraced her tightly. "Hang on to me, and don't let go."

She wrapped her arms around his neck and gripped her hands together. "Are you sure this is safe? There aren't any weight restrictions or—"

Everything went black.

She stumbled and blinked as brightly lit candles spun around her, reflecting off gold walls.

"Easy, love." Jack steadied her.

The room stopped spinning, and she realized there were paintings on the walls and ceiling, all outlined with gleaming gold-leaf stucco work. Candles glowed in golden wall sconces and from three ornate chandeliers. Antique furniture was clustered around an enormous fireplace with a marble mantelpiece.

Her feet were firmly planted on a polished terrazzo floor. This sure wasn't Kansas. "Wow."

Jack released her. "Are you all right?"

She looked around the room again. "Wow."

Jack chuckled. "Welcome to my home." He strode toward some French doors and pushed them open. "And welcome to Venezia."

Chapter Thirteen

*J*ack smiled at the expressions that flitted over Lara's face. Shock transformed into wonder as she gazed around the Great Room. He felt a surge of pride, for the room was impressive when all lit up. Mario and Gianetta weren't very nimble in their old age, so it was probably their grandson, Lorenzo, who had lit all the candles before leaving on his assignment.

A cool breeze swept through the open French doors, causing the flames to flicker and the gold to gleam.

Lara gave him a wry look. "Just a small *palazzo*, huh?"

He shrugged. "There are over two hundred *palazzi* in Venezia. It's no big deal."

"Right. Everybody has one." She followed him onto the balcony. "I can't believe it. We're really in Venice?"

"Yes. Venezia." He breathed deeply of the cool, humid air. Candles glowed behind beveled glass on each side of the French doors. A bistro table with two chairs was nestled in the corner of the balcony.

He glanced over the balustrade at the water below. Lights sparkled on it, reflecting the moonlight and lights from neighboring *palazzi*. The water gate was directly below him on the ground floor. The lamps from the water gate illuminated the red-striped poles in front of his home.

Jack always loved coming home. And now he had someone to share it with. "How do you like it?"

"It's incredible. Very . . . old." Lara gave him an odd look, then shivered.

"Are you cold?" He wrapped his arms around her and pulled her close. "I was afraid it might be too chilly for you. I'll have Gianetta find you something warm."

"Thanks." Lara looked around curiously. "It's not just the cooler weather that's bothering me. I'm in shock that we're actually here, and I'm still freaked out by our mode of transportation."

"It was quick and painless, no?"

"The moment of sheer terror was over quickly, but my confusion is greater than ever. How are you able to do such a thing?"

With a sigh, he stroked her hair. "I really don't know how it works. It's simply a gift, and I'm grateful for it."

"Well, it does beat ten hours on a plane." She turned in his arms so she could look over the balustrade. "I didn't realize the canals were this big."

"Most of them are not. This is the Grand Canal."

"Oh. Nice address." She glanced back at his home. "Not too shabby for a palace."

He grinned. "Unfortunately, many of the *palazzi* are in bad shape. This one dates from the sixteenth century, and there is always something that needs repairing."

"But you love it," she said quietly.

"Yes. I do. It's my anchor. A constant that is always here for me and never changes."

She regarded him, her eyes narrowed. "There's something so old-fashioned and . . . noble about you."

That was high praise for someone born a bastard. "*Cara mia*, thank you." He kissed her brow.

"Giacomo! You have arrived," a voice said in Italian.

Jack turned to find Gianetta at the open French doors. "*Bellissima*." He gave her a hug and kissed her plump cheeks. She was wearing a thick bathrobe over her nightgown, and her long gray hair lay in a braid against her ample bosom. He responded in Italian, "I'm sorry you had to get up in the middle of the night."

She patted his cheek. "It's always good to see you. And I'm thrilled you brought a girl with you. I've waited so long for this."

About fifty years, Jack figured. That's how long Gianetta and her husband, Mario, had been taking care of the *palazzo*. They'd started out as servants, but over the years, they'd become loyal and treasured friends.

"She's mortal, no?" Gianetta whispered in Italian.

"Yes, she is. Her name is Lara Boucher," he answered in Italian. "She's American."

"And very pretty." Gianetta nodded in approval, then spoke in heavily accented English. "I am very happy to meet you."

"Thank you." Lara grinned. "I'm delighted to be here."

"She needs a coat or jacket," Jack told Gianetta. When she looked confused, he translated into Italian.

"Ah, I have just the thing. And I'll bring refreshments." Gianetta bowed and left the balcony.

"She seems very nice," Lara said.

"She approves of you, which is good, since she and Mario are like family to me."

Lara snorted. "Everyone keeps playing the matchmaker around us."

"As if we need any encouragement." He wrapped his arms around her from the back and pulled her against his chest.

She rested her head on his shoulder. "The stars are lovely, but I wish there was more light. When does the sun rise?"

"Too soon." He nuzzled her neck. They had less than three hours before he'd have to teleport them back to New York City. He couldn't risk falling into his death-sleep in front of her. "This is a good time to be here. The city is quiet. All you can hear is the lapping of water against the buildings and the occasional hoot of an owl."

She folded her arms over his. "I've always wanted to see Venice. Thank you."

"*Bellissima*, we have barely begun." Jack pointed in the distance. "Do you see the light on the water? That is our gondola, coming to pick us up."

"This is so cool." Lara turned toward him, smiling. "Thank you for dragging me here against my will."

"Hmm." He smoothed a hand down her back. "What else can I make you do against your will?"

With a laugh, she slid her hands around his neck. "You know what they say—where there's a will, there's a way."

He nudged her nose with his own. "I want my way with you."

"Mmm." She pressed against him and raked her hands into his hair. "I can't ever resist you, Jack."

"*Cara mia*." He kissed her brow, her cheeks, her nose, and his heart soared. Lara wanted him, and he hadn't used any vampire tricks. She was the first and only woman he'd met whose mind he couldn't invade and read, and yet, their minds seemed to be of one accord.

He captured her mouth with his own and indulged

in a long, leisurely kiss. She melted against him. Lara in his arms in Venezia—life didn't get any better than this.

A throat cleared. "*Scusi,*" Gianetta whispered at the entrance to the balcony.

Lara stepped back, blushing slightly.

"I bring . . . food," Gianetta spoke in English. She set a wooden tray on the small bistro table. "And I bring cape for the *signorina.*" She removed the cape that had been draped over one shoulder and shook it out.

"Oh my gosh, it's beautiful." Lara stroked the midnight blue velvet.

While Lara was busy admiring the cape, which Gianetta was settling on her shoulders, Jack sidled over to the table to check the food. Sure enough, Gianetta had filled the bronze goblet with warmed-up synthetic blood. He chugged it down before Lara could see the contents.

She laughed. "You sure were thirsty."

"Yes." He set the empty goblet on the tray. "You look wonderful in the cape."

With a grin, she pirouetted and let the long cape swirl around her. The velvet material came to rest in long folds that reached her ankles. "Isn't it gorgeous? It's lined with silk and has a hood, too."

She lifted the hood, and Jack caught his breath. Her eyes looked as deep blue as the velvet framing her lovely face. Her cheeks were flushed with excitement, making her fragrant with the scent of pulsing blood. He was tempted to forego all the sightseeing and whisk her straight upstairs to his bedroom. But no, he needed to court her first. He needed her to love him. That way, if she ever found out the truth about him, he'd have a better chance at not losing her.

"Very nice cape," Gianetta said in English. "Giacomo

give me cape ten years ago for Carnival. Giacomo very nice man."

"Oh." Lara cast a curious look his way. "I guess he was about eighteen at the time?"

Gianetta gave Jack a confused look and spoke in Italian. "She doesn't know?" When he shook his head slightly, she frowned at him. "You have to tell her."

"Something wrong?" Lara watched them both.

"Yes." Jack switched to English and pointed at the tray on the table. "Your *gelato* is melting. Come, have a seat."

"Yes." Gianetta rushed to the table and set the bowl of ice cream, a linen napkin, and a glass of water in front of a chair. "*Gelato* from Venezia very good. You try."

"I'd love to." Lara sat in a bistro chair, carefully arranging the velvet cape around her.

Jack handed the empty bronze goblet to Gianetta.

"Here." She passed him a small package of Vampos, the after-dinner mint for Vamps who wanted rid of blood breath.

"*Grazie.* You think of everything." He popped a mint into his mouth and handed the package back to Gianetta, who quickly slipped it into her bathrobe pocket.

Lara glanced at the empty tray, then at Jack. "You're not going to have any ice cream?"

"No. I'm . . . lactose intolerant." He sat across from her at the table. "But I'll be happy to watch you enjoy it."

She gave him a sly grin. "You like to watch?"

He chuckled.

She aimed a seductive look at him as she brushed the hood off her head. He swallowed hard while his wayward mind imagined more clothes coming off.

She lifted the spoon to her mouth and touched the *gelato* with the tip of her tongue. Then she licked it. "Mmmm. So sweet and creamy."

He arched a brow at her. For a sweet angel, she could be wonderfully wicked. "You like it?"

"Oh, yeah." She opened her mouth slowly and inserted the spoon. "Mmmm." She drew the spoon out slowly.

His groin tightened.

"Oh, yes." She closed her eyes and tilted her head back. "Yes. *Yes!*" She pounded a fist on the table.

He shifted in his chair.

Gianetta grabbed Jack's shoulder and whispered in Italian, "Is she all right?"

"Yes." His voice sounded strained. "She really likes ice cream. That'll be all, Gianetta."

"Humph." Gianetta grabbed the empty tray and headed out the door, mumbling about strange American ways.

Lara grimaced. "Sorry. She probably thinks I'm crazy, but I just couldn't resist."

He smiled slowly. "*Cara mia*, I am counting on you not being able to resist."

She spooned more ice cream into her mouth. He continued to watch, amazed that he could get a hard-on from something so simple and innocent.

"This is really good." She finished the last bite. "And this bowl is beautiful."

"It's from Murano, where the glassblowers work."

"I'd love to see that."

"They're not open now, but I can arrange it for another trip." He stood and looked over the balcony. The gondolier was approaching the water gate. "Tonight, I want to show you the *basilica* and *campanile* at the *Piazza San Marco*."

She dabbed at her mouth with the linen napkin. "I'm guessing *basilica* is a church, but what's the other thing?"

"The *campanile*. A bell tower."

"Oh, cool! But aren't they closed at night?"

"I have . . . connections."

She grinned. "From being a choirboy?"

He chuckled. "Not exactly. Our gondola is arriving. Do you want to see?"

"Oh yes." She jumped up and peered over the balustrade. "Oh my gosh, he's wearing a striped shirt and hat, just like in the movies."

"Shall we go?" Jack gestured toward the French doors.

Lara accompanied him across the Great Room to the staircase. About fifty years ago, he'd had the stairs wired for electricity so no one would trip in the dark or have to carry a candle.

Lara glanced at the ascending staircase. "How many floors are there?"

"Four." He led her down the stairs. "The water floor is below. I live on the second and third floors, and Mario and Gianetta live on the fourth with their grandson."

Gianetta met them at the bottom of the stairs. "Mario has taken care of everything," she told Jack in Italian. "Father Giuseppe will be waiting for you in the *piazza*, and Lorenzo will be there shortly."

"*Grazie mille.*" Jack gave her a hug. "I may not have time to come back here."

"I understand." Gianetta smiled at Lara and switched to English. "Giacomo very good man. Never bring girl here before."

"Really?" Lara's eyes lit up.

Jack gave Gianetta an annoyed look, then escorted Lara to the garden. "I want to show you this before we go."

Lara gasped when they stepped into the garden. Long strands of white twinkle lights outlined its square shape. A path of paving stones circled the fountain in the middle. An arbor entwined with wisteria arched over a stone bench. The scent of gardenia and roses filled the air, along with the sound of trickling water from the fountain.

"It's so beautiful," Lara whispered. "And so peaceful. No wonder you love it."

Jack gazed up at the windows on the third floor where his bedroom was located. He was tempted to teleport Lara straight there. But their gondola was waiting, and he was determined to court her properly. He refused to act like his father, treating each woman like a conquest before moving on to the next. Lara deserved better. And if she could love him, he would remain devoted to her forever.

"Come." He led her back down the arched hallway to the water gate.

Mario was waiting for them where the gondola had tied off. Jack gave the old man a hug and introduced Lara.

Mario shook her hand. "*Brava, bellissima.* Giacomo very good man."

Lara gave Jack a wry look. "You must pay them well."

He laughed. "I do, actually."

He stepped into the gondola and helped Lara board. They settled on the cushioned seat beneath a canopy that afforded them some privacy.

"*Piazzo San Marco*, please," he called to the gondolier in the back of the boat.

"Of course," the gondolier replied and moved them quickly into the canal.

Lara snuggled close to Jack. "This is so romantic."

"I'm glad you like it." He looped an arm around her shoulders and turned toward her so he could see her face.

She looked about curiously as they moved slowly

down the Grand Canal. He pointed out several *palazzi* that had been transformed into hotels. They were lit up, and some even had luxury yachts parked in front.

Her mouth fell open. "Look at that bridge."

He glanced at it. "That's the Rialto." The center arch was illuminated at night.

Lara's eyes glittered with excitement. "This reminds me of a movie I loved when I was little. I thought it was the most romantic movie ever. *Lady and the Tramp.* Have you seen it?"

"No."

"Well, the Tramp takes Lady to an Italian restaurant, and the waiters bring them a big plate of spaghetti. Then the waiters serenade them with the song '*Bella Notte*,' and it's so incredibly sweet."

"'*Bella Notte*'?" He'd have to tell Mario about this.

"Then the Lady and the Tramp start sucking on the same spaghetti noodle, and he accidentally kisses her snout."

"Her . . . what?"

"Snout. Oh." Lara laughed. "Did I forget to mention that they're dogs?"

He gave her a dubious look. "Romantic dogs?"

She laughed again and swatted his arm. "I was five years old. And that spaghetti-noodle kiss was really hot. Lady turned away with this sweet blush like she was all embarrassed, and Tramp has this wolfish grin on his face like 'Yeah, baby, let's do that again.'"

With his own wolfish grin, Jack tapped the end of her nose. "So if I kiss your adorable little snout, will you be my Lady?"

True to her role, Lara looked away and blushed. "I'm not sure you could be a Tramp. I don't think he ever lived in a fancy *palazzo.*"

"Ah. But I'm a bastard, so I should still qualify."

She poked him in the chest. "You're not a bastard. You're a sweetheart."

"Must I prove I'm a bastard?" He reached underneath her cape and tickled her ribs. "Take that. And beware, or I will jab you with the comfy cushions."

She wiggled away from him, giggling. "Stop it, you . . . tramp."

With a laugh, he pulled her onto his lap. "My lady."

Her laughter faded as she slid her hands around his neck and gazed into his eyes. "Jack."

He squeezed her hip. "Woof."

She smiled. "A real bastard might try to take advantage of me." She nuzzled her nose against his cheek.

"I'll do my best." He turned his head to take her mouth. Her lips opened, inviting him in. He circled his tongue inside her mouth and stroked her tongue.

She moaned, then suddenly broke the kiss. She glanced over his shoulder at the dark canopy separating them from the gondolier. "I forgot we're not alone."

"They're used to it. Venice has always been a place for lovers."

She raked a hand through his hair. "Is that what you want us to be—lovers?"

"Mmm-hmm." Underneath the cape, he skimmed his hand down her skirt till he reached bare skin.

She ran her fingertips along his jaw. "Everyone keeps telling me what a good man you are."

"Mmm-hmm." His hand crept under the hem of her skirt. "I'm as trustworthy as a priest."

"So I hear. Shanna said I could trust you."

"Mmm-hmm." His fingers inched up her bare thigh. "I'm practically a saint."

She glanced down at the cape where his hidden hand made a bulge that continued to move up her thigh. "What exactly are you doing?"

His mouth twitched. "Searching for the Holy Land?" He reached the edge of her panties. Lace, by the feel of it.

She frowned. "Perhaps you should know that I'm not—I mean, I don't normally—" She gasped when his hand slipped under her panties. "Jack, you . . . bastard."

"That's me." He squeezed her bare rump.

"Jack," she breathed. "We shouldn't . . ." She glanced nervously at the canopy.

"I know. You're just so hard to resist." He patted her bottom, then started to slide his hand out from under her panties.

Her panties came with him. With a gulp, he quickly moved his hand so the panties would be in place. Then he slowly moved his hand down. There was a tug on his ring, and the panties moved with him.

Merda! Her lace panties had snagged on his ring, the signet ring he'd inherited from his father, Giacomo Casanova. His father had seduced hundreds of women without any problems whatsoever, and he was having trouble with just one. This was the real reason he never used the Casanova name. He could never live up to his father's reputation. The old man was probably laughing in his grave.

Chapter Fourteen

$\mathcal{N}$ ine circles of hell," Jack muttered.

"Hell?" Lara asked. "I thought I was the Holy Land."

"You're paradise. Unfortunately, I am stuck there."

Her eyes widened. "Stuck?"

"Normally, I would love being stuck to your lovely bum, but it might look odd if we go sightseeing with my hand under your skirt. Especially in the *basilica*."

She glanced down. "How can you be stuck?"

"My ring. It's caught in the lace. See?" He moved his hand down her hip, dragging her undies down a few inches.

"Okay, stop." She bit her lip, frowning, then suddenly giggled. "I can't believe this has happened."

"I assure you, as much as I had hoped to get your clothes off, this was not part of my original plan."

She snorted. "No problem. Just rip yourself loose."

"Are you sure? It will destroy your undies."

She narrowed her eyes with a seductive look. "Rip it."

"Very well." He jerked his hand away, but the panties came with him. He yanked his hand back and forth, but the lacy, latex material simply stretched with him. "*Santo cielo*, they are indestructible."

Lara laughed.

He continued to wage battle, but to no avail. "They could use this material to build spaceships."

She shook her head, grinning. "Maybe you should try taking your ring off."

He pushed at it with his thumb, but it didn't budge. "I would need to put my other hand up your skirt."

"A likely story." She cast him a sly look. "I think the only option left is for you to do the gentlemanly thing and cut your hand off."

"I prefer it attached, if you don't mind. And you might enjoy what I could do with it." While she snorted, he lifted her slightly. "Fortunately, I have another option." He slid his hand and the panties down her legs.

She gasped. "What are you doing?"

"It will only take a moment." He pulled the panties over her shoes.

"You'd better give them back." She quickly adjusted the cape to make sure she was covered from head to ankles.

"I will." He tried to free the panties from his ring. "You don't happen to have any scissors, do you?"

The gondola jolted as it came to a stop. Lara grabbed his shoulders to steady herself.

"*Piazza San Marco*," the gondolier announced as he tied the gondola off. His steps sounded closer as he came around the canopy.

"Oh no," Lara breathed.

Jack yanked the ring off his hand and stuffed it and the panties into his jacket pocket. "I'll get them back to you."

"I can't believe this." With a grimace, she stood and wrapped the cape around herself. The gondolier helped her disembark.

Jack could practically hear his father's mocking laughter as he led her toward the *piazza*. And like a true Casanova, his thoughts kept returning to her lack of panties. It was as if the gauntlet had been tossed. The castle walls had been breached. The inner sanctum was his for the taking. Before the night was over, he would touch paradise.

He couldn't force her, though. He needed to be smooth, like his father. Of course! He pulled out his cell phone and made a quick call to Mario with new instructions for Lorenzo. Mario assured him that everything was going according to plan. He rang off just as they reached the entrance to the *piazza*.

"Wow. It's bigger than I thought it would be." Lara squinted as she surveyed their surroundings. "I wish I could see better. Shouldn't we come back during the day?" She gave him a wry look. "Fully dressed?"

"There are too many tourists then."

A breeze swept past them, billowing the cape around Lara's legs. She shivered.

"Are you cold?" Jack wrapped an arm around her.

She gave him an annoyed look. "I'm feeling a slight draft."

He smiled. "Don't worry. The place is deserted. No one will see you but a few pigeons. And a priest. Come, I want to introduce you to Father Giuseppe." He spotted the old man across the *piazza* on the church steps.

Lara strolled beside him. "Isn't the church closed?"

"Father Giuseppe will let us in. He's an old friend."

"You get special favors from the Church?"

He shrugged. "I told you, I'm practically a saint."

"I'm practically naked," she muttered.

"Miracles do happen." Jack ascended the steps. "Thank you, Father, for meeting us."

The old priest embraced Jack, then spoke in Italian. "Have you been behaving yourself, Giacomo?"

"Of course, Father. May I introduce Lara Boucher from America?"

"*Signorina*." The priest bowed to Lara and switched to English. "It is a pleasure. You wish to see the *Basilica San Marco?*"

"Yes, I'd love to. Thank you."

"This way." Father Giuseppe fumbled through a large ring of keys as he led them toward a side door. He unlocked it, then flipped on some lights. "Come in, please."

Jack and Lara followed the priest into the nave of the cathedral. Their footsteps echoed through the large building, and statues stared down at them. Jack slipped some euros into a collection box.

"I just realized I don't have my handbag," Lara whispered. "I can't give a donation."

"It's all right. We left it at Romatech. We'll get it later."

Father Giuseppe gave them a tour, but his yawns grew longer and more pronounced as time slipped by.

"You're tired, Father," Jack finally told him in Italian. "And I have interrupted your sleep. We can continue on our own, if you like."

"Very well. I'll take you to the *campanile*."

Father Giuseppe gave him a worried look as they left the church. "She's a nice girl. You must treat her well, my son."

"I will." Jack ushered Lara down the steps.

A cool breeze fluttered her cape, and she pulled it close to her.

The priest stopped in front of the *campanile* and fumbled through his keys. "Does she know who you are?"

Jack sighed. "She knows my personality and character."

"That's not what I meant, and you know it." Father Giuseppe unlocked the door, then turned on the lights. He regarded Jack sadly. "You will have to tell her."

Jack swallowed hard. He knew from past experience that telling a woman the truth meant losing her. He couldn't risk going through that kind of pain. "I don't want to lose her."

The priest rested a hand on his shoulder. "You must have faith, Giacomo. Love does not judge, nor will it be unkind." He turned to Lara and made the sign of the cross in front of her. "May God bless you," he spoke in English.

"Thank you, Father," she whispered.

"*Grazie*." Jack hugged his old friend, then escorted Lara inside the bell tower.

The priest closed the door behind them, and the loud click echoed through the tower.

"He's not locking us in, is he?" Lara whispered.

Jack shrugged. "If he does, I can always teleport us out."

Her eyes narrowed. "You could have just teleported us to the top, right?"

"I could have, but I wanted you to have the full tourist experience." He led her inside the elevator and punched the button for the top floor.

With a lurch, the elevator began its ascent.

She shook her head. "I can't believe I've been talking to a priest with no underwear."

Jack smiled at her. "I'm fairly certain he was wearing underwear."

She scoffed. "So how do you manage to get preferential treatment around here?"

"I told you, I'm practically a saint." He pressed a hand against his heart.

She made a face at him. "You didn't answer my question."

"Very well. The original *campanile* fell down in 1902. There was no money to rebuild it till 1912 when . . . my family gave them a very large donation."

The elevator doors opened, and they exited onto the observation floor of the bell tower.

"Come see the view." He motioned toward the open window.

Lara remained in front of the elevator. "Your *family* gave them a donation in 1912?"

"Yes." *Merda.* Was she onto him? He lifted a hand toward her. "Come have a look."

"It wasn't your family, was it?" she whispered. "It was *you.*"

His hand dropped by his side. *Nine circles of hell.* He should have known she'd start figuring things out.

Her face grew pale. "I'm right, aren't I? It would be so easy for you to say that I'm wrong, but you can't bring yourself to say it."

His hands balled into fists. "Lara—"

"Just tell me the truth. How old are you?"

He turned to look out the window. Stars twinkled over a sea of red-tiled roofs. His heart raced. How much should he say? "I have come here so many times over the years, but I was always alone." He looked at her. "Till I met you."

She moved toward him. "Can you be honest with me?"

"Lara, I am falling in love with you."

She inhaled sharply. "Oh God." She pressed a hand to her mouth. "But how can we—is there any hope for us?"

"I've been told that when there is love, there is hope."
You must have faith, the old man had told him.

Lara's eyes glistened with tears. "I'm afraid you're
so much older than me, and so different from me."

"Inside, we are the same."

A cool breeze swept around them and fluttered her
hair. She shivered and wrapped the cape around herself. Music drifted up from the *piazza*. An accordion
played, then a baritone voice began to sing.

Jack glanced down. Lorenzo was playing the accordion, and he'd brought one of Venezia's finest singers
to the *piazza* to perform for Lara.

"Oh my God." She peered down from the window.
"He's singing '*Bella Notte.*'" She looked at Jack with
tears in her eyes. "You arranged that for me?"

"Yes." He took her hand. "Will you be my lady, Lara?"

"I want to be."

"Then no power on this earth can stop us." He pulled
her into his arms and kissed her with all the passion
he'd kept locked up for so many nights.

This was the night—the *bella notte* when she would
become his. He'd wanted to share Venezia with her.
There was so little he could share, so little information
he could tell her, that this had felt like the only way to
get close to her. And the way she was responding gave
him more hope than he'd had for almost two hundred
years.

She was clinging to him, opening to him, melting
against him. He invaded her mouth, and she sucked
on his tongue. He smoothed his hands down her back
and cupped her rear. When he pulled her against his
swollen groin, she moaned.

"Lara." He kissed a path across her cheek and down
her neck. She swayed her hips from side to side, rubbing against him.

Santo cielo. She wanted him. His passion escalated into a frantic need. He swept the edges of the velvet cape over her shoulders, then he undid the buttons down the front of her dress, stopping at her belt. He pushed the bodice and sweater back only to discover some sort of modern, strapless contraption barring him from heaven.

"It's not glued to you, is it?" He didn't want to rip something off her delicate skin.

Lara smiled and caressed his cheek. "It unhooks in the front. Shall I show you?"

"I can manage." He wrestled with the strange plastic hook, then suddenly, the clasp popped open. He sucked in a breath at the lovely sight. "*Paradiso.*"

She shook her head, smiling and blushing at the same time. "They're just breasts."

"No, love." His eyes met hers, and he smiled. "They're *your* breasts."

Her blush deepened, and the scent of her sweet, rushing blood ignited his frantic need once more.

"I want you." He unfastened her belt and with vampire speed, he undid the rest of her buttons before the belt hit the floor. He pushed her dress wide open, then gripped her around the waist. Her creamy skin was shaded pink from the red glow of his eyes. He slid his hands up over her ribs, then he cupped her breasts.

"Yes." She arched her back, leaning into him so the pink-tinted mounds filled his hands.

With his thumbs, he circled the plump, rosy nipples. They pebbled before his eyes, and his groin seized up tight. He rubbed the tips of her breasts and felt them harden beneath the pads of his thumbs. His erection grew hard. With a tortured moan, he pinched the tips of her breasts and tugged slightly.

"Oh God." Lara grabbed his shoulders as her knees buckled.

"I've got you." He grasped her bottom and lifted her up. She wrapped her legs around his waist.

He pressed her back against the wall and raised her higher so he could feast on her breasts. He shoved her dress aside with his face and latched onto a nipple.

She shuddered in his arms. "Jack." She held his head tight.

He suckled her and nibbled on the hardened tip of her breast. Then a slight dizziness swept over him, making him freeze for a second. The sun. It was approaching the horizon. *Merda*.

"Jack, please," Lara breathed as she gripped his hair in her fists.

He nuzzled his cheek against her breasts as he fought to remain strong. He had maybe five minutes left before his energy would completely seep away. If he fell into his death-sleep here, the sun would kill him.

He inhaled deeply, and the scent of Lara's arousal stirred him. So rich and heady. *Santo cielo*, he would make her scream before leaving.

He adjusted his hold on her so he was supporting her with one arm. With his free hand, he burrowed under her skirt.

"Look at me," he whispered as he slid his hand up her bare thigh.

She did. "Your eyes are so red."

"Yours are so blue." He reached the slippery folds, and she gasped.

"Oh God." Her eyes flickered shut.

He stroked her till she was quivering in his arms. He teased her clitoris with feathery strokes, then suddenly tweaked it.

She cried out. Her heels dug into his back. More moisture drenched his fingers, and he moaned. She was so sweet, so responsive.

He leaned forward and whispered in her ear. "*Cara mia*, I love you."

"Oh Jack." She panted, her breath erratic against his cheek.

His death-sleep tugged at him once again. He'd have to teleport very soon. He slipped a finger into Lara's wet vagina, and her inner muscles gripped him greedily. She was so close. His erection pushed painfully against his jeans.

The sun crept closer to the horizon. Sweat broke out on his brow. He inserted two fingers and stroked her slippery inner walls.

"Jack!" Her muscles clenched and she stopped breathing.

All was deathly silent for a moment. Even the serenade from below had stopped. Jack pulled his fingers out and tugged at her clitoris.

With a scream, she shattered. Her body convulsed. Pigeons, scared from their roosts, circled the bell tower with a flurry of beating wings. Jack leaned against the wall, dizzy with weakness as the sky lightened, announcing the imminent arrival of the sun.

With the last of his strength, he teleported them to his room at the townhouse in New York City. He collapsed on the bed with Lara landing beside him.

The alarm blared, set off by them teleporting in. Fortunately, no one was around to hear it, other than him. Phineas would be at Romatech, working. Jack fumbled in his jeans pocket for his keypad, then punched the button to turn off the alarm.

"What . . . what happened?" Lara whispered.

He breathed deeply as super vampire strength poured back into his body. The night was still young in New York. He had hours now that he could spend making love to Lara.

And that was exactly what he planned to do.

Chapter Fifteen

Lara pressed a hand to her brow as she waited for the room to stop spinning. Everything had happened so quickly. She'd had such a huge orgasm, she thought she'd passed out. But now, she realized they'd teleported.

Jack shifted position beside her, causing the bed to jiggle slightly. Bed? She was on her back in a bed. On a black-and-red-striped bedspread.

Jack propped himself up on an elbow and peered down at her. "Are you all right?"

She caught her breath. He'd said that he loved her. "Jack." She touched his cheek.

"*Cara mia*." With a smile, he skimmed his fingers down her neck, then down between her breasts. "Where were we?"

"Where *are* we?" She glanced around the room. The black furniture and plain, cream-colored walls looked awfully modern for a *palazzo*.

He cupped her breast. "My bedroom."

"We . . ." She shuddered when he teased her nipple. An aftershock from her orgasm shot through her. "Oh God." He was so good. And he'd said that he loved her.

He removed his leather jacket and tossed it on the floor.

"We—we teleported, right?"

"Yes." He stretched out beside her.

"To your bedroom at the *palazzo*?"

He hesitated, then kissed her brow. "It doesn't matter. We're together, and we have all night."

"I . . ." She had trouble concentrating when he was nibbling down her neck. "Are we still in Venice?" She felt his sigh against her skin.

"We're in New York."

She frowned. "But I was having a great time in Venice."

"I noticed." He untied the ribbons that fastened the cape around her neck. "You were shuddering in my arms, drenching my hand, and nearly ripping my hair out."

Heat rushed to her cheeks, and another aftershock hummed between her legs. She'd never had an orgasm like that before. She'd screamed so loud, she'd probably afflicted permanent trauma on all the pigeons. But it had been so incredibly romantic. And Jack had said that he loved her. "I loved it there. Why did we leave?"

"We only planned to go for a few hours, remember? We wanted to do more work on the Apollo case."

"We're not exactly working here."

He smiled as he circled a finger around one of her breasts. "I was distracted by the lure of heaven."

She took a deep breath. "Venice was very romantic."

"We can be romantic here." He gave her a hopeful look.

He wanted to make love to her. Lara swallowed hard. It was one thing to get blindsided with his declaration of love in Venice. She'd gotten swept into a whirlwind of passion, and it had been glorious. Unfortunately, another teleportation trip had knocked her back to reality.

She still didn't know jack about Jack.

She'd asked him flat out how old he was, and he had evaded the question. She'd hoped to find out more about him on the date, but he'd managed to tell her nothing—except that he loved her. "I'm feeling a little frustrated."

He glanced at his jeans. "You're not the only one."

"Do you really love me?"

"Yes." He met her gaze, his eyes intense and sincere. "I do love you."

Her eyes blurred with tears. "Why did you take me to Venice?"

"I wanted to share my home with you. I wanted to know if you could love it the way I do."

"Jack." She touched his cheek. "I did love it. I didn't want to leave."

"Then could you see yourself living there? With me?"

She gulped. "That—that's kinda sudden." How could she live with a man she knew so little about? She knew he was sweet and loveable. She knew he had to be human. He felt emotions like a human. He said he loved her. And right now, he looked genuinely worried. She sat up and located her bra squished inside her dress. She refastened it.

Jack sat beside her. "You don't have to go."

"I think I do." She buttoned up her dress. "I seem to have lost my belt."

"I'll call Mario, and he'll have someone collect it. I can return it to you tomorrow night."

"You could teleport back tomorrow night?" When he nodded, she continued, "But you can't go now?"

He looked away. "No."

"That's not making any sense to me."

He remained silent.

Her shoulders drooped. "You're not going to explain, are you?" She blinked back tears. How could he say he loved her, if he didn't trust her? She slid off the bed and retrieved her underwear from his jacket pocket. His ring was still stuck to it.

"Lara, you don't have to go."

He looked so sad, it was breaking her heart. "I—I don't have my handbag."

"I'll bring it to your apartment later."

"I need it now, so I can take a cab home."

Jack sighed. "I'll be back soon. Don't go anywhere."

"Okay." Lara perched on the edge of his bed. He vanished in front of her eyes.

"Oh, shit." She collapsed onto his bed and gazed at the ceiling. She was falling in love with him. He had all the wonderful qualities she'd ever wanted in a man. But those additional qualities, those supernatural powers, gave her pause.

She'd been forced to the conclusion that somehow he was genetically different from the average human. Some sort of strange mutation had occurred in the human species that gave some people super powers and incredibly long life spans. And he wasn't alone. There were others like him, and they wanted their existence kept secret. Maybe they were afraid of being misunderstood or exploited. They had a point. If others thought they had discovered the fountain of youth, they would be hunted down for the secret.

But she would never do anything to hurt Jack or his friends. Why wouldn't he trust her?

She closed her eyes and remembered their playfulness in the gondola and their passion in the bell tower. My God, what passion. She'd never experienced anything that wild and exciting before. It would be so easy to strip off her clothes and climb into Jack's bed.

She turned her head to look at the pillows. She could spend the night here. Jack would give her a night of glorious sex. And she wanted him. She wanted him so bad.

But she wanted answers, too! How could she make herself completely vulnerable to a man who wouldn't tell her anything?

He'd said that he loved her.

Dammit! Lara sat up. If he loved her, he needed to trust her. She wanted to love him, but how could she make that final plunge when he kept so many secrets from her?

With a sigh, she dropped her underwear on the bed. She hung the velvet cape in his closet. She couldn't resist grazing her fingers over his other clothes. Damn, she was in so deep.

She used the phone on Jack's bedside table to call a cab. Then she took her underwear into his bathroom to search for a pair of scissors. There was no mirror above the vanity. How strange. She rummaged through the drawers. Toothpaste, razors, dental floss, the usual stuff. For a supernatural being, Jack could seem awfully normal.

She found a small pair of scissors and snipped his ring free. It was a heavy, golden ring with some kind of elaborate insignia on top. Very old-looking. Strands of her underwear were still entwined in the design. She pulled the strands free and set the ring on the vanity.

"Lara?" Jack's voice came from the bedroom. He must have just teleported back.

She quickly put on her underwear, then opened the bathroom door. "I'm here." The look of relief on his face touched her heart.

He set her handbag on his dresser. "I'd like to take you out again." He gazed at her with that hungry look that made her knees weak. "We have unfinished business."

Good Lord, if the man was any sexier, she'd have a heart attack. But what a way to go. "I—I had a wonderful time." Sheesh, what a lame thing to say.

"You screamed."

"Well, yes." Her cheeks grew hot. "I don't usually . . ."

"I liked it." His eyes glittered with a softness that made her heart squeeze painfully in her chest.

Oh, she wanted to run into his arms. She wanted to love him. "Jack, I'm so . . . tempted by you."

The gold flecks in his eyes started to gleam. "*Cara mia*, let me love you."

She sucked in a ragged breath and prayed for strength. "I can't. I can't get more involved with you until you tell me everything." She lifted her chin. "So, here's your chance. Talk to me. Let me into your world."

He grimaced with a pained expression. "Lara, there are several reasons why I can't tell you. If it was only me, I might risk it. But there are others like me—dear friends who trust me. Their lives depend on my silence."

"I wouldn't do anything to hurt you or your friends."

He shook his head. "I can't risk their lives."

Dammit, why wouldn't he trust her? She clutched her hands into fists.

"I'm sorry, Lara, but I have to be loyal to my friends. Would you be able to respect me if I was the type of man to betray them?"

For the first time, she realized she was forcing him to choose between her and his friends. And if what she suspected was true, and he was centuries old, then he could have had these friends for a long, long time. Still, she was falling in love with him. Didn't she have the right to expect his trust?

She made a strangled sound of frustration. "What will it take for you to open up to me? Do we have to be married before it could happen?"

His eyes widened. "Are you proposing?"

"No!" She gritted her teeth. "I was being sarcastic."

His brows drew together. "Do not toy with me, Lara."

She groaned. "I only meant that if we're going to make ourselves vulnerable to each other, then we have to trust each other. I can't go any further until you trust me enough to tell me everything."

He dragged a hand through his hair. "Isn't it enough that I love you? That I would protect you with my life? And I will honor and cherish you for the rest of my life?"

That was beautiful, but still, she needed to know. "How long a life are we talking about exactly?"

He scowled at her. "It shouldn't matter. Not if you love me."

"Of course it matters! I'm not stupid, Jack. I'm guessing that you're really old. In fact, I have this bizarre theory that Giacomo Casanova is actually your father. Can you deny that?"

His face paled.

Her heart sank as time stretched out and he remained silent. He couldn't deny it. Her theory must be correct.

She pressed a hand to her mouth to keep from crying out loud. What was she doing here? She couldn't fall in love with someone who never aged. This was awful! He should have warned her.

He had. He'd told her to run like the hounds of hell were after her. He'd tried to avoid her. She was the one who had tracked him down at the wedding, at his townhouse, at Romatech. She'd pursued him relentlessly.

And now, he said he loved her.

Oh God, what had she done? "I need to go." She grabbed her handbag and strode from the room.

"Lara, I could teleport you home." He followed her as she headed down the stairs. "Or I could drive."

"I already called a cab." She was breathing heavily by the time she reached the ground floor. Her chest felt like it had been hit by a Mack truck.

"I need to turn off the alarm." He zoomed past her to the security panel by the door.

Tears stung her eyes. He was so different from her. Too different. "I won't tell anyone about you. You *can* trust me, Jack. You and your friends will be safe."

He frowned as he opened the door. "I want to see you again. We've come too far to give up now."

She stepped onto the front porch. It hurt too much to give him up entirely. "We'll keep in touch. We're working that case together, remember?" She descended the steps. "I was really impressed by all the work you did."

"When I am determined, nothing can stop me from obtaining my goal."

She paused at the sidewalk to look back at him. He was watching her with a fierce gleam in his eyes. She had to wonder if she had become his personal goal.

* * *

Lara dragged out of bed Tuesday afternoon about one. She'd been too upset to sleep when she'd returned to her apartment the night before. And she needed to stay acclimated to the night shift. So she kept herself busy printing off hard copies and studying all the material from the *Apollo* folder that she'd e-mailed to herself.

By five A.M., the kitchen table was covered with information, and her eyes were stinging too much to look at it anymore. She'd stumbled off to bed. Her last waking thought had been about Jack. She'd been right to back off. But when her eyes flitted shut, she remembered the soft way his eyes glimmered with love when he looked at her.

"Jack," she whispered and hugged the spare pillow to her chest. How could she not want him? She drifted off to sleep and dreamed of Venice.

After she awoke, she trudged into the kitchen, still bleary-eyed. She started the coffee machine and fixed herself a bowl of cereal. There was a dirty bowl and glass in the sink. LaToya must have been in a rush this morning before going to work.

Lara was sitting at the kitchen table, methodically spooning cereal into her mouth and wondering if Jack ever ate cereal, when she noticed the table was bare.

She blinked. Where the hell was all the stuff she'd printed out? She jumped to her feet and quickly checked the apartment. All the Apollo papers were gone.

LaToya. Lara grabbed the phone and called her.

"Hey, sleepyhead," LaToya told her. "I was just about to call to wake you up. I think they're going to want to see you."

"Who?"

"The special task force," LaToya said. "Can you believe it? This is so exciting. Here, let me get into an interrogation room here so no one can hear us."

"LaToya, did you take all my Apollo stuff?"

"Of course. You had so much information, girlfriend. It was amazing."

Lara's heart sank. "You shouldn't have taken it."

There was a pause, then LaToya whispered, "Are you serious? Girl, you can't withhold information concerning an ongoing investigation. People get arrested for that."

Lara winced. Her roommate had a point. "All right, but you should have asked me before taking it."

LaToya scoffed. "Why? Were you intending to keep it a secret? I thought we were working together. And I thought the idea was to catch the guy."

"Well, yes, but . . ." She'd wanted to work the case with Jack. If the police took over, she'd have no reason to see him again. Her heart sank deeper.

"Don't worry," LaToya said. "I wrote your name at the top of everything so the detectives would know that you'd done all the work."

"But I—"

"The guys were really pissed at first 'cause we weren't supposed to be doing it," LaToya continued, her words rushing out with excitement. "But when they realized you'd uncovered a serial kidnapper, they got real excited. They showed it to our captain, and he called your captain. Then they got together and called the police chief and the FBI!"

"Oh shit," Lara breathed.

"They're putting together a task force, 'cause it looks like this Apollo dude has kidnapped at least ten women from four different states. How did you find all that information so fast?"

Lara groaned. "I didn't."

"What do you mean? I heard you working last night. That damned printer is too loud."

"I didn't do it. Jack did."

"Oh. Damn." LaToya lowered her voice. "I sorta told everyone that you did it."

Lara sighed. "I can't take credit for Jack's work."

"Fine. You want to explain who Jack is to the police chief and the FBI?"

Lara winced.

"I think you should stop seeing that guy," LaToya said. "He's too strange."

Lara gritted her teeth. "That would really be ungrateful. He spent hours compiling all that information."

"Yeah, but he's got your mind messed up, girl. You're acting like the police don't have a right to this case, when it's Jack who's butting in where he doesn't belong. What's in it for him, anyway?"

Lara didn't know how to answer that. Why *was* Jack so interested in this case? If Apollo and Jack had similar mind control abilities, what else did they have in common?

"There's something really suspicious about him," LaToya muttered.

"Please don't tell anyone about him. I'm serious. Please." Lara had promised Jack that she wouldn't tell anyone about him or his friends.

LaToya paused, then whispered, "You know the truth about him, don't you?"

"Not really." Other than her theory that he was the son of Casanova and some kind of mutated human with supernatural powers. If she told her superiors that, they'd lock her up and lose the key.

"Why do I get the feeling you're not telling me something?"

Lara sighed. She was in the same predicament as

Jack—having to decide between him and her friends. "Jack did all that work just to help us. I don't want to cause him any trouble."

There was another pause. "Okay, then. If Jack's out of the picture, then you'll have to be the hero. I bet they make you a detective soon."

That was good news. It had been Lara's goal for the last six years. She'd wanted to put the pageant days behind her and do something meaningful with her life. Catching the bad guys and protecting the innocent—that had seemed like the most heroic thing she could do with her life.

No wonder she was so attracted to Jack. His goal was the same as hers. And whereas she aspired to be a regular hero, he was a superhero.

"Hang on a sec. Someone's at the door," LaToya said, and Lara heard mumbled voices. "Yes, sir. I'll tell her right away. Lara, you still there?"

"Yes."

"Get your ass into uniform quick," LaToya said. "A patrol car will be picking you up in ten minutes. The task force wants to see you."

Close to an hour later, Lara entered the precinct at Morningside Heights. As a sergeant led her through a sea of desks, dozens of heads turned to look at her. LaToya waved from across the room and gave her a thumbs-up.

"Boucher." Captain O'Brian from her precinct at Midtown North greeted her on the way to the conference room. "You've been briefed?"

"Yes, sir."

"You were told to take a week off after the Trent incident, and yet, you and Officer LaFayette took it upon yourselves to investigate a case you were not assigned to."

Lara swallowed hard. She hoped LaToya wasn't in trouble. "Yes, sir."

Captain O'Brian regarded her sternly. "It would appear the community will benefit from your utter disregard for the rules and your inability to grasp the concept of time off. Brilliant detective work, Butch."

Her cheeks warmed with a blush. She hated taking credit for Jack's hard work.

"They're waiting inside for you," the captain continued. "I told them you could do this, Butch. Don't let me down."

Do what? "Yes, sir."

Captain O'Brian opened the conference-room door and ushered her inside. At the sight of the police chief, Lara came to attention. There were five men at the table, all of them studying her silently. Captain O'Brian introduced them. Other than the police chief, there was the captain of this precinct, one of the NYPD case detectives, and two special agents from the FBI.

"At ease, Officer," the police chief said. He thumbed through some papers on the table in front of him. "Let's see, you graduated from our academy six months ago, and you were assigned to the night shift out of Midtown North."

"Yes, sir."

The chief turned to the special agents from the FBI. "What do you think?"

The one in the gray suit motioned to the Apollo papers on the table. "She's a good detective. She was able to uncover information that the case detectives didn't find."

The NYPD detective stiffened. "I interviewed those college girls myself. They didn't say a word about Apollo or this seminar."

"Maybe they were more comfortable talking to a

208 *Kerrelyn Sparks*

female officer," the second special agent suggested. "But the real question is, how will she perform in the field?"

"She does just fine," Captain O'Brian said. "Just a week ago, she subdued an armed man in a domestic dispute. He had shot and wounded her partner."

"She has the right look." The gray-suited FBI man motioned to the photos of Apollo's victims. "She has the right hair color, and she looks young enough to pass for a college student."

"Excellent." The police chief rubbed his hands together and regarded Lara grimly. "What do you say, Officer Boucher, to an undercover assignment?"

Lara swallowed hard. They wanted to use her as bait. Her mind raced. They were correct that she had the right look. What they didn't know, and what wasn't in those papers, was the fact that Apollo used mind control to abduct his victims and cover his tracks. She was immune to Jack's mind control, so hopefully, she would also be immune to Apollo's. If she was able to keep her wits about her, she could probably manage this.

She cleared her throat. "You want me to pose as a college student to help you locate Apollo when he comes on campus to do his seminar?"

"There's no law against him conducting a seminar," the NYPD detective said. "We need to know where he's taking the girls. Only then will we have the evidence we need to make an arrest."

"Exactly," the gray-suited FBI man agreed. "Officer Boucher, you'll have to let Apollo kidnap you."

Lara gulped. What would she do if he physically restrained her? What if he tried to rape her . . . or kill her? Maybe she should let a female officer with more experience do this. But what if that woman succumbed to

Apollo's mind control? She would have a worse chance of survival than Lara. And if she was murdered, how could Lara live with that? And how could she refuse this job and do nothing, when Apollo continued to kidnap a new girl every month?

She drew in a deep, shaky breath. "I'll do it."

Chapter Sixteen

"*A*re you crazy, girl?" LaToya demanded after she arrived home that evening.

"Don't fuss at me." Lara spooned chicken and sausage jambalaya onto two plates. After an hour of discussing her dangerous mission in the conference room, she'd come home frazzled. She'd decided to cook to calm herself down. "I wouldn't be in this fix if you hadn't swiped that Apollo file."

LaToya huffed. "You know we had to show it to them. Believe me, we would have been in a lot more trouble if we'd sat on that information for days before passing it on."

Lara winced. "Are you in trouble?"

LaToya shrugged, then retrieved a bottle of wine from the fridge. "They slapped me with one hand and patted me on the back with the other. They can't decide whether to be pissed or proud."

"Yeah, I got the some sort of thing." Lara set the plates on the table.

LaToya poured them two glasses of wine. "So you're really going to let that Apollo dude kidnap you?"

Lara sighed, wondering for the millionth time if she was making a huge mistake. A part of her wished LaToya had never taken the information. Then she could have continued working with Jack. But another part of her was ashamed. Those poor kidnapped girls were in danger, and here she was, hoping to use their sad circumstance as an excuse to keep seeing Jack. Why didn't she just face it? The relationship with Jack was doomed.

The timer on the oven dinged, interrupting her thoughts. The cornbread was ready.

"Well?" LaToya set the wineglasses on the table. "Are you going to do it?"

"Yes." Lara set the pan of cornbread on the stove and removed her oven mitts. "Those girls need help. I just hope they're still alive."

"Yeah, me too." LaToya gave her a worried look. "You could have refused, you know."

"I'll be all right." Lara cut two pieces of cornbread and put them on saucers. "They're going to put some kind of tracking device on me. The minute I arrive at Apollo's so-called resort, they'll swoop in and arrest him. It should be very quick and easy."

"That's what they always say." LaToya retrieved the butter dish from the fridge.

Lara brought their cornbread to the table. "I have a secret weapon, remember? I'm immune to mind control."

"Yeah, that's good." But LaToya still looked worried as she sat and smeared butter on her cornbread. "I—I may have been wrong when I told you not to see Jack anymore."

"You've decided he's okay now?" Lara gave her a wry look as she sat down.

LaToya shrugged. "I don't know what to think about him. He's suspicious as hell, but he does have some superpowers, and right now, I'm thinking it would be a good thing for you to have a superhero in your pocket."

Or in her pants. Lara squashed that errant thought. Her whole body just wanted to droop onto the floor. "I don't think there's any future for me and Jack."

LaToya stopped eating to look at her. "Why not?"

She sighed. "It's hard to explain."

"Oh shit. He's really an alien?"

A sorry excuse for a laugh escaped Lara. "I don't know what he is. He refuses to talk to me."

"A man who has trouble communicating." LaToya sipped some wine. "Now there's something completely different."

Lara made a face at her. "I can't get more involved with him when he won't talk to me."

"Does he treat you right?"

"Oh yeah." Lara drank some wine.

"Is he good in bed?"

She sputtered, and her eyes watered.

LaToya grinned. "I'll take that as a yes."

"We haven't . . . well, we sorta, but . . . okay, I would say yes." Lara's face flooded with heat.

LaToya snickered. "Then what's the problem?"

"There's more to life than good . . . great sex."

"Now I'm really worried about you."

"It's not funny, LaToya. My heart is breaking here. He says he loves me, but he won't trust me with the truth."

LaToya's brown eyes widened. "He says he loves you?"

Lara gulped down some wine. She hadn't meant for that to slip out.

"How do you feel about him?" LaToya asked.

She set the glass down. "Our food's getting cold." She rammed some cornbread into her mouth.

"You're in denial," LaToya announced.

Lara scowled at her, then swallowed down her food. "Right now, denial is my best friend. I'm not going to admit I'm in love with someone when the relationship is doomed."

"Didn't you just admit it?"

"And I'm not going to admit that I just agreed to an undercover assignment that could get me killed!"

LaToya sucked in a breath. "Take that back. Don't put those bad vibes on this. You'll make it through just fine. I know you will."

Lara took a deep breath. Her friend was right. She needed to keep a positive attitude. "It'll be all right. They'll be able to trace me." She wouldn't really be alone. She would survive this.

An hour later, LaToya left to go bowling with some friends from her precinct. Lara declined LaToya's invitation to join them, claiming she was too tired. Who was she kidding? She was hoping Jack would call.

She sat on the couch, flipping through channels on the television. She really ought to study the Apollo information on her computer, but she didn't want to think about it anymore. It would only make her more nervous, more worried that she was making a big mistake.

She wished she was back in Venice with Jack, floating down a canal without a worry in the world. But there was no such thing as a worry-free life. Even Jack had her confused and frustrated. If Casanova was his father, that would make Jack over two hundred years old. Was he aging super slowly, or was he stuck looking young and gorgeous for all time? Either way, it didn't look good for a lasting relationship.

She landed on a channel that showed a young woman in a white nightgown wandering around a dark, spooky house. She was carrying a lit candlestick, so apparently, the electricity was out. She gazed up a dark staircase that led to the attic, and thunder boomed. Creepy music swelled.

"Don't go up there," Lara told her.

She started up the stairs.

"Moron," Lara muttered and changed the channel.

A guy in a ski mask was chasing a girl who was running across the lawn. For some strange reason, she was in her underwear. The psycho killer waved a machete in the air. The girl looked back, then tripped and fell on her face.

"Get up, you idiot," Lara grumbled. "Run for your life."

The girl stayed on the ground and screamed. *Great. This was encouraging.* Lara changed the channel again. Was she being an idiot, too?

The phone rang, and her breath hitched. *Please be Jack. No, don't be Jack.* Dammit, she *was* an idiot.

After Jack woke up Tuesday night, he dashed upstairs to the fifth-floor office of the townhouse and chugged down some synthetic blood while he checked his messages. Lara hadn't called. Mario had sent him an e-mail to let him know that Father Giuseppe had found Lara's belt and delivered it to the *palazzo* that morning. The priest had also left a warning that he'd use the belt on Giacomo's hide if he didn't behave himself.

Jack sighed. The date had ended badly. Instead of drawing Lara closer, he'd managed to chase her away. He showered, dressed, then teleported to Venezia to fetch the belt. From there, he teleported to the grounds at Romatech. He looked around as he approached the side entrance. He swiped his ID card, then placed his hand on the sensor.

"Hey, bro," a voice spoke behind him.

He spun around to find Phineas. The young Vamp must have just teleported there. "*Merda*."

"Well, good evening to you, too," Phineas muttered. "We didn't see you at the townhouse."

"I had an errand to take care of. And I've just realized if a Malcontent timed it right, he could arrive like you did and take me by surprise." Jack motioned to the green light now blinking on the security pad. "You could have jumped me from behind and gained entrance."

Phineas frowned as he pushed open the door. "Howard would see it on the monitor and set off the alarm."

"True." Jack strode down the hall toward the MacKay security office. "Still, after Connor arrives, I'd like to have a meeting to discuss ways we can improve security here. We killed a dozen Malcontents last December at DVN. Sooner or later, Casimir is going to seek revenge."

"Yeah," Phineas agreed. "Those nasty vampires keep coming back." He glanced at the belt in Jack's hand. "Dude, you're not planning to wear that, are you? It's bad enough when some of the guys wear skirts, but a white belt—that's just not cool, man."

"It's not mine." Jack wound it up and stuffed it into a jacket pocket.

"Ooh, I see." Phineas's eyes lit up. "It's your *lady*'s

belt. I guess your date last night was a big success. So did you do a little bondage?"

"Excuse me?"

"You know, tie her up with the belt. Or maybe you used it for a little spanking."

Jack stiffened. "I would never spank Lara."

Phineas rolled his eyes. "Dude, you let the lady spank you. Believe me, the chicks really get into that."

"She probably thinks I deserve it," Jack muttered.

"Yeah." Phineas nodded. "That's what they always say to me. I'm an expert on these things, you know. But I figure you're the last person on earth who needs professional advice from the Love Doctor."

"Why is that?" Jack stopped in front of the security office.

Phineas snorted. "Dude, you're the son of Casanova. Seduction is your middle name. I saw you at the Gala Ball, sweet-talking all the ladies. You could have had any one you wanted. In fact, I bet you did have them all."

Jack groaned inwardly. Why did people always assume he had inherited some special talent from his father? All he'd inherited was a name that was such a curse, he'd stopped using it almost two hundred years ago. "I only danced with the ladies."

"Yeah, right. The horizontal mambo. I bet you were born with a condom on," Phineas continued. "A man like you could have any woman he wants."

But he only wanted Lara. "I don't want to lose her."

"What?"

"Nothing." Jack swiped his ID card in the keypad outside the security office.

Phineas leaned a shoulder against the wall. "Dude, what's wrong?"

"It's complicated."

"Love shouldn't be complicated, bro."

"It is when it's between a vampire and a mortal."

Phineas frowned. "Does she know you're a vampire?"

"No," Jack answered quickly. "I haven't told her anything. You and Connor can rest easy."

"Yeah, Connor's real touchy about keeping the big secret." Phineas rubbed his chin. "I gotta be honest with you, man. A little free advice from Dr. Phang."

"I'm not going to tie her up or spank her."

Phineas snorted. "I'm being serious now. If you love her, you gotta tell her the truth. You gotta make it real."

Jack swallowed hard. Lara kept asking him to tell her the truth. But what if she couldn't handle it? The women in his past had freaked out. He'd been able to erase their memories, but he couldn't do that with Lara. What if she lived the rest of her life remembering him with revulsion?

On the other hand, what if she was able to accept him? What if he'd finally found the *amore* that had evaded him for centuries? How glorious it would be to spend the rest of his life with Lara.

The door opened, and Howard peered at them curiously. "What's going on? You guys have been standing here for five minutes."

"Just talking, Papa Bear," Phineas said. "I'll go make the first round."

"Okay," Jack said. "And . . . thank you."

"Anytime, bro." Phineas zoomed back down the hall to the side entrance.

"Howard, can you stay till Connor arrives?" Jack asked. "I need to run an errand."

"Sure." Howard headed back to the desk. "I'll call the cafeteria and have them deliver my supper here."

Jack smiled. As long as were-bear Howard Barr was well fed, he stayed happy. "Thanks."

Jack hurried into the conference room across the hall and shut the door. He paced around the long table. Once he returned Lara's belt to her, what would he say? From the beginning he'd equated telling her the truth with losing her. But now, he realized he could lose her if he didn't tell her the truth.

Father Giuseppe, Gianetta, and Phineas all wanted him to tell her. Connor was strongly opposed to it. Angus had ordered him not to. What did *he* want to do?

He wanted her to love him. What if she hated him once she knew he was a Vamp? Jack took a deep breath. It was a chance he would have to take. There was no way to undo his status. She could either accept him as he was—or she couldn't. *You must have faith, Giacomo.*

Merda. Wasn't there a circle of hell for faithless bastards like himself? He made the call.

On the fourth ring, she picked up. "Hello?" She sounded hesitant.

"Hello, Lara. How are you?"

"I'm okay."

"I have your belt. I could return it to you now."

"There's . . . no hurry."

Was she reluctant to see him, or was this a bad time? He didn't want anyone else to see him teleport. "Are you alone?"

"I need to talk to you about the Apollo case," she said.

"We can work on it tonight, if you like," he offered. "I can teleport there and bring you back here to Roma-tech where I have all the information."

"I have the info here. I e-mailed it to myself."

"Oh." He had a bad feeling about this.

"I really appreciate all the work you did. We passed the info on to our superiors—"

"*What?*"

"We had to, Jack. We can't withhold evidence. And the minute Apollo started kidnapping girls across state lines, it became a matter for the FBI."

Nine circles of hell! Jack gripped the phone in his fist and paced around the table. "You shouldn't have done that. We were working on it together. We were making good progress."

"I know. I'm sorry, Jack, but it's not in your jurisdiction."

The hell it wasn't. This was a Malcontent crime, and it needed to be handled by Vamps. "How many people know?"

"Lots of people. The FBI and NYPD have set up a joint task force—"

"*Merda!*" He couldn't let them find Apollo first. The whole vampire world was in jeopardy. He couldn't believe Lara had done this. He stopped and leaned his elbows on the back of a chair. "I trusted you."

"Jack." Her voice was laced with pain. "I didn't mean to—I don't understand why this case is so important to you."

He took a deep breath. Fussing at her wouldn't fix the problem. "I'm sorry. I should have explained."

"There are a lot of things you could have explained," she grumbled.

"It'll be all right." He would get Connor and other volunteers to help. Ian and Toni were still on their honeymoon, but Robby was around. And maybe Phil Jones. "How much did you tell them? Do they know about Apollo's ability to control minds?"

"No. And I didn't tell them about you," Lara said. "You really can trust me."

"Thank you." He resumed his pacing. He needed to make some calls and set up a meeting.

"Unfortunately, they're giving me credit for all your hard work," Lara continued.

"That's all right. Maybe it will help you make detective."

She heaved a sigh. "They offered me an assignment under cover, posing as a college student."

Jack halted abruptly. "*What?*"

"I have the right look, so I'm going—

"*No!*" It felt like a wrecking ball had slammed into his chest. "No. You will not be bait."

"I already agreed."

He gritted his teeth. "You will *not* do it."

"You can't tell me what to do."

"Where are you? Are you alone?"

"There's no point in discussing it," she said. "My mind is made up."

Merda. He hoped she wasn't in a public place. He focused on her voice and teleported.

Chapter Seventeen

*L*ara gasped when Jack materialized in front of her. He looked quickly around the room.

"What—" Her throat constricted. He'd just focused on her with eyes that gleamed golden hot.

A frisson of fear pinned her to the couch. Jack was a man of supernatural power. What was he truly capable of?

Nonsense. She mentally shook herself. This was Jack. He'd made love to her the night before.

Somehow Venice seemed so far away.

Still glowering at her, he snapped his cell phone shut and pocketed it. He pulled her belt from another pocket and dropped it on the coffee table. "Maybe I *should* spank you," he muttered.

"Excuse me?"

His jaw shifted. "Forget I said that."

Like that would ever happen. She turned off her phone and placed it on the coffee table. "I gather you're a little miffed about the situation." She paused when a low growl vibrated in his throat. "Look, I'm not going to be intimidated by the he-man tactics. We can discuss this calmly and rationally."

"There is nothing rational about this." His hands fisted at his sides. "Using yourself as bait is ridiculous, foolish, and crazy!"

She sucked in a breath. "Why don't you tell me what you really think?"

His eyes narrowed into two golden pins of light. "You're not doing it."

"It's not your decision, Jack. In fact, none of this Apollo stuff is your business."

"You *are* my business, and you're trying to get yourself killed."

She snorted. "This may come as a surprise to you, but I'm not suicidal. Every precaution will be taken to ensure my safety. I'll be wearing a tracking device—"

"Those can be lost."

She glared at him. "As soon as they have a fix on Apollo's resort—"

He leaned over suddenly and with a swipe of one hand, he pushed the coffee table across the room. She caught her breath when he moved directly in front of her.

"You are not doing it." Anger seethed in his low, sharply clipped words.

Dammit, he was trying to bully her. Lara rose to her feet, her face inches from his stubborn chin. "No one tells me what to do."

He grabbed her by the shoulders. "I could teleport you someplace so remote you'd never find your way out."

She shoved at his chest. "Then you would be a kidnapper just like Apollo."

"No. I would be saving your life." His grip tightened

on her shoulders. "Stay away from Apollo. You have no idea what he's capable of."

"But *you* know?" She seethed with frustration. "What do you know that you're not telling me, Jack?"

He released her and stepped back. He dragged a hand through his hair and paced across the room. "When Apollo sees you, he's going to want you."

"We're counting on that. And with the tracer I'll be wearing, we'll be able to track him down."

Jack shook his head. "He'll teleport you someplace. He might teleport you several places in a row. You've seen how quickly it's done. By the time the police figure out where he is, he . . . Bloody hell, Lara, it will be too late!"

She swallowed hard. "I can buy some time. I won't be under his control like the other victims. That's why I'm the best choice for this job. I'm immune to mind control."

He scoffed. "You think that makes you safe? Lara, the instant he realizes he can't control you, he will kill you."

A shudder zipped down her back. *He's just trying to scure you into quitting.* Hell, maybe she should quit. What if she got in completely over her head? The special task force had already warned her that she couldn't take any weapons with her. It would blow her cover.

"You can't survive against Apollo," Jack continued quietly. He paced across the room, then turned to face her. His mouth twisted as if he found the words painful. "He'll feed on you."

Lara gasped and pressed her hand to her chest. "What?"

"He'll sink his teeth into you and take your blood."

She grimaced. "That's sick. You make him sound like a . . . a . . ."

"Vampire," Jack whispered.

She stared at him. My God, he was serious. "Jack, there's no such thing. Maybe he *thinks* he's a vampire. There are some crazy people out there who pretend they're vampires. But any guy who tries to bite my neck would get a knee in his groin faster than he could say Transylvania."

Jack scowled at her. "You don't believe me."

"I think you're trying to scare the hell out of me so I'll quit this assignment. I really should be pissed, but I realize you're worried about me 'cause you care so much."

"I'm in love with you."

Her heart squeezed in her chest. She would never get tired of hearing him say that. "I care deeply for you, too, but—"

"Lara." He stepped toward her.

"But" —she put up a hand to stop him— "I will not allow you to control me or manipulate me."

"*Merda.* I'm trying to keep you alive. He's a vicious vampire."

"There's no such thing!"

"That's what they want you to believe. They've used mind control to make everyone believe they don't really exist, that they're just make-believe monsters. But they feed on people, then erase their memories. It's been going on for centuries."

Her skin crawled with gooseflesh. "How can you know about vampires? How would you know that Apollo's one of them? Have you met him?"

"No, I haven't. But I recognize the signs. Apollo only appears at night. He can control people's minds and erase memories. He has super strength and speed. He can teleport."

She gasped. "You're describing *yourself*."

Jack winced. His eyes glinted with a wary look.

Lara stumbled back and fell onto the couch. Oh God, he wasn't denying it. He was either crazy as a loon, or he was actually. . .

"No," she whispered. "No. Vampires aren't real."

He regarded her sadly. "Why would I lie about it? What can I possibly gain from this, other than your disgust?"

She dragged in a shaky breath and pressed her hands against her eyes. Memories flitted through her mind. She'd never seen him eat. She'd never been able to reach him during the day. There was no mirror in his bathroom. There were thick shutters on the windows. He was over two hundred years old. He worked at a factory that manufactured synthetic blood. Damn, it was a grocery store!

All the pieces of the puzzle had been there, but she'd never been able to fit them together 'cause she hadn't known what the final picture looked like. She'd expected a picture of a superhero. Not a monster.

Her stomach lurched. Oh God, she'd kissed him. She'd let him touch her, make love to her.

She covered her mouth as a moan escaped.

"Lara." He stepped toward her.

She pressed back against the couch.

His face paled. "*Santo cielo*. Do not fear me. I would never hurt you."

"I think you'd better go."

"We still need to talk."

"No." Her eyes stung with tears. What was there to talk about? She'd fallen for a monster. She'd been a fool.

He frowned. "You know the truth about Apollo now. This is a matter strictly for vampires. You will let me handle it."

Anger sizzled deep within her. "How dare you. This is not just about Apollo. All of his victims are human, so don't tell me to butt out. And don't expect me to believe that there are monsters who care."

He stiffened. "We're not all bad, Lara."

"I want you to leave."

He rubbed his brow. "You're in shock now. In a few days, we can talk."

"*Go!*"

He lowered his hand, and his eyes glimmered with pain and sadness. He wavered, then disappeared.

Jack materialized in the woods surrounding Romatech. He trudged toward the side entrance. If only he knew how to materialize without a heart. His chest ached so much, it hurt to breathe.

He propped a forearm against a thick tree trunk and leaned forward, resting his brow against his arm. He closed his eyes, and images flipped through his brain, the expressions on Lara's face. Shock, horror, disgust, anger. Just like the women from his past.

He'd lost Lara.

You must have faith, Giacomo. Father Giuseppe's words echoed softly in his mind.

How? He was a creature of darkness, trapped in a circle of hell. How could he possibly have faith? He was losing Lara just like he had the others. How many years had he suffered after losing them? And Beatrice—losing her had been sheer torment. He'd always wondered if she could have accepted him, but she'd died before he could tell her. She'd died all alone, believing he had abandoned her.

Merda! He punched the tree with his fist. He would not abandon Lara, even if she hated him. He would not let her die.

If Apollo kept to his usual schedule, he'd take another victim the last Saturday in June. That gave Jack plenty of time to locate the bastard and eliminate him. Then he could do a mind sweep on the police and FBI to clean up loose ends, and the whole ordeal would be over.

Lara would be saved. He just needed to have faith. And the help of a few good friends.

He pulled out his cell phone as he walked through the woods. Robby MacKay would help him. He'd first met Robby in 1820 at Jean-Luc's fencing academy in Paris, when they'd been paired as sparring partners. They'd become good friends when they weren't trying to skewer each other.

Robby was now working as Jean-Luc's bodyguard. Since Jean-Luc was hiding in Texas, Robby was there, too.

Robby answered the phone. "Hi, Jack. How's it going?"

"A problem's come up. Can you spare a few hours? I could use your help."

"Thank God. I'm bored out of my skull here. Last night Jean-Luc's daughter asked me to play dolls with her, and I nearly said yes. That's how desperate I'm getting."

"Then it's your lucky day," Jack said. "In fact, I may need you for a week or so. Phil, too, if he can come."

"I'll check with Jean-Luc, but I'm sure he willna object. See you soon." Robby rang off.

Jack pocketed his phone and strode toward the entrance.

"Hey, bro." Phineas zoomed up to him. "I was making a round when I heard your voice."

"I was on the phone. Did Connor arrive?"

"Yeah, he's in the office." Phineas cast a sidelong

glance at Jack. "Are you all right, dude? You look kinda wasted."

Jack winced. "I want you and Carlos to live at Romatech for the next week or so. There are a few bedrooms in the basement, right?"

"Yeah. What's wrong? Are the Malcontents up to something?"

"No, but the police might come to the townhouse. We don't want to be caught there in our death-sleep."

"Damned po-po." Phineas halted. "Shit. Did you tell that cop lady about us?"

Jack gave him an irritated look. "Didn't you just advise me to?"

"Well, yeah, but since when does anyone take my advice? So I guess it didn't go well, huh?"

Jack shook his head.

"Damn," Phineas muttered. "I thought women were into vampires. I thought she'd be cool with it, man."

A jab of pain sliced through Jack's chest. "She wasn't."

"Shit. Do you think she's gonna tell her police buddies about us?"

"I don't know. She might. So grab whatever you need from the townhouse and bring Carlos here, okay?"

"Okay. Sorry, dude." Phineas teleported away.

Jack reached the side entrance, swiped his card, and used the hand sensor. He was halfway down the hallway when the security door opened and Connor leaned out.

"I saw Phineas teleport away," Connor said. "Where did ye send him?"

"To the townhouse to fetch Carlos. They're going to stay here for the next week or so."

Connor's eyes narrowed. "And why is the townhouse no longer safe?"

"It may be perfectly safe. This is just a precaution." Jack strode past the Scotsman into the office. He heard the door shut behind him.

"Bugger," Connor whispered softly.

Jack turned to face him.

"Ye told her."

Jack widened his stance and folded his arms across his chest. "I did what I had to do."

Connor snorted. "I gather it dinna go well."

Jack shrugged one shoulder.

"Ye told a police officer about vampires," Connor muttered. "Did ye really expect it to go well?"

"She knows I love her."

"Och, and that is supposed to make a difference?" Anger flashed in Connor's blue eyes. "Do ye seriously believe that rubbish about love conquering all? How many mortals have we loved, only to watch them succumb to death. All the love in the world canna stop them from dying."

"I know that." He'd lost Beatrice when an outbreak of typhoid had swept through Venice. "Love is fleeting. That doesn't make it worthless. It just makes it more special."

Connor glowered at him. "It makes it more painful. Ye must know that. I can see the pain in yer face."

Jack swallowed hard. He couldn't deny that.

"Have ye even considered what this great love of yers will do to her?" Connor asked. "Ye'll be dragging her into a world that she may no' want any part of."

Jack winced. He had to admit Lara had not reacted well. Still, other mortal women had adjusted to the vampire world. "Shanna is happy. And Emma and Heather."

"Ye canna expect every woman to want to live with the Undead," Connor grumbled. "I brought Darcy

Newhart into our world, and she hated me for it. Ye wouldna want to live with that kind of guilt."

Jack wondered if Connor had felt more than just guilt. "Darcy's very happy now. And she still works with us."

Connor waved a dismissive hand as he strode toward the desk. "Let's get back to this friend of yers. Is she going to tell her superiors about us?"

"I don't know. Maybe not." Lara wouldn't want them thinking she was crazy.

Connor took a seat, still scowling at Jack. "I'm sorely tempted to put a dent in yer skull, but ye look so miserable 'twould be like kicking a dog."

"Gee, thanks."

"Did she make any threats? I could teleport her someplace where she couldna tell anyone about us."

"No." Jack gritted his teeth. "You will leave her alone."

Connor snorted. "I wouldna harm her. 'Tis better than having the New York Police Department hunting us down."

"I don't think she's a threat to us. She's more of a threat to herself. She leaked all of my information on Apollo to her superiors."

"Bugger," Connor muttered.

"The police and FBI have formed a special task force, and they've asked Lara to go under cover. On the fourth Saturday in June, Apollo will be trolling universities, giving his seminar, and looking for the perfect victim. If the police have their way, that victim will be Lara."

"Bloody hell." Connor looked appalled. "We have to stop it. Apollo could kill her."

"That's why I told her the truth," Jack said. "I was trying to scare her into quitting the assignment."

Connor nodded. "All right. I can understand that."

"We're in a race for time," Jack continued. "We have

one month to find Apollo and kill him. I've asked Robby to help."

"We have plenty of time." Connor motioned to one of the surveillance monitors on the wall. "Robby has arrived. And he's no' alone."

Jack peered at the monitor. Robby had teleported onto the grounds, and he'd brought Phil with him. As a day guard, Phil wasn't able to teleport. But as a shape shifter, he had other talents that made him valuable.

"There's Phineas and Carlos." Connor pointed at another monitor.

Jack spotted Phineas materializing outside the side entrance with the day guard Carlos. They were joined by Robby and Phil, and the four men entered the building.

Jack smiled grimly. He'd assembled his own special task force. Counting himself and Connor, he had four vampires plus a werewolf and a were-panther. Lara should be safe now.

Apollo wouldn't live long enough to hurt her.

Chapter Eighteen

$\mathcal{T}$he next night, Jack paced around the conference room, wondering if it was too soon to call Lara. Everything else was under control. Roman had sent word to all the coven masters in North America to be on the lookout for a spa with classical Greek architecture. Already, a few leads had come in, and Robby and Phil were checking them out. Phineas was guarding Romatech. Carlos, who worked during the day, was sleeping in the basement, on call if they needed him. Howard had offered to help, but he also doubled as the day guard for Roman's family, so his time was limited.

Jack considered investigating some of the missing girls, but he figured Apollo's MO would remain the same. He lured pretty girls to his seminar on staying young and beautiful forever, then he selected a victim.

Jack halted his pacing. What if Apollo was making good on his promise to keep the girls young and beautiful forever? He might not be killing them. He could be transforming them.

Jack winced at the thought of controlling a harem of vampire women. *Merda*, he couldn't even control one mortal woman. At least there had been no police snooping around the townhouse. No police had come to Romatech, either, so it looked like Lara was keeping quiet about vampires. Most probably she feared her superiors would think she was crazy. But Jack hoped she still harbored some protective feelings toward him. If only her feelings for him could survive. If they could outlast her initial reaction of horror and disgust, he might have a chance.

You must have faith, Giacomo.

He called her apartment. The phone rang once. Twice. If she had Caller ID, she would know it was him. Three rings. She might be avoiding him. Four rings.

"Hello, Jack."

It was LaToya, her roommate. "Hello. Is Lara—"

"Save your breath. She's not here. And she doesn't want to talk to you. Ever. Good-bye."

"Wait. Is she . . . is she all right?"

"She's totally bummed out, you moron. I don't know what you did to her. I've never seen her so upset. She won't even talk to me. And she's always talked to me."

"She didn't tell you anything?" Jack felt a flicker of hope. Lara was keeping his secret.

"All she said was that she never wanted to see you or talk to you again. In case your super hearing didn't catch that, the operative word was *never*."

The flicker of hope sputtered out.

"And I am really pissed at you," LaToya continued. "You've got Lara moping around like the world has come to an end, when she really needs to be on the top of her game right now. Your timing really stinks!"

"She's going ahead with the undercover assignment?"

"Shit. You know about that?"

Jack wondered if he could find an ally with LaToya. "I don't want her to do it. I think it's too dangerous."

"Oh."

"I'm trying to locate Apollo myself, so Lara won't have to put herself in danger." There was a pause, and Jack hoped LaToya was reassessing the situation.

"I've got to go. Bye." She rang off.

Jack sighed. He'd keep trying.

By five A.M., Robby and Phil had checked out four locations, all false leads. They promised to return the next night, then teleported home to Texas.

Four more nights passed. The month of June began, and Apollo's location remained secret. By the second Saturday in June, Jack was beside himself with worry. Only two weeks were left. Still no sign of Apollo.

And no word from Lara. Was she trying to forget him?

The following Monday, he tried calling again.

"She still doesn't want to talk to you," LaToya said.

"How is she?"

"She's sad and depressed. I've heard her crying a few times in her room. Does that make you happy?" LaToya growled.

In a sad way, it did, although Jack knew better than to admit to it.

"Have you found that Apollo guy yet?" LaToya demanded.

"No." Jack was beginning to wonder if Apollo's Greek-style resort even existed. He could be showing bogus pictures in his seminar. "We're still trying."

"Well, you'd better try harder. Lara's going under cover in a couple of days."

"Where?"

LaToya snorted. "Like I would tell you?"

"I'm worried sick about her."

"Well, that makes two of us." LaToya hung up.

Jack paced around the conference room. Lara's undercover work would obviously be at a university. The special task force had probably enrolled her under a false name, and she was living in a dorm. But which university?

He sat in front of the laptop and checked his information on the missing girls. They came from ten different universities. He made a list of the past twenty months in chronological order, then listed the universities that Apollo had targeted each month. There was definitely a pattern. Two universities in Connecticut, four in New York, two in New Jersey, two in Pennsylvania, then back to Connecticut. Apollo's last hit had been Columbia University. If he followed his pattern, Syracuse University would be next.

"Jack." Phil strode into the conference room. "We've got a new lead. A place called Apollo's Golden Chariot, in Massachusetts."

Jack stood. "Is Robby back yet?"

"No, he and Phineas are still in Hoboken, checking out the Grecian Goddess Spa and Resort."

"All right," Jack said. "You and I can go. Do you have the phone number?"

"Right here." Phil passed him a slip of paper.

"Are you armed?"

Phil opened his brown leather bomber jacket to reveal a forty-four Magnum in a shoulder holster. Jack had a dagger strapped to his calf and another sheathed beneath his black leather jacket. If they ended up in a skirmish, he would call Robby and Phineas for immediate backup.

"Let's do it." Jack punched in the number on his cell phone.

"Apollo's Golden Chariot," a feminine voice answered. "Macy speaking."

"Hi. Can you give me directions from . . . Connecticut?" Jack asked.

As the speaker launched into a long explanation, Jack focused on the voice. He grabbed Phil's arm and teleported them both. He quickly scanned their new surroundings. A small office, a file cabinet, a messy desk, the harsh smell of chemicals in the air, and a blonde, staring at them with hot pink lipstick outlining her gaping mouth.

"Aack!" She let out a high-pitched squeal and dropped the phone.

"It's all right." Jack unfurled a wave of psychic energy to take over the woman's mind, but before he could gain control, she jumped to her feet, let out another squeal, then collapsed into a dead faint.

"*Merda.*" Jack frowned at the sprawled body on the floor. "We scared the poor woman to death."

Phil snorted. "That's not a woman."

"She screamed like a woman." Jack's gaze ran over the hot pink miniskirt, black hose, and hot pink boots. They looked feminine enough, but the black tank top revealed broad shoulders and a flat chest. A man.

Jack hunched down beside the unconscious man and swept into his mind. *Macy, you will not fear us. We walked into the office, looking for Apollo. You will awaken now.*

Macy's green-shaded eyelids flickered open.

"Are you all right?" Jack asked. "You fainted."

"Oh my God, this is so embarrassing." Macy sat up and tugged at his pink miniskirt. "It must be this new diet I'm on. I swear, I'm so woozy."

"Here." Jack helped him stand.

"You're too kind." Macy looked at him. "Oh my." His eyes widened, and he glanced at Phil. "*Oh my.*" He patted his long blond hair. "What can I do for you two?"

"We're looking for Apollo," Jack said.

"Well, he should be in the studio. I can't believe you missed him. Or that he missed you." Macy inspected them with an appreciative gleam in his eyes. "Come on, big boys. Follow me." He clonked past them in his platform boots and cast a sidelong glance at Phil. "Mmm."

Phil shot Jack an annoyed look.

"Come on." Jack headed for the door.

Phil caught his arm and muttered, "This can't be the right place. Let's get out of here."

"We might as well meet this Apollo," Jack said.

Phil scowled. "I have a bad feeling about this."

"You think it'll turn violent?" Jack asked.

"Worse," Phil grumbled.

Macy glanced back with a frown. "Come now, you two, stop bickering. Apollo doesn't allow any love spats here."

A low growl vibrated in Phil's throat.

Jack smiled. "We're coming." He joined Macy in the hallway with Phil trudging behind him.

As they entered the studio, Jack noticed the walls were painted lavender and decorated with hot pink hearts and cupids. He passed a line of pink reclining chairs and sinks for washing hair. He came to an abrupt halt as he noticed all the styling cubicles. Each one was lined on three sides with mirrors. And each cubicle was occupied by a male stylist and customer.

He couldn't possibly get past all of them without their realizing that he didn't reflect in the mirrors.

"Let's go," Phil hissed. "It's just a beauty salon."

Macy spun to face him with an appalled expression. "*Just* a beauty salon? Don't you think this world needs more beauty in it?"

Heads popped out from cubicles as stylists tried to get a peek at the offensive strangers in their midst.

Jack stepped back, not wanting to be near all the mirrors. "I'm sorry. I'm afraid we can't . . . go any further. This was a mistake."

"Don't say that. You two are gorgeous together." Macy whirled around to face the cubicles. "Apollo! We have an emergency! Cupid alert!"

More heads popped out to look at Jack and Phil.

A slender young man with short platinum blond hair, a black fishnet shirt, and a pink utility belt rushed from the first styling cubicle. "What's wrong?" He jammed a long comb into one of the slots on his utility belt. "This had better be super serious. I'm in the middle of a perm."

"These two guys came to see you." Macy pointed at Jack and Phil, and his bottom lip trembled. "But now they want to break up!"

Apollo's eyes widened as he looked them over. "Oh my. You poor dears. You have to work it out. I mean, look at you. You look fabulous together." He turned back to the stylists and customers who were filling the center aisle. "Aren't they absolutely gorgeous?"

"Just kill me now," Phil muttered.

"We shouldn't have come," Jack said. "Is there a back door we could use?"

Macy gasped. "You mustn't be ashamed! You're beautiful the way you are."

The audience all murmured encouragement.

"Yes, a lovely couple like you should shout your love from the rooftops." Apollo came closer and motioned to Phil's hair. "Macy, have you ever seen such a delicious blend of colors? There must be twenty shades of brown, auburn, and gold in his hair. It looks fabulous."

Macy pressed a hand against his flat bosom. "I

would die to have hair like that. Who on earth is your colorist?"

"I . . . don't have a colorist," Phil mumbled.

Apollo jumped back. "It's *natural*?"

A series of gasps reverberated through the audience.

Apollo touched Phil's hair, and the shape shifter stiffened. "It's incredibly thick," Apollo said. "Very rugged and manly, but a little too shaggy for my taste. I'm thinking layers and a tad bit shorter."

"Oh yes," Macy breathed, and the audience murmured in agreement.

"And *you*." Apollo circled Jack, studying him. "All that dark hair and black leather. It just screams 'bad boy.'"

"Mmm." Macy eyed him as he twirled a strand of blond hair around a finger.

"I'm thinking we'll keep your hair long." Apollo scrutinized him carefully. "You have such interesting gold flecks in your eyes. I'm thinking" —he tapped his chin— "*gold highlights*."

Macy gasped. "Brilliant!"

The audience applauded.

Jack cleared his throat. "You wouldn't happen to have a few female college students around here, would you?"

Apollo blinked. "Females?" He exchanged a confused look with Macy, then burst into giggles. He slapped Jack's arm. "You're so hilarious."

Macy joined in the laughter, and chuckles spread across the room.

Phil grabbed Jack's arm. "Let's get out of here."

"I can see you're very busy here." Jack retreated down the back hallway. "We'll come back another time."

"Oh please do." Apollo looked at them fondly. "And don't forget. I do weddings!"

"Thank you." Jack spotted a back door and pulled it open. He and Phil dashed into the back alley.

He grabbed Phil's arm to teleport back to Romatech.

Phil muttered a curse. "If you say one word about this to the other guys, I will stake you in your sleep."

"Don't worry, sweetheart. If they find out about this, I'll stake myself."

The next night, Jack considered going to Syracuse University. It would be easy enough to teleport into the admissions office and access the list of new students. He didn't expect there would be too many in June, so even if Lara was using a false name, he could track her down fairly quickly. He paused, ready to punch in the phone number for the admissions office. He'd simply use their recorded message as a beacon to teleport straight in.

Merda. He was starting to feel like a stalker. If Lara didn't want to see him, he shouldn't force himself on her. What kind of future could she have with him? Even if she fell madly in love with him and agreed to marry him, he could only be there for her at night. If she had children with him, they wouldn't be fully mortal. And sooner or later, she'd be faced with a terrible decision—whether to join him as one of the Undead.

Did he have the right to force such decisions on her? If he behaved like his famous father, he would satisfy his desires today and not worry about tomorrow. But he had never made a good Casanova. He knew deep inside that love should be unselfish. He should leave Lara alone.

But he couldn't let her walk into Apollo's clutches

unprepared. He had to do his best to make sure she survived. Then, if she wanted never to see him again, he would leave her alone.

He called her apartment, and LaToya answered.

"You again," she muttered. "Don't you ever give up?"

"I'm still worried about Lara. We haven't been able to find Apollo."

"No shit."

"I know Lara feels that her immunity to mind control gives her an advantage. I was never able to control her."

LaToya snorted. "Tough break, creepazoid."

"Her ability to resist is definitely good, but her inability to hear the psychic voice could spell disaster for her. Once Apollo figures out that he has no control over her, he will probably kill her."

There was silence.

"She'll be safe as long as he's giving psychic orders to a group," Jack continued. "She can mimic the other girls. But if he gives her a direct order, and she can't hear it and obey, the jig will be up."

"I see what you mean," LaToya said quietly.

"I could work with her and help her develop the ability to hear the psychic voice."

"What if she loses her ability to resist his control?" LaToya asked.

"I'll teach her how to listen but not succumb. I strongly feel that she needs to do this."

There was a pause. "Maybe."

"I could find her myself," Jack said. "I believe she's at Syracuse University."

There was a sharp intake of breath. "I'm not confirming that."

As far as Jack was concerned, she just had. "I don't

want to force my presence on her, so will you tell her what I said? If she agrees to see me, I'll try to help her."

There was another long pause. "I'll tell her."

"Thank you."

"Don't thank me," LaToya growled. "You try any tricky stuff with my girlfriend, and I'm coming after you. You'll wish you'd never left your home planet." She hung up.

As the third Saturday in June approached, Jack was ready to rip his hair out. Every lead that he and his team had checked out had proven false. The damned resort could be anywhere. They had assumed Apollo would stay close to his hunting grounds, but with teleportation, he could be anywhere. Even Greece, although teleporting east, into the rising sun, was always a dangerous proposition for a vampire.

Roman extended their search parameters by asking coven masters around the world to report any leads in their areas of jurisdiction. This kept Jack and his team busy every night. Still, with a growing sense of despair, he realized time was slipping by. And LaToya had not called him back.

Lara must really hate him if she was willing to risk more danger rather than see him again.

When Saturday arrived, he paced around the conference table. One week to go before Apollo would strike again. His heart squeezed painfully in his chest. He hadn't seen Lara in almost a month, but his love for her was stronger than ever. His desperation to keep her alive was overwhelming. He was sorely tempted to hunt her down, grab her, and teleport her far away. She would never forgive him, but so what? He was already in hell without her love. How could it get any worse?

His phone rang, and he whipped it open. "*Pronto?*"

"Jack, is that you?" LaToya asked.

"Yes." He held his breath and sent up a silent prayer.

"Lara wants to see you."

Chapter Nineteen

*S*unday night, Lara left the Graham Dining Center on the north campus of Syracuse University and strolled down the street to her new home. The special task force had found her a room in Day Hall, since the last victim from Syracuse had lived there. No doubt Apollo found it amusing to kidnap a girl who lived off Mount Olympus Drive.

She could have taken the passageway from the dining center to the residence hall, but she wanted to get away from the constant noise of jabbering students. How could she worry properly if she couldn't hear herself think? And she had a whole lot to worry about.

She glanced to the west, where the setting sun was gleaming pink and gold off the Carrier Dome. Jack would be up soon. *Rising from the grave*, she thought with a shudder. Would he call her? She was so nervous about the prospect of seeing him again that she'd hardly touched her supper.

She'd asked LaToya to call him last night. LaToya

was supposed to give him her new cell-phone number and ask him to call tonight. Lara had been a nervous wreck all day.

Damn that man! She'd tried so hard to put him out of her mind. And her heart. She'd immersed herself in the preparations for her assignment. Hours of martial arts, strength training, and coaching on how to handle stress and the criminal mastermind. And still, Jack had crept into her thoughts. With every muscle in her body aching from exhaustive workouts, she still felt the ache in her heart.

It was akin to mourning, she'd decided. She'd lost the man who could have been the love of her life.

She'd tried denial at first. There were no such things as vampires, and poor Jack was simply crazy. He couldn't be a vampire. He didn't act like a monster. Sure didn't kiss like one. Or make love like one. But she refused to think about that. Denial had worked well. For about two hours.

Then anger had taken root, growing into rage. How could such monsters exist unknown for centuries? And how on earth could she fall for one? How could she have missed all the signs? And how dare Jack pursue her as if a relationship was actually possible? A mortal would have to be clinically insane to marry a vampire.

Then she recalled Shanna and her beautiful children. Shanna was obviously a happy woman. But how could anyone marry a monster who fed on people? She had to admit, though, that Jack had never tried to feed on her. He'd always behaved like a perfect gentleman. Well, more like a naughty gentleman, but he was a Casanova, after all. The few times she'd seen him drink, he must have been drinking synthetic blood. Did that mean he didn't like to bite people?

And then the revelation had hit. Jack could have been transformed against his will. He could have been a victim, much like the poor girls who were kidnapped by Apollo. He could have been forced to bite people for years just in order to survive. Was that why he referred to the nine circles of hell so much? He was trapped in a living hell.

Lara shook her head as she entered Day Hall. She couldn't allow herself to feel sorry for Jack. He was over two hundred years old, so he'd obviously bitten a lot of people. She ought to feel sorry for his victims, not him.

She stepped into an elevator and punched the button for the eighth floor. Great. A couple was kissing in the back corner. She kept her back to them and ignored the moans of passion. The memory flitted back of her elevator trip to the top of the *campanile* in Venice. Jack had been so romantic, so sweet. Why couldn't he have been a normal guy? *Would you have been so fascinated with him if he were a normal guy? Would you have fallen in love?*

"I'm not in love," she muttered, and the elevator lurched to a stop on the fifth floor.

"Then find another guy," the young woman said with a laugh as she exited the elevator with her boyfriend.

Lara groaned and pushed the button to close the elevator. Another guy? There was no one who came close to Jack. No other man had that combination of cleverness, old-world charm, and mouthwatering good looks. She'd been totally intrigued by his unusual powers and the mystery surrounding him. Until she'd found out the truth.

Her vision blurred with unshed tears as she recalled the look on his face the last time she'd seen him. She'd yelled at him to leave, and there had been so much pain and sadness in his eyes. Poor Jack.

"Aargh!" She was doing it again. Jack was not a poor, abandoned puppy. He was a vampire. She exited the elevator and trudged down the hallway to Room 843.

The problem was, now that she was under cover, she had too much time to think. It had been easier when the special task force had kept her busy.

They'd given her a new identity—Lara Booker. Everything was set. Her only job now was to check the bulletin boards every day in the twenty residence halls spread over the huge campus. She was waiting for the flyer from Apollo to show up.

The FBI had determined that Syracuse University was the most likely place for Apollo to strike next. Even so, they were covering all the bases. Female special agents were checking bulletin boards at several colleges. Whenever the flyer appeared, Lara would be called into action. She'd attend the seminar and get herself kidnapped.

But what if Jack was right, and her immunity to mind control backfired on her? It wasn't a problem she could discuss with the special task force. How could she tell them about mind-controlling vampires? The only one who would understand was her friendly neighborhood mind-controlling vampire, Jack.

Her heart raced as she entered her single dorm room and locked the door. Would he call soon? Would he come to see her? Did he still love her?

No! She wouldn't think about love. She would accept his help, then say good-bye. But what if he looked at her with that pain and sadness in his beautiful eyes? She couldn't bear to hurt him.

We're not all bad, he'd told her.

She leaned over the desk to peer through the window

blinds. The sun was completely gone now. She removed her new cell phone from her handbag and set it on the desk. She stared at it, willing it to ring.

If what Jack said was true, then there could be good vampires and bad ones. Did the good ones attempt to keep the bad ones in line? LaToya had told her that Jack was trying to locate Apollo, but hadn't succeeded so far.

She paced across the room. The damned phone would never ring as long as she stared at it. What was Jack doing now? Was he drinking synthetic blood? Taking a shower? Getting dressed? Did he still love her?

The phone rang. She whirled to face it. *Jack.* She approached slowly, letting it ring again. "Hello?"

"Lara."

The sound of his voice poured over her like a hot bath. She just wanted to soak in it for hours. She mentally splashed cold water on herself. This was strictly business. "Hello, Jack. LaToya mentioned your offer to help me hear psychic voices. I'm willing to learn, if you're available."

There was a pause. She wondered what he was thinking.

"I have cleared my schedule for the next few hours," he said finally. "We could start immediately."

Lara exhaled with relief. He was acting businesslike, too. Thank God. "Just a moment, please. I'll check my schedule." She glanced down at the bare desk and drummed her fingers on the wooden surface. *One-one thousand. Two-one thousand.* "Yes, we're in luck. I can fit you in this evening. Do we need to do this in person?"

"Yes, we do."

She frowned. There was a strange echo on her phone. "You can hang up now," he told her.

"Excuse me?" She heard a click behind her and turned. "Ack!" Her phone tumbled to the carpet.

With a hint of a smile, he slid his closed phone into a pocket of his black leather jacket. His gaze drifted to her bare desk. "So kind of you to fit me in."

She grabbed her phone off the floor and set it back on the desk. "You shouldn't sneak up on people like that."

"I thought you were expecting me." He walked toward her.

She jumped out of his way.

He paused briefly, frowning, then continued past her to the desk. With a silent groan, she realized he had been headed for the window all along.

He peered through the blinds. "This is Syracuse University?"

"Yes. Day Hall. The girl Apollo kidnapped from here last August lived in this same dorm."

"Does anyone remember her?" Jack asked. "Is her roommate still here?"

"The roommate graduated last December. I asked around, but everyone thinks the missing girl dropped out of school and went home." Lara perched on the edge of the narrow bed that was pushed against a wall. "She never made it home."

Jack paced back and forth down the length of the tiny room. She cast a few furtive glances his way, not wanting to be caught admiring his lean, graceful stride or his broad shoulders.

"Is there any way I can convince you to quit?" he asked.

She lifted her chin. "I'm not a quitter."

"Are you sure about that?" he muttered under his breath as he continued to pace.

Was he referring to their relationship? Lara's cheeks heated with indignation. He was a two-hundred-year-old vampire, for Pete's sake. Was she supposed to be happy about that?

"I'm not a quitter, either." He removed his leather jacket and draped it on the back of her desk chair. "I'm going to find Apollo before you end up doing something foolish."

"Oh, thanks for the vote of confidence." She glared at him.

He glared back as he sat down. "You're plenty tough for a mortal, but you're still no match for a vampire."

She looked away. "Exactly. I shouldn't be matched with a vampire."

"Let's get started." His voice sounded strained.

"Fine by me." She turned back to him and clasped her hands in her lap. "What do I need to do?"

"Nothing. I do all the work, and you just try to be . . . receptive to me."

She gripped her hands tighter. "Okay."

He leaned forward, his elbows braced on his thighs, and studied her intently. The gold flecks in his eyes seemed to grow until the entire iris was gold and gleaming.

Lara looked away, uncomfortable with the fierce energy radiating from his stare. The room seemed awfully hot. Her skin began to tingle all over. Especially her breasts. The tingling sensation took a sudden turn south. She pressed her thighs together. She was suddenly desperate to feel a man inside her. And not just any man. *Jack*.

"Do you feel that?" he whispered.

She gulped. His eyes were actually glowing now. "What are you doing?"

"Turning up the power. This is how a vampire lures people in."

She stiffened. "So you can bite them?"

"I haven't bitten a woman since 1987, when synthetic blood was introduced."

"How considerate of you." She lifted her chin and gazed nonchalantly across the room. "I guess you're a bit rusty, 'cause I'm not feeling much of anything."

"Maybe you're just insensitive."

She shot him an annoyed look.

His mouth twitched. "You *are* feeling it. Your heart is pounding. Your temperature has increased. I can feel the heat coming off you like—"

"All right." She clenched her teeth. "Is there a point to this? I thought we were going to concentrate on hearing voices."

"I'm trying to assess your capabilities. Your sense of touch seems to be working fine. I think it's only your hearing that's off-kilter."

A blast of cold air nearly knocked Lara on her back. With a shiver, she righted herself.

"You felt that." He watched her closely.

"Yes." The cold air swirled around her, sweeping icy tendrils across her brow. "You're trying to invade my mind?"

He nodded. "Normally, I would be in by now."

She wrinkled her nose at him. "You don't make people squawk and do the chicken dance, do you?"

Now he gave her an annoyed look. "Do you hear anything at all?"

She shut her eyes and focused. There was a buzzing behind her ears that sounded like radio static. "Are you saying something now?"

"Yes."

She wondered what. She squeezed her eyes more tightly shut, frowning with all the concentration she could muster. The buzzing sounded louder and more masculine, more like Jack, but she couldn't distinguish any individual words.

With a sigh, she opened her eyes. "This isn't working. All I'm getting from you is a buzz."

His mouth curled up. "Was it good for you?"

"No." She scowled at him. "It's like having a pesky mosquito in my head."

"Damned bloodsuckers. I hate them."

"Isn't that the pot calling the kettle black?"

He smiled slowly and leaned closer to her. "I need to touch you. Now."

She gulped. "I . . . but . . ."

"On your head," he explained, still smiling. "I can make a stronger connection that way."

"Oh." She recalled how he had touched Megan's head in order to release her suppressed memories. "I guess that will be all right."

Her heart speeded up when he sat on the bed beside her. Icy currents swirled around her, brushing against her skin and raising goose bumps. She shivered.

He rested a hand on top of her hand. "Concentrate."

She closed her eyes, and the buzzing returned. It was deep and masculine now. It ricocheted from one ear to the other, a jumble of words that she couldn't isolate. The harder she tried, the more her temples throbbed.

"Can you hear me?" he whispered.

She shook her head.

His fingers tightened their grip, digging into her scalp. A sudden burst of pain stabbed like an icy dagger between her eyes. With a gasp, she fell back and broke contact.

"Ow." She rubbed her brow. "What the hell was that?"

"I used too much power. I'm sorry."

"It's just a headache." She massaged her throbbing temples. "It'll be worth it if this helps keep me alive."

"I would do anything to keep you alive."

"That makes two of us." She scooted back on the bed so she could rest her back against the wall. She closed her eyes and breathed deeply, willing the pain in her head to subside.

I'm still in love with you.

Her eyes flew open. "We shouldn't talk about that."

"I didn't say anything."

"But . . ." She could have sworn she'd heard him speak. Had it been wishful thinking? She caught her breath when she realized what had happened.

She'd heard his thoughts. He was still in love with her! Before she could think of a response, her mind filled with static. The throbbing increased, then she heard a few words.

. . . hear me?

"I heard the end of that." She gave him a wary look. "Can you hear *my* thoughts?"

He shook his head slightly. "Not very well. I mostly feel your pain."

"Oh, sorry." Though she was greatly relieved that he couldn't read her mind. She sure didn't want him to know that she still loved him. *Don't even think that. Think about pink elephants.* She winced as a damned elephant galloped across her brain.

At least the cold air had dissipated. That had to mean that Jack had stopped trying to communicate with her telepathically.

She motioned toward her desk. "I have some aspirin in my handbag."

Apparently, he could take a hint. He jumped up and passed the bag to her. "Do you need anything to drink?"

"Yes. There's a vending machine down the hall."

"I'll be right back." He left the room.

"Aargh." Lara collapsed on the bed. His incredible thought kept echoing in her aching head. *I'm still in love with you.* What was she going to do? The most wonderful man on earth loved her, but he was a vampire.

Her reclining position made her head hurt even worse, so she sat back up. She retrieved the aspirin bottle from her handbag and struggled with the child-proof cap. Dammit. She'd be able to do this if her hands weren't shaking. *I'm still in love with you.*

Jack slipped back into her room, carrying a diet cola and bottled water. "I didn't know which one you'd want."

The world was a bizarre place when the most considerate man she'd ever met was a vampire. "I'll take the water. Thanks." She popped two aspirin in her mouth and drank.

He set the cola on her desk, then sat in the chair.

Lara rested her head against the wall. *Talk about something safe.* "So . . . do vampires ever get sick?"

"It hurts like hell if we're deprived of blood," he answered quietly. "We can be poisoned, burned, or wounded, but we usually heal during our death-sleep."

"Death-sleep?" She grimaced, then stopped because it hurt too much. "You're actually *dead* when you sleep?"

He gave her a wry look. "That's why we're called the Undead."

She shuddered. No wonder he'd never returned her calls during the day. He wasn't being rude, just dead. As far as excuses went, it was pretty good, but she hated to think of him as dead. "Are you fully alive now?"

His mouth thinned with annoyance. "You've heard my heartbeat. I'm as alive as any mortal right now. And, in case you've forgotten, I'm fully functional."

She looked away to keep from glancing at his jeans. She'd felt an erection there several times. Time to change the subject. "So . . . are you really the son of Casanova?"

His frown deepened. "Yes."

She'd fallen for a real Casanova. "Why don't you use the Casanova name?"

He shifted in his chair. "Are you feeling any better now?"

"Not really." She wondered why he'd changed the subject. "You didn't answer—" She stopped when he suddenly removed one of her athletic shoes. "What are you doing?"

He pulled off the other shoe, then removed her socks. "You're in pain. I want to help you relax." He scooted the chair forward so he could rest her feet in his lap.

She stifled a moan when his thumbs pressed into the soles of her feet. It felt so good. Her feet had been sore from wandering all over campus to check the residence halls for Apollo's flyer. "Have you ever had trouble before? I mean, invading someone's mind?"

"No. You're the only one." He tugged gently on her toes. "I think it has something to do with the car accident you were in."

She winced. "You know about that?"

He nodded and turned his attention to her other foot. "I read a newspaper article about it online. I'm very sorry for the suffering you endured."

"Thanks." Her current suffering was actually declining. Jack's foot massage was doing wonders. *He could do more than your feet.* She chased that errant thought away. Thank God he wasn't reading her mind right now. "I was in a coma for a week. They didn't think I'd make it."

Jack continued the massage. "You're a fighter. I admire that about you."

He admired her? That felt even better than the foot massage. And the massage was damned good. "The accident changed my life. It nearly killed me, but in a weird way, it was the best thing that could have happened to me."

His hands stilled. "How can that be?"

She gave him a wry smile. "It ruined my mother's plans for world domination. She wanted me to be Miss Louisiana, then Miss USA, and then of course, Miss Universe."

He resumed the massage. "That's not what you wanted?"

"I didn't know any better. As soon as I could walk, my mother was entering me in pageants. At the age of four, I won the prestigious title of Little Miss Mudbug."

He grimaced. "Mudbug?"

"It's a crawdad." When Jack still looked confused, she waved a hand in dismissal. "It doesn't matter. Suffice it to say, my mom is crazy. She's fifty-two years old and still entering pageants. If she can't find one to enter, she invents one, like Miss NOLA Plus Size. She'll actually wear a sash and tiara to go shopping."

"How . . . odd." Jack slipped a hand into her loose cargo pants and massaged her calf.

Lara sighed with pleasure. Her legs had been sore ever since the FBI had tried to kill her with marathon exercise sessions. She wondered why she was telling Jack her life story, but he was such a good listener, not to mention massage therapist, that she didn't want to stop.

"Mom was so excited when I won Miss Teen Louisiana. But after fourteen years of entering pageants, I wanted to quit. Mom would go ballistic every time I even mentioned quitting. So I made sure my pageant career was ruined."

Jack switched to her other calf. "What did you do?"

"When I was nineteen, I was a finalist in the Miss Louisiana competition. They did the part where they ask you a question onstage. It's usually something like, What change would you like to see in the world? and the usual answer is, 'World peace.' "

Jack smiled. "What did you say?"

"That I wanted to increase the use of capital punishment. I thought it would be great fun to bring the whole community together for a nice, old-fashioned hanging."

Jack chuckled. "Naughty girl."

Lara grinned. "You should have seen the judges' faces. My mother actually screamed. Obviously, I placed fifth out of the five finalists. My mother was hysterical. She insisted it was too embarrassing to be seen at the hotel. So we drove home that night."

Jack's hands grew still. "Is that when it happened?"

Lara nodded. "It was dark. And we were so busy arguing, we didn't see the truck." She closed her eyes, thankful she couldn't remember the actual accident.

The bed jiggled, and she opened her eyes.

Jack was settling on the bed beside her. "It must have been terrifying."

She nodded. "Mom had multiple fractures. I broke an arm. And I took a bad blow to the head."

"I'm so sorry." Jack stroked her hair that now covered the scars.

Lara's eyes misted with tears. "The first thing I heard when I came out of the coma was my mother talking to my dad. She said thank God it was my head that was damaged and not my face."

Jack sucked in a sharp breath. "*Cara mia*, that is terrible."

"I knew right then that I could never enter another pageant. I wanted to use my head and not my face." Lara blinked back the tears. "Unfortunately, my head wasn't working too well. I couldn't remember how to read and write."

Jack leaned closer. "You had to learn all over again?"

She nodded. "LaToya was sharing the hospital room with me. That's how we met. She'd been working at a convenience store when an armed robber came in. She took a bullet to the shoulder. We were already in physical therapy together, so we decided to exercise our minds together, too. Her reading skills weren't so hot, but they were a lot better than mine, and it made her feel good to help me. And she said if I could work my ass off, then so could she."

Jack smiled. "That's how you became best friends."

"Yes. We worked together every day, and after a few months, we were reading Nancy Drew books to each other and solving the mysteries. Then we progressed to harder and harder books, till finally, we decided we wanted to be detectives and catch the bad guys. Make the world a better place. So here we are today."

"You're amazing," Jack whispered. "I've never met a woman as amazing as you." He took her hand and kissed it.

Her skin tingled where his lips had touched. He turned her hand over and kissed her palm. The tingles spread from her hand up her arm to her breasts.

When he lifted his gaze and met hers, his eyes were

brown and warm with love. No gleaming gold flecks, she realized. No vampire power being used to lure her in. Only love.

And she wanted it so badly.

His gaze lowered to her mouth. If she didn't stop him now, she'd never be able to resist.

She pulled her hand from his grasp and scooted to the edge of the bed. "Well, I think we did enough for the night. My head's too sore to do any more."

"I understand." Jack stood and slowly put his jacket back on. "I'm honored that you would share your story with me, but I have to wonder why. Maybe you didn't realize it, but it makes me want to be with you more than ever. Did you mean to encourage me?"

She gulped. "I—I think we could be friends. Maybe."

"You could be friends with a vampire?"

She looked down and plucked at the chenille bedspread. "I don't want to be . . . judgmental. You don't seem like a very bad vampire."

"Gee, thanks."

Her cheeks grew warm. "It occurred to me that you might have been attacked and changed against your will." She glanced at him with a hopeful look. "Is that what happened?" *Please tell me you didn't want to be a monster.*

He dragged a hand through his hair. "I'd rather not talk about it, but yes. I was attacked." He shifted his weight. "Shall we continue tomorrow night?"

He'd changed the subject. Maybe he was trying to spare her some gruesome details. After all, she assumed he must have been murdered. Sorta. She wasn't quite sure how vampires were made. But she was fairly certain it had not been at all pleasant for him. Poor Jack. "Yes. Let's meet tomorrow night. I think we made some progress."

He smiled. "Yes, I think we did." He disappeared.

Lara sighed. The man was far too tempting. But far too different. Did she really want to be a part of his world? Did she want a boyfriend who was dead during the day and could live forever without getting older? Where would that leave her? As far as she could tell, she had two options with Jack. She could grow older and end up alone, forgotten, and heartbroken. Or she could stay with him forever as a vampire.

She shuddered. How could she do that? How could she be a police detective if she was a vampire? How could she give up daylight and good food and chocolate? How could she tell her family? How could she have a family?

No, she was going to have to be sensible about this. Jack would make an interesting friend. But no more than that.

She would have to love him at a distance.

Chapter Twenty

*J*ack arrived at Romatech in a good mood. Lara had heard his psychic voice, and she knew that he still loved her. The meeting had started off a bit awkward, but by the end of it, she'd allowed him to touch her and comfort her. She'd shared important moments from her past. She'd offered her friendship. That had to mean she was willing to trust him. In time, their relationship could grow into something deeper. She was such an amazing woman. So strong, brave, clever, and beautiful. There was no doubt in his mind that Lara was the one for him.

But she was still in danger. His happy mood evaporated as he strode toward the MacKay security office. A month had gone by with nothing to show for it but one botched attempt after another to find Apollo. Jack's muscles tensed and his hands curled into fists. When it came to his work as an investigator, he was not accustomed to failure.

He grudgingly admitted that so far they had failed

to find Casimir. But the wily Malcontent leader stayed constantly on the move. This Apollo had a base. He was staying put. It was ridiculous that they couldn't locate the bastard.

Jack entered the office and found Phil sitting at the desk, studying something on the computer. "Where is everybody?"

Phil didn't even blink at the anger in Jack's voice. "I guess your meeting didn't go well?"

"It went fine, but we're running out of time. Where is everybody?"

"Robby's still chasing leads in Europe. He said he'd probably crash at your place."

"Fine." Jack always offered his *palazzo* as a sanctuary for Vamp friends who were traveling. "And Connor?"

"Connor and Phineas are investigating a place in Ohio," Phil continued. "And I've been scouring the Internet for any place that mentions Apollo or a sun god."

Jack paced across the office. "How many false leads have we followed?"

"Over a hundred," Phil muttered.

Jack slammed a fist against the chain-link cage that housed their weapons. "It shouldn't be this damned hard. There are Vamps all over the world. Why can't we find this one sick bastard?"

Phil leaned back in the chair, frowning. "I have a theory about that."

"To hell with theories. I need results!" Jack paced toward the door. *Merda.* He needed to get a grip. Anger was not going to help Lara. "Okay, what's the damned theory?"

"Well, now that you ask," Phil began with a wry twist to his mouth. "I've noticed over the years that Vamps tend to live in well-populated areas. Of course, in the past, you probably wanted to be close to your food source, and the more people who were available to bite, the less likely you were to be noticed."

Jack kept pacing. "Go on."

"You like to hang out with each other, too. And party a lot. It's been hard on Jean-Luc, going into hiding in the countryside. I think he'd be crazy by now if it weren't for Heather and her family. I know it's been tough on Robby."

Jack nodded. "And your point is?"

"If Apollo's resort is far away from any city or towns, then there aren't any Vamps around to notice it. Not many mortals around, either. That's why Apollo kidnaps people. He has no other food supply."

Jack sighed. Phil was probably right, but it made their chances of finding Apollo sound hopeless.

Phil leaned forward, propping his elbows on the desk. "Now shifters are completely the opposite. They avoid civilization. We enjoy roaming the more remote areas of the world."

Jack halted. "You think a wolf pack could find Apollo?"

"I think it's worth a shot. I could ask the Pack Masters across the country to help us." Phil frowned. "I offered to do it last night, but Connor didn't like the idea. He didn't want to involve the werewolves in Vamp business."

Jack resumed his pacing. He understood Connor's reaction. For centuries, the vampires and shape shifters had coexisted with a tense attitude of mutual distrust. They stayed away from each other, wary that another species knew of their existence. Angus had tried to breach the gap by offering shifters high-paying positions of trust.

Even so, Jack knew that most of the shifter employees at MacKay S & I were considered traitors to their own kind. Howard fared better since male bears tended to be loners. But Phil was a wolf and expected to be a member of a pack. A rogue wolf was a bizarre and dangerous phenomenon.

"Would the werewolves help us?" Jack asked.

"They might." Phil dragged a hand through his shaggy brown hair. "The truth is, they would like to have you indebted to them."

"Ah." That was why Connor had refused. He didn't want to owe any favors to a pack of wolves. But Jack was desperate enough to make a deal with the devil if he had to. "Ask them to help. Any debt incurred will be mine."

"Can you hear me now?" Jack asked again. It was Wednesday night, and this was his third session with Lara.

"Just a few words here and there." She sighed. "This is so frustrating."

"Tell me about it," Jack muttered. He'd had high hopes for the meeting on Tuesday, but it had ended after only ten minutes because it made Lara's head hurt too much. He knew she was in pain, for he could feel it, too, and he hated being the one who caused it.

"Do you need an aspirin?" he asked.

"I took one before you came." She massaged her temples. "It's either kicked in already, or I'm getting better at this. The pain is not as bad tonight."

"That's good. Your brain could be adjusting." He settled on the bed beside her. She didn't give him that wary, skittish look, so he took that as another good sign. She was adjusting to him, personally.

He believed he was slowly regaining her trust. He

wanted more. He wanted her love, but he could be patient.

He had a few new leads to check out later tonight. A western wolf pack had spotted two isolated mortal compounds in Nevada and Utah. He doubted either place would pan out. They were so far away, and they'd been described as log cabins. But still, he was desperate enough to look anywhere.

"I can't let you do this, Lara. Apollo could teleport you anywhere, and I'd never be able to find you."

She frowned. "I'll be wearing a tracking device. I'm getting it tomorrow."

"Tracking devices can be lost."

"The FBI is aware of that. They have something special planned." She gave him a stern look. "This *is* going to happen, Jack."

"No, it's not. I can't let you do it, so I have an alternative plan. When Apollo shows up for the seminar, Robby and I will grab him and teleport him to Romatech. We'll hold him prisoner in the silver room there."

Her frown deepened. "What about the other girls? We have to know where he's keeping them."

"We'll make him tell us."

She winced. "How?"

"Depriving him of blood might do the trick. Or we can try taking over his mind."

She was silent for a while, thinking it over. "Your plan might work, but how do we explain it to the police and FBI?"

"We don't. We erase their memories." When she started to object, he continued, "We have no choice. Whether we teleport Apollo away, or he teleports you away, that's still more than we can let any mortals see. We sure can't allow them to discover Apollo's resort.

If we find the girls, we'll send them home with their memories altered. We have to protect the secret of vampire existence."

Lara scooted off the bed and paced toward the door. She spun around and shot him an angry look. "If you have your way, no one will remember anything. What about making Apollo pay for his crimes?"

"Believe me, he will pay."

She planted her hands on her hips. "What about all my hard work? It would all be for nothing."

"You'll be alive. I wouldn't call that nothing."

She glowered at him. "I trained a month for this assignment. I can handle it."

"I will not let that bastard kidnap you. I'll do anything to protect you."

Her eyes narrowed. "It sounds to me like you're more concerned with protecting the precious vampire secret."

He clenched his jaw. "That *is* important, but nothing is more important to me than protecting you." *My life would be meaningless without you. I love you too damned much.*

She gasped. "Don't say that."

He stood. "Did you hear my thoughts?"

"Oh my gosh." She touched her forehead.

I want to throw you on the bed and strip your clothes off.

"Stop that." She glared at him.

He smiled. "You *are* hearing me."

"Uh, maybe." She rubbed her brow. "Just a little."

I'm going to nibble on your little toes, then kiss my way up your long, luscious legs until I reach—

"Enough!" Her cheeks blushed pink.

"But I was just getting to the good part."

She shook her head. "I'm trying to have a decent

argument with you, and you're describing an X-rated movie in my head."

Jack glanced at her bed. "We could make it real."

"I have a headache." She folded her arms across her chest. "I think you should go."

"Lara—"

"And I don't need to see you till after it's all over. We can call the lessons a big success. Thanks to you, I'll be able to hear Apollo's every little perverted thought."

Jack frowned at her. He had to try one more thing, just to be sure. He hurtled a wave of cold psychic energy at her, and she stumbled back. *I am your master, and you will obey. Take off your clothes now.*

She snorted. "In your dreams."

He stepped toward her, ratcheting up the power. *You are under my control. You will make love to me.*

Her eyes flashed with anger. "Get out, now!"

He took a deep breath and let the power fade away. "*Brava, bellissima.* You can hear, but you can still resist vampire control. That is very good news."

She eyed him warily. "That was just a test?"

He nodded. "I needed to make sure."

She looked away, but not before Jack noted the tears in her eyes. "You told me once that you would never use your powers to get me in bed. I thought you had betrayed your promise."

"Lara, I would never force you or manipulate you. It is true that I . . . long to have you in my bed, but more than anything, I want to have your love. Given freely."

"I can't do that," she whispered.

He paced toward the desk with despair settling heavily in his chest. What if he could never win her heart? He couldn't make her love him. But no matter what, he would keep her safe. "I will not let Apollo kidnap you."

She was still turned away from him, her arms crossed and her shoulders hunched over.

Merda, this was hurting her as much as him. "Goodbye, Lara." He teleported away.

"There's no point in meeting tonight," she told Jack when he called her Thursday night. "I appreciate you helping me, but it's done, and don't you dare teleport here while I'm talking."

Merda. She knew him too well. "Our plan is on for Saturday night. We're kidnapping Apollo."

"No, you're not! Jack, I'm serious. You will stay out of this."

"Have you seen a flyer yet? Is Apollo coming to Syracuse?"

"I'm not discussing this with you. I swear, if I see you or any of your friends here, I'll have you arrested."

"Lara—" The long beep indicated that she'd hung up on him. Stubborn woman. Well, he could be just as stubborn.

He spent the next few hours with Phineas, investigating a compound in Colorado that a wolf pack had reported. It turned out to be a survivalist training camp. When they returned to Romatech, Robby had arrived from Europe. Jack called a meeting to discuss their plans for Saturday night.

At three-thirty in the morning, he teleported into Lara's dorm room. Since he'd teleported there before, the location was embedded in his psychic memory. With his superior vision, he spotted her in the dark room. She was in bed, sound asleep, just as he had hoped.

He moved silently toward the door. He hadn't come to see her, but to check if Apollo had posted his flyer downstairs in the lounge.

A high-pitched beep sounded in his ears, very faint. He waited, and it beeped again. It was strange. He almost sensed it more than heard it. It was a repeating pulse of energy. He glanced at the bed.

It was coming from Lara.

He eased toward her. The FBI must have put the tracer on her. *Merda*. If he could hear the damned thing, Apollo would, too. He would know the mortal authorities were after him. He'd be tempted to kill Lara immediately.

Jack leaned over, trying to zero in on the homing device. She wasn't wearing a necklace. No earrings. Was it under her skin?

She moaned and turned on her side, facing the wall. Her hair spilled across the white pillowcase—thick, wavy, and . . . beeping. He gently touched the strands. Soft and silky. Wait. This felt different. Harsh and foreign. He stroked her hair again to be sure. He'd have to cut the fake hair off before Saturday.

"Mmm." She moaned and turned onto her back.

He stifled a groan. Her thin T-shirt left little to the imagination. He could see the round fullness of her breasts, the plump nipples begging to be coaxed into hardened tips. It would be so easy to slip into her mind and give her a round of vampire sex she'd never forget. She'd enjoy it so much, she'd beg him for the real thing.

But he'd promised not to use his vampire powers to get into her bed. *Merda*. Life would be easier if he could be a scoundrel like his father.

"Jack," she murmured.

He caught his breath. The heaviness in his heart lifted slightly. Maybe there was still a chance. *Don't give up on me, Lara. I will always love you.*

He slipped into the hall and zoomed toward the elevator. On the first floor, he located the bulletin board, and there it was. A pink flyer. *Do you want to stay young and beautiful forever?*

He phoned the security office at Romatech. "We've got him."

Chapter Twenty-one

Lara couldn't shake the feeling that she was a lamb going to slaughter. The two special agents assured her she was perfectly safe. They claimed the electronic tracking device in her hair weave was absolutely foolproof.

Could fools possibly work for the government? Somehow, Lara didn't feel so secure. It would be just her luck if Apollo decided all of a sudden that bald women were hot and had her head completely shaved.

Besides, how could she be safe with a vampire abductor? All her martial-arts training wouldn't help her against his superior vampire strength and speed. If he tried to rape her or kill her, would she be able to stop him?

As Saturday night arrived, her stomach clenched into knots. The two FBI guys were the only ones who were going to be at the student services building. They didn't want a big police presence there in case it scared Apollo off.

She paced in her dorm room. She glanced at the clock. Eight P.M. The FBI guys would be at the student services building soon. She was supposed to stroll in on her own, pretending not to know them. She was supposed to walk right into Room 102 and get herself kidnapped.

Not a problem, they'd said. The device in her hair weave could be picked up by satellite. They could find her anywhere in the world. She stopped pacing, with a chilling thought. They'd be able to track her even if she was dead.

"Hello, Lara."

With a gasp, she whirled around. "Dammit, Jack. What did I tell you about sneaking up on people?"

He smiled. "Feeling a little tense, *bellissima?*"

"This isn't funny, Jack." She didn't know whether to strangle the handsome rascal or throw herself into his arms. She'd told him not to come by till it was all over, but she was so glad to see him. He, at least, truly cared about her. With the FBI, she was starting to feel like an expendable crew member.

He looked her over. "Are you all right?"

"I'm great," she lied. "What are you doing here?" *And how dare you look so sexy, all dressed in black?*

"We're going ahead with our plans tonight."

She decided to go ahead and strangle him. "I told you to stay out of this."

"We have no choice, Lara. We thought we would find Apollo before tonight, but we didn't. Tonight, we know exactly where he'll be, so we have to do it. It's the best solution all around."

He must have seen the pink flyers. She frowned at him. "You just want to keep your vampire secret safe."

"And *you* safe. No one is more important to me than you."

She didn't want to admit how much she loved hearing him say that. And she wasn't really opposed to staying safe. She just found it irritating the way he breezed in and announced he was taking over. "I don't see how your plan can work. Too many people know about this case."

"It's already working. Connor and Robby are at the twenty-sixth precinct right now. Between the two of them, they can easily take over a hundred minds at once. They'll erase every thought of Apollo and every trace of him on paper or computer."

This irritated her even more. Vampires found human minds so easy to manipulate that they could do a *hundred* at a time? "The FBI knows, too."

"Connor is headed there next." Jack shrugged one shoulder. "We've done this sort of thing many times over the centuries. We know what we're doing."

Lara had no doubt that his vampire friends could pull it off. She'd seen how well Jack had erased all signs of the party at the Plaza hotel.

"Before we take Apollo, there's one loose end I need to take care of." He stepped toward her.

She moved back, bumping against the desk. "Don't you dare erase *my* memories."

He paused. "I wouldn't even try. I want you to remember Venice, and remember us."

Her heart squeezed in her chest. She didn't want to forget, either.

He removed a pair of scissors from his jacket pocket. "The problem is your hair. Or rather, the hair that isn't yours."

"What?" How could he tell? The expert from the FBI had matched her color perfectly.

Jack stepped closer. "I'll feel much better once the fake hair is removed. Just to be safe."

She smoothed her hand over the false lock of hair. "It's my only link to the FBI."

"You don't need it, Lara. You're not going anywhere. And once we're done with the FBI, they won't know they're supposed to track you. They won't remember who you are."

She winced. "You're completely taking over, whether I like it or not. I thought you were my friend."

He frowned. "I am your friend. I can hear the device, Lara. I can sense the electronic pulses. And if I can feel it, Apollo can, too."

Her skin chilled. My God, how close had she come to walking into a death trap?

"I would have cut it off earlier, but I didn't want to alert the FBI." Jack grabbed the lock of synthetic hair and snipped it off. He tossed it on the bed along with the scissors, then pulled her into his arms.

She stiffened. "What are you doing?"

"Making sure I got it all." He nuzzled his face in her hair. "Your heart is racing."

"You . . . you surprised me."

He grazed a hand over her hair. "I know you're angry. I hope you can forgive me someday."

A part of her wanted to melt against him and thank him for rescuing her from a dangerous assignment, but another part was still annoyed that he'd taken control against her wishes. "You had better find those missing girls."

"We will." He kissed her brow. "Tell your roommate not to speak to anyone about this. You're the only two who will remember."

Lara exhaled with relief. They would leave LaToya alone.

Jack released her and stepped back. "It's over for you now, *bellissima*. You can go home." He vanished.

She stared at the space he'd just vacated. "Are you kidding?" She couldn't leave now. She wanted to see this Apollo creep get captured.

Fifteen minutes later, she strode into the student services building. She passed the food court and headed for the meeting rooms. As she neared the end of the main hall, she heard Jack's voice in her head.

You will return to your offices. You will have no memory of being here at Syracuse. You will have no memory of Apollo or any of his victims.

Lara peeked around the corner and saw Jack with the two FBI guys. She looked to the right and spotted Room 102. Robby was sitting at the end of the hall in a chair, pretending to read a newspaper. He'd traded in his kilt for a ragged pair of jeans.

She glanced back to the left. Jack had finished with the two FBI guys and was talking to a young black man. Another vampire?

The FBI guys strolled toward her, and she retreated to study a vending machine. As the two special agents rounded the corner, she glanced their way with a smile. They nodded and kept going. No recognition in their faces at all. Damn. It looked like the FBI and the police were officially off the case.

The black guy came around the corner and looked her over as he passed by. He must not know who she was, because he made no attempt to talk to her. He took a seat at the food court, apparently watching the front and side doors.

Lara's heart rate speeded up. Any minute now, Apollo would saunter through one of those doors. Unless he teleported in closer to the room. But Robby and Jack were both in the hallway, so they should see him.

A group of girls strolled past her, laughing and talking. Three brunettes and a blonde. One of the brunettes was holding a pink flyer in her hand. They reached the end of the main hall and turned right. Lara assumed they were headed for Room 102, but they should be safe. They all possessed the wrong hair color.

"Hey, are you going to the seminar?"

Lara turned to see another young woman clutching a pink flyer in a well-manicured hand.

The young woman smiled. "It might be fun."

Lara's stomach lurched. The girl's hair was bright red. Oh God, no. The FBI guys had planned to stop any other redheads from going into the seminar. But they weren't here to stop this girl. "I—I don't think it's worth going to. I figure they're just trying to sell us something, you know?"

The pretty redhead shrugged. "Well, I heard we might get some free samples. And they're giving away a big prize." She strode down the hall and turned right.

Lara groaned inwardly. What if Jack and his friends missed Apollo? As a vampire, he would be super fast. He might teleport away. And take that redheaded girl with him.

Damn. She had to get that girl out of there. She marched down the hall and turned right. The redhead had already disappeared inside Room 102.

Lara was not surprised when Jack grabbed her arm.

"What are you doing here?" he whispered. "I told you to go home."

"And what on earth led you to believe that I would obey?"

He blinked. He opened his mouth to respond, then closed it with a confused look.

Lara smiled. She'd actually rendered him speechless. "A redheaded woman just went into the room. I'm going to get her out."

With a frown, Jack released her. "All right, but be quick about it. It's almost nine."

"I will. And try not to look so conspicuous. You look more like a macho, he-man warrior than a college student."

Jack's eyes lit up. "I do?"

She shook her head as she entered Room 102. There was a giant screen set up at one end. About eight rows of chairs faced the screen. Most of the seats were empty. Two clusters of girls sat in the first four rows. They were busy talking to one another and barely noticed her. Not a redhead among them.

The redhead she'd seen earlier was sitting in the back by herself.

She smiled as Lara approached. "I'm glad you came. You want a seat?" She touched the chair beside her.

"Thanks." Lara sat, wondering how she would get this girl out of the room. Maybe she could yell *fire*?

"I'm Thina," the redhead said. "Weird name, I know. I just transferred here from Utica."

"I'm new here, too," Lara said. "And I'm starving. How about we grab something to eat at the food court?"

"That sounds good." Thina stood, then glanced toward the screen. "Oops, looks like it's starting."

Lara rose to her feet as she saw someone step around the screen. A tall, handsome man with short blond hair and very blue eyes. *Apollo*. He was carrying a laptop.

"Wow," Thina whispered.

The girls in the room were too busy admiring Apollo to notice that he'd never actually entered the room. He must have teleported in behind the screen. And that meant Jack and Robby were not aware that he had arrived.

He strode to a side table and set down his laptop.

Lara assumed he had his PowerPoint demonstration on it.

A wave of cold air swept across the room.

I am Apollo, and you will obey. His sharp blue gaze drifted over the girls in the first four rows, then zeroed in on her and Thina. He smiled.

Lara gulped. "Let's get out of here."

A flash of movement zoomed through the door. Lara exhaled with relief as Robby dashed toward Apollo. Jack was close behind. He turned to make sure she was okay, but in that tiny millisecond, Apollo grabbed his laptop and teleported away.

"No!" Robby shouted.

Lara gasped. It had all happened so fast. She'd barely realized that Jack had failed when an iron grip seized her arm.

"What—?" She pulled, but the grip was too strong. Super strong, like a vampire. Oh God, no. Apollo had an accomplice.

"Let's go," Thina whispered.

Lara heard Jack's shout just before everything went black.

Lara stumbled as her feet landed on a solid floor, and she used her body's momentum to pull away from Thina's grasp. She jumped back, poised and ready to fight. She had to assume Thina was a biter.

Thankfully, Thina didn't pounce. She merely looked down her nose at Lara like she'd smelled something foul.

That was fine by Lara. While Thina was busy with her snooty act, she had time to scan the surroundings.

Small room. White walls. Two male guards by the door, holding swords. Bad news. They both had the deadpan expressions that signified they were under vampire control. Really bad news. Their skimpy white togas showed off their waxed chests and legs. There was only one door. No windows. Nothing lying around that she could use as a weapon. So much for escaping right off the bat.

"You are braver than most mortals," Thina sneered. "Most are on their knees by now, crying for their mothers."

Lara gulped. In her determination to stay alive, she'd forgotten she was supposed to act scared and clueless. She affected a frightened look. "Oh my God! What did you do to me? Where are we?"

Thina smiled, apparently pleased by the show of fear. "All will be revealed in time to those who are deemed worthy."

Lara wanted to jam a foot into Thina's smug smile. "Could you be a little more specific?" She turned to the two guards. "Oh, I get it. This is a frat party! Wow, great togas! Why don't you bring us some beers?"

"Silence!" Thina ordered. "Kneel before me."

Lara glanced at the two hunky guards. "You heard the lady. Down on your knees." She winked. "Let's see what you can do."

"Enough, maiden!" Thina's eyes flashed with anger.

Lara tilted her head with a confused look. "Were you talking to me?"

A blast of cold air hit Lara hard, and she stumbled back. Invisible icicles jabbed at her head. To stay alive, she would have to play along and pretend she was under control. She cleared her face. She would have to behave like the guards, and not show any emotion at all.

Thina walked up to her and slapped her across the face.

Lara stood still, trying hard not to show any pain

or surprise. Still, her eyes watered a bit. She couldn't help it.

Thina smiled. "That's more like it. Now kneel before me. Bow down to the floor."

Lara fell to her knees and leaned forward till her forehead touched the cold stone floor. This was better actually. Her face was hidden this way.

"I am Athena, daughter of Zeus and goddess of wisdom. You will address me as All Wise Athena."

Lara wrinkled her nose. Was this lady serious? She certainly had a healthy ego.

You will obey me in all things. Respond to me now.

"Yes," Lara answered. She gritted her teeth. "All Wise Athena." Thank God Jack had taught her how to hear psychic vampire voices.

The full depth of her situation washed over her. She was so screwed. She had no tracers on her. The FBI and police didn't even know to look for her.

Jack would look for her. He would be frantic, looking for her. She winced, imagining how upset Jack must be. She should've stayed out of the room. She'd made a big mistake, trying to be noble.

Well, she would make up for it. The FBI had given her plenty of training in how to effectively manage an escape. She didn't need a knight in shining armor, or a vampire in tarnished armor, to charge to the rescue. She'd get herself out of this mess. She hoped.

"You will obey Apollo in all things," Athena announced. "You will address him as My Lord Apollo."

"Yes, All Wise Athena," Lara murmured.

"When a guard gives you an order, you will obey and answer, 'Yes, master.'"

"Yes, All Wise Athena." What a fun resort this was. Maybe she could at least get a good wax job like the guards. Another blast of cold air swept over Lara, causing her arms to prickle with goose bumps.

Athena's voice reverberated in her head. *I will now bestow a small measure of my wisdom upon you.*

Oh, goody. Lara hoped this wouldn't take long. Her knees were starting to ache. The floor was hard as a rock. Actually, it was rock. Marble, maybe. White and spotless.

"I have rescued you from the mortal plane of existence," Athena announced. "You may thank me now."

Lara rolled her eyes. "Thank you, All Wise Athena." Goddess of Baggy Underwear. She slapped herself mentally. She needed to be more careful with her thoughts, just in case Athena could overhear her. *Athena is awesome.*

"I have brought you to the Elysian Fields," Athena continued. "The mortal realm is closed off to you. You can never return to Earth. Do you understand?"

"Yes, All Wise Athena." *You are such a cool goddess.*

"If you attempt to leave this place, you will find yourself in Hades, a land of eternal torment. If you displease me or Apollo, you will be sent to Hades. Do you wish to spend eternity in hell?"

"No, All Wise Athena." So that was how they got the other girls to stay without attempting an escape. The girls actually believed there was no way back to Earth, and they lived in fear of going to hell.

"You are now a maiden. You have no name. You are here to serve the gods. That is your sole purpose."

Lara gulped. She could guess how Apollo wanted to be served. A little bed and breakfast, with her as the menu. She wasn't going to be getting manicures and massages. This wasn't a resort. Or a spa.

It was a bizarre vampire cult.

Chapter Twenty-two

$\mathcal{J}$ack slammed a fist through the back wall of Room 102. The college girls screamed and huddled together.

Robby grabbed his arm. "Go back to Romatech. Now. I'll clean up here."

Jack pulled away. "I failed her! How could I fail her?"

"Get a grip, Jack." Robby glanced at the doorway as Phineas dashed in. "Phineas, take him back to Romatech."

"I'm not leaving," Jack growled.

Robby seized him by the shoulder. "*She's no' here.*" His face softened. "We'll find her, Jack."

"Oh, shit." Phineas approached them. "Apollo's got—"

"Yes, he does," Robby interrupted. "Now get Jack out of here. I'll be along shortly."

"I don't need a babysitter." Jack teleported away. He arrived on the grounds at Romatech and ripped a branch off an unsuspecting tree.

Phineas ducked as the branch flew over his head. "Dude, I'm sorry. We're gonna find her, you know."

Jack stalked toward the Romatech entrance. "I'm going to rip Apollo apart." He fumbled in his pockets for his ID card. *Merda*. His hands were shaking.

"I got it, man." Phineas swiped his ID and activated the hand sensor.

Jack turned and gazed at the woods surrounding Romatech. Lara could be anywhere. *Lara! Lara, can you hear me?*

"Whoa! That was loud." Phineas held open the door. "How far can a psychic message go?"

"No more than a hundred miles or so." Jack closed his eyes and concentrated. Nothing. She couldn't hear him.

How could he fail her? After all his promises to keep her safe, he'd failed her. His heart twisted with fear. *Stay alive, Lara. Stay alive till I can find you.*

It was happening all over again. He'd failed his first love, Beatrice. He hadn't been there for her, and she'd died, thinking he'd abandoned her. And now he wasn't there for Lara.

Robby appeared. "I altered the lassies' memories, but there wasn't much I could do about the hole in the wall." He strode toward them. "We'll find her, Jack."

"Yeah, we will," Phineas agreed. "She's gonna be all right, dude."

Jack wondered if prayers could be heard from the ninth circle of hell.

Lara was still kneeling on the hard marble floor. She tried to take her mind off her fear and aching knees by remembering her lessons on escape. First, she needed to gather information. She couldn't decide where to escape to until she knew where she was.

She would have to stay out of trouble, and hopefully, remain unbitten so she could keep her strength up. She needed to look for anything that could be used as a weapon. She needed a means of communicating with the outside world. And she needed to assess the other prisoners here to see if any of them could become allies. The guards were out of the question. They looked completely brainwashed, and they were armed.

"Guards," Athena spoke. "You will fetch two maidens."

"Yes, All Wise Athena," they answered in unison.

Lara tilted her head a little so she could see. The guards opened the door and left. The sandals on the taller one made a high-pitched squeaky noise with every other step.

She heard different footsteps approaching.

"Athena." It was Apollo.

Lara swallowed hard. She hoped he wasn't hungry.

Athena glanced back at her. "Stay."

"Yes, All Wise Athena." *You're so wise and awesome.*

Athena walked outside the room. "Yes, My Lord Apollo?"

Lara strained to hear their conversation. They didn't bother to lower their voices very much. She guessed they didn't consider her much of a threat.

"Those two vampires nearly caught me," Apollo grumbled. "They looked really angry."

"They're probably some of those stupid, bottle-drinking Vamps," Athena hissed. "I swear I hate them and their self-righteous attitude, like they're so much better than us. We have every right to a fresh meal."

Lara grimaced. They made her feel like a whole meat patty minus the sesame-seed bun.

"I think they were expecting me," Apollo said. "We're going to have to find new hunting grounds."

"No problem," Athena answered. "There are colleges all over the Northeast."

Now that was interesting. They must be somewhere in the Northeast.

"At least this location is still secret," Apollo said. "They didn't follow us here, so they obviously don't know where we are. What about the new girl? Do you think she could be working with them?"

Athena laughed. "No way. She's even more foolish than the usual ones."

Lara rolled her eyes. Great. Well, she would continue to act clueless until she was ready to escape.

"Good," Apollo said. "Get her ready. I'm going to do the Selecting Ceremony in five minutes." He strode away.

Lara heard two female voices in the distance. "Greetings, My Lord Apollo."

"Come, maidens," Athena called to them. She returned to the room. "Rise, maiden."

Lara figured that was her. She rose stiffly to her feet and looked around. There was an electric light overhead. Fancy that. The Elysian Fields had electricity. These other girls were totally messed up with vampire control if they didn't realize they were still on Earth.

The room was bare except for a large wooden trunk and a bookcase filled with folded gowns. No books. Well, who needed books with All Wise Athena around?

Two redheaded young women rushed into the room. They bowed. "Greetings, All Wise Athena."

"We have returned early tonight with a new maiden," Athena said. "You will prepare her for the Selecting Ceremony, which will begin in five minutes." She strode from the room.

Lara recognized the two girls from the case photos. One was Vanessa Carlton, who had disappeared from

Columbia University in May. The other was Kristy Robinson, who had vanished from NYU in April. What a relief to see them both alive. "Hi, I'm Lara."

They winced and glanced toward the open door.

Vanessa quickly closed it. "You'll get in trouble if you use a name," she whispered. "We're maidens. We only get a name when we become a Chosen One."

Kristy clasped her hands together, grinning. "And one of us will be chosen tonight!"

"Oh boy." Lara attempted a smile.

"Hurry." Kristy dashed to the bookcase. "Take off everything but your underwear. We have to get you dressed." She plucked a folded white gown off the shelf and shook it out.

Lara inspected the two girls as she kicked off her shoes. They were both dressed in long white tunics that were clasped on the left shoulder, leaving the right shoulder bare. Two long strips of white linen were attached to the tunics beneath the arms. These strips were wrapped around, crossing the midriff in front and back, then tied off in front at the waist.

Lara pulled her T-shirt off, then removed her jeans. "Do you guys know where we are?"

"We're *maidens*," Kristy repeated. "Didn't All Wise Athena explain it to you?"

"She said something about the Elysian Fields." Lara pulled off her socks. "I don't suppose she means the Champs Elysées in Paris?"

The girls gave her blank looks.

"You know. France? You don't want to die without seeing Paris."

Vanessa's shoulders slumped. "It's too late for us. We can never go back." Her eyes filled with tears. "I miss my family and my friends."

"Don't cry," Kristy hissed at her. "If you look bad,

you'll never be chosen. Besides, you'll get to see your family again someday."

"Yeah." Vanessa frowned. "After they die."

"Why would you have to wait?" Lara asked. "We could just leave here and go home."

"We can't go home," Vanessa wailed. "We're *dead*!"

"Shhh." Kristy poked her. "They'll hear you. You know the gods have super hearing." She looked at Lara. "Whatever you do, don't make the gods angry."

"Why?" Lara asked. "What can they do to us?"

"They're *gods*," Vanessa whispered. "They can vanish and reappear. And they have super strength. I've seen them rip trees from the ground and throw boulders like they were pebbles. They can take over our minds and make us do whatever they want."

"That's true." Kristy nodded. "One time, a guard made Athena angry, and she made him slice himself with his own sword. And then, Apollo used his holy blood to heal him."

Vanessa shuddered. "If you make them really angry, they could send you to Hades forever."

"But we don't mean to frighten you," Kristy said. "You must be really nice, since they brought you here."

Vanessa smiled. "Only special people like us get to live here and serve the gods."

"And if you please them, you can become a Chosen One, and they'll make you a goddess," Kristy added with a grin. "Hurry up! The Selecting Ceremony will begin soon."

Lara slipped off her bra, and Vanessa tossed the white tunic over her head. As Lara smoothed it down, Kristy used the bronze pin to fasten it on her left shoulder. Vanessa grabbed the linen strips, and with Kristy's help, they wrapped them around Lara and tied them at her waist.

A loud gong sounded in the distance.

"Oh no! They're starting." Vanessa ran to the bookcase and grabbed some white leather sandals. "Here. Put these on."

Lara slid her feet inside while Vanessa helped to fasten the sandals. Kristy gathered up all of Lara's discarded clothes and tossed them into the wooden trunk.

"What's going to happen at this ceremony?" Lara asked.

"Apollo will select a new Chosen One," Vanessa explained. "It's usually a maiden who's been here for a while, so we're not likely to be picked."

Kristy fluffed up her long auburn hair. "I can't wait until it's my turn."

Lara winced. The Chosen One was probably dinner.

The gong sounded again.

"Let's go." Kristy grabbed a red gown from the bookcase and opened the door.

"Are you sure we're dead?" Lara whispered. "I feel awfully excited for a dead person."

Kristy grinned. "It is exciting, isn't it? We're on a whole different plane of existence. And we get to live among the gods. How cool is that? We are truly blessed."

Truly brainwashed was more like it. They walked across a foyer to some ornate double doors. Kristy and Vanessa each opened a door, and Lara gasped.

It was like the Parthenon, but all shiny and new.

Vanessa smiled. "I gasped, too, the first time I saw it. It's really awesome, isn't it?"

"Hurry." Kristy shooed them in. "The other maidens are already in place."

Lara gaped at her surroundings as she walked into the temple. On each side of the rectangular room, a series of six marble columns soared to the high ceiling. In between the Corinthian-style columns, bronze braziers rested on tripods. A fire blazed in each brazier, tinting the white marble in shades of gold.

At the end of the temple, three golden thrones sat on a dais. Above them, hanging from the ceiling and surrounded by torches, a large bronze sun glimmered in the firelight. To the side, a guard in a short white toga struck the gong once more. The deep, metallic sound echoed across the large room.

In the center of the temple, nine red cushions lay on the floor in three rows of three. Six maidens dressed in white stood behind the first six cushions.

Vanessa came to a stop behind a cushion in the last row and motioned for Lara to stand next to her. Kristy dashed over to the gong and laid the red gown on the floor next to the guard. Then she hurried back to the last row of cushions.

"Behold, the Chosen One Calliope." The guard struck the gong again.

From behind the thrones, four guards marched forward, carrying a golden litter on their shoulders. As they circled to the front of the thrones, Lara could see the young woman who lounged on the golden pillows. She was dressed all in red. Her gown was similar to the white ones of the maidens, except for the red scarf around her neck. Lara winced. That had to be hiding bite marks.

The four guards lowered the litter to the floor, then two of them helped Calliope stand. Was she that weak? Lara watched with increasing alarm as the guards assisted her up the stairs to the dais. Calliope sat on the smaller throne on the left.

Lara could see her face now, and she recognized her from the case file. The Chosen One Calliope was Britt-

ney Beckford, the girl who had disappeared from Columbia University last July.

The four guards carried the litter away, taking it
somewhere behind the thrones. Lara suspected there
must be rooms back there.

The gong sounded again. "Behold, the gods are
among us," the guard announced. "All Wise Athena,
daughter of Zeus and goddess of wisdom."

"All Wise Athena," the maidens repeated in unison,
then knelt on their red cushions.

Lara followed suit, grateful there was a cushion this
time. She peeked up as Athena marched in. The vampire had traded in her jeans and T-shirt for a long toga
of purple silk. A wreath of golden leaves adorned her
head. She ascended to the dais and sat on the throne
on the right.

"My lord Apollo, son of Zeus and god of the Sun,"
the guard announced.

Apollo strode into view, wearing a long toga of shim-
mering gold. He was followed by the four guards, each
carrying a sword. That made a total of five guards, Lara
figured. They all appeared completely under control.

The maidens all sighed as Apollo passed by. Lara
supposed he was a good-looking man, but with all the
cold air swirling about them, she knew he was exud-
ing vampire power to make himself irresistible.

Apollo stepped onto the dais and turned to face with
them with an imperial sneer.

"My Lord Apollo." The maidens leaned forward in
a deep bow.

Lara copied their movements.

"It is time once again for me to select a new Chosen
One," Apollo announced. "It is the greatest honor a
mortal can ever hope to achieve. If you serve me well,
I will make you a goddess."

Lara heard several maidens whispering, "Please, pick me," under their breaths. She hated the thought of one of them getting bitten, but it was for the best if it gave Brittney the night off. That poor girl needed to regain her strength.

Apollo motioned to the guard by the gong. "Bring the red robe."

"Yes, My Lord Apollo." The guard picked it up and moved toward the nine maidens.

Apollo stepped down from the dais and walked slowly around the maidens. "Sit up, so I may see your faces."

They straightened, still kneeling on the cushions. Lara tried to hunch over and look unattractive, while the others were thrusting their chests out and flipping their hair behind their shoulders.

"First row, stand up," Apollo ordered.

The first three girls rose to their feet.

Apollo eyed them carefully, then stopped in front of the middle girl. "Bare yourself."

"Yes, My Lord Apollo," the girl whispered, and unhooked the bronze pin on her shoulder. Her white shift fell down to where the linen straps circled her rib cage, leaving her breasts exposed.

Lara fought to keep her disgust from showing on her face. Pervert. Lying bastard. Promising to turn these girls into goddesses when he only intended to bite them.

Or maybe he did give them eternal life. Her gaze wandered to Athena. She looked like a redheaded college student. Could she have been one before she became a vampire?

Apollo stepped back, his blue eyes starting to gleam. "Behold, the new Chosen One. She will be known as Aquila."

The guard marched forward with the robe in his arms. The two maidens in her row helped Aquila put it on. They looked bummed out, but Aquila was beaming with happiness.

Lara swallowed hard. The poor girl had been chosen for dinner. Apollo took her hand and led her around the thrones to the rooms in back. Damn. There was nothing Lara could do about it.

Athena followed with two guards. Lara wondered if they were her supper. Two more guards assisted the Chosen One Calliope from the dais and led her around the thrones.

The gong sounded.

"That's it." Vanessa stood. "We go to our room now."

As Lara rose to her feet, she eyed the nine red cushions. Only eight maidens now. She followed them toward the double door.

One of the rejected ones burst into tears. "Why doesn't he ever pick me? I've been serving the gods for months."

"You must be patient," another maiden said. "The gods know when the time is right for each of us."

They crossed the foyer and exited through another pair of double doors. Cool, fresh air swept around Lara, and she breathed deeply. There was a scent of pine in the air. It was too dark to see well, but the sky was so clear, she had to assume they were in the country.

The girls walked toward a smaller, square-shaped building. Behind that, Lara spied a still smaller building. She glanced back at the temple. It was the largest building on the compound. As far as she could tell, it was closed off only by a low stone wall. Easy enough to get over. A few torches illuminated the wall, but there were plenty of dark spaces where she could slip over unnoticed.

She could probably escape, but where to? She had no idea which direction to go, and the compound appeared to be surrounded on all sides by a thick, dark forest. She could end up wandering for days.

The maidens led her into the square building, which reminded her of a Roman villa. Four sides enclosed an inner courtyard. In the courtyard, she spotted a pool.

The girls turned right, and they entered a long dorm room with five beds lined up on each side.

"This is where we sleep," Vanessa told her. "The guards sleep on the other side of the courtyard."

"But stay away from them," Kristy warned her. "We have to stay pure for Apollo."

"Right." Vanessa lowered her voice. "The guards are serving Athena. She'll be furious if you even look at them."

"I understand." Lara took a shower in the large bathroom the maidens all shared, then she put on the plain white nightgown Kristy gave her. She was told which bed to sleep in.

She pretended to sleep while she waited for the other girls to doze off. She hoped to do some late-night snooping around to gather information. Or maybe she should try checking on the Chosen Ones to see if they were all right. Unfortunately, she didn't know exactly where they were, and she couldn't risk walking in on a vampire. She sure couldn't risk letting the vampires see that she wasn't under their control. They might kill her on the spot.

She hated what was happening to these girls, but the best way for her to help them was to stay alive and be very careful. She sighed. One of the rejected girls was still awake, crying softly in her bed. Lara slowly succumbed to sleep.

* * *

"Wake up, sleepyhead." Vanessa shook her. "It's daytime."

Lara sat up abruptly, hoping she had dreamed about Elysian Fields and Chosen Ones and vampires masquerading as gods. But no, she was there in the dorm room for maidens.

"Come on," Vanessa urged her. "Get dressed. We have chores to do."

After thirty minutes of helping Vanessa and Kristy clean the bathroom and dorm room, Lara was feeling more like a maid than a maiden.

"Where are the other maidens?" she asked.

"Some are cleaning the temple, and some are guarding Apollo," Kristy explained as she tossed dirty towels and nightgowns into a wicker basket. "We take turns guarding him during the day."

Lara sighed as she made up another bed. "If he's an all-powerful god, why does he need guarding?"

"It's only his body we're guarding," Kristy said. "He leaves his body during the day."

"Right." Because a vampire was dead during the day. Lara wondered if she could get her hands on a knife or stake. She could stake Apollo during the day while he was in his death-sleep. "Do I get to guard him?"

"Of course," Vanessa said as she swept the floor. "We do it two at a time and sit outside his room."

"You don't get to go in?" Lara asked.

"Oh no, the room is locked." Vanessa swept a small pile of dust into a dustbin. "We're just there to honor him. He has to leave his body before dawn, so he can become the sun."

"And when the sun sets, he returns to his body," Kristy continued. "He's very tired and hungry then. The Chosen One helps him to recover his strength."

"I bet she does," Lara said wryly.

"I believe we're done." Kristy looked about the room approvingly. "Let's go eat breakfast."

Lara accompanied them to the smaller building in the back. There, one of the maidens was busy cooking.

Kristy wrinkled her nose at the food on the table. "You burned the toast again."

"So?" The cook glared at her. "You try cooking three meals a day for fifteen people. I'm sick of this job."

Vanessa gasped and glanced toward the open door. "You mustn't complain. One of the guards might hear you."

"And it's a pleasure to serve the gods," Kristy added.

"I hardly ever get to see the gods," the cook grumbled. "I'm always slaving away in here."

Lara grinned. This was the perfect place to not get noticed. "I'll help you."

"Shhh." Vanessa tugged at her gown and whispered, "You don't want to work here."

"But I want to serve the gods," Lara insisted. "And I love to cook."

"Seriously?" the cook stared at her. "You—you would help me?"

"Of course." Lara strode into the kitchen and looked around. Hallelujah, there were knives here! She could serve Apollo *stake* for supper.

The cook grabbed her hand. "Bless you. I can't tell you how many times I've rushed late into the Selecting Ceremony with food stains on my gown. Apollo never picks me. He says I stink like mortal food, and it offends his immortality." Her eyes filled with tears. "Maybe now I'll have a chance."

"Don't mention it." Lara felt a twinge of guilt. Was she saving herself at this girl's expense? No, she had to save herself in order to save the rest of them.

She opened the pantry and studied the boxes, cans,

and bottles. She spotted a bottle of maple syrup from Vermont. It looked like it had been bottled locally. Maybe they were in Vermont. "Where does this food come from?"

The cook shrugged as she scraped a heap of scrambled eggs onto a platter. "It arrives every week. The gods have provided a way for it to come from the mortal plane."

"Right." Lara needed to be on hand when the supplies arrived. If she could get a message to the delivery man, then she might be able to save all them.

She set the bottle of maple syrup on the counter. "Who wants pancakes?"

"I do, I do!" Kristy and Vanessa waved their hands.

Another maiden rushed through the kitchen door with a tray of eggs, bacon, and toast. "Oh my gods." She set the tray down and pressed a shaking hand to her chest. "I think it's happened."

"What?" Vanessa asked.

The maiden motioned to the tray of food. "I was taking Calliope her breakfast in the temple, and her room was empty. She wasn't there."

Kristy, Vanessa, and the cook all gasped.

"Are you sure?" Kristy whispered. "She wasn't with one of the gods?"

"No." The maiden shook her head. "I asked the guards, and they said she ascended last night."

There was another gasp.

Lara walked toward the maiden. "What do you mean by 'ascended'?"

The maiden's eyes filled with tears. "She ascended to a higher plane. Calliope has become a goddess."

"May the gods be praised," Kristy whispered.

"Really," Vanessa added. "That is so cool. I hope I can be a goddess someday."

Lara shuddered as a chill skittered down her spine. She recalled how weak Brittney Beckford had looked the night before. She covered her mouth as bile rose in her throat. She had an awful feeling that Brittney Beckford was dead.

Chapter Twenty-three

*W*hen the guards arrived for breakfast, the cook informed them that Lara had volunteered to work in the kitchen. The tall guard with the squeaky sandal appeared to be in charge. He carried a clipboard with him and gave out assignments. He told Lara that she would be on guard duty that afternoon from one to four. After that, she could return to the kitchen to help prepare supper.

"Yes, master." Lara set a plate of pancakes, eggs, and bacon in front of him and noticed the puncture wounds on his neck.

As she served the other guards, she noted more wounds. Apparently, Athena didn't like to limit herself to a single Chosen One. She preferred the five-man buffet.

Lara stayed in the kitchen to help prepare and serve lunch, then shortly before one in the afternoon, she accompanied one of the maidens to the temple to do guard duty. It was the maiden who had stayed up late the night before, crying.

As they crossed the compound, Lara surveyed the surroundings, now more visible in daylight. There was the temple, the villa-style dormitory, and the kitchen, all enclosed by a stone wall. A thick forest loomed on the other side of the stone wall.

"What a pretty forest," Lara said. "Maybe I'll take a walk there later."

The maiden halted with a gasp. "You can't leave the Elysian Fields! It is forbidden."

Somehow that wasn't too surprising. "There might be some berries I could pick to make us all a nice cobbler."

The maiden shook her head. "You can't go into the forest. Apollo says there are ferocious beasts there with great gnashing teeth!"

Lara stifled a snort. She was a lot more worried about Apollo's gnashing teeth.

The maiden shuddered. "Apollo says that if one of those beasts captures you, it will drag you to Hades."

"Well, we wouldn't want that to happen." Lara sighed. These girls were so brainwashed, they couldn't even detect sarcasm. She followed the maiden into the temple.

The maiden led Lara around the thrones to a hallway in the back. There were three doors on each side of the hallway. Two doors were painted red. Rooms for the Chosen Ones, the maiden explained.

Lara noticed one of the male guards standing in front of a purple door. That had to be Athena's room. Kristy and Vanessa were sitting on red cushions in front of a golden door. They stood when Lara and the maiden approached.

"I hope you left us some lunch," Vanessa said. "We're starving." She and Kristy headed off to the kitchen.

Lara sat beside the other maiden. She pushed her cushion against the wall so she could lean back and stretch her legs in front. Her new position earned her a frown from the other maiden.

She tried not to think about Apollo's dead carcass on the other side of the door. At least they were safe from him during the day.

Where was Jack? In his death-sleep at the townhouse on the Upper East Side? She recalled how he'd told LaToya there were usually dead bodies in the basement, and she'd thought he was kidding. That rascal. He was so different from the vampires here.

Athena and Apollo considered humans nothing more than walking meals, foolish and easily controlled. Jack had always treated her with respect and kindness. He truly cared about her feelings and her safety. Had he spent the night desperately searching for her?

She thought back to how he'd been with Mario and Gianetta in Venice. They were mortals, but he considered them family. He'd showed respect and affection for Father Giuseppe. And he'd tried so hard to please her that night with the ice cream, the gondola ride, and the serenade.

He was such a good man. And she missed him so. He could make her laugh. He could make her hot. He made her feel beautiful and smart and cherished. He was the perfect man, except for the little *Undead* problem.

Was it crazy to fall in love with a vampire? Or was it even crazier to refuse him because he was a vampire? It wasn't Jack's fault that he'd been transformed. He had been attacked. Hadn't he suffered enough? It would be too cruel to reject him and make him suffer more.

Apollo rejected girls simply based on their hair color. But wouldn't the real God judge people according to their hearts and not their looks? Would Love reject anyone for being different?

A sensation of peace settled on Lara like a warm blanket. She knew what she had to do. She couldn't reject Jack. She couldn't bear to hurt him. Even if it meant the total upheaval of her own life, she would rather take the pain upon herself than cause him to suffer anymore.

It was the way of love. And she loved him with all her heart.

She closed her eyes and remembered how he'd made love to her in the bell tower. What a sexy man he was, her vampire Casanova. She couldn't wait to see him again, to let him know that her mind was made up. She belonged with him forever. *Please, Jack, find me soon.* She imagined how happy he would be, how he would make mad, passionate love to her.

The other maiden poked her in the shoulder. "Don't fall asleep. It is forbidden."

"All right," Lara grumbled as her romantic dream fizzled away. "Do we really have to sit here for three hours? This is so boring."

"Shh!" The maiden glanced at the guard down the hall. "Don't speak like that. He'll hear you."

"Okay. My name is Lara. What's yours?"

The maiden gasped. "Stop that!" She glanced again at the guard. "We cannot use names."

"Let me guess. It's forbidden?"

"Yes," the maiden hissed. "Behave yourself."

"Okeydokey." Lara decided to call this girl No Name. No, Miss Forbidden was better. She couldn't recall seeing her photo in the case file. "What college did you go to?"

Miss Forbidden shot her an angry look. "That life is over. We do not speak of it. I realize you are new, so I won't report you, but you had better learn to curb your tongue, or you'll end up in Hades."

Lara reluctantly agreed that she needed to behave. She didn't want to draw attention to herself. "I'm terribly sorry. I really do want to serve the gods." She pointed at the bronze doorway at the end of the hall. "Whose room is that?"

"It is the Most Holy Sanctum," Miss Forbidden whispered. "When Zeus comes, he stays there."

"Zeus comes here?" Lara figured he was another vampire. And he stopped by to mooch a free meal off of Apollo. "That is so exciting."

"I know!" Miss Forbidden's eyes lit up. "He comes by every few weeks to visit his children, Apollo and Athena. But of course, he usually lives on Mount Olympus."

"Of course. What does he look like?"

"No one knows," Miss Forbidden whispered. "He never leaves the Most Holy Sanctum. Apollo selects a Chosen One for him. And the next morning, the Chosen One doesn't remember him. He works in mysterious ways."

"Right. So how many gods drop by?"

"A few." Miss Forbidden smiled. "One time Hermes came to visit, and he chose me."

"How . . . wonderful for you." Lara couldn't see Miss Forbidden's neck since her long reddish blonde hair was in the way.

Lara spent the rest of the guard duty trying to glean more information from Miss Forbidden. Then she returned to the kitchen to help Cook prepare supper for five guards, eight maidens, and the new Chosen One, Aquila. It couldn't be a coincidence that Aquila was chosen just as Brittney Beckford disappeared. Apollo must have known she was about to die. That bastard. He actually had these girls eager to become his next victim.

She and Cook were cleaning up after supper when the sun set.

Kristy ran into the kitchen. "Hurry! Zeus has arrived. There's going to be another Selecting Ceremony."

"Oh my gods." The cook dried her hands on a dish towel. "We need to get cleaned up, fast." She ran to the dormitory.

Lara followed, and Kristy gave them new white robes to wear. They rushed into the temple just as the first gong sounded.

Lara took her position in the last row of red cushions in the center of the temple. Vanessa and Kristy were next to her. Three maidens stood in front of her. On the first row, only two maidens stood—Cook and Miss Forbidden. The third pillow was unclaimed. It had been Aquila's.

The gong sounded again, and the guard announced the Chosen One. Aquila strode in, dressed in her red robe. Lara was relieved to see her still looking strong, though the red scarf around her neck was creepy.

Athena was announced, and then Apollo. Lara knelt and bowed with the other maidens.

"We have been honored by a visit from my father, All Mighty Zeus." Apollo circled the maidens. "First row, stand."

Cook and Miss Forbidden rose to their feet.

"You will be his Chosen One for tonight." Apollo motioned to Miss Forbidden. "See that you please him well."

"Yes, My Lord Apollo," Miss Forbidden breathed. "Oh, thank you, my lord."

With a sad face, Cook helped Miss Forbidden put on the red robe.

Lara's stomach churned. She didn't want to think about what was going to happen to Miss Forbidden.

Apollo led Miss Forbidden to the hallway behind the thrones. She was going to the Most Holy Sanctum, Lara thought. She hoped the poor girl would come out alive.

As the ceremony ended, Lara noted there were only seven maidens now. Fear surged inside her, threatening to explode into sheer panic.

They walked to the dormitory. The air was cool and crisp, but she was finding it hard to breathe. Her heart raced. She glanced up at the clear night sky. Jack would be up now. Was he looking for her? *Jack, please hurry. I'm starting to freak out.*

She couldn't wait for a rescue. She had to get out of here. Aquila and Miss Forbidden could die. The other maidens were in danger. Hell, *she* was in danger.

"I think I'll go to the kitchen and check supplies," she told the other maidens. "I'll be along later."

She dashed to the kitchen and gathered up supplies for her escape. A knife, a small box of matches, an empty bottle filled with water, some crackers. She emptied potatoes out of a burlap sack and put her supplies inside.

With the sack in hand, she crept out of the kitchen. These damned white sandals were not good for a long trek through the woods, but what choice did she have? And this white gown made her way too visible.

She spotted two guards walking along the stone wall. They were headed away from her. She rounded the kitchen and spotted an overgrown dirt road in the back, leading to an iron gate. Great! This was probably the road the delivery truck used to bring in food supplies. It might lead to a nearby town.

She looked around. The coast was clear. She pulled her long white gown up to her knees and dashed to the gate. She slipped underneath. She was free!

A long howl echoed eerily around her. She scanned the woods and gasped when a pair of golden eyes looked back at her. What had Miss Forbidden told her? There were ferocious beasts in the woods with gnashing teeth? They would drag her to Hades?

She shook her head. No, that was brainwashing. She couldn't believe that.

The golden eyes moved closer. Lara pressed against the gate. Her heart thundered in her chest. Another howl came from the forest. Undergrowth swished and crackled.

She fumbled in the burlap bag for the knife. Just in time, too, for a huge, gray wolf appeared from the forest. She gulped. She'd never seen such a huge wolf. Actually, she'd never seen a wolf before at all. She tightened her grip on the knife.

The wolf's gold eyes gleamed in the dark. He snarled, and two more wolves emerged from the forest.

Oh God, there could be a whole pack of them. Lara eased back underneath the gate. She retreated slowly, keeping her eyes on the three wolves. They stood still, watching her.

She circled the kitchen, then ran inside and slammed the door shut. Dammit! Vampires and wolves. Either way, she was a goner.

Oh, Jack, please find me.

Jack strode into the security office at Romatech. "Give me another place to check out. Hurry."

Phil looked up from where he sat behind the desk. "No luck with the place in West Texas?"

"No." It was just past midnight, and already Jack had investigated four isolated compounds across the country. "Wasn't there one in Colorado?"

"Robby's at that one." Phil referred to the yellow legal pad on the desk in front of him. "And Phineas is in Virginia."

Jack paced across the office. The three Vamps had split up so more locations could be checked. Phil was manning the phone as more reports were called in from wolf packs across North America. Unfortunately, they were getting a lot of reports from the western states, and Jack still believed Apollo was somewhere in the east, close to his hunting grounds.

Phil tapped his pen on the yellow paper. "I've got one in Minnesota."

"Call the pack master, and I'll teleport there." Jack had to stay busy, or he'd go crazy. If he even stopped to think about how Lara could be suffering, he would rip a tree out by its roots.

As Phil reached for the phone, it rang. "MacKay Security and Investigation. Phil speaking." He paused. "Yes, I'm that Phil."

Jack's superior hearing could pick up the deep, gruff voice on the line. A pack master from northern Maine. This sounded promising.

Jack leaned over the desk, so he could hear better. A female body had been discovered in the woods.

His heart lurched. *No, not Lara.*

Phil gave him a worried look. "Can you describe her? You have a photo? I'll give you our fax number." He recited the number.

A chill stole over Jack. The voice on the phone described the girl as tall, slim, with reddish blonde hair and blue eyes. The fax machine was so damned slow. Jack's stomach roiled, and for the first time in his long vampire life, he thought he might lose his dinner.

Finally, the photo arrived. Jack ripped it from the machine. It wasn't Lara.

He drew in a shaky breath. "It's not her. But this girl looks familiar." He grabbed the case file and rummaged through the photos he'd collected. He pulled out a photo that closely matched the fax. Brittney Beckford. Apollo had dumped the poor girl's body in the woods.

"Greek-style architecture?" Phil sat up. "Are you sure?"

"Put him on speakerphone," Jack said. "We'll go there now."

Phil punched the button and warned the pack master that they were on their way. Jack grabbed Phil's arm and teleported to the sound of the werewolf's voice.

"Welcome to Wolf Ridge." A tall man with thick gray hair and amber eyes stood behind a desk, wearing a police uniform and a grim expression. "Everyone around here calls me Chief."

Jack glanced at the empty jail cell behind him. "You're the chief of police here?"

"Yes, and pack master." The werewolf extended a hand toward Phil. "It's good to meet you. I know your father."

"I'm sure you do," Phil muttered and shook Chief's hand. "This is Jack from Venice."

Chief eyed Jack warily as he shook his hand. "My sons and I found the dead girl in the woods. I think one of your kind killed her. She has tooth marks on her neck, and she's completely drained of blood."

Jack ground his teeth. "The vampire who killed her is *not* one of my kind. I only drink synthetic blood, and

I protect mortals from those who would kill them for a meal."

Chief nodded. "Good. I don't allow my pack to attack mortals, either."

"We need to see the compound you discovered." Jack called Robby and Phineas, and the two Vamps teleported there.

Chief looked them over. "So we have a vampire from Venice, one from Scotland in a kilt, and one from . . . ?"

"The Bronx," Phineas finished the werewolf's sentence. "You got a problem with that?"

"No." Chief smiled. "I'll take you to the compound. If there's a vampire there who's killing women, I want him stopped, too."

Chief led them out the door, and they all piled into his SUV. Thirty minutes later, they arrived at Chief's hunting cabin, deep in the forest.

"I'll take you the rest of the way on foot." Chief stepped behind the big hood of the SUV and removed his uniform. "It'll be faster for us wolves if we shift." He glanced at Phil. "Ready?"

Phil's jaw shifted. "I'll stay as I am."

Chief winced. "Sorry. I got the impression that—"

"Don't mention it," Phil grumbled. "I'll be right behind you all. And I'll bring your clothes."

"Thanks." Chief left his clothes stacked on the hood. As he walked toward the woods, his body began to waver. Within a few seconds, he had shifted into a large, gray wolf.

"Holy shit," Phineas said. "That was fast."

"He's an Alpha." Phil grabbed the police chief's clothes. "They can shift easily at any time. He doesn't need a full moon."

"Oh." Phineas glanced up at the crescent moon. "So I guess you're not—"

"Enough," Robby interrupted. He pointed at Chief, who was already loping into the forest. "Let's go."

The three Vamps dashed after the running wolf. Phil sprinted along behind.

After a few miles, they arrived at the compound. Jack grinned when he saw the Greek temple. *I've got you now, Apollo.*

"Bingo," Phineas breathed. "This has got to be it."

Chief sat on his haunches, panting, with his tongue hanging out.

"As soon as Phil catches up, there'll be five of us," Robby said. "We could attack right away."

It was tempting, so tempting to rush in and rescue Lara. But was it wise? "We can't be sure how many vampires are in there," Jack said. "We know Apollo has at least one accomplice. There could be more."

He walked slowly around the compound, keeping to the woods. The others followed. He wished he could send a psychic message to Lara that he had arrived, but he didn't dare. Vampire telepathy was like broadcasting on a radio. Every vampire in the vicinity would hear it.

Phil arrived. He set Chief's clothes behind a tree, and the wolf shifted back to human form.

Phil eyed the compound. "This looks like the right place. It's got to be, since one of the missing girls was found close by."

"Yes, but I want more information before we attack." Jack spotted two guards. "Mortals. Armed with swords."

"I bet they're heavily under vampire control," Robby said. "They may be programmed to kill the women and themselves if the compound is breached."

"Shit," Phineas muttered. "That's cold."

"You could be right." Chief rounded the tree, buttoning his shirt. "I doubt this guy will want to leave any witnesses. Come, I want to show you something."

Chief led them through the woods till they came upon a dirt road and a gate. "This leads to another town, a mortal one, about thirty miles from here. I think the town is delivering food supplies here."

"Really?" Jack turned to Phil. "How would you like a new job?" With vampire control, it would be easy enough to convince a store manager that Phil was their new delivery man.

Phil nodded. "Sounds good. But I would be here during the day when the vampires are in their death-sleep. I may not be able to find out much."

"I'll come here at night to find out more," Jack said.

"Ye're thinking of going under cover?" Robby frowned at him. "I doona like it, Jack. Ye've killed enough Malcontents that they know yer name. And Apollo saw you for just a second before he teleported away."

"That's all right." Jack smiled. "I can change my name and my looks. I know a really good hairdresser in Massachusetts."

The next day, when Lara was helping Cook clean up after lunch, she thought she heard the sound of an automobile engine. She grinned with relief.

Cook frowned in confusion. "This isn't delivery day. But I guess I'd better unlock the back door." She wandered into the back storeroom with a key.

Lara looked around frantically. She ripped a paper towel off the roll and grabbed a bottle of ketchup. She squeezed a small drop onto the tip of her finger, then wrote *Help! Bring police* on the paper towel.

She flapped the towel in the air, so it would dry

quickly. Then she folded it and slipped it inside the bodice of her white gown.

She found Cook standing by the open back door. In the distance, she spotted a delivery van parked on the other side of the gate. The driver, a young man dressed in jeans and a flannel shirt, was opening the gate.

She ran toward him.

"Stop!" Cook yelled. "We're not supposed to be seen."

The driver moved toward her, watching her carefully with his light blue eyes. "Can I help you, miss?"

"Yes!" Lara slowed down and reached inside her bodice. "We need—"

"Maiden!" a guard's voice bellowed behind her.

She stopped short, six feet from the delivery man. Damn! She couldn't pass him the note without being seen.

"Maiden, return to the kitchen immediately!" the guard shouted.

She glanced back. It was the head guard with the squeaky sandal. He was followed by two more guards. She shot one last pleading look at the delivery man. "We're prisoners," she mouthed, hoping he would understand.

His blue eyes narrowed, and he nodded ever so slightly.

Lara ran back to the kitchen.

"Oh no," Cook muttered. "You're in big trouble now."

Squeaky Sandal marched up to the delivery man. "What's going on here? You're not the usual driver. And we're not expecting a delivery for two more days."

The delivery guy shrugged, apparently unfazed by the head guard's beefy muscles and belligerent attitude. Lara smiled to herself. The guard would be a lot more ominous if he didn't squeak with every other step.

"Look, buddy." The delivery man crossed his arms over his broad chest. "The regular guy quit, and I'm going on vacation tomorrow. So there won't be any more deliveries for two weeks. Take it or leave it."

Squeaky glared at the delivery man. "All right. Pull the van up closer to the kitchen."

The delivery guy jumped back into the van and drove closer to the kitchen. To Lara's dismay, there was no writing on the van. She had hoped to catch the name of a local town.

"Stop!" Squeaky yelled, and the van halted.

The two other guards opened the back of the van and began unloading. The driver grabbed a box and strode toward the kitchen.

"Stop." Squeaky held up a hand. "You cannot enter." He took the box and brought it into the storeroom.

Damn. Lara had hoped the driver would come in so she could pass him her note. She peeked out the door. The delivery guy nodded at her.

"You should not be seen." Squeaky pushed her aside as he exited. He glared at the driver. "Wait inside the van."

"Sure," the driver muttered. "Nice toga. Bet it gets a little chilly in the winter." He strode back to the van.

Lara hovered just inside the door. It looked like she wasn't going to be able to pass her note. Still, she had a feeling that the delivery man understood. Or was that just wishful thinking?

The last of the supplies were brought in, and the guards slammed the van doors shut.

The driver sauntered toward the kitchen with a box in his hand. He spotted Lara peeking from behind the door. With a grin, he shook the box. "How about a snack?"

"Give me that." Squeaky grabbed the box. "And you can leave now."

The driver cast one last look at Lara, then climbed into the van and drove through the gate.

Lara's heart sank. What if he hadn't understood? There wouldn't be another delivery for two weeks.

Meanwhile, the guards inspected the box from the driver.

"There might be a special decoder ring inside," one guard said.

"Yeah, that guy seemed a little suspicious to me," the second guard said.

Squeaky ripped the box apart, and caramel corn scattered all over the dirt road. "There's nothing here." He tossed the box on the ground, then glared at Lara. "Clean this up, maiden."

"Yes, master." Lara grabbed a garbage sack, then rushed outside. She scooped handfuls of sticky pop-corn into the bag while the guards strolled away.

When it looked like they'd lost interest in her, she picked up the pieces of the torn box.

Her breath caught. *Cracker Jack.* A sound, halfway between a laugh and a sob escaped her mouth.

Jack had found her.

Chapter Twenty-four

Soon after the sun set, Vanessa ran into the kitchen. "Another god has come to visit. There'll be another Selecting Ceremony!"

Cook gasped and pressed a soapy hand to her chest. "This could be my night." She glanced down at her damp gown. "I need to change." She dashed from the kitchen.

Lara finished loading the dishwasher. Just what the world needed—another god. Miss Forbidden had returned to the dormitory this morning wearing a red scarf around her neck like a badge of honor. She claimed she couldn't remember anything, but the bruises on her arms spoke volumes. That Zeus had been an almighty abusive pig.

"What are you doing?" Vanessa asked. "You need to get ready."

"I'm coming." Lara trudged from the kitchen. "So which god is here tonight?"

"I don't know. The guards didn't say."

"Well, let me think." Lara glanced up at the clear, starry sky. *Jack, this would be a good time to rescue me.* "It might be Ares, the god of war."

"Oooh." Vanessa shivered. "He sounds hunky."

Lara snorted. "Or it could be Hermes or Poseidon."

"You're so smart to know their names," Vanessa said. "I wish I'd paid more attention in school. For some weird reason, I thought all that Greek god stuff was made up."

"Yeah. How could we be so wrong?"

"I know." Vanessa brushed her hair back over her shoulder. "It's just so cool that it's real. I mean, people back on Earth don't know about it, but we get to know the secret. It makes me feel really special."

"You *are* special," Lara told her. "You don't need gods to tell you that."

"But it feels so good." Vanessa gasped. "Here we are talking, and you're not ready. Hurry!" She grabbed Lara's arm and dragged her through the dormitory to the bathroom.

While all the maidens were primping in front of the mirrors, Lara took a hot shower. Then she put on a fresh gown and towel-dried her hair.

"The first gong has sounded!" a maiden called from the dormitory, and the maidens rushed from the bathroom.

Miss Forbidden looked back at Lara and grimaced. "What are you doing? Your hair is still damp. You can't go before the gods looking like that."

Lara tossed her towel into the wicker laundry basket. "I know this may come as a big surprise to you, but I don't want to be chosen."

Miss Forbidden gasped and looked around to make sure they were alone. "You mustn't say that. It's a great honor to serve the gods."

Lara grabbed her arm and pointed at a large green-and-purple bruise. "This is what that god did to you."

The maiden's eyes filled with tears. "I don't remember it," she whispered. "I must have displeased him somehow. May the gods forgive me."

"He abused you." Lara pulled the scarf away from Miss Forbidden's neck to reveal the puncture marks. "He bit you."

With a cry, Miss Forbidden pulled away. "I don't believe you. I can't." She ran away.

Lara took a deep breath, then put on her sandals and followed the girls to the temple. They filed inside and took their places behind the red cushions.

The Chosen One Aquila was announced. She strode into the room and sat on her throne. Lara was relieved that she still looked well. Athena was announced. Her smile looked especially malicious tonight. Not a good sign.

Apollo marched in with his escort of four guards. The maidens bowed before him.

"Tonight we are honored by the presence of a very powerful god." Apollo stepped down from the dais. "He will select one of you to be his Chosen One."

"Yes, My Lord Apollo." The maidens remained still, but Lara could feel their excitement mounting.

Apollo stopped in front of them. "I should warn you that this is one god you must never displease. Your eternal fate will be in his hands. His name is Hades."

The maidens gasped.

Lara winced. This was bad. If Zeus had bruised his Chosen One, what would a vampire called Hades do?

Up on the dais, Athena snickered. Lara's hands curled into fists. That damned bitch enjoyed seeing them scared to death. Vanessa was shaking beside her.

Cook whimpered. She probably feared she was next in line to be chosen.

Footsteps approached them.

"Here comes Hades now," Apollo said.

Lara glanced up and caught a glimpse of short blond hair. She tucked her head back down, not wanting to draw attention to herself. She'd already spent the afternoon cleaning the guards' dormitory and bathroom as a punishment for speaking to the delivery man. Would they give her to Hades as a further punishment?

Apollo chuckled. "Which one of you will attend to the god of the underworld? If he's not pleased, he's threatening to take someone to the nine circles of hell."

Lara flinched. She lifted her head. Could it be? He was dressed in a burgundy silk toga. Those broad shoulders looked familiar, but the short blond hair was strange. He turned toward the maidens, and she gasped.

Jack.

His eyes met hers briefly, then looked away. She ducked her head and bit her lip to keep from grinning. Jack was here to rescue her, to rescue all the girls. She wanted to leap around the room and dance for joy.

"You have some lovely maidens here, Apollo."

His accent was different. Lara recalled that he'd spent his first years in Bohemia, speaking Czech.

"Thank you, Hades," Apollo said with a smug tone. "I believe you will find them very accommodating."

"I had better." Hades strolled around the maidens, who were visibly shaking. He stopped beside Lara. "This one looks interesting. You will stand, maiden."

Lara rose slowly to her feet, keeping her eyes downcast and her face blank.

Apollo sighed. "I would suggest another. This one is new and still untrained. She did not behave well today."

"Then she is perfect for hell," Hades said wryly. "It would please me to teach her a lesson."

"Very well," Apollo said. "Maiden, bare yourself."

Oh shit. She was going to have to pretend to be under his control. "Yes, My Lord Apollo." She reached up to unfasten the brooch on her shoulder.

"Not necessary." Hades waved a dismissive hand. "My mind is made up. This is the one."

Oh thank you, Jack. She would gladly give him a private showing later.

Apollo motioned to a guard. "Bring the red robe."

Vanessa and Kristy helped Lara slide the red gown over her white one. They looked at her with tears in their eyes.

She grabbed their hands and gave them a reassuring squeeze.

The gong sounded. Athena left with two guards, while Apollo escorted his Chosen One Aquila to his room. Hades took Lara's hand and led her around the thrones.

She glanced back and saw the maidens huddled around the entrance doors to the temple, all watching her with worried looks. Poor girls. They really believed she was about to be bedded by the god of the dead. She squeezed Jack's hand. She couldn't wait to be alone with him.

He led her down the hallway. Apollo and Athena were already in their rooms. A guard stood in front of their doors.

Jack stopped by a blue door. "This is a guest room." He opened it and ushered her inside. He turned to lock and bar the door.

She glanced around the room. Big canopy bed. Blue sheets and blue gauzy curtains hanging from the canopy. When Jack turned toward her, she flung herself at him, wrapping her arms around his neck. "Oh, thank you, thank you, you wonderful man. You glorious, incredible man."

He chuckled as he held her tight. "I guess you're glad to see me."

She covered his face with kisses. "I'm thrilled. I'm ecstatic. I knew you would find me."

He took hold of her shoulders and moved her back so he could look her over. "Are you all right? I swear, if they have harmed you in any way, I will—"

"I'm fine." She jumped at him again, circling her arms around his neck and squeezing against him tightly. "I missed you so much. Don't ever let me go."

"I was so worried about you." He pressed a kiss against her brow, then glanced over his shoulder. "We should move away from the door," he whispered.

She hung on to him as he maneuvered them to the center of the room and accidentally trampled on his foot. "Sorry. I'm so glad you found me. I tried to escape, but there were wolves in the woods. And I didn't know where to go, 'cause I don't know where we are."

"Northern Maine."

"Oh. Well, thank God you found us. I think one of the girls is *dead*."

"Shh." He put a finger on her lips and glanced at the door. "Not so loud. There are guards in the hall."

"They're probably waiting for their turn with Athena," Lara muttered.

Jack glanced at the bed, which filled half the room. "These rooms do seem designed for one purpose."

Lara looked at the bed, then at Jack, and a surge of longing swept through her. She wanted him to know that she'd made up her mind. "Jack." She cradled his face in her hands.

A tint of red shaded his eyes, then he closed them.

"We need to talk." He opened his eyes, and they were back to their usual golden brown color. "I need all the information you can give me, so I can return to the guys and formulate our attack."

Her hands dropped to his chest. "You're not taking me with you?"

He squeezed her shoulders. *"Cara mia*, I can't. It would look too suspicious. But we plan to attack tomorrow at dusk. You'll only have to stay one more day. Can you do that? Will you be all right?"

"Yes. We're fairly safe during the day. We just cook and clean and do laundry." She glanced down at her red robe. "I was really tempted to wash one of these with the guards' white togas, so they'd end up wearing pink."

Jack chuckled. "I'm so glad you're still you, that they didn't manage to brainwash you."

"Oh, there's some serious brainwashing going on around here." Lara pulled the red robe off and tossed it on the floor. "These poor girls actually believe it's a great honor to be a Chosen One." Her eyes filled with tears. "Thank God you found me before it happened—"

"Shhh." Jack pulled her into his arms. "You're all right now. *Cara mia*." He kissed the top of her head.

She wanted to tell him that he was her Chosen One. She stepped back. "Jack, I need to tell you—"

"Yes, I need to know everything. We have to come up with an attack plan that will eliminate the vampires here without causing any harm to the mortals."

She groaned inwardly. Hadn't they discussed business long enough? He was here, her knight in shining armor who had charged to the rescue. And she was madly in love with him. Shouldn't they be celebrating? She glanced at the bed. Shouldn't he be ravishing her right now? "You need a plan?"

"An attack plan, yes."

"Okay. I'll tell you how to attack." She wrenched the bronze brooch from her white gown and tossed it on the bed. "First, you should start with the breasts." Her gown tumbled down to the ties around her midriff.

His gaze dropped to her bare breasts. "I'm . . . trying to do business."

"I *mean* business." She cupped her breasts. "I believe you've met these before."

The gold flecks in his eyes started to gleam. "La—" He halted when a noise sounded outside their door.

Lara figured one of the guards was hoping for a cheap thrill.

"Down on your knees, woman!" Jack thundered. "Bow before me."

"Yes, My Lord Hades," she called out as she dropped to her knees and prostrated herself.

Jack winced and whispered, "You don't have to really do that."

She sat up, grinning. "Oh, My Lord Hades! Please don't hurt me. I'll do anything to please you. Anything!"

He gave her an annoyed look.

"Why, My Lord Hades! Look at you! You're so well endowed! Careful with that. You'll put someone's eye out. Oh, what a mouthful!" She made a loud strangling noise.

Jack's eyes widened as he watched her.

"Oh, yes, yes! Take me, Hades!" She let out a long squeal, lifting her arms in the air like she was riding a roller coaster. "Oh, that was good. Let's take a nap now."

Footsteps moved away from the door.

Jack arched a brow. "Are you done now?"

"Yes, but I feel strangely . . . unsatisfied."

He chuckled. "So do I. You made me last about two seconds."

"Well." She glanced at the bed. "I'm sure you could do better."

"We still need to talk."

Her Casanova was being terribly unromantic, but she'd fix that. She stalked toward him on all fours. "What kind of attack plan did you have in mind? Full frontal?" She rose up on her knees, rubbing her breasts against his toga.

He closed his eyes with a moan.

She slipped her hands underneath his toga and skimmed up the back of his bare calves. Higher, to his bare thighs.

"Lara." He opened his eyes. They were red. He gritted his teeth. "This is not a good time—"

"Oh!" Her hands had reached his buttocks, and he wasn't wearing any underwear. "Oh my." Tingles spread out over her skin. Her nipples tightened, her back arched, and she succumbed to an urge to press her breasts against him.

She splayed her hands over his rump. Her fingers stroked the skin, so smooth and soft. Suddenly, his muscles flexed, tightening beneath her hands, creating a delicious concave curve. Her knees felt weak. She struggled to breathe. Heat sizzled between her thighs. "Oh my God."

"Talking to me?" He knelt in front of her.

She leaned toward him, but he held her back by the shoulders.

"Lara, I realize you're grateful that I'm here."

"Does this look like gratitude to you?" She fumbled with the linen strips tied at her waist.

"Then it's adrenalin and excitement. But those feelings will pass once you're back home."

"Don't tell me what I'm feeling. And don't you dare say my feelings are temporary." She loosened the strips, and her gown pooled around her knees.

He sucked in a sharp breath. His eyes gleamed red hot. "Then tell me exactly what you're feeling. Because I can't take you just for the hell of it. If I make love to you, I will never give you up. Never."

She gazed into his glowing eyes. "I know that. I'm counting on that."

"Forever is a long time for a vampire."

"I know that, too." Her eyes filled with tears. "I'm in love with you, Jack. Forever. You're all I want. All I need. No matter what happens, I'll never give you up."

His grip on her shoulders tightened, and his red eyes glimmered with moisture. "Are you sure?"

"Yes! Now stop being so dense and make love to me."

With vampire speed, he tossed her on the bed, ripped off her underwear and his own toga, then jumped into bed beside her. He covered her face with kisses. "*Cara mia*, Lara *mia* I love you."

She planted kisses all over his face, too, till their mouths finally met in a hot, urgent kiss. Their tongues stroked, their hands groped, their bodies rolled.

Lara was panting by the time he kissed his way to her breasts. Licking, suckling, tweaking, pinching. She let out a long moan and wrapped her legs around him. His erection pressed against her hip.

She felt hot and wet and aching with need. "Oh God, Jack, let me have it."

He chuckled, his breath tickling her damp, tight nipples. "Are you begging, *cara mia*?"

"I'm demanding!" She slapped his rump.

He lifted his head to look at her. "What was that?"

"I-it wasn't very hard. Sorta . . . playful, you know?"

His mouth twitched. "Now you've asked for it."

"Well, duh, yes. I have been asking—" She squealed when he suddenly dove between her legs. "Oh, oh!" All that licking, suckling, tweaking, and pinching had moved to a new location. She made a mental note to slap his rump more often.

"Jack, Jack," she breathed. Pleasure spiked and spiraled, growing more and more tense. She strained, lifting her hips to meet his mouth. He grabbed her bottom and pressed her against him. With another squeal, she climaxed, and he groaned with satisfaction.

She struggled to catch her breath. "Oh, Jack, that was—" He dragged his tongue over her with one long slow lick, and aftershocks rocked her body.

He rose to his knees, leaning over her. "*Cara mia.*"

"Hmm?" She blinked a few times to bring him into focus. The blunt tip of his erection nudged against her highly sensitized skin. More moisture seeped from her.

His eyes gleamed, still red. "I'm going to enter you now."

Like she wouldn't have noticed? She gasped when he drove into her with one swift stroke. And he kept coming. "Wow." He was big. Her inner muscles spasmed with another aftershock.

He winced. "I won't last long with that kind of torment."

Was he actually worried about his performance? "I'm not keeping time. We have our whole lives together."

He kissed her brow. "I love you, Lara."

"I love you, too. Just the way you are."

He smiled. "Then I'm home."

He started slow, but soon they lost all semblance of control. It was as if he couldn't get close enough. He rose onto his knees and grasped her hips, grinding himself against her. She screamed as another climax jolted through her. He let out a long groan, then suddenly threw his head back as his fangs popped out.

Lara screamed again.

He released her and collapsed on the bed. "Sorry. Didn't mean to scare you." He grimaced. "*Merda.*"

She sat up. He looked like he was in pain. "Are you all right? Are you . . . hungry?"

He shook his head. The fangs were already starting to recede. "I drank plenty before coming here. I—I just lost control. I'm sorry I scared you."

"It was just a bit dramatic, that's all." She decided not to let the fangs bother her. He couldn't help having fangs. He actually had good control, since he hadn't made any attempt to bite her. And he couldn't help being a vampire. She loved him the way he was.

She smoothed a hand over his chest and down his belly. He was a beautiful man. Well-defined muscles. She trailed her fingers down the line of hair that led to his groin.

"You're magnificent." She stroked the length of his manhood. Even relaxed, it was long and thick. She traced a vein. "How did it happen?"

"What?" He lifted his head to look, then dropped his head back onto the bed. "I was born with that."

She snorted. "I meant, how did you become a vampire?" She moved her hand down and cupped his balls.

"I'd rather not talk about it."

"Oh come on." She squeezed his balls gently.

His mouth curled up. "Are you threatening me?"

"No, of course not." She tickled him. "I'm just trying to persuade you to talk."

"Playing with a man's balls does not lead to conversation."

She stretched out beside him and rested her head on his shoulder. "I want to know all about you. Please."

"I'm a bastard."

"That's a given."

He snorted. "My father was a terrible womanizer." He stroked her hair. "I'm not anything like him."

"One woman is enough for you?"

"Definitely." He smiled at her, and his eyes had returned to their warm golden brown color.

"Tell me more."

His smile faded. "I inherited my father's personal papers. Things that he didn't want included in his memoirs. Imagine a twelve-year-old boy reading about his father's struggle with the pox and his search for a cure."

"Eeuw." Lara wrinkled her nose.

"Exactly. Now you know why I don't like to speak of it. My father was in Paris when an attempt was made on the French king's life, and he met the man responsible for saving the king. There were some rumors about Jean-Luc Echarpe. Rumors that he had super strength and was invincible. My father asked him what his secret was, hoping to find a cure for his syphilis, but Jean-Luc refused him."

"This Jean-Luc was a vampire?" Lara asked.

"Yes. My father didn't give up. He suspected Jean-Luc knew a way to defeat old age and disease. Eventually, my father's investigations led him to Transylvania. He took a job nearby at the Castle Dux in Bohemia. That's where he seduced my mother. I never knew her, but I heard she died years later in an insane asylum."

"Oh, Jack, I'm so sorry."

"So was I. I feared my mother had died from syphilis, given to her by my father. And I feared I could have it, too. I was determined not to pass it on, so I decided to become a monk. My uncle persuaded me to go the University of Padua first. Then, when I was twenty-four, something terrible happened."

Lara sat up. "You were attacked?"

He smiled. "I fell in love."

She swatted his arm. "That's not terrible."

"It is if you think you have a disease that could kill. I wanted to keep Beatrice safe, so I used my father's notes to try to find a cure. A year later, my travels took me to Transylvania. I was riding toward a small village as the sun set. Three beautiful women appeared on the road."

"And they were vampires?" Lara asked.

Jack nodded. "I introduced myself, and when they heard the name Casanova, they jumped me. The next thing I knew I was in an old castle with the women biting me. I tried to fight back, but . . . they were very strong, and I grew weaker as they drained every drop of blood from my veins."

"That must have been terrifying."

"I woke up in a dungeon with a horrific hunger." He grimaced. "I wanted blood. I didn't know what had happened to me. I didn't realize I could simply tele-port away. They encouraged me to bite their wrists. I did, but there was always a price for survival. They thought I would be a skilled lover like my father. You can imagine their disappointment to find out I barely knew the basics."

Lara winced. She had been right. Jack didn't realize he was a wonderful lover.

"After a few months, they threw me out in disgust. Said I would never live up to the Casanova name." Jack sighed. "I've never used the name since then."

"Well, they were idiots. If you were any better in bed, I would have had a heart attack."

He smiled. "They would have thought our love-making too tame. No swinging upside down from a chandelier or dangling over the parapet of a castle tower."

Lara laughed. "You've got to be kidding." When Jack shook his head, she gasped. "They really did that stuff?"

"Yes. They attacked a circus after I left, and they were much happier with a trapeze artist."

Lara snorted.

"I nearly died again, trying to make my way across Europe to Paris. I found Jean-Luc there, and he taught me how to be a vampire. Then finally, I went back to Venezia, hoping that Beatrice could still love me."

"What happened?"

Jack sighed. "She had died a month earlier during an outbreak of typhoid fever. I have always feared that she died believing I abandoned her."

"Oh Jack." Lara touched his cheek. "I'm sure she still loved you. How could she not love you?"

He took her hand and kissed the palm. "I have always been unlucky in *amore* till now. Over the years, I fell in love twice more, but the women rejected me when I told them what I was. I was afraid you would reject me, too."

"I love you too much to lose you. And it's about time you found happiness." She frowned at his blond hair. "But I have to tell you I'm not crazy about the new hairstyle."

"I had to change my appearance." He pulled her close, so he could whisper. "Too many Malcontents know about Giacomo di Venezia."

"Malcontents?"

"That's what we call the bad vampires who enjoy

killing. They call themselves the True Ones, since they believe they're following the true nature of the vampire—hunting and killing. They were cruel, violent mortals, and becoming vampires has only magnified their brutality."

"So you and your friends are fighting them?"

"Yes. I've investigated so many of them over the years that I know how to act like one. I came here with my new look, speaking Czech, and calling myself Henrik Sokolov."

"Which is your real name," she whispered.

"Yes. I pretended to be an old friend of Jedrek Janow, who died last December, so he can't confirm it. I dropped some other names, and I knew so much, like the location of this place, that Apollo bought it."

"Thank goodness." She raked her hand through his short blond hair. "You took a big risk."

"The others are close by. They would have charged in if I'd put out a psychic message for help. Robby wanted to attack tonight, but I wanted to make sure you were all right first. And I wanted whatever information you could tell me."

"Of course." Lara explained the routines and how many maidens there were, how many guards, and how many vampires. "There was a guest vampire last night called Zeus. We never saw him. A maiden was chosen for him, and this morning she had no memory of him. But she was covered with bruises."

Jack shook his head, frowning.

"When I first arrived, the Chosen One was Brittney Beckford. The next morning, she was gone, and I'm afraid—"

"She's dead," Jack said quietly. "Her body was found."

"Oh no. That poor girl."

"The wolves found her body in the woods."

Lara winced. "I saw the wolves. They scared the hell out of me."

"They won't harm you. And they told me where to find you. They've agreed to help us tomorrow night."

"Whoa." Lara lifted a hand. "They . . . talk?"

"They're werewolves. Shape shifters."

She gasped. "No way."

"The delivery man who left the Cracker Jack is a werewolf. Works for MacKay S & I, just like me."

She shook her head. "This is getting too weird."

"We're worried that the minute we attack, the guards may be under orders to attack the women."

"What?"

"If the compound comes under attack, Apollo may have the guards programmed to kill all the witnesses."

Lara shivered. "God, I hope not."

"We hope not, too. We need you to help keep the other girls safe. Can you do that?"

"Yes." She would find some reason to get them all into the kitchen. They would have a supply of knives there.

"One more thing." Jack took her hand. "It will look very suspicious if you're here in the morning without my mark on you."

"Your . . . mark?"

He nodded. "On your neck. I'm sorry, but it will have to be done."

She swallowed hard. "You want to bite me."

Chapter Twenty-five

*I*s it going to hurt?" Lara asked.

"It could." Jack stroked her hair. "Some vampires, like the Malcontents, enjoy causing their victims pain and terror. But if a vampire takes the time and effort, he can make it very pleasurable."

"I vote for the second option."

His mouth curled up. "Are you sure? I was still undecided, myself."

She swatted his arm.

With a grin, he pushed her down and leaned over her.

She gave him a wry look. "You want to be on top again?"

"It's easier for biting." He frowned, considering. "I guess I could bite you from behind."

"Or you could hang upside down from the canopy."

He chuckled. "I knew I shouldn't have told you that story."

Lara gave him a weak smile. She was joking around in a sad attempt to delay the inevitable. Surely it wouldn't hurt too badly. Jack had said he could make it pleasurable. "Are you going to . . . feed from me?"

"Just a little. I don't want to leave you weak."

"Okay." She turned her head to expose her neck and squeezed her eyes shut. "I'm ready."

She waited. Any minute now. Sharp fangs jabbing into her neck. She curled her hands into fists. And she waited.

She opened her eyes and glanced his way.

He was propped up on an elbow, smiling as he leisurely inspected her body.

"What are you doing?"

"Admiring the view." He touched a spot close to her left hip bone. "You have a little mole here." He leaned over and kissed it.

"I thought you were going to bite me."

"I am." He skimmed his fingers across her belly, then circled her navel. "I'll have to use Vamp power to make you conceive pain as pleasure and heighten your senses."

"Oh."

He dragged his fingers up to her breasts and circled them. "You'll need to open your mind to me."

"Okay."

He looked at her, and she suddenly felt herself caught in the intensity of his gaze. A wave of cold air swept around her. Her skin chilled. The gold flecks in his eyes expanded, turning the entire iris gold and glittering.

She was mesmerized, unable to move or think.

I am with you. His words whispered in her head.

Heat surged through her, and her skin turned pink, flushed with rushing blood. Her heart pounded. It felt like her blood was racing, racing toward him, on fire with the need for him to take it. It was bizarre. She actually wanted him to bite her.

"Jack." She reached for him. "This is so strange."

He brushed a thumb over her nipple, and she cried out as a jolt sizzled through her. All her nerve endings were extra sensitive and burning for his touch.

She wrapped a leg around him. "Jack, I need you."

"It's the Vamp power." He stroked her cheek. "It's just an illusion. It will pass."

"I don't want it to pass." She gritted her teeth. "I want you. Now."

"I'm only going to leave my mark. It will be over soon. I promised I would never use my powers to trick you into sex."

"You're released from that promise." She held his face in her hands. "And this isn't sex. It's love. I love you. I love everything about you, even this—this strange thing you're doing to me."

His eyes turned red. "Then hang on, *cara mia*." He grabbed her hips and thrust deep inside her.

She shattered with a powerful orgasm. He arched back, and his fangs jutted out. He fell on her, and she shivered with pleasure as his fangs gently scraped her neck.

Her blood was throbbing in her veins, desperate to be released. He licked her neck, and she felt the same sensation magnified between her legs. He eased in and out of her vagina. She was swirling, drowning in pleasure and barely felt the pop on her neck as his fangs slid into her. He continued to rock in and out as he sucked on her neck.

I love you, his voice echoed in her mind.

"I love you, too."

He pulled away from her neck. She had a glimpse of blood on his lips before he licked it off.

"You're still bleeding a little. I can stop it." He leaned over to nuzzle her neck.

Every lick of his tongue caused a shudder of plea-sure. Tension coiled inside her, begging for release. He scooped her up into his arms and sat back, settling her on his thighs.

She wrapped her arms around his shoulders and pressed herself against him. He seized her hips, sup-porting her and pulling her to him with each powerful thrust.

The room spun around Lara, and she held on tight. He slid a hand between them and tweaked her clitoris. A strangled moan escaped as another orgasm ripped through her. He pumped into her, his eyes flaming red hot. Then, with a long groan, he tumbled onto the bed with her. They held each other, still breathing heavily.

"Oh Jack." She stretched, still lingering in a lovely, sensual daze. "You're so good. You're going to kill me someday."

He flinched, then rolled onto his back and stared at the ceiling.

She winced. What a stupid thing to say. She hadn't meant it literally. She hadn't even been thinking properly.

A chill stole over her. If she wanted to stay with Jack forever, and she did, then he would have to turn her into a vampire. He *would* have to kill her someday.

She sat up. "I'm sorry. I didn't mean it the way it sounded."

The look he gave her was so full of pain, it wrenched her heart. "You know I never want to hurt you. If there was any other way . . ." He grimaced. "If you want to change your mind about me, I won't stop you. I would never force you."

"Shh." She placed her fingers over his beautiful mouth. "I'm not going to leave you." She lay down beside him and nestled her face in the crook of his neck.

He held her tight. She relaxed against him and grew drowsy. She drifted off to sleep.

"Lara," he said softly, "it's getting close to sunrise. I need you to wake up."

She blinked awake. She was still in bed with him, and at some point during the night, he'd pulled the covers up over her. And he'd dimmed the light. "I didn't mean to sleep."

He smiled. "It's all right. I enjoyed holding you."

"I guess you don't sleep?"

He shook his head. "I need to go and finalize the plans for tonight."

"I understand."

"Try to keep the girls safe. See if you can get them to leave the compound. The werewolves will be waiting, in human form, about half a mile down the road with a few SUVs. They'll take the girls to town. We'll come later to alter their memories."

Lara sat up, frowning. She had serious doubts she could convince the girls to cross the gate.

He touched her shoulder. "I hate to leave you here."

"I'll be fine. The girls will be amazed that I'm still here and not getting punished in Hades. They'll think I served you really well."

"Oh, you did." He chuckled when she made a face. "I'll see you tonight."

Fear gripped her as she envisioned him fighting armed guards and Apollo. She threw her arms around his neck and hugged him tight. "Please be careful."

"I will." He kissed her brow. "You be careful, too."

They shared one last kiss, then he vanished.

* * *

That evening, in the dark cellar of Chief's hunting cabin, Jack jolted awake. He heard the quick intake of air as Robby and Phineas also woke from their death-sleep. The sun had just set. This was it. The night Apollo would pay for his crimes against humanity.

As usual, within seconds of waking from his death-sleep, Jack's thoughts turned to Lara. Was she all right? How had she fared during the day?

The basement door creaked open and light spilled down the staircase.

"Are you guys up yet?" Phil asked.

"Yes, we're coming." With vampire speed, Jack inserted his knife into the sheath strapped to his calf. He'd put on some jeans and a T-shirt when he'd teleported back to the cabin before dawn. He'd been so worried about leaving Lara behind, that he hadn't realized he was teleporting naked. He'd taken some ribbing for that.

He slid a longer dagger into the sheath underneath his left arm, then put on his leather jacket. Phineas was similarly armed, but Robby had opted for his Scottish weapons—a knife beneath one knee sock and a claymore in the long sheath on his back.

The three Vamps rushed up the stairs. Phil handed them bottles of blood from the ice cooler. With no electricity at the hunting cabin, the Vamps were drinking their meals cold. Connor had teleported to the cabin the night before, delivering bottles of blood, swords, and handcuffs.

Jack gulped down his bottle of blood, then stuffed some handcuffs into a jacket pocket. These were for the mortal guards. If at all possible, they hoped to keep the guards alive.

"You know Connor came here twice last night," Phineas said as he jammed handcuffs into his pockets. "He kept wondering why you weren't here. He thought you might have gotten lost in the woods."

"I told him ye were at the compound gathering information," Robby said, his green eyes twinkling. "All night long."

"Hmm." Phineas finished up his bottle of blood. "Jack must have studied every inch of that compound."

Jack ignored them and selected a sword from the stash Connor had brought.

"Let's see." Phineas rummaged through the swords. "I need a really strong blade. One like Jack has, that'll last all night long."

"Enough," Jack growled. "This isn't a picnic we're going on. So get serious, Phineas."

The black Vamp shrugged. "How hard can it be? We've got three Vamps, and Phil, and the element of surprise."

"We thought it would be easy to locate Apollo's compound, but it took over a month," Jack said. "And then we thought it would be easy to capture the bastard, but he got away. We can't afford to take this lightly."

"I got you, bro." Phineas selected a sword. "Just keeping it positive, dude. We're gonna kick ass."

"Good. Then let's go." Jack glanced at Phil. He was barefoot, with a pair of gym shorts and a T-shirt on. "Aren't you going to arm yourself?"

"I'm keeping it simple so I can shift."

Jack exchanged a confused look with the other Vamps, then turned back to Phil. "There's no full moon tonight. Only an Alpha wolf can—oh, I see."

"Well, I don't see," Phineas grumbled. "If you're an Alpha, why didn't you shift the other night with Chief?"

"I have my reasons," Phil muttered. "Can we get going now?"

"That's why you insisted Chief and his people park half a mile down the road," Jack said. "You don't want them to know what you can do."

"Oh, Big Bad Wolf's got a secret," Phineas said.

"And we'll keep it for him," Robby said. "Let's go."

The three Vamps had practiced teleporting close to the compound the night before, so the location was embedded in their psychic memory. Phil grabbed on to Robby to hitch a ride, and within seconds, they arrived about fifty feet from the gate.

In the distance, Jack spotted Lara and the other women, strolling toward the kitchen. Their white gowns gleamed in the moonlight.

Phil pulled off his T-shirt as he stepped behind a tree. After a few seconds, he returned as a huge wolf.

"Let's do it." Jack headed to the right with Robby, while Phineas and Phil turned left to circle the compound.

There were usually two guards marching around the perimeter of the compound each night. It was Phil and Phineas's job to capture them. Once they were handcuffed, Phineas would teleport them to the jail at Chief's office. One of the Chief's grown sons would be there to watch them. Later, when the attack was over, the Vamps would alter the guards' memories and set them free.

Jack and Robby weaved through the forest till they neared the dormitory. They jumped the wall, then unsheathed their swords before entering the dorm. It was empty. Good. Lara had managed to get all the women out.

They hurried to the temple next. Phil loped toward them and met them at the base of the stairs.

"You caught the two guards?" Jack whispered.

Phil dipped his head and growled softly.

Phineas would be gone for a few minutes while he transported the guards to the jail at Wolf Ridge.

Jack ascended the steps to the temple. "There should be three mortal guards and one mortal woman inside."

Robby cracked the door and peeked inside. "Coast is clear." He widened the door, and Phil slipped inside.

They crossed the foyer to the next set of double doors. Jack scanned the temple as he eased inside. The room was lit by the small fires in the bronze braziers located between the columns. At the other end on the dais, a guard was lounging on the center throne and munching on chips. He obviously didn't expect any trouble. He was entirely focused on his bag of potato chips. His sword rested on the throne next to him.

Jack moved silently to the row of columns on the right. Robby eased to the left. When Phil followed him, his claws made a small clicking noise on the marble floor. Robby looked back at him, then at the guard.

The guard sat up. His eyes widened at the sight of a wolf and an armed, kilted Scotsman. His bag of chips tumbled to the floor. He grabbed his sword, jumped off the dais, and ran to the gong to sound the alarm.

"Nay!" Robby charged at him.

Jack and Phil were close behind. When the guard saw how fast they were zooming toward him, he threw his sword at the gong. It clanged just as Robby tackled the guard.

The impact from the sword knocked the gong free and it rolled past a lit brazier before it went into a rotating spiral that created a whooshing, metallic sound that echoed across the large room. Phil pounced on it, and it stopped with one loud clash.

Even though Robby had the guard pinned to the floor, the mortal was still struggling and yelling for help.

"Be quiet," Robby muttered and clonked the mortal on the head with the handle of his sword.

Jack handed him a pair of handcuffs. "We'll teleport him later."

Robby cuffed the unconscious guard and dragged him behind a column.

Meanwhile, another guard came running from the back hallway. He rounded the thrones, shouting and brandishing his sword. Jack engaged him, and within a few seconds, he sent the guard's sword flying through the air. It fell with a clamor in front of the dais.

The guard stumbled back, his eyes wide with fear.

Jack held his sword to the side. "I don't want to kill you. You only have to surrender."

"Under attack. No hope," the guard whispered. He stiffened suddenly, and his eyes turned glassy. "There can be no survivors." He reached inside his toga and pulled out a knife. He turned the knife, pointing it at his own chest.

"No!" Jack dropped his sword and teleported behind the guard. He seized the man's wrist just as he attempted to stab himself.

Jack wrenched the knife from the guard's hand and knocked him on the head with the handle. When the guard slumped forward, Jack dropped the knife and caught him.

There can be no survivors. Jack muttered a curse. He tossed the guard over his shoulder and strode to where Robby had stashed the first guard.

"Did you hear what he said?" Jack dropped the guard on the floor.

"Aye, no survivors." Robby cuffed the guard.

"Phil, make sure Lara's all right," Jack ordered. "And the other women, too. They're in the kitchen."

Phil raced to the double doors. He reared up on his hind legs to push a door open, then dashed through.

"You can find the other mortal woman in the back," Jack whispered to Robby. "Behind a red door."

Robby nodded, then a voice rang out.

It was Apollo.

Jack pulled Robby behind a column. "I'll take care of him. You get the girl," he whispered.

"What the hell is going on?" Apollo strode around the thrones. His golden toga was all askew as if he'd thrown it on in a hurry. He stopped when he saw the sword on the floor and the bag of spilled chips on the dais.

"Hello, Apollo," Jack greeted him in Czech as he walked over to where he'd dropped his sword. He'd discovered the night before that Apollo was actually Anton, from Prague.

"Henrik, what are you doing here?" Apollo answered in Czech. "You've got the stupid guards thinking we're under attack."

Jack needed to say the right things to make Apollo stay, or the bastard would simply teleport away. He picked up his sword. "You *are* under attack. I've taken four of your guards."

Apollo stiffened, then his face flushed red with anger. "You scum-sucking pig! I welcomed you here. I even gave you a maiden to fuck. And you repay my generosity with betrayal? Why?"

"I want to keep the girl." Jack glanced quickly to the right. Robby was still hidden behind the column, waiting for his chance to run to the back rooms.

Apollo scoffed. "Well, shit, you idiot! Why didn't you just say so? I've got eight women to spare. If you want one of the bitches, just take her." He gave Jack a disgusted look. "But you'll need to hurry, 'cause my head guard just left to kill them all."

A chill crept across Jack's skin. Lara had to be all right. Phil was there. And Phineas should be back by now.

Apollo leaned over to pick up the sword in front of the dais. "You've screwed up my whole operation, you bastard. I should kill you."

"You're welcome to try." Jack retreated, hoping to draw Apollo away from the thrones and make it easier for Robby to sneak to the back rooms.

"You asshole." Apollo stalked toward him. "I'll have to start over and completely restock."

"No." Jack switched to English. "You're not starting over. You're finished."

Apollo's eyes narrowed. "Your accent is different tonight. Who are you?"

"I am Giacomo di Venezia."

Apollo's face turned red, and he visibly shook with rage. "You're one of the butchers from the DVN massacre!"

"Yes, I killed six of your friends that night. And I saw Jedrek Janow die. He was so pathetic and weak that a mortal killed him."

"No!" Apollo ran at him, swinging his sword.

From the corner of his eye, Jack saw Robby zoom toward the back rooms.

Jack jumped to the side and parried Apollo's attack. He spared one last prayer that Lara was safe, then focused all his attention on staying alive.

Chapter Twenty-six

*Y*ou make the best cookies ever." Vanessa stuffed another chocolate chip cookie into her mouth.

"Thanks." Lara stacked more on a plate and set it on
the table. She'd spent all afternoon baking so she could
lure the girls to the kitchen. "More milk, anyone?"

Several hands went up. Lara grabbed the milk jug
from the fridge and circled the table, refilling glasses.

Miss Forbidden gave her a confused look. "Why are
you being so nice to us? I thought you hated being
here."

"I saw how worried you were last night when Hades
chose me." Lara returned the jug to the fridge. "I was
really touched. This is my way of thanking you."

"I thought I'd never see you again." Vanessa shuddered. "I thought Hades would take you to hell."

"Me, too." Kristy bit into a cookie. "How—how was
he?"

All seven maidens turned to Lara, eager for her
answer.

"He was . . . great. Hades is a real gentleman."

"I don't think Zeus is," Miss Forbidden muttered as she glanced at her bruised arms.

"Shh," Cook hushed her. "Someone might hear you."

Kristy finished her cookie and reached for another. "I swear I'm going to gain five pounds tonight."

The other maidens commiserated. While they complained about being overweight, Lara wedged a steak knife underneath the linen ties around her rib cage. She wanted a weapon, just in case Jack was right and Apollo sent a guard to attack them. Jack had also wanted her to get the girls down the road to where the werewolves were waiting with the SUVs. Convincing them to go through the gate would be tough.

She approached the table. "If you really want to lose some weight, you should get some exercise. We could take a walk down the road."

The girls gasped.

"We can't leave," Cook said. "It's forbidden."

"And there are terrible beasts in the woods," Kristy added. "With great gnashing teeth."

Vanessa grimaced. "I heard they drag people to hell."

"I asked Hades about that," Lara said. "And he said the woods are perfectly safe. The beasts know that we're special, so they would actually protect us."

The maidens remained silent while they pondered this new information.

Cook shook her head. "I'm not sure we can trust anything Hades says."

"And you think you can trust Apollo?" Lara asked. "He kidnapped us all from college. We were taken from our friends and families. Vanessa, I met your friends."

Vanessa jumped in her chair. "You know my name?"

"Yes. And I met your roommate Megan. And your

friends Carmen and Ramya. They're worried sick about you. All of you have friends and families who are worried about you."

"So?" Cook frowned. "What's the point? We can't go back."

"Yes, you can." Lara pointed in the direction of the road outside. "Half a mile down the road, there are people waiting for us. Nice people, and they want to take us back home. You could all go back to your real lives."

"Are you serious?" Miss Forbidden's eyes widened with a hopeful look.

Vanessa wrinkled her nose. "But I'm failing three of my classes."

"I was flunking, too," Kristy grumbled. "Life is a lot easier here."

"What life?" Lara asked. "You're told what to wear, when to eat, when to clean, when to guard a false god—"

"Don't say that!" Cook looked around nervously.

"I like it here." Vanessa bit into another cookie. "Life is too hard back on Earth."

"It's not supposed to be easy," Lara said. "If it was always easy, we would never grow or learn. And when awful stuff happens, that's when we stretch beyond ourselves and become better than we ever thought was possible."

She thought back to how much she'd grown since the car accident. Now she could be grateful for the suffering and the struggle, because it had left her strong enough to handle this situation and strong enough to embrace a future with Jack.

"And sometimes, we have to make really hard decisions that will affect the rest of our lives." Lara knew her decision to stay with Jack could ultimately cause her to become a vampire. But it was the right decision, and she would stick by it.

She was pulled from her musings by a voice yelling outside. One of the guards. Her heart lurched. What if Jack was right, and the guard meant to kill them? She ran to check the lock. What if the guard had a key? She grabbed a chair and wedged it under the doorknob.

"What are you doing?" Cook stood.

"Is the back door locked?" Lara asked.

"Yes," Cook answered. "But what—"

The doorknob rattled. "Open the door!" the guard yelled.

Lara recognized his voice. It was the head guard, the one she called Squeaky.

"Let me in!" He pounded on the door.

"Yes, master." Cook headed for the door.

"No." Lara held up a hand to stop her.

The other maidens stood.

"We can't disobey a guard," Kristy said.

Squeaky banged on the door. "I order you to open this door. The Elysian Fields are under attack!"

The maidens gasped.

"What should we do?" Vanessa whispered.

"We must open the door." Cook stepped toward the door.

Lara pulled out her knife. "Stay back."

Cook's eyes widened. "You—you're in league with Hades! You're trying to get us all taken to hell!"

"I'm trying to save you," Lara said.

"There can be no survivors," the guard yelled.

Lara gasped. Jack had been right.

"What does that mean?" Vanessa asked.

Lara pushed against the door as the guard shook it. "It means Apollo has ordered the guard to kill us."

The maidens gasped. A few stumbled back. Vanessa started to shake and whimper. Lara heard footsteps moving away from the door. What would Squeaky try next?

"No," Cook whispered. "Apollo is a god. He would never kill us."

"He's not a god," Lara said. "He's been lying to you."

"You're wrong, you're wrong," the maidens said.

"I have to stop you." Cook ran into the kitchen and grabbed a knife. "You're going to get us all dragged to hell."

"No!" Miss Forbidden shouted, and all the maidens turned to her. Her eyes filled with tears, and she rubbed her bruised arms. "She's right. They're not gods."

The kitchen window shattered. The girls squealed. Glass flew into the room.

Squeaky used the hilt of his sword to clear all the glass away. "There can be no survivors."

"He's coming in!" Vanessa cried.

"Stay back!" Lara yelled at the girls. She ran to the window with her knife, ready to stab Squeaky if he tried to climb through the window.

A howl sounded close by. Squeaky shrieked just before a huge wolf knocked him down.

The maidens screamed.

"It's one of the beasts from the woods," Kristy wailed. "He's come to drag us all to hell."

"No, he's saving us." Lara looked out the window. The wolf had pinned Squeaky to the ground. "Come and see."

The girls slowly crept forward to peek out the window.

A young black man strode into view. He was dressed all in black and carrying a sword. Lara recognized him as the Vamp she'd seen before at Syracuse.

"Oh my, look at *him*," Vanessa whispered. "He's as handsome as Denzel."

He jabbed his sword into the ground, then pulled handcuffs from his jacket pocket and cuffed the guard. He patted the wolf on the head, then plucked his sword from the ground.

"Wow," Vanessa breathed. "Who is he?"

"He's amazing," Kristy added. "Did you see him tame that scary wolf?"

Since the girls persisted in their belief of Greek gods, Lara decided to use that. "He's . . . Ares, god of war."

"Ooooh," the maidens sighed.

Miss Forbidden pulled Lara aside and whispered, "Who is he really?"

"He's a good man who's come to help us," Lara said. "He can take you to the nearest town, so you can go home."

A tear rolled down Miss Forbidden's cheek. "Thank you." She hugged Lara. "My name is Sarah."

"Will you help him get the girls to safety?" Lara asked.

"Yes." Sarah pulled the chair away from the door and unlocked it. "Come on, let's go."

The maidens filed outside.

"Where are we going?" Vanessa asked.

Lara approached the black Vamp. "Hi, I'm Lara."

He looked at all the women and grinned. "Hello, ladies. Allow me to introduce myself—"

"Oh, we know who you are," Lara interrupted. "You're Lord Ares, the god of war."

"Say what?"

"You're Ares, the god of war," Lara repeated with a pointed look. "And you've come to rescue all these fair maidens."

"Oh yeah. That's me, baby. I'm the god of war."

Lara smiled. "And you're going to lead all these women down the road to the SUVs."

"Sure." He motioned to the gate. "Come on, ladies."

"Oh Lord Ares." Vanessa fluttered her eyelashes at him. "You're so brave."

"I love the way you tamed that horrible wolf," Kristy added.

The wolf grunted.

The black Vamp grinned at the wolf. "Oh yeah, he's bad. He's big and bad. But don't worry, ladies. I'll protect you with my mighty sword."

The girls followed the black Vamp to the gate. He opened it, and they all walked down the road. Sarah glanced back at Lara and waved.

Lara waved back. The girls were safe. Squeaky was on the ground with his hands cuffed behind his back.

"There can be no survivors," he whispered over and over.

Lara shuddered. Apollo had intended them all to die.

With a jolt, she realized Jack could be fighting Apollo right now. She grabbed Squeaky's sword and started running to the temple.

The wolf dashed in front of her and stopped with a growl. Lara moved to the right, but the wolf moved, too. She ran to the left, but the wolf blocked her again.

"Oh come on," she yelled. This had to be the werewolf Jack had told her about. Did he understand English?

"Are you the delivery man who left the box of Cracker Jack?"

The wolf grunted and dipped his head.

"I need to get to the temple."

The wolf growled low in his throat.

"We can't just stand here all night, glaring at each other."

The wolf sat on his haunches and regarded her with his pale blue eyes.

"Look. I want to help Jack. He might need us. What if something happens to him while we're standing here? How could we live with ourselves?"

The wolf cocked his head. Then he turned and loped toward the temple.

"Thank you." Lara ran after him.

Where the hell was Robby? Jack asked himself for the tenth time. Apollo was a surprisingly good swordsman. Still, Jack could have defeated him five minutes ago if Athena hadn't arrived.

First the female vampire had shrieked at him, calling him a dozen foul names. Then she'd tried to free the two guards in handcuffs. When that failed, she'd picked up the sword from the first guard. She was obviously ignorant about fencing, didn't even know how to hold the sword properly. But she was able to be a dangerous nuisance.

While he parried with Apollo, she dashed behind him to try to stab him in the back. He spun, knocking the sword from her hand, then continued his fight with Apollo.

Where the hell was Robby? He was supposed to teleport the mortal Chosen One to Wolf Ridge, then come right back.

Jack lunged at Apollo, forcing him to retreat. Then suddenly, in his peripheral vision, he saw something flying at him. He ducked as a knife flew over his head. That damned Athena.

The doors opened, and Jack saw Phil slip inside. Good. Maybe he could take care of Athena.

Then Jack did a double take when Lara came in, carrying a sword. *Merda*. She was supposed to be safe with the other girls, not putting herself into danger here.

Athena spotted her. "You bitch! Kneel before your gods!"

"Go to hell." Lara moved toward her, holding her sword in both hands.

Athena flung her knife at Lara. Jack froze a second in fear, then jumped to the side as Apollo took a swing at him. He glanced back. Lara had ducked in time. Thank God.

With a ferocious growl, Phil charged at Athena, but she dashed with vampire speed to pick up her sword. She retreated around a column, swinging the sword wildly to keep the wolf from pouncing on her.

Athena squealed as Phil chased her around another column. She passed by one of the tripods holding a lit brazier. Lara kicked the tripod over, and the brazier crashed onto the floor next to Athena.

Athena screamed as the fire leaped onto her long purple toga. The flames spread quickly. She fell on the floor, rolling and screeching. Her body writhed, then went still.

"Athena!" Apollo roared with rage. He charged at Jack, abandoning all form in a wild quest for revenge.

This was exactly the opportunity Jack had been waiting for. He knocked Apollo's sword aside and skewered him in the chest. Apollo's eyes widened just before his body disintegrated into a pile of dust.

Jack turned to Lara. "Are you all right?"

"Yes." She looked at the floor and grimaced. "Is that what happens when you—"

"Look out!" Jack ran toward her.

She spun around. Athena was charging at her, her body blackened and burned. She lifted a sword with her charred arm and bellowed with rage.

Lara held her sword steady. With a growl, Phil leaped on Athena from behind. The force pushed her right onto Lara's sword. Athena crumbled into a pile of burnt ash.

Lara dropped her sword and stepped back. Jack grabbed her in his arms. Her body was trembling.

"It's all right." He tossed his sword down and held her tight. "It's all right. It's all over."

She wrapped her arms around his neck. "I was so scared for you."

"I was scared for you, too." Jack rubbed her back. "You should never try to fight a vampire. It's too dangerous."

"I had help from the wolf. What's his name again?"

"Phil Jones." Jack looked around the temple. Phil had crossed the room to check on the guards. "Thank you, Phil."

"Yes, thank you!" Lara added.

Phil looked back at them with a wolfish grin.

"Are the girls safe? What happened?" Jack asked.

"They're fine. They're with the black vampire."

"He's Phineas McKinney, also known as Dr. Phang."

Lara laughed. "I have a whole new world to get used to."

The door opened and Robby rushed inside, holding his claymore ready.

"And that one is Robby MacKay," Jack drawled. "Also known as mud."

Robby looked around and grimaced. "I guess I'm a wee bit late."

"About ten minutes late!" Jack yelled. "Where the hell were you?"

"Bugger." Robby slid his claymore into the sheath on his back. "I did as ye asked and found the mortal woman in the back behind the red door."

"The Chosen One Aquila," Lara said. "Was she all right?"

"Nay. The guard had already stabbed her in the chest. She was near death, so I teleported her straight to Romatech." Robby sighed. "Roman tried to save her life, but she had too many internal injuries. I wiped her memory and took her to a hospital. I doona know if she'll survive."

"That poor girl," Lara whispered.

"You did all you could," Jack said quietly.

Robby crossed his arms, frowning. "So is everything done here?"

"Just about." Jack motioned to the guards. "They have to be teleported to town."

"And there's another guard by the kitchen," Lara said.

"I'll get him." Robby strode from the temple. Phil trotted alongside him.

"Where's the wolf going?" Lara whispered.

"He's probably going to his clothes so he can shift back. Lara, we're the only ones who know that Phil can shift when the moon isn't full. Don't tell any of the people in Wolf Ridge. I'm not sure why, but Phil wants to keep it secret."

She nodded. "Okay. I guess I'll have a lot of secrets to keep from now on."

He touched her cheek. "It's no secret that I love you and adore you and want to spend my entire life with you. You can shout that from the mountaintops."

She grinned. "I'll just shout it from the top of a certain bell tower I know in Venice."

Jack laughed. "It's a date."

Lara sighed as hot water sluiced down her body. She hadn't wanted to spend one more minute in that white gown. While Jack stayed in the temple, watching the guards, she'd gathered her old clothes from the trunk in the side room. Then, she'd run back to the dormitory to shower and change.

It was all over, she thought, as the last of the soap and shampoo spiraled down the drain. No, it was actually just beginning. Her life would be an exciting adventure with Jack. He'd assured her that he just wanted her to be happy. She could return to her job as a police officer on the night patrol. She could continue to work toward her detective badge. Or she could start as a detective right away, working for MacKay Security and Investigation.

It was tempting. Very tempting. She already knew about Vamps and Malcontents and shape shifters. How could she go back to her regular job when she knew about this strange new world? She would have to find a way to explain it all to LaToya. She turned off the water and stepped out of the shower stall.

"Hello, *bellissima*."

She gasped. "Jack." He was standing across the bathroom, leaning against the vanity with his arms folded. His reflection didn't appear in the mirror behind him. "How long have you been here?"

"Long enough." His golden brown eyes twinkled.

She snorted and grabbed a towel to dry off. "I thought you were going to stay in the temple to watch those guards."

"Robby just teleported the last one away, and I was there all alone, getting worried about you. I wanted to make sure you were all right." He smiled slowly. "You are definitely all right. All over."

She grinned as she towel-dried her hair. "You should have joined me in the shower."

"I seriously considered that. I also considered using

one of those beds in the dorm room. But they're expecting us to teleport to Wolf Ridge. If we don't show up in a few minutes, they'll come here looking for us."

"Oh, I'd better get dressed." She pulled on some underwear.

Jack watched with a wistful look. "Well, it was nice while it lasted."

She grabbed her bra. "Thank God I can wear this again. I was so tired of flopping around in that gown."

"Yes, it was a very sad thing to watch."

She scoffed. "I was afraid my breasts would start sagging."

"They look perfect to me." His gaze focused on her chest. "They perk right up when I see them."

She laughed and put on her bra, then her jeans.

"Jack, are ye here?" Robby's voice called from the dormitory.

"*Merda,*" Jack grumbled. "Coming!" He strode into the dormitory.

Lara quickly donned her T-shirt, then her socks and shoes. She ran into the dorm room.

Robby nodded at her. "I was just telling Jack that we've altered the memories of the guards and most of the lassies. There was one, though, who wanted to retain her memory. Her name is Sarah."

"Oh, right." Miss Forbidden. Somehow, Lara wasn't that surprised. "Sarah was starting to figure things out. She was given to some creep who called himself Zeus, and he abused her."

"Aye." Robby frowned. "She couldna remember Zeus, so I helped her regain those memories. It was verra hard on the puir lass. She knows now that he raped her and bit her."

"Then she knows about vampires," Jack said.

"Aye. We'll have to be verra careful with her. I'm

teleporting her straight to Romatech, where we can keep an eye on her until we decide whether or not to let her keep her memory." Robby turned to Lara. "Ye know her better than we do. Do ye think she can be trusted?"

"Yes, I do." Lara had to admire Sarah. She'd made a tough decision to keep those awful memories. It would have been so much easier to have them simply erased.

"Normally, I would just erase her memory anyway," Robby continued. "But she's studying to be a school-teacher, so I thought I'd let her talk to Shanna first."

Jack nodded. "I heard she needs more teachers."

"Teachers for what?" Lara asked.

"A school for special children," Jack said. "Shape shifters or kids like Constantine who have some Vamp DNA. I'll tell you about it later."

"Please do." Lara was really curious about the pos-sibility of having children with a vampire.

"One more thing," Robby said. "When I brought back her memories of Zeus, she was able to describe him. Tall, dark eyes, Russian accent, and a left arm bent at a strange angle. He wore a glove on his left hand."

Jack stiffened. "Nine circles of hell."

"What?" Lara asked. "Do you know him?"

"We've been hunting him for several years," Robby explained. "The most recent reports had indicated he was in Eastern Europe."

Jack gave Lara a worried look. "He's Casimir, the leader of the Malcontents. And he's here in America."

Lara gulped. This had to mean more battles. More deaths. More mortals in danger.

"I'm going straight to Romatech to alert Roman and Connor," Robby said. "Then I'll call Angus. He'll want to transfer every available man here."

Jack nodded. "Go. I'll take Lara to Wolf Ridge."

Robby vanished.

"Let's go." Jack wrapped his arms around Lara.

"Wait." She pressed her hands against his chest. "Just how bad is this? What does Casimir want to do?"

"He's building an army of vampires who were criminals in their mortal lives. He plans to kill every decent, bottle-drinking Vamp like me. And then they'll terrorize the mortal world, feeding and killing with no one to stop them."

Lara shuddered.

Jack brushed her damp hair away from her face. "I'm sorry, *cara mia*. I didn't mean to drag you into this."

"It's all right." She touched his face. "After the car accident, I wanted to do something really important, something that made a difference in the world. This is it. I can't think of anything more important than this."

"You are so brave, *cara mia*." He kissed her brow. "But I have to disagree with you. There is something much more important than Casimir and all his nasty followers."

Lara smiled. "Are you talking about love?"

He nodded. "*Amore*. With love on our side, we can never be defeated."

Epilogue

T hree nights later, Lara was standing in the *campanile* of the Piazza San Marco, gazing over the moon-lit rooftops of Venice. She leaned back against Jack's sturdy chest, and he wrapped his arms around her.

"It's so beautiful, so peaceful," she whispered.

He rubbed his chin against her hair. "This is where I first told you that I love you."

"Mmm. It was very romantic." She jumped when music started below. "What's that?" She peered down from the bell tower and laughed when she saw Lorenzo playing his accordion. The strains of *"Bella Notte"* drifted up to her.

"Oh Jack." She touched his face. "You're so sweet."

"I wanted everything to be perfect."

She gave him a wry look. "Are you trying to recreate that first date?"

He winced. "Not really. You left me at the end of that date."

"Well, yes. But you did make me scream. I'm afraid I permanently traumatized the pigeons."

He held up his hands. "I learned my lesson. Tonight, we will teleport to my bedroom at the *palazzo*, and there, I will make love to you all night long. I promise to do my best, but the screaming will be left to your discretion."

She laughed. "You rascal. You always make me scream."

He grinned. "And then tomorrow, while I'm totally useless in my death-sleep, you will be taken on a tour of Venezia. Gianetta's niece works at a museum, and she'll spend the day as your personal guide."

"Oh, that's wonderful. Thank you, Jack."

His eyes sparkled. "And I have another surprise for you. You won't be sightseeing alone. I gave LaToya a first-class ticket to Venice. She'll be arriving in the morning."

Lara gasped and pressed a hand to her chest. "Jack, that's the most wonderful gift ever."

"She's been a good friend to you. I don't want you to lose her just because you're with me."

Lara's eyes filled with tears. She hadn't told LaToya everything yet, but it shouldn't be difficult to convince her best friend that Jack was the most wonderful man in the world. Because he simply was.

She leaned from the bell tower window. "I love Giacomo di Venezia!"

The pigeons, startled from their roosts, flapped wildly around the tower and *piazza*.

Jack laughed. "There you go, scaring the poor pigeons again."

She flung her arms around his neck. "I do love you, Jack. I will always love you."

He held her tight. "You are my angel, Lara. I have another surprise for you in my pants."

She snorted.

He placed her hand on the bulge.

She glanced down. "I seem to remember you being a lot bigger than that." She moved her hand to the center. "Oh yeah, now we're talking."

He chuckled and removed the smaller bulge from his pocket. "I think you'll like this, too. At least I hope so." He opened the small black box.

Lara gasped. It was a beautiful sapphire surrounded by glittering diamonds.

"I know it's not exactly traditional, but the sapphire reminded me of your lovely blue eyes."

She stepped back. Her skin prickled with goose flesh. She knew this was a moment she would cherish for as long as she lived. She would remember the cool night air blowing through the *campanile* and the sound of *"Bella Notte"* drifting up from the *piazza*. And she would remember Jack, standing there with a ring and so much love glimmering in his golden brown eyes.

He knelt before her. "Lara Boucher, will you marry me?"

She fell to her knees in front of him. "Yes, yes, I will." She wrapped her arms around his neck.

He held her tight. "Well, that's a relief."

She leaned back. "I do have one condition, though."

He looked worried. "What is it?"

She smiled and caressed his cheek. "You have to stop saying 'nine circles of hell.' "

"Oh." He looked surprised. "I can do that." He stood, then pulled her into his arms with a grin. "You are right, *cara mia*. You have brought love into my life, and we have found our way to *Paradiso*."

Turn the page for a sneak peek at

Forbidden Nights With a Vampire

by

KERRELYN SPARKS

Coming May 2009
From

Avon Books

*A*lthough Phil knew about Vanda's nightclub, he'd never been inside before. The entrance to the Horny Devils was hidden at the dead end of a dark alley to keep unsuspecting mortals from stumbling across the place.

A huge bouncer stood guard at the plain black door. His nostrils flared as he took a sniff. Phil knew he didn't carry the usual mortal scent. Since most Vamps didn't know about shapeshifters, they didn't realize the significance of Phil's different scent. They simply thought he was a strange-smelling mortal.

"Place is closed," the bouncer grumbled. "Get lost."

"I'm here to see Vanda Barkowski."

"You know Vanda?" The bouncer took another sniff, and his beady dark eyes narrowed. "You're an odd duck."

"Not even close." Phil showed his MacKay Security and Investigation ID card, knowing the Vamp bouncer could see it in the dark. "I'm returning Vanda's car. The black Corvette. She left it at Romatech."

"Well, okay." The bouncer still eyed him suspiciously. "I'll have to frisk you."

"Fine." Phil raised his arms to shoulder height so

the bouncer could pat his navy Polo shirt and khaki pants— the MacKay uniform for guards who didn't wear kilts.

"You're clean." The bouncer opened the door. "Go on in."

Phil was instantly bombarded with loud, pounding music and red and blue laser lights slashing across the large renovated warehouse. As his eyes adjusted, he noted the stage was empty. The male dancers must be on break.

A group of scantily-clad Vamp women were writhing on the dance floor. A few Vamp men sat at tables, drinking tall glasses of Bleer topped with pink-tinted foam while they watched the women dance. Their eyes narrowed when they spotted him. Competition.

He scanned the huge room but couldn't see Vanda anywhere. He recognized the woman behind the bar though—Miss Cora Lee Primrose, former member of Roman Draganesti's harem. She'd shed her ruffles and hoop skirts in favor of more modern garb—hip-hugger pants and a sparkly halter top.

She did a double take when he eased onto a barstool. "Phil? Is that you?" she yelled over the loud music. "Land sakes, I haven't seen you in ages."

"Hi, Cora Lee. You're looking great."

"Why, thank you kindly." With a giggle, she flipped her long blonde hair over her shoulder. "You're looking pretty good yourself. Would you like something to drink? We have a few mortal drinks like Coke or beer."

"I'll have a beer." He stood so he could pull the wallet from his back pocket.

"No you don't. It's on the house." She cast a flirtatious look at him as she filled a glass. "Land sakes, you've filled out nicely over the years."

"Thank you." He settled back onto the barstool. "So, is Vanda here?"

With a sigh, Cora Lee set the beer in front of him. "Dang it, I should have known you'd come to see her. The way she used to talk about you—goodness gracious, we were all scandalized."

His first sip of beer went down with a gulp. "Why? What did she say?"

"What didn't she say? I swear that woman would editorialize on your manly physique, from the top of your head down to your toes." Cora Lee gave him a sly smile. "She was quite poetic about your buttocks."

He didn't know what to say, so he gulped down more beer.

Cora Lee wiped the counter, still smiling. "She always claimed you had a crush on her."

His hand tightened around the glass. "Did she now?"

"You're darned tootin'. According to Vanda, she can make you do anything she wants, like a trained puppy."

He downed the last of his beer and slammed the glass onto the bar. "Where is she?"

Cora Lee pointed to a series of doors along the back wall. "The first one is her office."

"Thanks." Phil slid off the stool.

"Don't forget to knock," Cora Lee warned him. "Vanda's got the dancers in there. It could be kinda awkward if you just barge in."

He stiffened. "Why? What's she doing with them?"

Cora Lee shrugged. "The usual. She has to personally check out the costumes and dances before the guys go on stage. Quality control, you know."

Phil's jaw clenched. "You don't say."

"Oh, I do. I went in there once when Terrance was prancing around naked." Cora Lee giggled. "Vanda told him to put a sock on it."

"Enough," Phil growled. As he stalked toward her office, the music ended. With his superior hearing, he recognized Vanda's voice through the door.

"Oh my God, Peter, it's huge!"

"They don't call me the Printh of Peckerth for nothing," a male voice boasted.

"You can't let him on stage with that," another male voice protested. "He'll make us look small."

"You *are* smaller than me," Peter insisted.

"We are not!" a third male shouted. "Vanda, do something!"

"Calm down!" Vanda's voice sounded agitated. "Peter, I'm glad you've come back, but this is not acceptable. You're supposed to get the girls excited, not scare them to death. You'll have to lose a few inches."

"No!" Peter screamed. "I won't let you touch it!"

"Don't tell me what I can't do!" Vanda yelled. "Where are my scissors?"

Peter squealed.

Phil threw the door open and charged inside. "Vanda, stop! You can't cut off a man's——" He halted, stunned to see Vanda standing behind her desk with her scissors poised on a sparkling red sheath.

It wasn't a dong. It was a thong. With a long sheath stuffed like a sausage.

Vanda's mouth fell open. Her eyes widened. "Phil, what are you doing here?"

He glanced around the office, noting that the three slender young men were fully clothed and regarding him curiously. "What are *you* doing, Vanda?"

She glanced at the scissors and sparkly thong in her hands. Her cheeks grew pink as she lowered the thong to the desk. "I was conducting a business meeting."

"Vanda," one of the male dancers whispered. "Won't you introduce us to your handsome young friend?"

"Sure, Terrance," Vanda spoke through gritted teeth. "This is Phil Jones." She gestured to the other male dancers. "Terrance the Turgid, Freddie the Fireman, and Peter the Great."

"Oh, I remember you," Peter said. "You were at the coven meeting. You thaid you would help Vanda with her anger problem."

"I don't have an anger problem!" Vanda pointed the scissors at Peter, then at Phil. "And I don't need your help."

Phil arched a brow at her. "As your sponsor, I suggest you put the scissors down."

She slammed them onto the desk. "You are *not* my sponsor."

Terrance smiled at him. "You can be *my* sponsor."

Vanda groaned. "Phil, we're trying to have a costume meeting here." She handed Freddie a thong that looked like a fire hose and Terrance a thong covered with ivy.

Terrance dangled his costume in front of Phil's face. "Isn't it fabulous? I'm doing an ode to Tarzan."

"That's nice," Phil mumbled.

Peter made a grab for the red sparkly thong.

"No!" Vanda snatched it from his hand. "You're not dancing in this monstrosity. *I* design the costumes, and I'll tell you what to wear."

"That'th not fair," Peter whined. "I had that cuthtom made to fit me perfectly."

Freddie shuddered. "It's hideously grotesque. You would have to use padding."

Peter huffed. "I never uthe padding."

"You would have to." Frowning, Vanda set the costume on the desk. "There isn't a man on earth who could fill that thing."

"I'm not so sure about that." Terrance glanced at Phil and winked.

Phil had had all he could take. "This meeting is over." He gave the men a warning look and motioned to the door. "You will leave."

"*What*?" Vanda's look of disbelief quickly shifted into anger. "You can't do that! This is my"—she paused when Peter and Freddie scurried from the room—"office."

Terrance stopped halfway out the door and grinned at her. "Be nice, girlfriend. This one's a keeper."

"Out," Phil growled.

"Oooh." Terrance shivered. "Me, Tarzan, you, Phil." He ran out.

Phil shut the door. "Now we can talk."

Vanda glared at him. "I'm not talking to you. You're acting like a caveman."

"I suppose you prefer those pretty little boys who are easy to control."

She grabbed Peter's costume off the desk and threw it at him. "Get out!"

He caught the thong with one hand and turned it over as he examined it. "Why, thank you, Vanda. It's just my size."

She snorted. "A man would have to be aroused to fill that up."

He lifted his gaze to meet hers. "Not a problem."

She gulped audibly, glancing down at his pants before jerking away. "What—why did you come here?"

He walked toward her. "You left Romatech in a hurry. We were in the middle of a conversation."

Her eyes darkened to a stormy gray. "The conversation was over."

"You left your car behind."

"Like I had any choice! That damned Connor confiscated my keys." She blinked when Phil jingled the keys in the air. "You—you brought my car?"

"Yes. It's parked across the street."

"Oh. Thank you." She skirted the desk and approached him. "That was very kind of you."

"You're welcome." He dropped the keys into her outstretched hand. "Now, about my sponsorship. . ."

Her hand fisted around the keys. "There is no sponsorship. You can't force me to take anger management."

"I believe we can. It was a court decision. If you want the lawsuits against you dropped, then you have to comply."

She tossed the keys on the desk. "Do I look like the kind of person who *complies*? Only cowards and trained monkeys comply. I'm a free spirit. Nobody's going to tell me what to do."

Phil couldn't help but smile. Vanda's words were almost identical to the speech he'd given his father nine years ago before he'd stormed out of Montana. "Then what do you plan to do about your anger problem?"

"I don't have an anger problem!" she bellowed. With a groan, she pressed a hand to her forehead. "I wouldn't get angry if people would stop trying to force me to do things against my will."

"Believe me, I understand." Phil's father had tried to force him into a pre-planned life. At eighteen, he hadn't possessed the maturity or strength to fight him. Phil simply left. Then his father had banished him from the pack. "Things don't always go the way we want them to. And it's very frustrating when there's nothing you can do to change it."

Vanda frowned at him. "Are you sympathizing with me just to get me to agree to the program?"

"I'm saying if you want to talk, I'll listen."

Her eyes glinted with moisture, then she blinked it

away. "Why should I believe you care? You haven't bothered to see me in three years."

She'd counted the years? Phil swallowed hard. What if he'd misinterpreted things? He'd felt sure that Vanda had considered him nothing more than a toy to relieve her boredom. Good God, what if she had genuinely cared about him? "I didn't realize you wanted to see me."

Her eyes narrowed. "What do you need, an engraved invitation?"

"You opened a male strip club, Vanda. You're surrounded every night with available men. Half-naked, vampire men." He tossed the damned costume onto her desk. "I really didn't think you were lacking for companionship."

She lifted her chin. "I get all the companionship I need."

He gritted his teeth. "Good."

"Excuse me for thinking you might want to keep in touch. I had thought we were friends."

"We were never friends."

She gasped. "How can you say that? We . . . we talked."

"You taunted me."

She stiffened. "I was nice to you."

He stepped toward her. "You were bored and you tormented me for the fun of it."

"Don't be silly. It was just a little harmless flirtation."

He advanced another step. "It was sheer torture."

She moved back. "But—but you liked it."

"I *hated* it. Every time you touched me, I wanted to rip your little catsuit off and make you purr."

Her mouth dropped open, then shut suddenly with a snap. Her cheeks flushed. "Then why didn't you?

Why did you let a stupid rule stop you? Ian didn't let anything stop him from going after Toni."

He grabbed Vanda by the shoulders so quickly, she gasped. "I would have taken you in a second if I had thought you actually wanted it."

Her cheeks grew a deeper red. "How would you know what I really want?"

He leaned close. "I was on to you, Vanda, from the start. You're a tease. You like to get a man hard, then leave him panting. You enjoyed watching me suffer."

"That's not true. I—I really liked you." She winced as if she'd admitted more than she had wanted to.

He brushed his nose across her cheek and whispered in her ear, "Prove it."

She trembled in his arms. He could feel her breath coming quick against his skin.

He moved his mouth closer to hers. "Show me."

Next month, don't miss these exciting new love stories only from Avon Books

Forbidden Nights With a Vampire by Kerrelyn Sparks

Vanda Barkowski is a vampire with a hot temper, and now her employees at the nightclub she owns have filed complaints, sentencing her to anger management class. Worse, Phil Jones has agreed to be her sponsor, but can she resist her attraction to this forbidden mortal?

A Scotsman in Love by Karen Ranney

Margaret Dalrousie is a talented artist who lets no man interfere with her gift. But she has dark memories that haunt her, and she has not painted a portrait in ages. Yet she soon discovers that there is nothing so dangerous—or tempting—as a Scotsman in love.

The Angel and the Highlander by Donna Fletcher

After Alyce Bunnock's father tried to marry her off, she fled, taking shelter at Everagis Abbey and disguising herself as a nun. But when Lachlan Sinclare arrives to return her to her family, Alyce fears for her freedom—yet the sight of him weakens her with desire.

Night Song by Beverly Jenkins

Cara Lee Henson knows no soldier can be trusted to stay in one place—and that includes handsome Sergeant Chase Jefferson of the Tenth Cavalry. Dallying with the dashing man in blue could cost the independent Kansas schoolteacher her job and reputation, but Chase has a lesson of his own to teach her.

At Avon Books, we know your passion for romance—once you finish one of our novels, you find yourself wanting more.

May we tempt you with . . .

- **Excerpts** from our upcoming releases.

- Entertaining **extras**, including authors' personal photo albums and book lists.

- Behind-the-scenes **scoop** on your favorite characters and series.

- **Sweepstakes** for the chance to win free books, romantic getaways, and other fun prizes.

- Writing **tips** from our authors and editors.

- **Blog** with our authors and find out why they love to write romance.

- **Exclusive content** that's not contained within the pages of our novels.

Join us at
www.avonbooks.com